QUEST OF THE CHOSEN

M. L. Chamaschuk

ATHENA PRESS
MIAMI LONDON

QUEST OF THE CHOSEN

ISBN 1 931456 06 2

First Published 2002 by
ATHENA PRESS PUBLISHING CO.
1001 Brickell Bay Drive, Suite 2202
Miami, Florida 33131

Printed for Athena Press

QUEST OF THE CHOSEN

Prologue

Almost 1,000 years ago, this world, this small and beautiful globe slowly turning beneath the binary suns of its home system, had once been home to nearly a billion people spread out over five main continents. It had been a time of high technological advancement; each continent and nation sharing its resources and cooperating with one another in a world of relative peace and prosperity.

Then had come the cataclysm, the terrible day that astronomers on the floating city of Quayvern sighted a rogue comet hurtling through space on an inevitable collision course, heralding a frightening end. The leaders of that time had been confident that in their unity of thought and resources they would find a way to deflect or destroy the comet, and many attempts were made at great expense.

It was all in vain. In the end, they had only managed to break the comet into smaller fragments that continued to bore down on the planet. Literally millions of people died in the ensuing bombardment, while millions more were to perish from the effects on planetary weather patterns that ravaged peoples, cities and ecosystems for year upon endless year afterward.

With the destruction of the infrastructure that had supported the people, the survivors on the continent of Primus eventually banded together into small communities centered around the remnants of the old civilization. Unfortunately, they found life very different, very primitive compared to what they had enjoyed before, and in their need to pin blame on someone for the cataclysm, each ascribed it to the remnants of their neighboring nations. Wars were fought over everything from the possession of surviving technologies to the basics of land ownership and the distribution of food supplies. The Great Division had begun.

Then, in the middle of this dark and dangerous time, arose a Legend and a Prophecy whose stories were to be forever intertwined and whose origins remained a tantalizing mystery.

The Legend told of how the Sky Lords of Quayvern had helped many of the displaced people of Primus relocate after the Great Division, using their technology for the benefit of all. Scions of generosity and mercy, the Sky Lords, nonetheless, found themselves shunned and reviled as the very people they strove to help turned against them in their envy and desire to claim for themselves the beautiful floating city of Quayvern that the Sky Lords inhabited. Disheartened, the Sky Lords left Primus. Where they could have gone when the world was in ruins, no one could begin to imagine, but there was hope for their return in the pages of a Prophecy whose text brought hope for the future.

The Prophecy told of the day the Sky Lords would return to Primus to select the Chosen, a young man and young woman who would each make fantastic journeys to every kingdom and land. Both were to be absolutely impartial, forthright, peace loving, brave and possessing a myriad of other lofty traits that only the Prophecy could hold them to. The young woman, known as the Observer, would travel anonymously, going out amongst the common folk of the lands in an effort to discover their fondest hopes and their most pressing needs. The young man would be the Gatherer, whose task it would be to bring together representatives of the kingdoms and lead them to Quayvern. Once there, the Chosen would mediate between the kingdoms, leading them into a new era of peaceful cooperation, a Final Reunification, that would rival that of the generations that had lived before the great cataclysm.

⋆

Now, the floating city of technology had appeared in the skies of the northern regions of Primus less than a year ago. There was great rejoicing as the Sky Lords landed their magical ovoid airships in every kingdom, announcing that the time of the Chosen was close at hand. Old enmities were being cast aside; hate was turning to forbearance and intolerance to acceptance as the kingdoms waited, preparing for the day the Chosen would arrive in their land to summon forth a representative for the Final Reunification.

Chapter One

From her vantage point on a plateau above the valley Kingdom of Eristea, Aurori shaded her eyes with one hand against the early morning light of the twin suns and took one last look back at the shining glass towers of her home. Far enough away that she could no longer pick out the forms of her mother, father and two sisters from the knot of people gathered at the base of the largest tower, she still knew with certainty that they were there and would be looking for a last glimpse of her amongst the trees that lined the road on which she stood – the road that was taking her away from home.

Eristea, the Healers' kingdom, lay nestled in a valley in the midst of the Arttorian Mountains that bisected the southern tip of Primus, one of the smaller land masses remaining habitable after the Great Division. Rather small in size with a population of only 10,000, Eristea was nonetheless graced with a beauty that was dichotomous, pairing the breathtaking spectacle of primal wilderness with the glacial severity of the glass constructs of man. The five amber-colored glass towers that comprised the heart of the city rose from the valley floor to heights varying from fifty to over 200 feet. Unable to challenge the majesty of the surrounding blue-green mountains, they instead altered and reflected the colors and hues of the forest mountains and clouds in their polished mirror facets. The effect on the valley was stunning, as though a passing giant had dropped a jewel at the mountain's foot.

Aurori had always planned to make a journey like this one day. Hundreds of her people had walked this same road, had probably even taken this last look back as she has, for the Healers of Eristea had often left their mountain home, going out with the singular purpose of using their gift of healing in the aid of the people of the other kingdoms scattered across the continent. As a daughter of the King of Eristea, it was highly unusual for Aurori to be making such a journey unaccompanied, but it was her duty to do so and she was honored to have been chosen for it. She just hadn't expected to feel so alone and frightened.

The feeling of anticipation and excitement she had felt only a day ago now paled in comparison to the homesickness already gnawing at her. As a child, she had delighted in hearing the many wonderful stories connected with her people. Now, with her fears at the forefront, she could only recall the very few tales of hardship that had been scattered among those recounts.

Scrubbing one hand across her tearful eyes, she inwardly chided herself to turn and walk away, afraid that if she looked too long at the green lushness of her mountain home, she may not have the courage to do what she must. For this journey, for the duty that lay ahead, she would have to become a simple peasant, become the servant where once she had been the mistress. Gone now were the flowing robes she had worn as a member of the Royal Court. In their place, her lithe frame and traveler's clothes were obscured by a simple hooded white cloak that all Healers wore, and her thick auburn hair had been neatly braided in a utilitarian style in an effort to minimize the striking elegance of her delicate features and emerald eyes.

With a sigh of resolution she shrugged the pack she carried higher onto her shoulders, forcing herself to turn and walk away; one step, then another; the first of many on a journey to reunite the people of her world.

★

Early morning mist rose from the forest floor to swirl around the feet of the great felinae as it stalked silently through the thick brush dotted between the trunks of the giant keyta trees, its hot breath creating a mist of its own in the cool air. Six feet high at the shoulder with impressive musculature, massive clawed paws and four-inch fangs, this feline predator was highly prized by the people of Kingdom Kaethos as a beast of burden and battle mount. This particular felinae's long coat of silky white and black fur marked it as being from a particular herd belonging to the royal family, as did the gold and silver diamond emblem embossed on the boots of its rider.

The rider, who at the moment, was leaning so far forward over the neck of his mount as to be practically prostrate, was Terien, Prince and Heir to the throne of Kingdom Kaethos. Tall and leggy, he was a pleasing mix of his muscular father and delicately graceful mother. Sapphire eyes and dark hair with forelocks perpetually playing across his eyes added to Terien's roguish good looks, belying a cool intelligence softened by a quick wit.

"We've got him now," Terien whispered into the felinae's left ear, causing it to twitch slightly. The beast softly rumbled its assent somewhere deep in its throat. If the words weren't perfectly understood, the intent certainly was. Moving forward slowly, crouching close to the ground, the felinae edged out from behind the low shrubs it had been concealed behind. Their quarry, another felinae and rider, was in full view, standing not more than fifty feet away. The great cat quivered in anticipation as Terien shifted weight from left to right to sight his weapon past its right ear, which conveniently flattened down and out of the way as had become habit. The soft hiss of gas entering the weapon's priming chamber lasted a heartbeat, followed almost immediately by the pneumatic rush of its discharge.

A startled human yelp split the quiet morning air, accompanied by an angry felinae's roar. "Bones of the ancestors! That's the third time this week!"

Terien urged his felinae from their hiding place. "Fourth time, Duncan," he called out, smiling as he held up a corresponding number of fingers. His smile grew as he appraised the sticky blue splotch of wetness, on the front of Duncan's white shirt. "The maid will have a fit this time for sure!"

Duncan, second in command of the Royal Guard and long-time friend to the Prince, slid down from the back of his own felinae and wiped ineffectually at the spot, managing only to spread it further. "My bright idea of filling pneumatic guns with colored water for battle practice has a definite downside," Duncan muttered, grimacing. "You know, Terien, I think you're really having too much fun with this," he said accusingly, now trying to dry his shirt by holding it away from his chest and shaking it vigorously.

Terien swung down from his felinae's back, folded his arms and leaned nonchalantly against the beast's side, grinning at his friend. "It is fun, Duncan, and you know it. Training the felinae has always been boring work. Until now. Besides, where's the harm in having a little fun? You should try it sometime."

"Is that a royal decree, then?" Duncan asked with cocked eyebrow as he reached back to stroke the wet spot on his felinae's mottled cinnamon and cream fur.

Terien blew an exasperated breath between his teeth. "As if that would help," he groused. "You were so serious as a kid that there were times I wanted to kick you." He paused to swat the bangs out of his eyes. "You still are and I still do," he said with mock conviction.

Duncan snorted his disapproval. "Training the troops and the felinae is serious business. Kaethos hasn't been attacked in over thirteen years, but that doesn't mean it can't happen. The treaty we signed with Glaybor is one thing, but there are other kingdoms who would be just as happy to raid our lands for keyta trees." Turning, Duncan grabbed a handful of his felinae's fur and hoisted himself onto its back once more. "We have to be ready," he said firmly.

Terien rolled his eyes, pushed away from his mount and thrust a hand at his own huge cat. "Shangra and I have been ready for years! So are you. So is every man in the Royal Guard." He posted his hands on his hips and stared up at Duncan with an intensity meant to burn the truth out. "You're my best friend, Duncan. True, you've always been a straight-faced royal pain who pushed himself harder than anyone I've ever known, but you've been brooding over something for weeks now. I've asked you what's on your mind and you just keep talking about how the men need more battle drills, how this or that strategy should be practiced." Terien's eyes narrowed to slits. "Do you know something I don't, or have you been nipping into the wild berry wine before breakfast?" he asked slyly.

"Terien! I wouldn't, I mean… you know I never… that's not even funny!" Duncan sputtered, dismayed.

One look at the blossoming smile on Terien's face told Duncan he'd done it again. Time and again Terien would tease him mercilessly and he'd make the mistake of taking his friend seriously. After all these years you'd think he'd learn. He sighed heavily. "Permission to dismount and kick myself?"

"There's a line forming for that and you're nowhere near the front," was the retort. "Now, spill it," Terien said, his tone making it a command not to be refused.

Duncan's gray eyes flicked away in embarrassment. The two of them had never stood on ceremony and he had always been more than comfortable with the familiarity of the friendship shared between Prince and commoner, but with the increased demands on Terien's time, not to mention the increase on his own in recent months, Duncan had found himself holding back on burdening Terien with some of the minutiae of his daily life. No, this didn't qualify as minutiae. This was more like hiding a guilty secret. And keeping secrets from Terien had never been his strong suit, guilty or not.

Running a hand through the briar patch of his sandy blond hair, Duncan worked to get some moisture into his suddenly dry mouth. "Komak is getting old," he said at last, referring to the warrior who was Captain of the Royal Guard and his immediate superior.

"That's an understatement," Terien snorted, impatient with being told the obvious.

"Yeah, well, I sort of... overheard him talking to your father a few weeks ago." Overcome with the need to move, Duncan bounded down from the back his felinae, Tiagra, and started pacing back and forth, hands clasped behind his back, head down. "They were talking about all the things I've been saying for the last few weeks. You know, about training and strategies and all that. And – well – Komak told your father he was getting too old to be Captain of the Guard and that he just didn't think he was able to do the job anymore." Duncan stopped mid-stride and met eyes with Terien. "They were discussing *me*, Terien. They think I should be promoted to Komak's position when he retires."

"That's great!" Terien crowed, throwing his arms up.

"No. It's not," Duncan said, adding emphasis to his flat denial by slashing a hand horizontally through the air. He started to pace again, faster this time, missing the look of total bewilderment that puckered Terien's face. "I was happy being second, but... to be Captain! That's a lot of responsibility. Screening new candidates, setting training drills, picking felinae for the stables, acting as advisor to the King, attending diplomatic functions, not to mention actually leading a battle if we ever go to war again," he listed, ticking them off on his fingers. "Damn it! I'm not ready for it. What if I give lousy advice to the King when he's negotiating a treaty? What if I choose a battle strategy that gets a whole division killed? What if..."

"Duncan."

"What if..."

"Duncan, stop." Terien moved to intercept Duncan's pacing, catching the smaller man's shoulders in his hands. "I can't believe this is what's had you so tied up in knots. You are the most capable warrior I know. Besides me, of course," he teased gently, and was pleased to see his friend's head come up a fraction, revealing the barest quirk of a smile tugging on his lips. "You and I trained side by side under Komak's direction. He's the best warrior Kaethos has ever known, and if he thinks you're the man to succeed him, then you know he's right," Terien told him, giving Duncan's shoulders a shake before releasing them and stepping back. "Besides, you're already doing most of everything you're so afraid of taking responsibility for. Or hadn't you noticed that Komak has been delegating more and more duties to you? Never mind. Knowing you, you probably didn't notice. Anyway, seconds become first eventually. Sure, it may be a little sooner than you expected, and sure, you might make a mistake here or there, but who doesn't?" An easy grin lit Terien's face. "I know you're up to the job, and you'd realize it too if you weren't always so busy looking for the cloud in the silver lining."

Duncan took a breath, his confidence visibly returning. "I suppose you have a point or two."

Terien swung an arm around Duncan's shoulders in a one-handed bear hug. "In any event, you'll still have me around to make sure you're not making an ass of yourself. Or at least, not a bigger one than usual," he gibed, smacking his free hand against his friend's chest, eliciting a coughing laugh.

His mouth opening for a retort, Duncan was cut short by a

sound like whistling thunder coming from somewhere beyond and above. Their heads snapped back in unison to track the sound while the felinae shifted uneasily behind them. A visible wave of shimmering heat preceding it, an ovoid airship glided over the tops of the trees. Sending a warm blast of air surging down on to them, it forced them to turn away and cover their eyes until it had passed into the distance.

"That was a Sky Lord's flyer!" Terien choked out past the dust eddying through the air.

"And it was heading in the direction of Kaethos," Duncan added excitedly, swinging up on his mount and reining it in towards the kingdom. "The Sky Lord visited Kaethos almost seven months ago. Why would he come back a second time?"

Terien was sure his heart had just stopped. The Sky Lord who had visited Kaethos those many months ago had said that the time of the Chosen was at hand and that the kingdoms should expect their arrival. He hadn't stayed long, a single week, during which he had discussed the ideological and political views held by Terien and his father, King Koren, but no mention had been made of the Chosen diverging from the text of the Prophecy by arriving in flyers. Which left the question – why was the Sky Lord returning to Kaethos?

"Come on. We won't find out sitting here and debating it with the trees," Terien said. With an economy of movement, Terien vaulted onto Shangra's back and squeezed his knees into the cat's sides. Bellowing a throaty roar, Shangra reared, hind claws digging deep to find purchase as powerful muscles launched him and his master into a high leap. The great cat was running the moment his paws hit the ground, sending up clouts of loamy earth in his wake.

"Hey! Wait for me!" Duncan yelled at Terien's back, spurring Tiagra into motion.

Though they had been less than fifteen minutes from the castle, Terien could barely contain himself as the triple spires of the castle finally came into view. Situated with its back facing the edge of the forest, Castle Kaethos was the largest single structure in a city that was composed mainly of homes and businesses made

from the wood of the majestic keyta trees that were the crux of the economy in this region of rolling hills and woodland. Home to over 50,000 with another 20,000 in the four adjoining towns that it allied with, Kaethos was well known in the southern regions as being a peaceful kingdom whose King was just and compassionate, traits that were also evident in his son, Terien.

However, patience was not among those traits. Charging straight through the open gate of the fence surrounding the castle grounds, he and Duncan flurried into the stables in record time, handed their reins over to waiting stable boys and set off up the stairs leading to the main buildings, taking them two or three at a time.

A harried looking vizier met them at the top just outside the doors to the castle. "Prince Terien! Thank goodness you're back," he breathed, hands flailing the air. "They're in the library, waiting for you!"

Without a word, Terien slipped past the vizier, Duncan right behind him. Together they ran through the main doors, ignoring the ceremonial guards holding them open. A sprint across the great hall, around a corner, down a passage, and they skidded to a halt before the gilded double doors of the library.

Reaching for the door handle with one hand, Terien raked the other through his tousled hair.

"Wait!" Duncan barred the door with his arm. "You can't go in there like that."

Terien glanced down at himself. "You mean windswept, sweaty and dressed for a ride in the woods?"

"Well, yeah."

"Heh! Maybe I'll start a new fashion trend."

Pushing the doors open, Terien gave Duncan a beckoning wave and strode into the library. Designed as a quiet, contemplative place for study or thought, the room also served for small meetings. It boasted walls covered with row upon row of book-filled shelves, a vaulted ceiling with a skylight and several high-backed chairs ringing a low round table near the giant fireplace on the back wall. It was there that Terien could see his mother, Aitia, sitting primly in the chair facing him, her lovely features an unreadable pale mask. His father, King Koren, stood beside her chair, one hand resting on his wife's shoulder while the other was repeatedly stroking his gray streaked beard – a sure sign of impatience in his usually rock-solid father.

"Father, Mother," Terien greeted formally, his long legs carrying him to the edge of the circle of chairs in just a few strides. His mother's hands moved to the arms of her chair as if to propel her to her feet and into the arms of her son, but she held herself frozen instead, her eyes locked on him. His stomach in knots, Terien was about to ask where the Sky Lord was when a figure rose from one of the chairs facing away from Terien.

Dark blue robes rustling, the elderly Sky Lord turned to him. "Greetings, Prince Terien." The voice was a velvety rich baritone, wholly regal in its precise enunciation; pleasant, as were the man's aristocratic features. He sported a white mustache and goatee that matched his close-cropped hair. His eyes, a gentle light blue, crinkled with a smile at seeing Terien. "I am delighted to finally meet you. I am Sky Lord Soloth."

Terien stared dumbly at the Sky Lord's proffered hand for a moment before regaining himself. He grasped Soloth's hand and was mildly surprised at the strength of the vigorous shake he received. "I am honored to meet you, sir."

"The honor is mine, I assure you," Lord Soloth said, still smiling.

"What brings you to our kingdom, Lord Soloth?" Terien asked, smiling politely while his questioning eyes slid to his parents. This wasn't the same Sky Lord who had visited before.

"You do, Prince Terien."

Terien's smile faded. "Me?"

"I shall get right to the point of my visit." Lord Soloth cleared his throat and tucked his hands into the opposing sleeves of his robe, his demeanor becoming very formal and rigid. "Terien, Prince and heir to the throne of Kaethos, you have been selected as the Chosen, the Gatherer, whose duty it will be to travel to every Kingdom of Primus and escort their representatives to Quayvern for the Final Reunification."

The silence was total, a tangible thing that seemed to blanket the room with the electric cold of new fallen snow. Even the air seemed to have suddenly fled the room. Knees turning to water,

Terien's mind reeled at the announcement. *The Chosen? He had been selected as the Chosen?*

"Perhaps I should have thought to ask you to sit first," Lord Soloth chuckled, taking hold of Terien's elbow and directing him to a chair.

Brows knit, fingers dug into his thighs so hard it hurt, Terien struggled to find a way to give voice to all the questions flooding his mind and only managed a pitiful disjointed stammer. "Me? The... Chosen? I... can't... how did you... when..."

Lord Soloth laughed, a hearty belly laugh that broke the tension of the moment. "All in good time, young Prince. I will answer all your questions, one by one. There is plenty of time."

"Why me? How was I...?"

"Ah! Suffice it to say that the selection process for the Chosen is known only to the Sky Lords." He offered an apologetic shrug. "It is enough to know that you have been Chosen, and should you accept the role of the Chosen, I will instruct you on a great many things."

"Should I accept...? You mean, I have a choice whether to be Chosen or not?" Terien asked, incredulous.

"Of course, my boy. We would never force anyone into such a challenging role. But know this," he stepped close to Terien and put his hand on his shoulder, "you are our first choice and the best choice. There is another, but we believe that you and you alone possess the attributes best suited to the task." Soloth returned his hand to the fold of his sleeve and straightened. "Before your arrival, I briefly discussed this with your mother and father. If you like, I can leave you to discuss the matter with them," he offered.

Terien looked first to his father. The look of pride was unmistakable. He had long believed that the Prophecy would come true and when the Sky Lord had come to Kaethos to announce the coming of the Chosen, he had been ecstatic. To now find that his son was that Chosen... well, he looked ready to do a cartwheel. Mother? Fear in her eyes, and a tight, brave little smile he knew all too well. She, too, would honor his decision, pushing her own wishes aside. It had been she who had first told him the Prophecy about the Chosen, and he could still hear her soft voice reciting it to him as she tucked him into bed at night as a child. Duncan? He looked cataleptic, but his thoughts on the matter were clear from the huge smile plastered on his face.

The question was, did he want to do this? To be the Chosen, to be a part of something so important for the people of Primus… it was a dream come true. Now, he suddenly felt unworthy. Who was he that he should become the Chosen?

He found the answer in the eyes of Lord Soloth, eyes that were looking at him with utter calm and composure, eyes that seemed to be at peace with the selection that had been made.

Terien stood, relieved to find that at least his knees didn't feel like they were about to give out anymore. "There is no need to discuss this." He drew a breath. "I accept the role of the Chosen."

Queen Aitia was out of her chair and in her son's arms in an instant, hugging him with all her might. "I am so proud of you, Terien," she whispered. "Just promise me that you'll be careful."

King Koren enveloped them both in his arms. "He will be," he said.

After a long moment, King Koren pulled away from his son and wife and turned to Duncan. "You have been my son's best friend since you were both infants and I cannot imagine separating you now," he told him. "I think Komak's retirement will have to wait. Will you accompany my son on his journey as the Chosen?"

"I would be honored, Your Majesty," Duncan replied with a bow, his voice hoarse with emotion.

"This is unprecedented, but the Kingdom of Kaethos will now have two First Captains of the Guard. Congratulations, my boy," King Koren said.

Duncan swallowed hard and began to bow again, but instead found himself caught in a bear hug from the King, followed by a somewhat gentler hug from the Queen.

"Your parents would have been so proud of you, Duncan," Queen Aitia said. "As am I."

"Thank you," Duncan said softly, struggling to maintain composure. When his parents had both died in a landslide when he was fourteen, the King and the Queen had taken him in. His father had been the King's friend and one of his advisors, and since he and Terien had practically been raised together, it had been a logical decision. While Duncan had always been treated kindly and with affection by the royal couple, with the exception of a few rare occasions, they had not been overly demonstrative towards him. This was one of those occasions and it was making Duncan a bit uncomfortable.

Terien laughed at the look on Duncan's face and made it three for three by grabbing him up in a bear hug of his own. "And you were worried about replacing Komak. See how things have a way of working themselves out," Terien said, slapping Duncan's back before stepping back and smiling. "Good thing I'll have you along."

"To... guide you?" Duncan asked uncertainly.

"No, to keep me from making an ass of myself."

"Oh. Is that in my job description?"

"It is now, Captain," Terien said with pride.

Even Lord Soloth laughed at that, amused by the exchange between the two long-time friends. "I can see that the Chosen will be in good company."

"That reminds me," Terien said, turning to Soloth. "Has the other Chosen already been selected?"

"Yes. She has already begun her journey."

"I don't suppose you'll tell me who she is?"

"I'm afraid not," Soloth said with a shake of his head. "Her identity is strictly secret. Only she has the right to reveal herself if she feels it is appropriate."

"Do you think our paths might cross?"

Soloth thought about that for a moment. "All things are possible, but I think it unlikely," he said at last.

Terien nodded thoughtfully, his mind already jumping ahead to the journey he faced.

"Come," King Koren invited, clapping his hands. "It is far past the noon meal and I'm sure the cook is wondering what's keeping us. I suggest we all get cleaned up," he said, eyeing Terien and Duncan's rough attire critically, "and meet in the dining room in half an hour."

"An excellent idea," Lord Soloth said, already following King Koren across the room. "We can begin your instruction after lunch, then," he said, smiling over his shoulder at Terien. "I have much to tell you before you depart, and you have much to learn, very much indeed."

Chapter Two

On the fourth day of her journey Aurori had awoken with the first light of the suns. The initial fear she had felt at her departure from Eristea had faded into mild uneasiness, but she had still slept fitfully during the nights, one ear and one eye on the alert for danger.

She had descended the mountains and entered the lower foothills around mid-afternoon two days ago. The forests here were no less lovely than those of her home, but they were much denser with more scraggly underbrush and taller, leafier trees. Though she had not yet encountered any larger animals, she had seen a vast number of songbirds, fuzzy rodents and large crawling insects that weren't native to her region. The latter had made her shiver. So had the temperature. It was early spring and the winter snows had already melted, leaving only pockets of resistance manifest in the odd mounds of dirty ice deposits defiantly lingering in shadowed nooks and crannies throughout the forest.

Aurori had kept to the winding dirt path that lead down from her mountain home and knew that it wouldn't be long before she came to the crossroads. To that end she set about packing up her meager camp as quickly as she could after finishing off a simple breakfast of water and cereal grains.

She could hardly wait to actually visit some of the other kingdoms and find out for herself how the people lived, what they thought, what technologies they still possessed. From what she had learned from other Healers, villages, towns and cities had sprung up from the ruins of the old civilization, sometimes with the remnants of the old structures incorporated into their plan, as in Eristea. That was not a common practice, however. After so much time, a great majority of the old buildings were simply too frail and had been torn down. Eristea's own shining amber towers, defiant vestiges of an era long gone, were actually barely functional after the hundreds of years they had endured. Though still quite structurally sound, only their lower floor rooms were still utilized as individual dwellings and offices. The higher floors had been cordoned off, for electricity and water had not flowed for centuries anywhere on Primus, making the arduous climb up dozens of flights of stairs unrealistic. Instead, most of Eristea's inhabitants lived in the wood and log dwellings that surrounded the base of the towers. Their lives were simple and hard with most tasks done by hand or by beasts of burden.

Few of the old technologies remained in the hands of the Eristeans, but those that did were a closely guarded secret that had earned the Healers a reputation that was nothing short of mythical. While physicians could be found in most of the larger population centers and were quite capable of tending the people in their care, Healers were renowned for their extensive knowledge of natural medicines and seemingly magical skill in tending all types of illness and wounds. Many believed that Healers were capable of physically healing a person by their touch. Others proclaimed they used an old technology long forgotten. The truth was a fuzzy in-between that Healers rarely revealed.

Stuffing the last pieces of her camping gear into her pack, Aurori shouldered her burden and straightened her cloak. One last pass of her hand over the remains of her campfire assured her it was out. She was going to miss its warmth, she realized with a shudder, deciding that her first order of business would be to make a stop in the village of Donellin and purchase a riding animal of some sort. Her people kept only animals that were used for work or food, but there was no sense in walking all the way to Quayvern, after all. She shuddered again. Perhaps an investment in some warmer clothes would be wise, as well. She had seriously underestimated the unpredictability of the weather at this time of the year and now wished she had listened to the advice that it was likely to be a hard spring.

Pulling out the map Lord Soloth had prepared for her, Aurori traced a finger up the squiggly line from Eristea, north to the crossroads and then west. The village of Donellin, which lay inside the territory of the Kingdom of Kaethos, was only a few miles out of her way. She could make her purchases, double back to the crossroads and then continue north towards Glaybor.

She set off at a good pace, hopeful to be in Donellin before nightfall.

Hours passed. The winding tree-lined dirt road widened and the more severe terrain of the high foothills gave way to the gentle hillocks that would soon smooth into the prairies. Cresting the small hill she had been laboring up, Aurori nearly cried out with joy at the sight in front of her. At the bottom of the gentle slope before her, the road she was on conjoined with three others – the crossroads at last.

Despite being fatigued from hours of walking, Aurori felt a surge of renewed energy at the sight of her first goal. She practically ran down the hill, stopping only when she arrived at the very center of the crossroads. She spread her arms and twirled around on the spot, glorying in the pure joy she felt at the moment. Feeling a little giddy, Aurori took in the surroundings. Wooden signposts marked each offshoot of the crossroads. The road north was wide and flat, hard packed from much use. The roads east and west were slightly less broad but looked well traveled. And the road south – well, she knew what *that* looked like – poor south road.

Deciding this would be an excellent place for a rest, Aurori strode a short distance up the west road and into the shelter of a particularly large tree, several paces from its edge. She swung her pack to the ground and plopped down beside it, immediately rummaging inside for her water canteen. A long draught later, she set the canteen aside and leaned her back against the tree's massive trunk. She closed her eyes and relaxed her head against the tree, letting her hands fall limply into her lap. Her feet throbbed and her hands felt slightly puffy. The feel of alternating cool and warm washed over her as clouds scudded across the sky, successively occluding and revealing the binary suns. Birds chirped and trilled, now near, now far, and the wind sighed through the forest.

Aurori sighed, thinking how perfectly pleasant it felt to simply sit and rest when distant sounds tickled her ears. A bovine bray and the clatter of wooden wheels jolting over hard packed earth.

The staccato beat of shod hooves and the garble of voices too distant to be little more than noise at the moment.

Someone was coming.

Aurori's eyes flew open, scanning the crossroads to identify the direction the sounds were coming from. Her heart beat faster and she chided herself for being silly. It was just some other travelers. What was she afraid of?

After a few minutes she spotted them coming down the east road and was torn between fleeing into the forest or staying put. There were three men. Two were riding large gray equines and the third rode on a covered wooden wagon drawn by a single woolly bovine of a kind Aurori had never seen before. They looked older than she, somewhere in their thirties, all with long hair pulled back in ponytails, and the identical long black cloaks they wore made her wonder if they could be military men. The two riders sported brambly beards while the wagon driver looked grizzled beneath the stubble of a few days' growth. They looked rather dashing, if somewhat tired and scruffy. As they drew abreast of where she sat, Aurori realized she was holding her breath.

The rider closest to her slowly turned his head as though sensing her scrutiny. He pulled his mount to a stop when he spotted her. "Hey, hold up!" he called out to his companions who halted a few paces ahead and looked back in his direction as he silently motioned an arm at Aurori.

The wagon rider's face lit with a broad, friendly smile. "Hi-O, girl! Are ya in need of assistance?"

"Ah… no!" Aurori called back, climbing to her feet. "I'm fine. Just… resting."

"Travelin', then? But what's a girl like you doin' in the middle of nowhere all by her lonesome? Only fools and Healers would travel on foot and all alone!"

Aurori hesitated over an answer, a little miffed at his harsh proclamation. She finally decided on the truth. Sort of.

"I'm traveling to Donellin to pick up some supplies and purchase a riding animal." She stood a little straighter, feeling defiant. "I may be a Healer, but I'm no fool."

The wagon rider jolted upright at that. "A Healer! Truly?" He exchanged a guarded look with his companions. "Well, praise the ancestors, girl! We've an injured comrade in the back," he said, jerking a thumb over his shoulder. "We were taking him to Donellin to see a physician, but maybe you could take a look?" he suggested, his face becoming a question mark.

Caught off guard, Aurori stood stock-still for a moment, staring back at the wagon driver's expectant face. "Oh! Of course!" Aurori said, quickly stashing her canteen in her pack before lugging it the short distance to the wagon.

The wagon driver jumped down from his perch, circled to the back of the wagon and lifted one flap of the canvas cover. Aurori stood on tiptoe and peered into the dim interior where a man lay on the floor of the cart. Wrapped in blankets, he was moaning softly, his face bathed in a feverish sweat.

"What happened to him?" she asked as she climbed into the cart, dragging the pack with her.

"Bandits," the wagon rider spat. "His name's Kale. Took a bad sword slash to the leg and got pretty beat up three days ago. Think he might have some busted ribs, too."

"Bandits," Aurori echoed in a whisper. She had heard tales of bandits from other Healers, but it had been said that they were an uncommon blight. How disheartening to find evidence to the contrary so early on in her journey. She would have to be careful.

"Hello Kale," Aurori said, critically assessing the dirty bandage swathing his left leg and the bruises on his face. He was holding a protective arm over his left side.

"Hi-O, miss. You really a Healer?"

"I am," Aurori confirmed. "May I?" she asked, reaching out to touch his bandaged leg with her fingertips.

With his nod of assent, Aurori gently unwrapped his leg. The cut was deep and long, a diagonal running from just above his knee to midway down his calf. The pressure from the bandage had stopped the bleeding and held the wound's edges together in a fair approximation, but it would still need tending. She turned her attention to the bruising and abrasions around his right eye and brow, expertly probing the area. Satisfied that none of his facial bones had been broken, she moved on to examine the left lateral area of his chest. No obvious breaks. All he really needed was rest and something for his pain.

"Except for your leg, you faired not too badly," she said with a reassuring smile, "and your leg will be as good as new in no time." She delved into her pack and withdrew a small ornate glass with lines etched into it and a matching vial capped with a cork stopper. She poured a viscous liquid from the vial into the glass until it reached the second etched line.

"I know this tastes terrible, but you need to drink it if I'm going to do anything for your leg," she said, holding the glass out to him. "It will relieve your pain, but it will also make you sleep for several hours. Do you understand?"

Nodding, Kale took the glass and sipped the contents. His face screwed up with distaste, but he drank it down and handed the glass back to her.

"How long will it take before... it... makes me... sleep–y..."

Kale's whole body deflated before he had finished the question, and by the last syllable he was as limp as a wilted weed, fast asleep.

"Damnedest thing I've ever seen!" the wagon rider exclaimed.

Ignoring him, Aurori positioned herself in such a way as to block the wagon rider's view and scooted herself in close to Kale's leg. She flicked her thumbnail against the first joint of her right index finger, then placed the tip of her finger at the apex of the wound. As she slowly drew her finger downward, the wound reopened, debriding and beginning to bleed as she went. When she had finished that task, she once again flicked her thumbnail against her index finger, then repeated the process with her middle finger. Pinching the edges of the wound together with her left hand, she began to draw her right middle finger down along the wound. A faint red glow surrounded her hands, accompanied by the unmistakable smell of burning flesh. Reaching the end of the wound, Aurori flicked her thumbnail against the joint of her middle finger one last time and surveyed her handiwork. All that remained of the jagged wound was a slightly raised pink line.

Turning again to her pack, Aurori drew out a stubby clay jar. Removing its wax seal, she dabbed her fingers into the shimmering green jelly-like contents, then smeared it over the abrasions on Kale's face. The jelly dried almost instantly, becoming a transparent film that would adhere to his wounds like a second skin, allowing his body time to repair the damage without fear of infection.

After stowing her potions in her pack, Aurori heaved a theatrical sigh and turned to smile at the wagon rider. "He needs to get some rest and he shouldn't move around too much for a few days until his ribs have a chance to mend a bit, but his leg is going to be just fine."

"No problem. He can just stay put in the wagon until we reach Mayquire," the wagon driver said with a shrug.

Aurori shouldered her pack and, placing a steadying hand on the wagon's tailgate, started to climb out.

"Hold on there, girl," the wagon driver said, his hand lashing out to grip her wrist and keep her from climbing down.

Uncertain of his intention, Aurori froze and her pulse quickened as she tried to figure out what was going on by looking in his eyes, but he was staring past her into the wagon.

"Remember the bandits I mentioned? Well, we had a run-in, right enough," he told her. "Who'd have thought a couple of guys dressed up so fine would be so much trouble? Poor Kale took the worst of it," he mused, shaking his head sadly. "Good thing for Kale we happened across you." He lifted his eyes to her now and she didn't like what she saw. A feral grin was darkening his rugged features. "Too bad for you, though."

Sudden realization landed a rock in the pit of her stomach. "You weren't attacked by bandits. You *are* the bandits," Aurori spat out, trying to jerk away from him without success. He tightened his grip, sending a shot of pain up her arm.

"Very bright," he laughed.

Real fear gripped Aurori's heart. "If it's money you want – I haven't got much, but you can have it."

"I might take you up on your generous offer, but it's not your money we want," he stated with a shake of his head. "I can't believe our stroke of luck. You have no idea what a handsome price a Healer will fetch in some parts."

That hit home. A handful of Healers had never returned from their journeys over the years. It had been speculated that they had either decided to make a new home for themselves elsewhere or had died in some distant conflict or accident. This was a possibility that had never been considered, to be abducted and sold as a slave.

"No!"

Her fear blossoming into outrage, Aurori's foot lashed out, catching the man square in the jaw and propelling him back. Unfortunately, he still had hold of her wrist and she went flying out of the wagon, landing in a heap beside him on the hard ground. Scrambling to get her feet under her while her would-be captor writhed on the ground, cursing and nursing his jaw, Aurori was dismayed to find the two riders already advancing on her, their mounts snorting and prancing as they tried to trap her between them. In a dangerous bid for freedom, Aurori tucked and rolled between one equine's legs, ending up in the tall grass edging the road. She fought to regain her footing, cursing the long cloak crippling her effort, but managed to hop, skip and generally jump her way into the forest. Clutching desperately at her offending cloak, trying to gather it up, she ran deeper into the woods on legs rendered rubbery and treacherous from the adrenaline rush pounding through her veins.

She could hear the shouts of the men and the thundering of hooves right behind her as she dodged through the trees and around rocks, refusing to give up. Outnumbered and outclassed in speed by the equine, she knew hers was a hopeless flight. *She was the Chosen! She couldn't let herself be sold off like some piece of jewelry! Whatever it took, whatever the cost, she had to get free!*

A startled whoop escaped Aurori's lips as her getaway was cut short by the lasso that seemed to materialize around her. One moment she was running, the next she was wrenched backward, her body twisting around in mid-air, arms pinned to her sides, legs splaying out uselessly. She landed hard on her left hip and her head snapped forward, hitting the ground. Shoots of pain exploded behind her eyes and her vision dimmed and then brightened into dancing sparkles. Unable to move, she lay panting, hurting and unable to think clearly.

The rider whose lasso had taken Aurori down now dismounted and knelt to examine her as his other two companions arrived, doubled up on one equine.

"She's alive," he announced after rolling her over onto her back and peering into her unfocused eyes. "Brained, but okay."

"She had better be!" the wagon rider snarled, still massaging his jaw. "Frag! We'd better get a good price for her after the trouble she's been."

"What now?" the kneeling rider asked.

"Tie her up and put her in the wagon," he ordered. "We'll camp outside Donellin tonight and head for Mayquire in the morning, just like we planned."

Aurori was aware of being pushed over onto her stomach, could feel the roughness of the rope being used to tie her hands behind her back and bind her ankles together. She gave half a thought to struggling and decided it would be utterly pointless.

Biting her lip to stifle a cry of pain as she was hoisted up and dropped, belly first, over the back of her captor's equine, Aurori blinked back bitter tears, ashamed of how naive she had proved to be. When she got out of this – and she vowed to herself that she would – she would be much more worldly-wise and on her guard. She had learned a valuable lesson. Never again would she take a person or situation at face value.

Enduring the discomfort of jolting along on the back of the equine as it was led back to the waiting wagon, Aurori put her mind to work plotting possible escape plans. At least she had her hidden Healer's gift to rely on. What she really needed now was an opportunity and a little luck.

Chapter Three

By the time morning arrived on the day after her capture, Aurori was thoroughly disgusted and bone weary. After traveling for hours the evening before, bouncing along inside the wagon while trussed up like a prize goose and gagged for good measure by her captors, she had still been in fairly good spirits when they had stopped to make camp for the night in the forest on the outskirts of Donellin. Certain that nightfall would provide the opportunity she needed to make an escape, she watched and waited after they had hauled her out, fed her and allowed her to sleep on the ground beside the fire.

These bandits weren't stupid, though. All through the night they had taken turns standing guard, though whether it was to ensure Aurori stayed put or against the possible threat from other bandits or animals, she wasn't quite sure. Regardless, she had forced herself to stay awake throughout the night, sometimes pinching herself to keep awake, sometimes drifting off for a few minutes. It made for a long night in any case. A long and fruitless night of waiting for an opportunity that never materialized.

When morning had dawned gray and raining, it only added to the misery Aurori already felt. Still, all was not lost. Night would have provided better cover for an escape, but it was a whole new day and that meant new possibilities, and at least her captors had fed her a decent breakfast before once again gagging her and putting her back in the wagon before resuming their trek towards the coastal town of Mayquire.

When Kale came to the back of the wagon to toss the last few items of their camping gear in with her, he paused and looked shyly at her, uncomfortably shifting from foot to foot.

"I, uh, well – I just wanted to say thanks for fixing my leg," he managed to say. "It feels real good. I don't know how you did it, but, well, thanks."

Surprised when he abruptly flung the flap shut, she listened intently to his footsteps, tracing his progress to the front of the wagon. The jostling of the wagon told her Kale had climbed onto the seat beside the nameless wagon driver. Moments later, when the wagon twitched into motion accompanied by the bray of its woolly bovine engine, Aurori knew her time had come.

Elation! She had expected Kale to ride in the back with her. Without his presence complicating matters, she was free to act.

Aurori activated the Healer's cutting tool in her right index finger and set about loosening the bonds on her wrists. It would be a slow and delicate thing to do with her hands out of sight behind her back. She would just have to be very careful, take her time – not too much time, though. They would inevitably stop somewhere along the line, and she simply had to be free before that happened.

★

The tearful goodbye he had exchanged with his parents had been difficult, but after two and a half days of the most intense and interesting study Terien had ever endured in his life, he found it was a relief to finally be on the road and at the beginning of what promised to be the adventure of his life. Too bad the day had decided to be so overcast and rainy or his mood might have been less pensive.

Riding on Shangra in the lead position, Terien twisted his upper body around to get another look at his entourage. Duncan and Komak had chosen twenty men to accompany him, all fine warriors with varying skills that might prove useful on this journey. While most were riding powerful ebony equines, three were also riding felinae from the royal herd, as were he and Duncan. Three canvas-covered supply carts pulled by teams of two equines brought up the rear, packed with all the goods necessary to sustain them. Overall, they were a rather impressive-looking bunch. Clothed in heavy ankle-length black cloaks to ward off the rain and conceal the dress uniforms they wore underneath, they all rode straight and tall, proud to have been selected for the task of providing security for their Prince, now revealed as the Chosen.

Aside from the selection of the men who would accompany them, Duncan had also been responsible for the other preparations for the journey. Deciding how much to bring, who would be responsible for what duties, and whether or not to bring along some of the antiquated but serviceable air guns had kept him very busy.

While Duncan had been kept in a state of constant nervous frenzy over these issues, Terien had spent hours with Lord Soloth, learning more about the kingdoms of Primus and receiving instruction on a few technological devices that would aid them on their journey, including a very interesting map.

There was much about Primus that no one knew. The most astounding was that there were four cities hidden on Primus where high technology had survived the cataclysm. One was hidden in the Teseni Desert that lay to the east of Glaybor. Another lay beneath the Merani Ocean off the west coast, not too far north of the town of Mayquire. Two more were hidden in the north, with one situated deep within the Kescate Mountains and another supposedly deep beneath the jungle in the region of Tekatan. While the Sky Lords had long ago lost contact with two of these cities and assumed their people had moved on, the city in the Kescate Mountains was still thriving, as was another in the Merani Ocean, and Terien had been given a key that would gain him entry to them when the time came, as had his anonymous counterpart. He now wore that key on a chain around his neck, and his hand strayed to touch its unfamiliar cylindrical shape beneath his cloak.

"You look troubled."

Terien was startled out of his thoughts as Duncan trotted up beside him on Tiagra.

"Not troubled, just thinking about things," Terien replied, stretching.

"Care to share?"

Terien fingered the collar of his cloak and sighed. "Just thinking about some of the things Lord Soloth told us about – the hidden cities, mostly. I still can't believe no one ever found them." Terien frowned. "I'm also a little worried about how people will react when we arrive in their kingdoms. Lord Soloth said that most had been happy to hear that the Prophecy had finally come to pass, but he also mentioned that some had been a little cool towards the whole thing, especially in some of the central kingdoms where there's still some fighting between towns." He sighed heavily. "I was also thinking about the Legend of the Sky Lords. Lord Soloth was rather vague about the origin of the Sky Lords and where they had been all this time. He kept asking me to trust him and trust in the rightness of what we were doing, promising a full explanation once we reached Quayvern, but I can't help but wonder." He pressed his fingers to his temple. "I think I'm getting a headache just talking about it."

"We've been through all this," Duncan said wearily. "It doesn't matter where the Sky Lords came from or where they've been or how the Legend and the Prophecy came to be. All that matters is that for the first time in generations, the leaders of Primus will be brought together and have the opportunity to unite themselves through peace treaties and trade agreements that will potentially benefit every person on the continent." Smiling, Duncan looked askance at Terien. "I, for one, am proud to be a part of that. We'll be making history, Terien."

"I know. Maybe it's just self-doubt talking. Gathering the representatives together and acting as mediator are a huge responsibility. I'm proud to have been chosen for it, but I can't stop worrying about everything, including the things I have no control over."

"Then I know just the thing you need – the perfect cure." Duncan alluded.

"And that would be?"

"You and I can scout ahead. Give the felinae a short run."

Terien dipped his head and gave Duncan a wide-eyed stare. "Do you always have to mix work with fun?"

"Work? What work?" Duncan protested. "We're not even at the Mayquire fork yet! It's not like we're actually going to be scouting for something."

"In that case—" Terien whipped his head around and shot a finger at the warrior directly behind him, "Elek, we're scouting ahead. Take over until you either catch up with us or we return. Give us an hour."

With the sound of snapping reins, Terien and Duncan took off, leaving a few raised brows in their wake.

Elek smiled to himself. Broad-shouldered and muscular, Duncan had chosen him as second in command because of his extensive battle experience. Oldest of the group, he had fought and earned many a medal in the days before the treaty between Kaethos and Glaybor. Nonetheless, he was a jovial sort with an easy smile that frequently lit his face, as it did now.

"Steady as we go, boys," he called out.

"Isn't it dangerous for the Prince to go off like that without us?" someone asked.

"Naw," Elek said with an easy shrug. "There's not much between here and the turn-off to Mayquire. They'll be fine."

Chapter Four

Standing at the window in his office on the top floor of the second tallest spire on Quayvern, Sub-Primary Leander, the second most powerful member of the city's ruling council, stared out over the city below, his hands clasped behind his back, enjoying the lofty view that his high position granted him.

He did not turn as a woman entered unbidden. His ice-blue eyes shifted focus to watch her reflection in the window as she approached his desk and silently stood before it, hands behind her back in a stance that mimicked his own, her sleek form adorned once again in the pale green bodysuit she favored. Choosing to let her wait for a minute, his eyes returned to considering the view of the Kescate Mountains that lay far below the floating city.

"I told my secretary that I did not wish to be disturbed, Idona," Leander said evenly after a time, idly running a finger along the windowsill.

Idona shifted to lean on the desk with both hands. "Primary Soloth just returned," she told him, taking his statement as permission to speak. "He's scheduled a conference for 18:00 to brief the councilors about his meetings with the two Chosen. He asked me to extend an invitation for you to attend."

Leander loosed a scornful sound. "How thoughtful of him to send his personal aide when he could simply have called me on the communications panel."

Idona's reflected image shrugged elaborately. "He asked me to extend the invitation. He didn't say it had to be in person." The corners of her mouth turned up in a coy smile. "I have the afternoon off."

Suppressing a smile of his own, Leander tugged down on the hem of his gray jacket and turned. "So, it has begun." He strode to his desk and smoothed a hand over the back of his black leather chair but did not pull it out to sit. "The Prophecy has been put into motion and the Chosen dispersed on their fantastic journeys.

How perfectly nauseating." He sighed and pinched the bridge of his nose between thumb and forefinger, feeling a headache coming on. "Returning to Primus was a popular proposal and helped consolidate Soloth's power base during the last election. I had hoped that once we arrived, the people would lose interest after a time and I would be free to build a campaign platform centered on going back to the outlier continents, but then the old fox got wind of this Prophecy business."

"Soloth is a shrewd one. His drive to help the people of Primus reunite their lands and forge trade routes is viewed as being totally altruistic. The people of Quayvern love the idea." Her expression souring, Idona straightened and brushed at a piece of lint on her arm. "Fools."

"Not so," Leander disagreed, holding up a slender finger. "Soloth is a highly scrupulous and idealistic man. That the people of Quayvern hold him in high regard as a result of this endeavor is hardly surprising. Unfortunately, Soloth's popularity has escalated to the point where he has practically guaranteed himself a win in the next election. As for the Prophecy and our participation in its fulfillment – I wish I had thought of it, actually. A stroke of genius, that."

Snorting, Idona flipped her long red hair over her shoulder. "You sound impressed by the old fox."

"I am," he said, then lowered his head, his eyes narrowing. "Understand this, though. I have no intention of letting Soloth sit in the Primary's chair, come next election. Whatever it takes, Quayvern will be mine to rule."

Idona hitched a leg over the corner of the desk and folded her arms. "What do you have in mind?"

Leander pulled out his chair and lowered himself into it, a smile slowly spreading over his aquiline features as he leaned his elbows on the desk and interlaced his fingers. "If the Chosen were to fail in their mission, Soloth would lose face with the council and his popularity would falter, leaving me as the only viable candidate."

"I see. I take it you've already taken steps to ensure their failure, then?"

Leander laughed; an unpleasant, guttural sound. "Assuming

that they survive past the first three cities on their itinerary, yes. I flew over the route they will take while on my way to Brinbourne to announce the coming of the Chosen. Primus has become a harsh and unforgiving place and there are only a handful of populated areas, separated by incredible distances. Considering that Soloth and the council voted in favor of letting the Chosen make the journey unassisted and unmonitored, I will be very surprised if they make it past the Teseni Desert, actually." Leander leaned back and rested his hands on the chair's arms, a predatory smile on his lips. "Soloth staked his own grave plot by so graciously appointing you to visit the Director of Merani Base to inform him about the Chosen. I am in your debt for introducing us, my dear. It turns out that the Director and I see eye to eye on many issues. He has many problems of his own and was quite willing to offer his assistance, especially after I promised to help him resolve a particular supply issue he has. He's a weaselly little man and not very bright. Steering him in the direction I wanted was far easier than I could have imagined. How he managed to accomplish what he has with Merani Base is astounding."

Idona knew better than to ask for details. He would tell her his plans when he was ready, not before. She stood away from the desk and bowed in acknowledgment. "One look at the Director's operations was all it took to convince me that you and he might benefit from meeting. He wasn't very communicative with me at the time, but I was certain you would fare better. You have a way with people," she said, giving him a meaningful look. "But, if I remember correctly, the Chosen won't be reaching Merani Base for some time. What do we do in the meantime?"

"We wait," Leander stated plainly, shrugging indifferently. "This gives us time to plan and prepare. There are two other councilors I intend to speak with, as well. Albeon and Edegan were against Quayvern's participation in this whole Prophecy business from the start and have expressed their interest in supporting me when the time comes. I must be cautious until I know exactly where they stand on the matter, but I'm confident that they will prove quite useful. Both have extensive holdings on Quayvern and many... associates... who might also render assistance."

"What do you want me to do in the meantime?"

Leander stretched languidly and ran a hand through his salt and pepper hair. "What you do best, my dear Idona. Watch. Listen. Be a lovely voice that sows dissent among the ranks." Pushing away from his desk, Leander stood and paced to Idona's side. He slipped an arm around her slim waist, pulled her close and kissed the tip of her nose. "18:00 is many hours away. Perhaps you and I can find something to occupy our time until then?"

Giving him a slow smile, Idona drew her hands across his back. "Perhaps we can."

⋆

The felinae seemed to be enjoying the freedom of their run as much as Terien was. The feel of the wind rushing past, stinging slivers of drizzle pelting his face, and the hypnotic blur of trees whizzing by drove all thoughts of recent days into a corner.

For a few minutes he was free.

Just ahead was the turn-off for Mayquire, the only fishing and shipping port in the region. Mayquire was semi-autonomous, governed by Elders who had long ago allied with Kaethos. Terien had pleasant memories of spending summers there, by the sea with Duncan.

Slowing now to an easy walking pace, Terien and Duncan rode in companionable silence until they reached the mouth of the path to Mayquire where they drew their felinae to a halt. Looking up the road, they could see two riders and a wagon slowly bumping its way through the potholes and water puddles a short distance away.

"The rain sure made a mess of that road," Duncan commented. "Good thing we're not going that way."

Terien nodded agreement, watching as the equine splashed up gooey water with every step. "That mud would certainly make a mess of the felinae's fur…" His voice trailed off as he saw a figure in a white cloak part the flaps of canvas covering the back of the wagon, glance side to side, then start to climb out of the moving wagon, positioning its feet on the narrow ledge of wood jutting out at the foot of the closed tailgate.

"What the...!" Duncan exclaimed.

They watched dumbfounded as the figure lugged a large pack out of the wagon and clutched it tight. The figure then dropped to the ground, rolled once through the mud and lay unmoving for several seconds before rising and making a crouching run into the ditch, heading for the woods. If the figure's slight build was any indication, it was a woman.

"So much for that white cloak she's wearing," Terien commented. "What do you suppose is going on?"

Duncan shook his head side to side. "Can't say." He looked to Terien. "So, what do we do? Go after her and ask why she was sneaking away, or alert those riders?"

"Neither, now," Terien replied, pointing towards the wagon.

One of the riders glanced over his shoulder as though he had heard something. He did a double take, shouting a warning as he caught sight of the muddy figure. He spurred his equine into action and took off after her, the other rider right behind him.

Coming up beside her, the closest rider leapt from his mount and tackled the woman to the ground. They rolled several times in a tangle of arms and legs before the rider got hold of the situation and pinned her to the ground by her shoulders. She was feisty, though, and kicked her legs up, hitting his backside hard enough to send him sprawling away from her.

The second rider didn't give her a chance to recover. He was off his mount and on her in seconds, grabbing her arms and pinning them behind her back as he hauled her to her feet.

"I won't let you sell me!" the woman screamed, struggling and kicking as the riders now joined forces to subdue her.

Her words sent a white-hot flash of electricity through Terien.

"Slavers!" he snarled, drawing his sword and smacking Shangra's rump with its flat edge in one fluid motion. The huge felinae crouched back on its powerful hind legs, let out a deafening, screaming yowl and leapt forward.

"Spit!" Duncan cursed angrily, his own mount following Shangra's lead as he drew his own sword.

Several things happened at once. The two riderless equines

reared and bolted for the forest, startled by Shangra's roar. The woolly bovine drawing the wagon let out a frightened bellow of its own and took off with the wagon sluing from side to side as it bounced over muddy potholes, its driver and passenger hanging on for their lives while hollering for the bovine to stop. They finally disappeared around a bend in the road.

The two men holding the girl had swords of their own and might have been trouble, but the sight of the two onrushing felinae and their sword-brandishing riders gave them pause. Instead, they forgot about the girl and ran after their own fleeing mounts.

They didn't get far. Terien caught up with one and took him down with a well-placed boot in the back, while Duncan felled the other by steering Tiagra into him, knocking the man flying.

Terien brought Shangra to a grinding stop and jumped down, his sword pointed at the two men. "Your weapons. On the ground. Now."

Both men grudgingly drew their swords and tossed them at Terien's feet.

"Go after that wagon, Duncan. I'll keep these two company."

"Terien, the girl's gone," Duncan informed him, scanning the forest urgently. "We can't just leave her out here all alone."

"You worry about that wagon. I'll worry about the girl."

Duncan nodded and took off down the muddy road.

Reaching a hand up to scratch behind Shangra's ear, Terien flashed a smile at his two captives and said, "Be good while I'm gone, kids." To Shangra he said, "Stay on guard", then strode away into the tall grass of the ditch, smiling to himself at the fretful look the two exchanged when Shangra edged closer to them and growled.

His charges in good care, he searched the edge of the forest until he came across his objective. The pack the girl had been carrying lay where she'd dropped it, forgotten in her desperate flight into the woods. Picking it up, he walked back to Shangra and held the pack up for the cat to sniff. Whiskers quivering, Shangra snuffled at the pack and then sneezed, shaking his huge head.

"Good boy, Shangra. Now fetch," Terien commanded,

thrusting a finger towards the forest. The big cat bounded away, tail high and waving like a flag. Returning his attention back to his captives who were now shifting restlessly and looking miserable, Terien held his sword diagonally across his chest, at the ready. "It might go easier for you two if you tell me the truth," he warned them. "What were you planning to do with the girl?"

Faces hard, the men stared mutely at him.

"'I won't let you sell me'," Terien quoted. "Are you slavers? Or was she just the opportunity of the day?"

The man on the left glanced sideways at his partner, then away to the forest. He seemed to be considering. Maybe all he needed was a little incentive.

"I'm sure the girl will be quite willing to tell her side of the story," Terien said, slowly pacing around them, stroking his chin as though seemingly deep in thought. "But then, her story is bound to be one-sided. She seemed terribly angry, and if she thought you were going to sell her, I'm sure whatever she has to say will paint an ugly picture."

The man on the right continued to stand there, staring resolutely at his feet, but the other was following Terien with his eyes.

"In these parts the law is rather – archaic," Terien went on. "If you *are* slave traders, they will immediately stretch your necks," he said, his eyes narrowing to dangerous slits. "However, if you were something like, oh – say thieves or the like – that had come across a golden opportunity to make some quick cash, then you'd probably get hauled away to one of the logging camps in the area. Years of back-breaking work maybe, but at least you'd have a back to break."

The man on the left came to a decision and lifted his head. "The boss came up with the idea out of the blue. We were just robbing people until he heard her say she was a Healer."

"Shut up," his partner growled.

"No, you shut up! Robbing people is one thing, but selling them is another. I ain't gonna get my neck stretched because that windbag got it into his head to sell the poor girl!"

"I said shut up!" The other warned, his hands balling into fists.

"I told you guys. I told you I didn't like the idea from the start," he said, angrily shaking a finger in the other man's face. "Not after she fixed Kale's leg and all."

Not that Terien wasn't rather enjoying the exchange between the two or the information it was bringing to light, but it probably would be best to end their argument before they came to blows. "Gentlemen!" Terien waggled his sword at them to get their attention. "You can argue later. Much later, preferably."

A shriek of terror echoed through the forest.

"That cat of yours won't... well, you know..." the man on the left asked, actual concern on his face.

Terien almost laughed, but managed to keep a straight face. "Nah. He's not hungry enough. Yet." His wicked grin drained the color from his captives' faces.

"Terien!"

Turning at the sound of the familiar voice, Terien smiled as Elek and four other men trotted towards him on their equines. The rest were some distance away at the mouth of the road with the supply carts.

"Hey! Reinforcements!" Duncan's voice rang out.

Terien looked the other way down the road to see Duncan arriving with two men tied together, walking sullenly behind Tiagra.

"Their wagon is a total write-off," Duncan reported. "That crazy bovine of theirs had it wrapped around a tree. These two were shook up, but okay otherwise."

"And the bovine?"

"I left it happily munching grass," Duncan replied with a laugh. "It looked so content I didn't want to disturb it. No sign of the two equines, though. Some farmer up the road will probably be happy to find them, I'm sure."

"You two have been busy," Elek interjected, grinning. "And here I thought you couldn't possibly get into trouble. I should have known better."

"Yeah, well, damsel in distress and all that," Terien said sheepishly. "These guys were planning to sell a young lady they had somehow acquired. This one says it was a spur-of-the-moment thing." Terien shrugged. "Regardless, we'll turn them over to the constabulary at Donellin on our way to the crossroads."

Duncan frowned. "What about the girl?"

At that moment the bushes at the edge of the forest rustled loudly and Shangra pranced into view, looking very pleased with himself. In his massive jaws he delicately held a rather muddy form. Unharmed and looking utterly furious, she was hanging face down, her hips securely clenched in Shangra's teeth. Her long braid, soaked and muddy, lashed her face with Shangra's every step.

"Let me go! Now! I mean this instant, you overgrown excuse for a house cat! Put me down!"

A chorus of laughter erupted and Aurori raised her head, surprise washing over her face as she took in the sight of the extra men that had arrived. One look at the emblems on their boots and on the bridles of their equines told her she would be safe, though. She had seen the eagle-and-diamond crest once before, when King Koren of Kaethos had visited Eristea almost eight years ago. These were military men, no question. How humiliating to be seen like this by them! And they were laughing at her.

Her cheeks burned with renewed anger as the cat proudly presented her to its master. Angry as she was, though, she still couldn't help but notice how handsome this tall man was, even with his dark hair soaked and plastered to his forehead. He was making an effort not to laugh, but his broad shoulders were shaking just the same.

"Make him put me down this instant!" Green eyes glittering, she folded her arms in a vain attempt to appear commanding.

"At once, my lady," Terien said, managing to keep a straight face as he sketched a bow. "Good boy, Shangra. Let her go." Shangra's jaws released on command, dropping the girl into the soggy grass at Terien's feet.

"Sorry about that," he apologized, bending at the waist and extending a hand to help her up. "Are you okay?"

Her foot lashed out, catching Terien behind the knees and pulling his legs out from under him. He landed with a squish in the wet grass, flat on his back, his sword falling from his hand.

Unhurt except for his pride, he raised himself up on his elbows and glared at her. "What did you do that for? I just saved your life."

"I know!" she shouted at him. Swiping the hem of her cloak into her hands she clamored to her feet and stared down at Terien, indignant. "That was for scaring the life out of me by letting that – that furry *creature* chase after me," she said vehemently, flinging a hand at Shangra. "Now we're even."

Elek and Duncan were practically falling off their mounts because they were laughing so hard, and Terien's disapproving glance only made them laugh harder.

Terien realized what a ridiculous sight he was and gave a short self-deprecating laugh. "Guess I deserved it, then." He picked himself up, made a half-hearted attempt at wiping his muddy hands on his soggy cloak, then stuck a hand out to her again, giving her his most dashing smile. "Let's start over, shall we? I'm Terien. And you are…?"

"Aurori," she introduced, taking his hand. Her expression softened beneath the caked mud. The intensity of his blue eyes and the gentle way he placed his other hand over hers melted all her fury. "I'm sorry about what I just did." She shivered, wet and cold. "I guess it… well, I was just so angry. And with everything that's happened to me… I didn't mean to take it out on you, but I… oh, this is embarrassing." She averted her eyes. "Thank you for coming to my rescue. You didn't have to." She could feel herself blush. This was ridiculous.

"You're welcome," he said graciously, as though she hadn't just dumped him on his rear. He found himself thinking she was quite lovely, even soaking wet and covered with mud. His smile suddenly died. "You're shivering," he remarked, giving her hand a squeeze before releasing it. "We'd better get you some dry clothes."

"We have spare cloaks in the supply carts," Elek offered.

"Right." Terien gave a short whistle to get Shangra's attention, then snapped his fingers and pointed to the ground. Obediently, the felinae crouched down on its haunches, its massive back now easy to access. Aurori gasped in surprise as Terien grasped her around the waist with both hands and effortlessly lifted her onto

Shangra's back. He reached down and picked up her pack in one hand and his sword in the other. He sheathed the sword and tossed the pack to Elek before hoisting himself into position behind Aurori. Reaching around her, he took hold of the reins and gave them a light snap, giving Shangra the cue to rise.

"One of your captors admitted to planning to sell you," Terien told Aurori as the group moved out onto the road and headed for the waiting supply carts. "We'll turn them over to the authorities in Donellin on our way through, but I'd be interested to hear how you managed to come into their possession before we hand them over."

"I had been headed for Donellin to pick up some supplies and purchase an equine when I met up with these four," she said, indicating her would-be captors with a thrust of her chin.

"You were all alone, Miss?" Elek asked over his shoulder.

Aurori nodded in confirmation. "Yes, I was."

"Really?" Duncan asked, amazed. "Only fools and..."

"I know! I know! Only fools and Healers travel alone," she finished for him, exasperated. She could feel Terien shaking with silent laughter and snapped her head to the side in an attempt to look at him, her wet braid slapping across his face. "I'll tell you the same thing I told them. I may be a Healer, but I'm no fool."

"A Healer, eh? I thought you might be when I saw your white cloak." Terien wiped away the muddy drops her braid had left on his cheek. "We had a Healer come through Kaethos a few years ago. Fascinating fellow." He chewed his lip in thought for a moment. "Donellin couldn't have been your final destination, though. Where were you headed?"

Aurori shifted uncomfortably. She would have to settle for a half-truth again. "I'm on a Healer's journey. I was heading... north."

"I see," Terien said. "Just... north?"

"Well, I planned on going to Glaybor, but after that – I don't know yet."

"We're headed to Glaybor as well," Terien said. "If you'd like, you can travel with us. We have some business there, but will be branching off to Brinbourne in the east after that. Your choice if you want to go on alone from Glaybor."

"That's very generous of you. Thank you. At least I won't have to worry about bandits," Aurori said with a rueful glance back at her would-be captors.

When they reached the waiting supply carts and had dismounted, Terien was met with a flurry of questions from the men. He and Duncan took turns explaining what had taken place while Elek immediately went to retrieve two new cloaks, one for Terien and one for the soaked and shivering Aurori.

Elek handed Aurori a towel with which she wiped the mud from her face and hands and sponged the excess water from her braid, then he held a brand new cloak out for her. Aurori shed her ruined white one, pleased to note that the white tunic she wore had remained clean. Unfortunately, the knees of her white pants and the soft doeskin boots she wore had not faired as well, but were still serviceable if somewhat mud caked. Slipping into the warm folds of the cloak Elek held out for her felt wonderful. For the first time in days she was finally warming up.

After giving Elek a nod of thanks, she turned to thank Terien who had been standing behind her. Butterflies filled her stomach and her words caught in her throat at the sight of him as he whirled the soaking wet cloak from his shoulders. Terien was a striking figure, resplendent in a black dress uniform. The long-sleeved black tunic had silver braid stitched at the sleeve edges and around the high collar. The same braid ran around the capped shoulders and down the front of the tunic in double lines that diverged just below his rib cage and looped to the back. An eagle in full flight with talons extended, clutching a single brilliant cut diamond, the emblem of Kaethos, was also embroidered on the left breast of the tunic, but was rendered in gold, a color reserved for the ruling family. A silver sash was slung around his hips and tied to the side, while a black belt and ornate scabbard hung from his left hip. A holstered weapon of some sort lay against his right upper thigh. Black pants, also with silver braid embroidered on the outer seams, black boots, and a silver-lined black cape completed the outfit.

However, it was the pendant he wore on a silver chain that struck Aurori. She felt dizzy just looking at it and actually stumbled backwards into Elek. It was a transparent cylinder, four inches long and one inch in diameter, filled with a kaleidoscope of shifting light. She wore an identical cylinder hidden under her own tunic. Soloth had given it to her, telling her it was a key that would allow her access to the hidden cities. And if Terien wore one, then…

"Aurori! Are you okay?" Terien was looking at her with concern. "You're staring at me like I suddenly sprouted horns!"

How was she going to explain *that* to him when he hadn't yet told her he was the Chosen? At this point no one else but the other Chosen and his own men would recognize the key he wore. Lord Soloth had told her that the other Chosen was the Prince of Kaethos, but she had assumed that their paths would not cross. Now, here he was standing right in front of her. He had even saved her life. Should she reveal herself to him? That was certainly an option, but she hadn't even considered it before now. No. Not yet. She wanted to be free to leave his company if she wanted to. If she told him who she was, he might expect her to accompany him and she wanted to be free to go her own way whenever she chose.

"Aurori?" he asked again, taking her shoulders and giving her a slight shake.

"You… you… you're a Prince," she managed to get out, stabbing a finger at the golden eagle crest on the breast of his tunic. She silently congratulated herself on the nice recovery she made.

His hand covered the crest self-consciously. "Yeah, well…"

"He's the Chosen, too," one of the men piped up proudly, beaming.

Terien's cheeks actually reddened and he shot a withering glance at the man.

Silently thanking her unwitting savior, Aurori gasped in surprise, her hands fluttering to her chest as she immediately went down on one knee before Terien. "Chosen! I am honored!"

Blowing out an exasperated breath, Terien reached down and lifted her to her feet. "Please don't do that," he said, his tone a mixture of annoyance and embarrassment.

"But you… you're a Prince! And the Chosen!" She averted

her eyes from him. Actually, now she felt twice as bad about kicking his legs out from under him. "I'm so sorry, Your Majesty. If I had known... I never would have..."

"Dumped me on my ass?" Terien asked, grinning.

Now it was Aurori's turn to blush. Well, at least he had a sense of humor. "Yes, Your Majesty."

"Just call me Terien," he told her, taking her hand and kissing her fingertips. "My friends all do, and I think you qualify by virtue of having caught me totally off guard."

"She deserves a medal," Elek said. "That move has failed me every time I tried to use it on you in practice." He leaned in close to Aurori and whispered loudly enough for everyone to hear. "Will you teach me how you did it?"

Aurori chuckled at that.

Releasing Aurori's hand, Terien turned to his men. "Well, it's already nearing noon and we need to stop in Donellin. We'd best be on the move."

Terien winked at Aurori as he once more signaled Shangra into a crouch and made ready to assist her onto the felinae's back. "Now, how about telling us the whole story of how you met these four?"

Chapter Five

The rain had stopped and the skies had cleared somewhat by the time Terien and his entourage arrived in the bustling town of Donellin an hour after midday. Leaving Aurori at the seamstress shop, the men went off to turn their four charges over to the authorities.

The matronly seamstress, who had previously worked for the royal family in Kaethos, warmly welcomed Aurori, fussing and clucking over the state of Aurori's clothes and hair. She had even insisted on drawing a bath for Aurori in her own private facilities, an offer that was gratefully accepted.

Emerging clean and refreshed a short while later, Aurori was shown an array of finely tailored clothes of every color and texture, including a beautiful replacement for the ruined white cloak that was the trademark of a Healer. Edged in green embroidery, it was feathery soft to the touch and reputed by the matron to be both water-resistant and wind-proof, fashioned from a material that was produced in a faraway land by people who still held an old technology for making exquisite fabrics.

Armed now with warmer clothes and feeling much more herself than she had in days, Aurori paid for her purchases, thanked the matron profusely and exited the store to find Duncan and Elek waiting for her. They had been busy in her absence, looking over the equines that were for sale at a nearby livery.

Excitedly ushering her over to the barn and up to one of the stalls, they pointed out the equine they had picked out for her. An Appaloosa mare named Mystafire raised her head over the rail to snuffle at Aurori's outstretched hand and it was love at first sight for both. Elek had teased that at least Mystafire's black-on-white dappled coat went well with Aurori's new white cloak and received a playful swat from her for the comment.

The long shadows of approaching evening were already slanting across the path by the time the group had finally gotten under way after sharing a hasty meal at the local tavern. They managed to get as far as the crossroads and turn north before it was decided to make camp for the evening.

That first night found Aurori feeling a little self-conscious about being the only female in the group, a feeling that was quickly dissipated by the easy acceptance afforded her by these rugged warriors. They made every effort to make her feel at ease, taking turns introducing themselves to her as they sat around the three fires that had been built.

They had even fussed over her comfort when it was time to bed down for the night, giving her tips on how best to pad the ground for her sleeping bag and arguing over which fire would be the warmest. It was a trend that was to continue for the rest of the journey, much to Aurori's delight and embarrassment.

As the journey to Glaybor progressed over the next couple of days, spirits were high as the weather improved and the terrain became more flat with areas of large open fields interspersed between the stands of trees, signaling their approach to the prairie regions. Though they passed through several small villages on their way, they never stayed more than an hour or two before moving on, preferring to spend the night along the road since their presence in the villages invariably created undue excitement and pleas for them to stay on for a few days.

Terien watched his men, amused with the effect Aurori's presence had on them. Generally a good bunch, they were not only a bit more polite than usual for those first two days, but took turns regaling Aurori with tales of their prowess as warriors, trying hard to impress the lovely lady in their midst. On the third night, however, Aurori stunned them all by asking if they would teach her some of the self-defense moves she watched them practice when they would break for the day.

"I thought Healers were supposed to be pacifists," Duncan remarked, taken aback by her request that Terien show her how to handle the quarterstaffs they had been using.

She had frowned at that. "Healers love peace and avoid conflict, but will certainly fight if the cause is sufficient," she had informed him, hands on hips. "There have even been stories of Healers fighting in some of the wars they encountered in their journeys. Of course, it's not something we take part in lightly, but there are times when violence is a necessary evil."

Unable to argue with that, the men took to teaching her a little about every discipline they were proficient in. Aurori soon found herself trying out the bow and arrow, hand-to-hand martial combat and even a few sword moves. Most evenings, though, she and Terien could be found practicing the quarterstaff – her weapon of choice – by the light of the fire. Afterwards, they would always rejoin Duncan and the others, resting, as they exchanged stories about their homes and lives, sometimes into the wee hours of the night.

It was a hard thing for Aurori to always lie about her life in Eristea and she was beginning to feel quite guilty about it, the more she got to know Terien and the others. She knew them by name now, knew every one of their individual quirks of personality, too. Her favorites were three that stood out from the rest.

The first was Haren. Taller than Terien and built like a brick house, he was as gentle and soft-spoken as a newborn with wispy blond hair and gentle brown eyes. Then there was Benem, the small one. Short and muscular with wavy dark hair and dark eyes, his gruff manner belied a heart that was twice his size. The friendship between the two was a joy to watch, with Benem constantly needling Haren over his slow and rigid mannerisms, and Haren good-naturedly rebutting him in his soft, precise way. The third was Elek, Duncan's second-in-command. A robust and jovial sort, he loved to sing. And he did – rather badly, too, but with gusto.

Terien and Duncan were another matter. While they were her absolute favorites above all the others, they also perplexed her. Duncan was so serious, she sometimes had trouble telling if he was teasing her or chastising her. As for Terien, he was proving to be a true leader and, in her opinion, the perfect choice for the Chosen. However, he didn't act at all the way she would have expected him to. She soon realized that he was simply not that self-absorbed. Even as a Prince he could have demanded the pomp and ceremony that was his due. Instead, he led his men by example, as a near equal, never berating them for a mistake made, and always showing them courtesy and respect. Even-tempered and unassuming, he was simply content to be himself, and that alone endeared him to Aurori more than anything else could have.

On the morning of the eleventh day of their journey they had awakened to a cloudless day. The binary suns shone down on the fields around them, setting the world aglow in their rich orange light. In the distance, the jewel of the prairie region was visible – Glaybor, ruling kingdom of the prairies.

"I can't believe that Glaybor and Kaethos warred with each other for so many years," Aurori commented to Terien as they made their way down the road. "They're so far from each other."

"Not far enough, I'm afraid. Remember, the keyta trees of Kaethos are the only ones in the region whose wood can be used for building, and Glaybor produces far more grains than we were capable of on the plots of land we cleared in the forests," Terien advised her. "The trade agreement we hammered out is almost thirteen years old now, but the wars fought before that were pretty brutal."

Excitement stirred in Aurori as they soon entered the outskirts of the city of Glaybor, their presence causing a fuss as they moved through the narrow streets. People would stop all activities to stand and watch the procession go by, the vast majority waving and smiling. Only a handful would fold their arms across their chests and watch them with guarded expressions.

Realizing she was lagging behind, Aurori nudged Mystafire into a quicker pace, her attention turning to the large building they were approaching. It was magnificent. Obviously rebuilt from the ruins of the old civilization, it had a circular design ringed by walkways that ran all around it on each of its five storeys. Its domed top shone like gold in the light of the suns and it was surrounded by a large fenced-off area of trees and grass that featured a huge statue of a winged equine around which water fountained into a pool below. A stone path lined by beautiful flowering trees, whose fragrance filled the air, led from the gate, swerved to the right of the fountain and continued to the front steps of the castle.

Approaching the four guards at the gate, Terien opened his cloak and draped the front folds over his shoulders to expose the crest of Kaethos on his tunic. A few brief words later he and his entourage passed through the gates and made their way to the front steps, while one of the guards ran ahead of them and into the castle, presumably to announce their arrival.

At the steps the men all dismounted and clustered around Terien. Aurori hung back, standing beside Mystafire and looking around at the manicured courtyard until moments later Terien left the knot of men and came up to her.

"I want you to accompany me inside to meet King Denid," he said without preamble, taking her hand.

Aurori gave him a sly look. "You expect to need a Healer?" she teased.

"I might," he said with a laugh. "Seriously, though, I know Denid has a great respect for your people." He released her hand and shyly glanced away. "I would be honored by your presence."

"And I would be honored to accompany you, Lord Terien," she said formally, giving him an abbreviated curtsey.

Offering her his arm, Terien strode to the steps and was greeted by a courtier who led them into the castle. Aurori noticed that Duncan walked with them half a step to the right and one step behind and that only half the men accompanied them, trailing in single file as they traversed the great hall and were ushered into the large throne room that was their destination.

The throne room was at the very center of the castle, directly below that great golden dome, with the throne itself on a raised dais right in the middle of the room. Seated there was a man only a few years older than Terien, arrayed in rich robes of gold and blue. His dark brown hair was swept back from his face, accentuating his high forehead and hawkish features. To his right, stood a man with his hands clasped behind his back, regarding them with a hard look. A few years younger than the King, his long blond hair hung loose around his shoulders like a curtain. His features were strikingly handsome, marred only by a scar beneath his right eye. When he spotted Aurori his pale blue eyes fastened on her long enough to make her squirm.

A dozen paces from the dais, Duncan took Aurori by the arm

and held her back with himself and the other men while Terien approached the King of Glaybor, halting at the bottom step.

"Greetings to you, King Denid," Terien said, offering a bow from the waist.

"Glaybor welcomes you, Prince Terien," Denid replied formally, leaning forward. "But I wonder what brings you to Glaybor so many months before the next scheduled meeting. And without your father, King Koren. A breech of protocol, I might add."

Terien's shoulders squared and his chin raised a fraction. "I do not come to you on behalf of my father or Kingdom Kaethos," he said, feeling a rush of apprehension wash over him as he worried what Denid's reaction to his next words would be. "I come as the emissary of the Reunification foretold. I come as the Chosen."

"Chosen? You?" The man standing at King Denid's side laughed out loud, a harsh bark of dismissal.

"Makhani!" Denid hissed, warning the blond man into silence with a ferocious glance. Standing now, Denid descended the steps until he was eye to eye with Terien, his hazel eyes searching Terien's sapphire ones for any hint of collusion. "What proof have you of such an outrageous claim?"

Taking that as his cue, Duncan stepped forward and placed a small black cube into Terien's outstretched hand, which Terien then held out to King Denid on the flat of his palm. He flicked a hidden switch with his thumb and a column of light emanated from its flat surface, coalescing into a three dimensional holographic image of the magnificent glass and steel spires of a city floating in the clouds. The view of the image rotated slowly for a few seconds, then evaporated, replaced by the image of an elderly man's face.

"I am Sky Lord Soloth, Primary of Quayvern, city of the Final Reunification," the image said in a voice that was somehow commanding and soothing at the same time. "Before you, stands Terien, Prince of Kaethos and the Chosen of the Gathering. The future of your people rests upon him. And upon you. Listen well."

Soloth's wizened visage faded away, replaced once more by the mesmerizing image of the floating city.

Denid stared wide-eyed at the message cube, his gaze never leaving the representation of Quayvern as his expression flickered, reflecting the shifting thoughts going through his mind. "*You will know them by the images of light they bring forth from the air,*" he quoted, his voice a barely audible whisper. "The Sky Lord said that I would know the Chosen by this, but..."

Terien glanced over to Makhani who stood frozen in place on the dais behind the King, his eyes narrowed and focused on the cube, but whether in concentration or disbelief, Terien couldn't be sure.

Eyes finally regaining their focus, Denid looked at Terien and took a hesitant step back as the image of Quayvern dissolved and Terien slowly lowered the cube. Astonishing everyone, King Denid went down on one knee before him. Head bowed, Denid's voice was shaky but clear.

"The Kingdom of Glaybor is honored by your presence, Chosen one."

Terien gave an irritated sigh and reached forward to clasp Denid by one bicep, pulling him to his feet. "Not the reaction I expected, but more than I hoped for," Terien observed wryly. "You and I have known each other for years, Denid. I'm still the same person you knew. Only my job description has changed."

"Yes, but..."

"We need to talk. I have much to tell you, as you can imagine," Terien interrupted before Denid could argue the point further.

Inhaling deeply, Denid nodded and motioned a hand at Makhani. "See to it that Terien's men are given accommodations and their mounts are taken care of. Send word to the nobles of Glaybor that there will be a banquet this evening in honor of our guest."

Makhani stiffened. "I would prefer to be with you to hear what he has to say."

Denid spun to face him. "Then have the servants make the arrangements. We will be in the conference room. You can join us shortly."

Makhani gave a curt nod of his head, clearly unhappy with that, but turned on his heel and stalked away to carry out his orders.

"A banquet is hardly necessary..." Terien started to say.

"You are the Chosen," Denid asserted. "I would offer a banquet for any noble traveling through Glaybor. How can I do any less for you?" he asked with a raised eyebrow. "Besides," he continued, walking over to Aurori and taking her hand, "it has been some time since our kingdom has been graced by the presence of a Healer, and I look forward to speaking with this one," he said as he kissed her fingertips, his eyes locking with hers. "You will join us tonight, won't you?"

Aurori curtseyed and gave him a demure smile. "I would be pleased to, Your Majesty."

Terien interposed himself between them as several servants arrived to escort Terien's men to their rooms. "I will see to my men and join you shortly, then."

"I'm sure you remember where the conference room is?" Denid inquired, to which Terien nodded his affirmation. "Good, then we shall meet there at your convenience."

Terien and his entourage were led from the throne room and into the great hall where the rest of the men waited. Following the servants, they were escorted through the brick-walled passages and up one flight of stairs to a set of elaborately decorated suites on the second floor of the castle. The men dispersed into the rooms in groups of four to share accommodations while Terien, Duncan and Aurori were directed to separate suites.

Hesitating at the door of Aurori's suite, Terien cleared his throat nervously. "Duncan and I will be busy for the rest of the afternoon, but... I will see you tonight, won't I?"

"Now, how could I miss out on the Chosen's first banquet?" she teased.

Smiling, Terien tossed her a mock salute as he spun on his heel and headed back down the stairs with Duncan. "Until later, then," he called over his shoulder.

"At the banquet," she confirmed, watching until he disappeared from view.

Stepping into her suite and closing the door, Aurori immediately went to the window and looked out over the city, scanning the rows of low mud-and-brick buildings that lay beyond the enclosure of the castle grounds. Terien was beginning his mission as the Gatherer and it was time for her to begin her own mission as Observer.

She moved away from the window and looked down at the comfortable canopied bed, thinking how nice it would be to spend the night somewhere soft after so many nights on the ground. That would have to wait, though. Instead, she deposited her pack on the bed and quickly left her room.

Finding her way down to the great hall, she asked one of the guards at the door for directions to the market and proceeded out, feeling a little nervous about going out alone in a strange city.

Chapter Six

The open-air market Aurori had been directed to was only a short distance from the castle and ran down a wide lane lined on both sides with single-storey buildings. At this late hour of the morning, it was filled to capacity with people bustling about and talking loudly as they haggled over their purchases. Brightly colored canopies flapped above most of the stalls and the smell of freshly baked breads wafted through the air, accompanied by the scent of spiced meats cooking over open grills. Aurori's stomach growled and she realized she hadn't eaten since early morning.

Stopping at a cart displaying delicious-smelling sweet breads, Aurori fumbled to dig out a gold chip from an inside pocket of her cloak and overheard two women at the next cart chatting about Terien's arrival in Glaybor.

"Did you see the size of those cats they ride?" one asked her companion.

"So who was looking at *them*," the other retorted. "That Prince is an eyeful! Did you see how he was dressed? I tell ya, he's here to look for a wife," she said with a conspiratorial wink.

"Hah! Shows what you two know," a third piped up. "With an entourage like that, he's here on business."

"Lousy Kaethosians," the cart vender muttered, curling his lip. "Wish they'd stay in the forest and just send us the lumber they promise us."

That caught Aurori's ear. "You have a grudge against them?"

The vender snorted and looked her up and down. "Where the hell are you from that you don't know about the wars we fought with them bastards?"

Aurori felt a tingle of shock at his harsh words. "I know about the wars, but I thought a peaceful trade agreement had been made."

The vender shrugged indifferently. "Peace is good. So is the trading. But it don't take away the fact that a lot of good men died in the fighting, including my brother."

"I'm sorry to hear that," Aurori told him sincerely. She paused for the space of a heartbeat before going on. "What has life been like in Glaybor since the trade treaty? I mean, is everyone happy?"

"Is everyone happy where you come from?" he asked in a patronizing tone. He shook his head. "People ain't ever happy."

Annoyed with him, Aurori slapped a gold chip on the cart and picked up a spiced sweet bread.

"Ignore him," one of the women at the other cart advised, dismissing him with a roll of her eyes. She leaned a hip against the post holding up the cart's canopy and folded her arms. "Life's pretty good in Glaybor for the most part. Ours is a rich city, what with all the good land we have for growing. And the King does right enough for us simple folk." She flashed Aurori a gap-toothed smile. "In fact, I think you might be interested to go down that alley over there, the one that's two stalls down and to the right."

Craning her head to see the alley, Aurori asked, "What's down there?"

"Well, you being a Healer, you ought to be interested to see what old Baruch is up to." The woman laughed when Aurori's jaw dropped open. "We had plenty of Healers come through Glaybor over the years," she explained. "Can't miss them white cloaks of yours. Only a Healer would wear a color that dirties so easily. Go on," she urged, motioning towards the alley. "Old Baruch is a physician. I'd imagine you two would have a lot to talk about. He's tending a missus down there who's about to give birth. Fourth door on the left."

"Thanks!" Aurori called over her shoulder, already hastening towards the alley as she popped the last piece of sweet bread into her mouth.

When she had turned down the dimly lit alley, Aurori found it easy enough to find the right place. A cluster of men was gathered around one doorway halfway down, pacing and conversing in hushed tones. As she approached, they all fell silent except for one young man who threw his hands in the air and seemed on the verge of tears the moment he saw her.

"Aw, no! They've gone and called for a Healer! I knew it! I

knew it was taking too long!"

Flustered, Aurori quickly swallowed the mouthful of bread. "No! It's okay," she blurted out. "I was just in the market and someone said I should come and see Baruch." Her face reddened. "I didn't mean to frighten you. I'm sure your wife is fine," she assured him.

He seemed to relax a bit, but only for a second. "But it's been so long," he wailed. "Maybe you could go and see?"

"Why aren't you with her?" she said, frowning. "Husbands are usually present at the birth of their children."

The men standing around tittered like old women, bringing a rash of heat to the young man's face.

"I... can't stand the sight of... blood," he admitted, his obvious humiliation eliciting another round of laughter.

Aurori shushed them with a glare.

"Okay, I'll go in and see how things are progressing," she assured him. Her hand on the handle, she stopped before pulling the door open. "How long has it been since she went into labor?"

"Two whole hours!" the man whined.

It took great effort to stifle the laugh that threatened to escape her lips, and it didn't help that the men were all grinning at her like mad rabbits. Seems they'd been deliberately having fun at the poor fellow's expense. Who knew what horror stories they'd been telling him!

Composing herself, Aurori entered the shadowed interior of the dwelling and was greeted by the sight of an old grandmother sitting in a chair and knitting. The room was clean and modestly furnished with a table and chairs made of a lovely dark wood. Handmade tapestries hung on the walls, depicting various scenes.

The old woman put aside her knitting at seeing Aurori and her wrinkled face lit up.

"Healer! Welcome! Welcome!" The woman exclaimed as she hobbled over to Aurori and grasped her hand.

Her clothes were of a simple design, but were clean and not very worn. These people were obviously quite well off.

"I don't mean to intrude, but I was directed here by a lady in the market. She said that the physician named Baruch would be here."

"Oh no, my dear. No intrusion at all. Healers are always welcome. Baruch will be out in just a moment."

"How *is* the mother doing?" Aurori asked. "The father outside is as nervous as a cat on hot coals. Of course, his friends aren't helping matters at all."

Grandma giggled like a schoolgirl. "I'm sure they aren't! This is my grandson's first child and I think he's had a worse time of it than his wife," she confided. "Anyhow, his wife's just fine. She delivered a healthy little girl a little while ago."

The door to the bedroom swung open and a middle-aged woman bustled out, cooing to the bundle in her arms and smiling hard enough to chase her wrinkles into her hairline.

"My first grandchild!" she exclaimed, proudly showing the baby to Aurori and the old woman. Still beaming, she went straight to the door and disappeared outside amidst a cheer from the gathered men.

The man that emerged from the bedroom could best be described as being a bear of a man. Of medium height, he was barrel-chested and large handed. His brown hair was cut short and gray-streaked, as was the full beard he wore. He radiated warmth and caring, his kindly brown eyes crinkling the second he saw Aurori.

"Well, well! Two blessed events on one day! A new life enters the world and a Healer arrives in Glaybor. Welcome, child. My name's Baruch, as I'm sure you've been told." He thrust a meaty hand out to Aurori and her own disappeared in his massive grip.

"I'm Aurori. I arrived with Prince Terien of Kaethos this morning. I was out exploring the city and was told I should meet you. So, here I am. I hope I'm not intruding."

"Of course you aren't," Baruch assured her with a broad smile. "Let me just finish here and I'll accompany you on your tour of the city."

The door opened then as the proud father came in, holding his baby daughter, followed by his mother and a few women from the neighborhood who were carrying baskets of food and items of clothes for the child.

Baruch took hold of Aurori's shoulder and steered her towards the door as he congratulated the father, gave them some last words of advice about the baby and said his goodbyes to them over the clamor of many voices all talking at once.

Closing the door behind him, Baruch turned to Aurori and indicated the way back to the market with a wave of his hand. "Now then, Healer. What would you like to see first?" he asked as they walked.

Aurori looked up at Baruch. "To be honest, I was planning on wandering around the city just to find out how well the people are doing here, to see if I could offer my services. But, from what I've seen so far, the people are quite well." She hesitated. "I take it you're not the only physician in Glaybor."

Baruch's ample belly shook as he laughed. "Oh, no. There are several throughout the city and in the surrounding countryside." He rubbed at his nose, looking a little uncomfortable all of a sudden. "Actually, I'm King Denid's personal physician."

That made Aurori's eyebrows rise. "And you still go out and tend the common folk?"

Again Baruch laughed his belly laugh. "I have to keep busy somehow. After all, the King's a young and healthy man!" His expression sobered. "In truth, I enjoy working with the people, and King Denid agrees that the best way for him to know how well the people are faring is if I go out amongst them."

"That's... very caring of him."

"King Denid cares very much for his people and their well-being. It was he who negotiated the trade agreement with Kaethos, after all. He couldn't stand to see his people suffering and dying in the battles led by his father."

"You mean to say that Glaybor was attacking Kaethos?" Aurori asked in surprise. Terien had never once assigned blame for the wars when the subject came up, instead making it sound as though each had equal reason to be in conflict.

"Yes. Old King Thyros was a mean spirited son of a..." Baruch broke off and huffed to himself. "Well, let's just say that there were few who mourned his passing, including Denid. Thyros wanted to harvest trees from land belonging to Kaethos. King Koren took exception to that and offered instead to trade keyta trees for grains and milled flour. Thyros refused and the rest is history, as they say."

"That's interesting. Denid doesn't seem at all like his father, then."

"Ah. He's his mother's son, that one. On the outside, he can be as haughty as his father ever was, but his heart is as golden as the fields of waving grain his mother loved." Baruch swiped away a tear from the corner of his eye. "Fine woman. Fine woman indeed. She raised a fine son, too; rest her soul." Baruch brightened and waved dismissively. "But enough of that. Tell me about yourself. You said you arrived this morning with Prince Terien of Kaethos? I should very much like to hear what a Healer is doing traveling in such a distinguished company!"

As the two of them wandered the city streets, Aurori gave Baruch a full account of her journey thus far, including a detailed description of the turn of events in the throne room that morning. For his part, Baruch pointed out various places and people of interest on their stroll, all the while giving her a good account of the history of Glaybor. It soon became obvious that the people were generally happy here, with poverty being extremely rare. There were always a few malcontents like the vender in the market, but in general the people had a good life and viewed the trade agreement with Kaethos quite favorably. Most blamed the former king's bloodlust for their own losses and not the people or the royal family of Kaethos, which was somewhat of a relief for Aurori.

By the time Baruch had escorted Aurori in a full-circle tour of the city and returned her to the castle, there were carriages arriving for the banquet, filled with finely dressed nobles talking excitedly amongst themselves about the arrival of the Chosen.

Taking Aurori in through the servants' entrance in order to avoid the commotion at the main doors, Baruch escorted her up the back set of stairs that led to the guest rooms before hustling away to his own rooms to prepare for the banquet.

After seeing how well dressed the arriving nobles were, Aurori was wondering to herself what she could possibly do to make her Healer's clothes a bit more presentable, but as she opened the door to her suite she was flabbergasted to find a an impatient-looking little man waiting for her. A tailor, by the looks of the pins jutting out from his vest, he was puttering around with a dress laid out on the bed, glancing from her to the gown and back again.

"Since you weren't here I had to guess at your size based on the description I got from that pair of brutes across the hall. As if they knew anything. How am I supposed to make you presentable if you're not here? Well, never mind, I think this white and pink gown should do quite well, don't you? Of course you do and so do I. Do you like pink? Well, you should with your coloring, anyway," he jabbered as he held the gown up to Aurori. "Oh, and that braid has got to go. I'll have the hairdresser here right away. Maybe if... oh, never mind. There isn't time." He shoved the gown at Aurori and stuck his hands on his hips, blowing a breath between his teeth. "What are you waiting for, girl! The banquet will be starting in half an hour!"

Clucking his tongue and shaking his head, he scurried from the room, leaving Aurori standing slack-jawed in the middle of the room, clutching the gown. "That was very, very scary," she muttered to herself.

Still feeling a little off balance after that encounter, Aurori set about getting herself ready for the banquet while she idly wondered how Terien's afternoon had compared to hers.

★

The afternoon had seemed to drag on for hours. Denid had listened intently and with great interest as Terien had explained at length about how he had learned he was the Chosen and about the long journey he was to make. The only sticking point came when King Denid appointed Makhani as Glaybor's representative for the Final Reunification. Makhani had at first flatly refused, expressing unwillingness to embark on such a long journey, but King Denid did not take kindly to that and asserted his will, basically giving him no choice; accompany the Chosen or be removed from his position as vizier. The dour look on Makhani's face made Terien wonder for a moment if he was actually going to defy King Denid, but in the end Makhani had bowed and resolutely submitted to the will of his King.

Now, standing at the doors to the great hall with Duncan to

one side and King Denid and Makhani at the other, Terien felt drained and had to stifle a yawn several times as he shook hands and greeted the nobles streaming in through the doors.

He was thinking he would have preferred to just get the banquet over with and retire for the night to the inviting bed in his suite until Duncan jabbed him in the ribs and motioned with his eyes towards the grand staircase in the corner.

"She looks like a princess," Duncan whispered.

Terien gaped at the vision he saw descending the stairs. Dressed in a white and pink gown, her hair coifed into a mass of curls that hung around her bare shoulders, Aurori could easily have been mistaken for the princess of the castle. He lost sight of her almost immediately in the crowd filling the great hall, but noticed that Denid whispered something to Makhani, who promptly left the doors and pushed his way through the crowd, heading in her general direction.

"Your Healer is quite a lovely lady," Denid said quietly, leaning towards Terien. "I've asked Makhani to find her and take her into the banquet hall. I hope you don't mind, but I've seated her next to myself."

Terien opened his mouth to deny ownership of Aurori, thought better of it and nodded instead. "By all means, Denid. I don't mind at all."

As the last of the nobles passed the receiving line, Denid, Terien and Duncan made their way to the open doors of the banquet room where Denid raised his hands for silence and addressed the gathering of about one hundred.

"We welcome Terien, Prince of Kaethos and the Chosen of the Gathering, to Glaybor, first city to be graced by his presence," Denid said loudly.

The nobles clapped and cheered, smiles all around.

"Our own Lord Makhani has been selected to accompany the Chosen on his journey, to act as companion and to represent the interests of Glaybor at the Final Reunification." Denid announced. "They will leave tomorrow, so I suggest that we honor them both without further delay, by retiring to the banquet hall and partaking in the feast that has been prepared!"

Another round of applause and cheers erupted but died down

quickly as the nobles moved into the banquet room where serving girls hastily directed them to their tables. Terien and Duncan were ushered to a table at the far end of the room, a place of honor, while the King and a handful of his guests would be seated at the opposite end of the room, near the main doors, as was the custom in Glaybor.

Terien scanned the crowd. Here and there throughout the hall he could see the rest of his men taking seats at various tables, instantly becoming the centers of attention. Then he caught sight of Makhani moving towards the King's table, Aurori in tow. They were laughing together about something as Makhani guided her to the chair next to the King and took the place next to her, sparking a momentary stab of jealousy in Terien. He forced his eyes away, inwardly rebuking himself for the feeling.

"You okay?" Duncan asked quietly, concerned.

"Fine. I'm fine," Terien told him. "Just tired."

"Sure. And you didn't notice how Makhani was looking at her, either."

"Who?" Terien asked innocently.

"Who else? I've seen the way you look at her." Duncan planted his elbows on the table and cradled his chin on his fists, fixing Terien with a wicked look. "You like her."

"I like the spunk she showed in trying to escape from those bandits. She's a nice person. Of course I like her," Terien said defensively.

"No. I mean you *like* her," Duncan emphasized.

"You're imagining things," Terien scoffed.

"You know I don't have an imagination. I'm the serious one, remember?"

No escaping from his best friend. Not now, not ever. "So she's nice looking. I can look, can't I? Besides, I'm on a mission. No time for romance. What's more, I don't even know if she's coming with us tomorrow or going off alone on her Healer's journey."

"So ask her."

"Fine. I will."

"When?"

"Duncan…"

Whatever Terien was about to say was cut short by the arrival of several nobles at their table. Three couples and two single maidens took seats around the table and began to engage them in conversation.

The maidens, though young and lovely in their vibrantly colored gowns, failed to hold Terien's attention. All through the dinner that followed they tried in vain to impress him by acting sophisticated and saying witty things. It was a relief for both Duncan and Terien when the dinner was over and the crowd started to move about the room, giving them the perfect excuse to do the same.

Everyone wanted to talk to him. Terien found himself repeating over and over again the same brief story about his encounter with the Sky Lord until he was ready to run screaming from the room, but his heart really sank into his boots when he saw that the tables in the middle of the room were being cleared away and an orchestra was setting up.

"When did the word 'banquet' become synonymous with the word 'ball'?" he groused to Duncan.

"About the same time you agreed to be the Chosen," Duncan deadpanned.

"Now I suppose I'll be expected to dance with every woman in the room," Terien said with a tired sigh and a grimace.

"Only the really ugly ones, I'm sure."

"You're enjoying this!" Terien accused.

"Yup."

"I thought you were the serious one!" he protested.

Duncan waved a finger back and forth. "Uh, uh, uh. You were the one who once said I needed to have a little more fun."

"Now is not a good time for you to start!"

Duncan simply grinned at him without remorse as one of the maidens who had been seated at their table accosted Terien at the very first strains of music from the orchestra, leading him to the dance floor.

Searching around for a familiar face, Duncan started to make a beeline in the direction of Haren and Benem who were seated at a table a short distance away, a bevy of beauties following their every word and gesture. He never made it. Intercepted by a rather gaudily dressed older woman, he found himself swept onto the dance floor. He could only silently curse the wicked grin Terien gave him when they crossed paths on the floor.

Several times throughout the evening, Terien would be dancing with another nameless noblewoman and would catch a glimpse of Aurori in her splendid gown, either dancing with Makhani or conversing with King Denid and a bearded gentleman seated at the table. Each time he did, he thought about his conversation with Duncan. *It wouldn't hurt to at least talk to her, would it*? He had to be practical. Inviting a Healer along for the journey could be a very wise move. Who knew what they may encounter?

Convinced by his own logic, Terien apologized to the next eager lady awaiting her turn with him when he saw Aurori slip out of an open side door and into the courtyard beyond. He quietly stole away from the ball, practically hugging the shadowed walls as he followed her out. The cool evening air was a refreshing change, and he soon found himself wandering the garden area until he saw her standing on the far side of the equine fountain.

"Beautiful evening, isn't it," he commented breathlessly when he reached her, inwardly wincing at how lame that sounded.

"It is," she agreed. Her voice sounded distant, like her mind was miles away.

Terien decided it was best to just come out and say what was on his mind.

"We'll be leaving for Brinbourne in the morning, and I was wondering... have you decided whether you'll be going on with us or heading north on your own?"

Aurori gave him a sad little smile. "I'm having trouble deciding about that," she said, sighing slowly as she hugged her arms around herself. The evening wasn't at all cold but she still felt chilled. "I was thinking it would be... interesting... to accompany the Chosen on his mission, but I really wasn't planning on making such a long journey." Not true, of course, but the best she could come up with. Even while still on the road to Glaybor she had been agonizing over whether or not to accompany Terien. She had decided not to reveal herself to him just yet, but that didn't mean she couldn't make the journey in his company. The question was – should she?

Terien was nodding sagely, his arm folded across his chest. "I understand. I should also warn you that Makhani mentioned that he had recently heard that there was some fighting going on between a couple of rival factions on the way to Brinbourne. I wouldn't blame you if you wanted to avoid a potential battle zone."

"I am *not* afraid," Aurori huffed firmly.

"I didn't say you were," Terien placated. "Look, I really would like you to come with us," he admitted. "Having a Healer along could prove... well, it would be..." he groped for the words, flailing a hand in the air.

"Useful?" Aurori supplied.

"A Healer would be a welcome addition," he amended. "I can't guarantee there won't be danger, but I can promise that we'd do our very best to protect you. My men would love to have you along." He flashed her a mischievous grin. "Besides, you never did complete your quarterstaff training. A few more lessons and you'll be ready to dump me on my rear!"

"I've already done that once, so you'd better come up with a better incentive," she laughed.

Terien smiled at her jibe and put a hand to his chin, making a show of coming up with a response to her challenge. "Well, it really is a shame that your people won't be participating in the Final Reunification. Maybe... you could be their unofficial representative?" Terien asked hopefully.

"Excuse me?" She gave him a blank stare on that one. What was he talking about?

Terien looked at her askance. "You mean you don't know? The Healer King refused to take part in the Gathering."

"He... did?"

"I'm afraid so. Lord Soloth told me that the King of Eristea didn't think there was a need for the Healers to take part in the Final Reunification. I suppose I can see his point. The Healers are already at peace with everyone else, and from what my father told me, they're pretty much self-sufficient anyway." Terien tipped his head to one side. "That's why I headed straight for Glaybor.

There was no need to go to Eristea."

Aurori chewed her lip and stifled a giggle. She hadn't considered how Lord Soloth might explain why the Gatherer was bypassing Eristea, but the story was plausible. Now, here Terien was asking her to accompany him as representative of Eristea when she already was. It was rather funny.

"I'm sorry," Terien said suddenly. "I… hope I haven't offended you."

"No. Oh no. I was just… thinking about what you said." In truth, the idea of traveling alone had not sat well with Aurori from the start. It had been the role presented to her and she had accepted it as her duty, nothing more. Encountering Terien had been a blessing. She'd be crazy to walk away from this handsome, caring man, especially when it would mean traveling by herself once more.

Her decision made, Aurori stepped close to him. Placing both hands on his chest, she looked up into his eyes. "I would be honored to accompany you, Chosen."

Covering her hands with his own, he smiled down at her. He had the urge to sweep her up and dance around the fountain. "Thank you," he said finally, settling instead for a more neutral response.

The moment was almost magical. The soft strains of a waltz were drifting across the courtyard from the banquet hall, filling the silence of the evening as they stood looking into each other's eyes, both uncertain about how they felt. A gentle breeze carried the scent of the flowering trees and caressed Aurori's hair, making her curls float around her lovely face. For a wild moment Terien considered kissing her, could almost feel her soft lips on his, could almost hear Duncan snickering triumphantly.

Terien gave his head a minute shake to clear the images from his mind and swallowed hard. Aurori was looking up at him expectantly. "You know, I think I've danced with every lady at the banquet except you," he said softly, ruing the heat rising to his cheeks. "You wouldn't like to dance… would you?"

A smile was just beginning to touch the corners of Aurori's lips when Makhani appeared on the scene and the moment came to a crashing end.

"I've been looking for you," Makhani stated as he approached.

"Ah... yes. Just came out for a breath of fresh air," Terien explained, struggling to keep his annoyance at the interruption from showing in his voice as he released Aurori and turned to face Makhani. "It was getting a little warm in there."

If Makhani was aware of having arrived at an awkward moment, he gave no indication. "King Denid noticed your departure and assumed you must be tired after the long day you've had. He thought you might want to know that the guests will be departing shortly and asked that I escort you through the servants' entrance to your suite so that you can avoid the crush," Makhani said with an indifferent shrug that made it clear he thought the courtesy was tantamount to coddling Terien.

"That's very kind of him," Aurori replied in Terien's stead. "I know I'm exhausted."

"This way, then," Makhani smiled, offering Aurori his arm.

As they made their way to their suites, Terien followed a pace or two behind, listening while Aurori informed Makhani of her decision to join them on their journey the next morning. Terien was hard pressed to keep his expression neutral and not roll his eyes as Makhani took the announcement in stride, commenting smoothly that it would be an honor to be in her company. The two men had never gotten along well and it had hardly been a surprise that Makhani had had such a strongly negative reaction to Terien's announcement that he was the Chosen Gatherer or that he had balked at being selected as representative for Glaybor. While Terien knew that Makhani would not allow his contempt to interfere with the Chosen's mission, he felt certain that the blond man would prove to be a thorn in his side during the journey, as he had been during every last meeting regarding the trade agreement between Kaethos and Glaybor. Not that Makhani had ever said or done anything to derail the negotiations – he had simply done nothing to hide his disdain for Terien, making snide comments and generally being a mouthy nuisance.

Terien was just thinking what an interesting journey it was going to be when they arrived at the door to Aurori's suite and bid her a goodnight just as Duncan came up the staircase, followed by the rest of the men. They all looked tired but were still chatting excitedly about their experiences of the evening.

Makhani took this as his cue to leave.

"King Denid will meet you downstairs in the dining room for breakfast before we leave. I will come for you then," he said, bowing to Terien before disappearing down the staircase.

"I look forward to it," Terien called after him, uncertain whether he meant it or not.

Once the men had all filed into their suites, Duncan turned to Terien with a frown on his face. "Where did you wander off to?" he asked, his tone making it clear he was annoyed. "I was beginning to think you'd abandoned us or been kidnapped or something!"

"I was in the courtyard with Aurori, convincing her to come with us."

Duncan's eyebrows shot up. "And?"

"And she's decided to come with us."

"That's it?"

Terien sighed. "Duncan, I already told you – I don't have time for romance."

"Yeah, yeah, I know," Duncan groaned, throwing his hands up in resignation. "Fine. I'll drop the subject," Duncan said with a weary sigh as he opened the door to his suite. He hesitated before entering and looked back at Terien. "For now," he warned, before slipping inside his room and slowly shutting the door.

Terien glanced once more at the door to Aurori's room before entering his own suite, his thoughts in turmoil.

Chapter Seven

The morning after the banquet in the Kingdom of Glaybor, Terien and his entourage got an early start on their journey towards Brinbourne. The men were delighted to find that Aurori would be accompanying them, but were somewhat less enthusiastic with the addition of Makhani to their group. Grim-faced and quiet, he hung back at the end of their procession, sitting ramrod straight on his chestnut equine, dark blue pants and white shirt with billowy sleeves setting him apart from everyone else. His blond hair hung forward over his chest, all but obscuring his face.

"I wonder why Makhani is so sullen," Aurori commented to Duncan as they rode side by side in the middle of the group.

"He's just not very happy to be coming with us. King Denid didn't give him much choice. Bad blood between him and Terien, too," Duncan whispered back, stealing a glance back at the subject in question.

"What happened?" Aurori asked, trying not to be obvious as she hazarded a glance back.

"Now there's a story. I'd suggest you find a way to ask Makhani about it sometime," Duncan said.

Aurori's head whipped around and she frowned at Duncan. "Not Terien?"

"You could," Duncan said, "but Makhani's the one holding the grudge. You might want to hear it from his perspective."

Aurori raised an eyebrow at him. "Fine. I'll go talk to him," she said, reining Mystafire around.

"I said ask him 'sometime'. I didn't mean right this instant," Duncan hissed after her, but she was already fast approaching the sour-looking representative of Glaybor. "Oh well," Duncan muttered, turning his attention away. He shrugged to himself. "Might do some good."

Makhani perked up the moment he became aware of Aurori's presence beside him and he flipped his hair away from his face. "Good morning, my lady," he said with a smile, dipping his head to her.

"You look very cheerful this morning," Aurori teased him, hoping to break the ice.

"My morning has just been cheered by your presence," he complimented.

"That's very flattering, but it doesn't tell me why you looked so unhappy a moment ago."

Makhani turned his eyes away and said nothing.

"You don't like being here, do you?"

Eyes flickering with uncertainty, he turned to study her. "It is my duty to Glaybor and to my King to be here, but it's not my choice. So, no. I'm not happy to be here." He turned from her, his eyes seeking Terien who was riding at the front of the procession. "Finding out that the Royal Boy over there was the Chosen wasn't exactly a thrill, either."

Aurori almost laughed at the appellation Makhani gave Terien but didn't want him to get the wrong idea. "You don't like him?" she asked, fishing for an opening.

Makhani remained tight-lipped for a long stretch before he finally shrugged to himself and looked over at Aurori. "Let's just say that his high-and-mighty attitude does little for me."

That description was as far away from the truth as it could get from what Aurori had observed so far, and she told him so. Makhani just shrugged and remained silent for a long while, until Aurori lost patience.

"Are you going to tell me what happened to make you dislike him, or do you plan on leaving me in the dark?" she asked with an edge in her voice.

Makhani's jaw muscles tightened and Aurori could almost hear him grind his teeth as he mulled it over. It was obviously a touchy subject for him and she almost wished she hadn't been so quick to ask him, but at last, with eyes resolutely fixed ahead, he began his story.

"It was during the last war between Kaethos and Glaybor. King Thyros had found out that King Koren was traveling to

Glaybor in hopes of initiating a peace treaty. I was with the battalion that was sent to apprehend King Koren. When we came across him on the road to Glaybor, we found that he was traveling with more men than we expected, but we still tried to accomplish our mission."

Makhani's eyes narrowed as he remembered. "I managed to reach the King's coach, but when I opened the door of the coach, a spindly kid jumped out and challenged me with a rapier. I was so surprised that I froze. He didn't. He whipped the rapier across my face, cutting me here," he said, running a finger along the scar under his right eye. "Before I knew it, he... knocked me down and had my own sword at my throat." Makhani's cheeks burned red, making the line of his scar stand out even more. "The battle ended with King Koren's men overwhelming us. He spared us, though, and sent us packing back to Glaybor. I became the laughing stock of the entire army for letting a child get the best of me."

"Terien was that kid with rapier, I assume?"

Makhani nodded. "He was twelve. I was eighteen."

Aurori considered her next words carefully. "One would think that the passage of time would have healed more than just the physical wound."

"It might have if he hadn't been so smug about it at the time." Makhani turned his pale blue eyes on her. "Not once did he mention the incident when we met again during the treaty negotiations, but I know he must remember it. How could he forget the time he humiliated a warrior of Glaybor? Must have been very satisfying for him."

Pondering that for bit, Aurori finally looked over at him with a knowing smile. "Possibly. But I can't help but think – if you ever forgive yourself for freezing at that crucial moment, you might even be able to forgive Terien."

Aurori spurred Mystafire into a trot, leaving Makhani to stare after her in stunned disbelief, his mouth hanging open.

Terien had known that the journey would be long and rather boring. He just hadn't expected the tedium of it. Day after day, night after night it was the same story. Plod along mile after mile, rest, eat, exercise, sleep, then repeat. Only the changing scenery and the ebb and flow of conversation held any interest. Even then, there were times when silence prevailed for mile after mile and the landscape seemed static.

One bright point was that Makhani was coming out of his shell for some mysterious reason. He had abandoned his shotgun post on the second day after leaving Glaybor and had actually struck up conversations with Terien and some of the men, offering them his thoughts on a variety of subjects pertaining to their journey and destination. His attitude was still a little haughty towards Terien, but overall his manner was almost friendly. Terien had even commented on this to Aurori and Duncan, who exchanged a conspiratorial look and changed the subject.

On the sixth day out, the landscape changed abruptly as the flat prairie gave way to the rocky buttes and scraggly trees of semi-desert. The road now skirted the southern edge of the Teseni Desert that lay to the east of Glaybor and stretched all the way to the coastal city of Brinbourne.

Makhani had explained that Brinbourne and Glaybor did not share trade. Each kingdom kept strictly to itself, and that soon became apparent as the road became little more than a sandy path winding between the rocks and buttes. On the positive side, the weather had become warmer, allowing them to remove their black cloaks and stow them away.

"You had mentioned that there were two rival factions supposedly fighting, out this way," Terien reminded Makhani. "Any idea where? I'd rather avoid them if we can."

"The Cohalili and the Penaro," Makhani confirmed. "They live further into the Teseni, so I doubt we'll encounter them at all."

"Not much out here," Benem observed, trotting up beside the two. "What would they even fight over?"

"They pretty much keep to themselves, but apparently they've been living out here for hundreds of years, scraping a living out of the desert." Makhani indicated the desert to the north with a sweep of his hand. "They say that the Penaro were here first and that the Cohalili came later. Part of their dispute is supposedly over territory. Fertile land and water are scarce out here, so they feud over the rights to it."

"They don't ever bother with Glaybor or Brinbourne? Ask to move in?"

"No. They leave us alone and we leave them alone. Both groups are fiercely independent. They won't even consider moving closer to Glaybor. A handful of Penaro will come to the city every now and then to trade fur pelts and skins for bovine, but beyond that they prefer to remain in the desert." Makhani made a face of distaste. "We prefer to avoid them. They're unpredictable."

When they made camp that night between two stands of rock, Terien went so far as to order an extra man to stand watch on every shift through the night, bringing the number to three, just in case the Cohalili or Penaro decided to be unpredictable.

Later, while sitting around the fires after dinner, the low growl of the felinae alerted them to the presence of something out in the desert. Falling silent, the men fanned out, weapons at the ready. Using hand signals, they searched the area around the camp, coming up with nothing out of the ordinary that would explain the behavior of the big cats. Spread out, each in eye contact with another member of the group, they waited and watched.

A mournful yelping disturbed the still night air, sending shivers through everyone.

"Probably just sentati," Makhani guessed, sheathing his sword. "I think your felinaes just heard them approaching before we did."

"What are sentati?" Aurori asked from where she stood, by one of the fires.

"They're about half the size of a felinae, a kind of reptilian creature with big snapping jaws and long fore claws they use for digging bugs out of the ground. Ugly things. The Cohalili make leather out of their hides."

"Dangerous?" Duncan inquired.

"They won't come near the fires," Makhani assured. "Besides, they sound as if they're quite faraway."

The yelping of the sentati continued intermittently for quite some time, making sleep difficult for almost everyone. Only Elek seemed immune to the haunting yelps, belting out a few snores that rivaled the sentati's calls. It was well past midnight before the sentati had quieted down and everyone but the watchmen was finally asleep.

Haren, Benem and another man, Shaygan, signaled each other to meet back at the fire in fifteen minutes to report before each went their separate way on his rounds.

Benem had just taken the opportunity to relieve himself behind a thorny bunch of bushes when an insect's sting sent a shot of pain into his neck. Slapping at it, he took no more than three steps before collapsing in a heap on the ground.

Haren was investigating a noise he'd heard behind a large boulder. Sword drawn, he was just slowly creeping around the rock when a soft buzzing sounded by his left ear, followed by a pinprick sensation in his neck.

"Blasted bugs," he cursed under his breath, rubbing at the spot he'd been stung.

He leaned forward around the rock, felt a wave of nausea ripple through his gut, and fell flat on his face, his sword falling from his limp hand.

Across the camp, Shaygan was whistling softly to himself as he strolled to the back of one of the supply carts with the intent of getting himself a midnight snack. He was leaning into the back when something stung his butt. He only had time to spin around for a look when he, too, dropped to the ground.

Shadows now separated from the rocky outcroppings, moving with uncanny silence as they darted in and out amongst the sleeping forms of men and beasts alike, while somewhere in the darkness the eerie yelping of the sentati chorused once more, growing closer.

Chapter Eight

His right cheek pressed uncomfortably into the sand, hands resting near his head in the grit, the first thing Terien thought when he awakened was that he had somehow slipped out of his sleeping bag in the middle of the night. The second thing he became aware of when he tried to lift his head was that he had a pounding headache behind his eyes. Moaning with the effort, he squirmed onto his back and pressed the heels of his hands into his eyes, trying to figure out why he felt like he'd had too much wild berry wine. Every muscle in his body ached.

"You must get up," an unfamiliar female voice urged.

Bolting upright and forcing his offended eyes open, Terien realized too late what a bad move that was. Nausea gripped his stomach and his head throbbed as though filled with too much blood. He swayed sideways where he sat and had to thrust a hand out to keep from pitching over, his eyes watering as he tried to focus on the form kneeling beside him.

"Who are you?" he managed to ask despite the dryness of his mouth.

"I am Quatina, First Speaker of the Cohalili," the woman stated.

After a few blinks, Terien was finally able to see her. She was slender and well muscled, wearing a short leather skirt and matching tunic with short sleeves. Her long black hair hung in many braids around her regal features, complimenting her skin, the color of polished keyta wood. Her dark eyes were fixed on him, unblinking.

Hazarding a glance around, Terien only confirmed what he already knew. He was dressed only in his black pants and sleeveless undershirt. His feet were bare. He wasn't outside in the camp they had made, but inside some sort of mud-and-wattle building, all alone except for the woman.

"Where am I? Where are my people?" he demanded to know,

anger chasing his headache away.

"You are in the village of the Penaro. Your people are here as well and will be fine," she gently assured him. "They were only made to sleep by the juice from the cactus the Penaro use in their blow sticks. That is why you feel so badly. Your animals are safe as well, guarded in the camp you made."

"Why have you brought us here?"

Quatina sighed, obviously uncomfortable with that question. "Nedak, the leader of the Penaro, came to my village under a flag of truce two days ago. He said that the Chosen of the Prophecy was in Glaybor and would be traveling through our lands. He proposed to me that the Chosen be… asked to settle the disputes of our people."

Rising to her feet, Quatina balled her hands into fists and crossed her wrists over her chest, distraught. "My people were eager to accept. We have fought with the Penaro off and on for generations. We are tired of the killing and the dying." She shook her head, setting her braids into motion. "We were amazed to find that the Penaro are as tired of it as we are, but I agreed to discuss this with them and came to their village with some of my people."

Terien lost none of his anger. "So you decided to drug us and steal us out of our beds in the middle of the night just to ask me if I would mediate a peace between your peoples? That doesn't even make sense!"

Quatina looked down at him, her dark eyes almost brimming with tears. "You do not understand. Nedak was convinced that the Chosen would not agree to take time to do this for us if we approached and asked. We know the Prophecy. The Chosen is to reunite the peoples of Primus, not settle feuds between such insignificant peoples such as the Cohalili and Penaro. Nedak insisted that you would have no choice this way. I did not agree with this, but could not find words to sway his mind. I am sorry."

Terien blew a breath out and struggled to his feet. He swayed for a moment, unsteady as his head swam from the after-effects of the drug. "Well, as long as none of my men have been hurt, there's no harm done." His head was starting to clear. "I would be happy to mediate between your peoples. You can tell Nedak he was wrong. There was no need to abduct us."

"I am pleased to hear that," a deep male voice said from behind Terien.

Turning, Terien beheld an exceptionally tall man dressed in leather pants and matching boots ducking through the doorway of the hut. Chest bare, his skin was a deep bronze and his hair was a pale sand color from exposure to the suns. He was well-muscled and sported tattoos on both biceps. His brown eyes were deep-set beneath heavy dark brows that made him look like he was perpetually frowning.

"I am Nedak, First Warrior of the Penaro." His eyes fastened on Terien with an intensity that was almost frightening in its frank appraisal. "You are not what I expected the Chosen to be," he said, his tone making it clear that he was disappointed in what he saw.

Terien was not a small man, standing over six feet, but he was still dwarfed by this giant warrior. "Appearances can be deceptive," Terien replied evenly but with steel in his voice.

"This we will see for ourselves," Nedak said. "You have agreed to mediate between our peoples, and that is good. But before the Penaro hear your words you must agree to participate in the Trial. Only then will my people believe that you are truly a warrior whose words have meaning."

"The Trial?" Terien looked questioningly at Quatina who immediately bowed her head in shame, leaving Nedak to answer.

"The Penaro are great warriors," Nedak proclaimed with pride. "Our leaders have always endured the Trial to prove they are worthy of leading the people in battle." He placed a mammoth hand on Terien's shoulder. "You must endure the Trial if you are to mediate a peace between the Penaro and the Cohalili. It will be a war of words and ideas, but a battle nonetheless."

"You have a very… unique way of choosing a leader," Terien told him. "But what exactly *is* the Trial?"

"You must fight the two best warriors of the Penaro. If you win, you will be declared Enaro, the winner, and your words will become the words of the First Among Warriors. You will have the respect of the people."

"And if I were to lose?"

A sneer curled Nedak's lip. "You would be Keynaro, shunned as less than worthless."

Disbelief shocking through him, Terien laughed derisively. "I can't believe this. You are the ones asking me to mediate for you." He stabbed a finger at Nedak's chest. "*You* came for me, *you* chose me, yet you still expect me to take part in some ritual just to prove to you that you're making a worthy choice for a mediator?" He stepped back and posted his fists on his hips. "I won't do it. I am already a warrior and a Prince. And the Chosen. I have fought in battles as you have. I have no need to prove myself to you or anyone else."

"You are the Chosen, this much I know." Nedak's eyes narrowed. "As for the rest, I see no proof. Or do you hide the scars of battle in shame?" Nedak challenged, picking at Terien's undershirt with a meaty paw.

Now that he'd mentioned it, Nedak did have a number of scars criss-crossing his chest. Terien glanced down at his own chest. If he removed his undershirt, Nedak would not find any scars there. He'd seen battle before but had never suffered any major wounds, attributing his good fortune to his skill with the sword and shield. He'd never before considered that a detriment. Until now.

Terien was about to restate his position on the matter when another massive Penaro warrior appeared at the door with two familiar faces in tow.

"These two just awoke, Nedak. I brought them as you ordered."

"Aurori! Makhani!" Terien rushed over to them, relieved to see them both. They looked well but a little groggy. He thumped Makhani on the back, smiling, then turned to Aurori. A stray hair hung over her face and he brushed it away. She looked disoriented, almost wild-eyed. "Are you okay?"

Aurori clutched a hand around his wrist. "I was about to ask you the same thing. What happened? Where are we? No one will tell us anything." Her tone was urgent, angry.

"Were the rest of the men with you?" Terien asked, concerned.

"Some of the others were just waking up when this walking tree trunk came for us," Makhani said, casting an angry glance at the warrior who had escorted them in.

Terien quickly filled them in on what had happened, their faces reflecting every emotion in the book as they listened raptly.

"What happens if you refuse the Trial?" Makhani wanted to know when Terien had finished his narration.

Terien shrugged one shoulder and looked to Quatina and Nedak.

"You are free to go," Nedak told them, folding his arms. "No one may force another into the Trial against his will. That is the law."

"Well, then. I suppose you'll just wish them a good day and get out of here," Makhani said to Terien, eyes narrowed in accusation.

"No!" Quatina went directly to Terien and put her hands on his chest. She looked at him with pleading eyes, then slowly lowered to her knees before him, hands pressed palm to palm as she bowed her head. "Please! Reconsider. If you refuse the Trial, our people will never be free of the feuds. Never before has there been anyone that both the Cohalili and the Penaro would accept as mediator. You must help us." She turned her tear-streaked face up to him. "Please, do not abandon us. I beg you, Chosen. Help us!"

Shocked into silence, Terien stared down at Quatina for what seemed like hours, pity warring with common sense as he considered. He had confidence in his abilities as a warrior and had been trained by the best teachers Kaethos had to offer. Though this matter truly did lie outside his purview as the Chosen, he couldn't simply abandon a call for help. That he would have to participate in some barbaric ritual to prove his worthiness grated at him, but he could swallow his pride long enough to endure the Trial if it would help end a feud that was generations old. He'd had his share of bumps and bruises before. That didn't bother him. Even if he failed, he could at least say he had tried, hadn't just walked away.

Terien lifted his head. "I accept the Trial."

"Terien, you can't!" Aurori blurted, clutching her hand

around his arm and digging her nails in so hard that he almost winced.

Makhani grunted and folded his arms. "You surprise me, Royal Boy. I thought you'd be too high-and-mighty to do the right thing."

"You stay out of this," Aurori snapped at Makhani. "This is not 'the right thing to do'!"

"We will take you to your men. You may eat and rest first, recover your strength. The Trial will begin in two hours, if that is agreeable," Nedak said, ignoring Aurori's protest.

"It isn't!" Aurori growled. "Terien, you can't be serious!"

"We'll discuss this later," Terien said evenly to Aurori, feeling a little puzzled by her uncharacteristic vehemence as he gently removed her hand from his arm. He looked back at Nedak. "Two hours will be fine."

★

Duncan and the men had been relieved to find that Terien, Aurori and Makhani were all fine and had listened as the three had taken turns explaining what had transpired. They weren't pleased with the fact that the Penaro had managed to catch them flat-footed, though. Embarrassment was the order of the day when they found out that it had been only five Penaro who had stolen into the camp and subdued them all without so much as a struggle.

As for the matter of Terien's agreement to participate in the Trial, no one seemed overly concerned about it. Duncan in particular seemed quite at ease with the notion of the Chosen taking part in the test, going so far as to remark that he was proud of Terien for his willingness to endure the Trial for the sake of peace.

"I can't believe this," Aurori shouted from where she sat on a low stool in one corner of the room. Her braid had come undone, leaving her hair to fly loosely around her shoulders, making her look as wild as she sounded. "Terien could be seriously hurt and you're all treating this like some sort of a game!"

"Eristea has never been at war, has it?" Elek asked, squatting beside her.

Aurori shot him a look full of arrows. "Of course not! We're Healers, not warriors," she grumbled.

"Well, let me tell you. Kaethos has fought many wars. We train constantly, even now, when we're at peace with our neighbors," Elek said. "As Prince, Terien has trained right alongside us. He's no stranger to a fight. Hell! He's been beating me in hand-to-hand combat for years!" A roar of laughter accompanied that comment. "He'll be fine," Elek went on. "Besides, you'll be here to patch him up afterwards, right?"

"That's not the point!" Aurori shot to her feet. "He's the Chosen, not a prize fighter!" she said emphatically. "I'm all in favor of helping these people settle their feud, but giving in to this... this... foolishness – it's just..."

"Typical male chest beating?" Makhani supplied.

She glared at him before turning fiery eyes to Terien, but her ire found a new target when Quatina entered the hut. "You! This is your fault!" Aurori cried, pointing an accusing finger at the woman.

"I'm sorry for her outburst," Terien apologized as Elek placed a restraining hand on Aurori's shoulder.

"Unreasoning anger is a common side effect of the drug the Penaro used, particularly in women. We do not know why." Quatina said.

"Unreasoning anger? I'll give you unreasoning anger!" Aurori growled at Quatina, her hands becoming claws as she took a step towards the other woman.

"Whoa, there," Elek murmured, catching Aurori by the back of her cloak and holding her back.

"It will pass in a few hours," Quatina promised, casting an amused glance at Aurori before turning back to Terien. "I wanted to thank you for your bravery, Chosen One. Whatever happens, I want you to know that your efforts will be appreciated." She gave him a small smile and bowed slightly, then reached into the bodice of her tunic and pulled out a small object on a chain. This she held out to Terien, dangling it in the air between them.

Aurori's anger melted into astonishment at the sight of the cylinder she was offering Terien. Simultaneously, Terien's and

Aurori's hands flew to their chests, searching for their own cylinders. Terien's was where it had always been, hanging around his neck, and Aurori also found that hers was still safely concealed beneath her tunic.

"Where did you get that?" Terien asked in awe.

"It has been passed down to every First Speaker of the Cohalili since the time the small sun died," Quatina said. "I give it now to you, Chosen One. May it bring you good fortune this day."

"I was wondering how they picked Terien out as the Chosen when they captured us," Duncan said. "You knew about the key?"

"Yes. We searched until we found the one who wore the sky crystal. My people knew that the Chosen would have one," she told them proudly. "My people once lived far from here in a great city hidden in the Teseni Desert. The storytellers say that our ancestors had to leave the Hidden Home when the small sun died. They tell that this sky crystal was the only thing they took with them to remind them of where they had once lived." Quatina took Terien's hand and pressed the cylinder into it, wrapping both her hands over his. "We have never returned to the Hidden Home, and I cannot imagine that we ever will since the storytellers have forgotten its location. Keep this with you, always."

"Thank you," was all Terien could find to say.

Terien and Quatina stepped apart as Nedak appeared in the doorway.

"It is time. Are you ready to face the Trial, Chosen One?"

"I am."

"Will we be allowed to watch?" Duncan wanted to know.

Nedak seemed uncertain. "You will not try to stop the Trial? Or interfere in any way?"

"You have our word," Duncan replied formally.

"Very well. Come with me."

As the group filed out of the building and into the bright light of the afternoon, Duncan hung back until he was walking beside Aurori. "You behave," he warned her. "I gave Nedak my word."

"Me?" Aurori asked, flabbergasted. Duncan laughed and it dawned on her that he was teasing her. "Unreasoning anger, indeed," she muttered to herself as Duncan trotted off to catch up with Terien.

It soon became apparent that the Trial was to take place inside a huge pit that had been dug into the ground. The sides were about ten feet high, smooth and perfectly vertical, making it difficult for someone to try and scramble out in the middle of a fight. People stood around the edge of the pit, mostly men from the Penaro and the Cohalili people, but there were also a few women in attendance.

Quatina showed up beside Terien, holding his very own pair of boots out to him. Where she had gotten them didn't even cross his mind as he quickly pulled them on before being lowered by a rope into the pit.

Another man was lowered in after him, a strapping Penaro with a series of scars on his chest that Terien thought vaguely resembled the outline of a felinae. He was huge, with arms as big as the branches of the keyta tree and legs like the trunks. The warrior grunted a greeting to him and promptly retreated against the wall of the pit to begin some warm-up exercises.

The other Penaro being lowered into the pit was a shocker for Terien.

"Nedak? You're going to fight me?"

Nedak inclined his head to Terien. "It is nothing personal, Chosen. I am First Warrior. It is my duty to face you in the Trial."

Raising his arms to quiet the people standing at the sides of the pit, Nedak addressed them all. "The rules of the Trial are this: The challenger fights two warriors. The two may not attack at the same time, but may switch places if one is tired or dazed. The Trial is over when the challenger is unable to continue the fight, or if both his opponents are unable."

"It's been nice knowing you," Makhani called out to Terien, grinning as he leaned over the pit with his hands braced on his knees. He received a hard elbow in the ribs from Aurori for the comment, but just laughed and slung an arm over her shoulder.

"Keep it up, Blondy. See if I invite you along the next time I'm executed," Terien called back, shooting him a bemused look.

Terien almost got his head knocked off an instant later when Nedak came at him with a roundhouse right. He noticed the movement in the periphery of his vision just in time and caught his wrist. Using the larger man's momentum against him, Terien sidestepped and flipped him over onto his back.

"Keep your mind on the fight, Royal Boy!" Makhani hooted. "Now's no time for making stupid jokes!"

"Would you stop it?" Aurori growled at Makhani, knocking his arm away.

"All right, all right," he said, holding both hands up in a shushing gesture.

"Unreasoning anger," Elek reminded Makhani with a conspiratorial grin.

Terien could hear every word but tuned them out as he lunged at Nedak. They both went down hard, landing in a tangle. Nedak retaliated by clamping his arms around him in a bear hug, but Terien butted him in the face. Blood streamed from Nedak's nose, which looked decidedly broken, dazing him for a second and leaving Terien the opening he needed. Grabbing hold of Nedak's shoulders, Terien rolled backwards, planting a knee in Nedak's stomach and hurling him back over his head. Nedak went flying, landing in a heap at the feet of the other Penaro who had to sidestep out of the way.

With Nedak down for the moment, Terien's other opponent advanced on him. Breathing hard, Terien circled slowly, trying to gauge what the other man planned for his first move. The big warrior spat on the ground between them, a clear challenge.

"Come, little man," the warrior taunted, moving closer. "I think Nedak was being too easy on you. I will show you how warriors fight."

Terien suddenly dropped to the ground and swept a leg out, pulling the warrior's feet out from under him. As he fell, Terien kicked out, straight for his head. The warrior's head snapped back and he landed on the ground with a resounding thump, but he shook it off and was already on his feet when Terien swung a left-handed punch at him. Cutting him off with a chop from his right arm, the warrior grasped Terien's arm and gave it a twist, trapping his elbow and exerting pressure upward. Terien grunted in pain, certain that the joint was about to explode. Before he could break the hold, the warrior slammed a meaty fist into his stomach and the wind went out of him in a rush. He felt himself being

released, only to catch a blur of motion as a fist smashed him in the mouth. He only had time to register that blood was spurting from a split in his lip before the warrior grabbed a handful of his shirt in one hand and one leg in the other as he was hoisted high in the air over the big guy's head. Belting out a yell, the warrior slammed Terien to the ground. The impact sent bolts of pain shooting down his arms and legs. Worse yet, bits of gravel on the pit's floor were stingingly driven into his back.

The big guy had long arms. Terien had to move faster and get in close where his opponent's advantage of a longer reach would be useless. Terien fought to catch his breath, scrabbling away on his elbows until he was far enough away to risk getting onto his feet. The warrior laughed, which was a bad move on his part, for it only made Terien all the more determined. As the Penaro rushed in, Terien dropped to one knee and threw the man over his head. The big man was just getting to his feet when Terien darted in close and grabbed his head, jerking it down as he thrust his knee into his face. The warrior groaned once and fell back, unmoving.

"Nicely done, Chosen One," Nedak complimented as he launched himself at Terien from behind.

Damn! Terien cursed himself for forgetting about Nedak as he went sprawling face down, slapping the ground with his hands to absorb some of the impact as Nedak rolled away to regain his feet. Pain lanced through Terien's left shoulder. Not a good sign. Forcing himself to roll further out of Nedak's reach, he felt another shot of pain, this time on his upper right arm, as he rolled right over another sharp rock. Shunting the pain aside, Terien pushed up into a low crouch and waited until Nedak was no more than two paces away. Springing up, Terien took one step towards the larger man before swinging his leg up and across his face, staggering him. He jumped up, landed a second kick with his other leg and followed it by a third from the same leg on the return swing. Nedak seemed to fall back in slow motion, blood now streaming from a cut over his right eye as well as from the earlier blow to his nose. He landed in the dirt, his whole body bouncing once before he settled in the dust.

Terien stood in a forward-ready stance, knees bent, fists raised and ready. Slowly, he became aware of the crowd around the pit. They had been silent the whole time during the fight, but now they were cheering wildly, pumping their arms in the air. He looked around until he found Duncan in the crowd. He was cheering and giving him two thumbs up. He had won.

He had won!

Terien lowered his arms and slowly uncurled his hands. Panting to catch his breath, he turned to see what had become of his other opponent. The warrior who had called him "little man" was sitting on the ground, just now coming around. His eyes slowly focused on Terien and he bowed his head in humble acceptance of his defeat.

Behind him, Terien heard Nedak moan a couple of times and he turned around to look at him.

"You fight like a demon," Nedak groused, dabbing his fingers at the cut above his brow. "Had I known, I would never have challenged you to the Trial," he admitted with a smile as Terien offered his hand to help him up.

"I had the best teachers," Terien told him, trying to smile despite his painful split lip. "Now. How about our patching things up between you and the Cohalili?"

Nedak laughed and pounded a hand on Terien's sore back. "Yes, but let us first see to being patched up ourselves!"

Ropes were quickly lowered into the pit to assist the warriors out. Unable to raise his left arm because of the pain in his shoulder, Terien held tight to the rope with only his right hand and let Duncan and Elek haul him up.

"Knew you'd win," Duncan said, smiling from ear to ear.

"Hell, yeah," Elek crowed. He almost slapped Terien's back in congratulations, but caught himself in time. He pumped Terien's uninjured right arm instead, which still shook Terien hard enough to bring a small grimace of pain to his face.

"Chosen!" Quatina came jogging up to Terien, tears streaming down her face. She dropped to one knee before him. "My people will never forget the sacrifice you made this day."

Terien made a face of exasperation. He would have reached down to lift her to her feet, but his back hurt too much. "Please get up, Quatina. You can thank me best by working hard with me to bring peace between the Cohalili and the Penaro."

Standing, Quatina swiped at the tears on her cheeks. "I promise I will," she said. "I will go now to make arrangements for your animals to be brought here to the village."

"I'll go with her," Elek said.

"Terien!"

For a split second Terien thought he was being attacked again and raised his arms up defensively as he instinctively turned in the direction he had heard his name being called. He staggered back, totally stunned as Aurori threw herself at him and hugged him around the waist.

"I was so worried! I could hardly stand to watch!" she cried.

His injured back protested her hug, as did his shoulder as he wrapped his arms around her, but he didn't care.

"Oh, I'm so sorry!" she apologized when he stiffened a little. "You're injured," she said, loosening her grip on him.

"I just thought I would give you something to do," he teased, unwilling to let her go yet. He tried to squeeze her a little tighter but gave up and let her go when his shoulder screamed at him this time.

"Very impressive, Royal Boy," Makhani said, sticking his hand out. "You're just as quick as you were when you were twelve."

Terien looked at Makhani as though seeing him for the first time. That same grim look, the scar on his right cheek, the reminder about their encounter as youngsters. It brought back a flood of memories. As well, it sparked a revelation.

"Thanks," Terien said, shaking Makhani's hand. "You know, I had heard that you were really given a hard time about that cut I gave you, and I feel that – well, that is to say, I'm really sorry for what you went through. It was a lucky shot. I never should have been... such a... a..."

"Smug little twerp?" Makhani offered with a wry smile.

"Yeah," Terien said with a grin that flamed pain into his lip. "Yeah. Sorry about that."

Makhani's smile faded, and his eyes narrowed to slits as he inclined his head to Terien in acceptance of the apology. "You really have changed. Makes it hard for a guy to hold a grudge."

"Maybe. But from now on, if you catch me being a smug little twerp, I expect you to deck me."

"You've got a deal," Makhani said, returning a genuine smile.

Aurori looked from one to the other, her own heart filling with emotion for both these proud men. She looped her arms around both of them. "Come on. Let's get Royal Boy cleaned up. He has a peace to negotiate."

Terien gaped at Aurori, then looked at Makhani with mock reproach. "You're a bad influence on her, you know that?"

Laughing together at that, they headed off for one of the huts, where first-hand experience of Aurori's talents as a Healer became a revelation for Terien. He was mystified and fascinated as he watched her hands move deftly over the cut on his right arm, making it literally disappear before his eyes. It had stung like crazy, as Aurori had warned it would, but he had weathered that as stoically as he could. She had apologized for his discomfort, but explained that she had no method of delivering a dose of anesthetic only to the affected area without rendering him unconscious. That admission had sparked interest in Nedak who was awaiting his turn for her ministrations, and he quickly summoned the village's own physician who had been hanging back, allowing the Healer to tend the wounded men.

After an abbreviated consultation between Aurori and the small Penaro physician, one which found Aurori giggling in delight, she returned with a series of small darts of varying size in hand. She selected the smallest of the darts, accepted the clay pot that the Penaro physician held out for her and proceeded to dip the dart's tip into its contents. Receiving a nod of approval from him, she then moved in close to Terien, warned him to hold still, and pricked his split lip with the tip of the dart. She then stood back and awaited his reaction.

Moments later Terien lifted his fingers to his lip, amazed. "It feels numb," he reported.

Aurori immediately turned to the Penaro physician, grinning like a Cheshire cat. He clapped his hands together, delighted to have been of service.

"You and I must compare notes later," Aurori said to the Penaro as she turned back to Terien and began to seal his wounded lip. "I suspect that I might have a preparation with me that would work just as well as this cactus juice your people use in their blow sticks."

"I assume that the Healer is learning some new tricks," Terien asked when she was done.

"Oh, yes! This is fantastic! In larger doses the cactus juice renders the recipient unconscious – as we already experienced – but in small intradermal doses it acts as a local anesthetic." Aurori frowned and heaved a sigh. "How I wish my people had thought of this method of intradermal delivery ages ago!"

After tending to Terien's wrenched shoulder by massaging a sour-smelling ointment into it and putting that arm in a sling, Aurori finished by cleaning the gravel out of his back and slathering a coating of the green jelly she had once used on the bandit's facial abrasions. At the moment, that seemed a lifetime ago, and best forgotten, she decided.

"Now then, who's next?" Aurori asked, laughing when both Nedak and the other injured warrior eagerly raised their hands at the same time.

Chapter Nine

The process of negotiating a peace treaty between the Cohalili and the Penaro, once begun, was to consume most of Terien's time and energy. He had started by asking for a tour of both the villages and lands currently claimed by each side, and had spent long hours that first day as he listened while the Penaro told him how they managed to survive in the harsh environment of the semi-desert. The following day he, Duncan, Aurori and Makhani had made the trip to the Cohalili village to begin the same routine there while the rest of the men remained in the Penaro village. Terien was startled to find how near each other they actually lived, for they were only a matter of a two-hour walk apart.

He soon learned that both groups planted and harvested a grain with large kernels as their staple food source, raised a few bovines that supplied milk and acted as beasts of burden, and that both had hunters whose job it was to supplement their diet by hunting small animals in the desert. They also lived in similar mud-and-wattle huts, wore similar leather clothes and had the same system of government, only with different methods of selecting their leaders. The Trial was solely the concept of the Penaro; the Cohalili cast votes every eight seasons to decide who their leader would be.

The histories of the two groups and the make-up of their populations were another matter. The Penaro had lived in the Teseni since before the time of the Great Division and their population consisted entirely of people of one race. They were all large and robust with bronze skin, eyes of various shades of blue or gray, and hair that rarely deviated beyond different shades of blond. In contrast, the Cohalili were relative newcomers to the area, having settled here only a few hundred years ago, and their people were widely varied. Skin tones ran from as white as unbaked bread to as dark as charred wood, with eye and hair color spanning the spectrum.

This crucial difference in the make-up of the Cohalili people gave credence to what Terien had already suspected when Quatina had mentioned the "Hidden Home" in the Teseni Desert, but this was confirmed by the tale related on the evening of his tour of the Cohalili village and lands.

After a delicious dinner prepared by the Cohalili women, Terien was sitting on the ground by the fire, legs stretched out and back resting against one of several large rocks that had been placed for that purpose. The night was warm and cloudless, giving a clear view of the stars. Duncan and Aurori sat on either side of him, also resting after the long day spent in touring, while Makhani, who had tagged along, was standing over the large fire, idly poking it with a stick and sending hot sparks twirling into the dark night. Nedak and two other men, members of the Penaro negotiation team, also sat conversing in soft tones by the fire with their three Cohalili counterparts, one of whom was Quatina.

"As you have seen," Quatina was saying to Nedak, "our people live well enough, but we must expand our fields if we are to support ourselves, and the only land good for growing lies in the direction of the Penaro."

"I understand this, but your expansion has made it necessary for you to divert the stream that lies between us to irrigate your fields. This leaves little water for the Penaro, and that is not acceptable," Nedak replied, chopping a hand through the air between them.

"The negotiations will begin tomorrow in the Penaro village, as agreed," Terien said loudly, cutting them off. "There will be plenty of time to argue the details at that time. Until then, I'd rather just sit and relax. Agreed?"

Quatina and Nedak exchanged sheepish looks and fell silent.

"What I would like to hear is the story of how the Cohalili came to be here," Terien said. "Quatina, you told us that your people had once lived in a great city hidden in the Teseni Desert and that they left when the small sun died. Is there more to the story?"

"Yes, but we do not know how much is truth and how much is myth."

"Would you tell us?"

Quatina shifted position until she was sitting cross-legged, wrists resting lightly on her knees, and began her tale. "In the Before Time, long, long ago, the Cohalili lived in a beautiful city made of stone and sand and had many magical devices as the Sky Lords do. The city survived the rain of rock that came from the sky and the Cohalili lived for many many years, lonely years, all alone in the desert. They planted and harvested, as we do now, but the land and the water kept changing because of the terrible effects of the rocks from the sky until only a few Cohalili were left alive." Quatina's eyes glistened in the light of the fire as she looked in turn to each person seated around the fire. "One day, the small sun died, for even the magical devices of the Before Time cannot last forever. Without it to warm them and give them light, the ancestors had to leave the Hidden Home, so they made the great journey across the desert, searching for a place they could live. They came here, and made a new home."

"The Penaro know the rest," Nedak said with a touch of heat in his tone. "Our two peoples lived for countless seasons without knowing about each other, until the Cohalili began diverting the waters to irrigate their crops." He folded his massive arms across his chest and looked away from Quatina, fixing his eyes on Terien. "We have feuded ever since, always fighting for land and water."

"We have been at peace from time to time, Nedak," Quatina said hotly. "You make it sound as though we have fought without pause since the beginning."

Terien pushed to his feet, commanding their attention before they could debate the matter further. He removed the two cylinders he wore around his neck, his and the one Quatina had given him, and held them out to dangle by their chains. "I have a story of my own to tell, one that the Cohalili should find enlightening." He smiled over his shoulder at Aurori and said, "You should find this interesting, too. I know Makhani certainly did."

"Of course!" Makhani said, brightening. "The story you told King Denid and me, the one about..."

"The Hidden Cities," Terien finished for him. He started to slowly pace around the fire as he spoke, causing people to shift position and pull in their feet. "Lord Soloth, the Sky Lord, gave me a map to follow before he sent me out. On it he had marked four places that he called 'Hidden Cities'. Like Quayvern, they are cities of technology that had survived the Great Division mostly intact. No need to go into detail right now, but he gave me this," Terien said, indicating the cylinder Soloth had given him, "and explained that it's a key for gaining entry to the four cities. He gave one to me and one to the other Chosen. Unfortunately, Lord Soloth said that the Sky Lords had lost contact with two of these cities, including the one in the Teseni Desert."

"Then, the sky crystal I gave you..." Quatina's eyes went wide. "My people have always thought it was just a keepsake. Is it actually a key to the Hidden Home?"

"Yes, I believe it is," Terien said. "The Cohalili once lived in a city of technology just like Quayvern. Lord Soloth called the city in the Teseni Desert a 'bunker'."

"After we leave Brinbourne we had planned to cross the Teseni on our way to Pergase," Duncan added. "We were going to bypass the city in the desert, but I'll bet anything that we're going to make a detour now," he said with sly smile aimed at Terien.

"That we are," Terien confirmed. "It may be deserted, but who knows what interesting things we may find there."

"I wish to come with you!" Quatina shot to her feet. "No one has ever returned to the Hidden Home. I would like to go with you to see where my people came from."

"You'd be more than welcome to come with us, but what about your people here?" Terien asked.

Breathing hard from the frustration welling in her, Quatina looked to the two Cohalili who had been sitting with her, then back at Terien. Her mouth opened and closed a couple of times, but nothing came out.

"You must go with them, Quatina," one of her people said quietly. "This is important. We will elect a new leader to take your place after you have finished the negotiations." He stood and placed his hands on her shoulders. "You must only promise to return one day and tell us all that you saw."

"He is right," the other Cohalili said. "Someone must go with the Chosen to see what is there. It is because of you that this opportunity has presented itself. It is only right that you be the one to make the journey to the Hidden Home."

Tears brimming in her eyes, Quatina embraced her friends and faced Terien. "Then it is settled. I will accompany you, Chosen."

"Glad to have you along." Terien and Quatina clasped hands, both smiling. "That reminds me..." Terien held out the cylinder Quatina had given him. "I think you'll be needing this."

Quatina stared at it for a long moment, then gently pushed his hand away. "No. It is right that the key should be in the hands of the Chosen."

Terien hesitated for a moment, uncertain, then took the chain and awkwardly tried to lift it over her head with one hand, his left still being trussed up in the sling. "I appreciate the sentiment, but the Chosen has decided that it should be the leader of the Cohalili that carries the key to her ancestral home. When the time comes, it should be your hand that uses it."

Quatina bowed her head to him and then suddenly reached out to stroke the side of his face. "Thank you." She spared his shoulder by taking the cylinder and chain from him and putting it around her neck herself. She held his eyes for a moment, then stepped back and addressed everyone. "You are welcome to sit as long you like, but my friends and I must go and make this announcement to my people," Quatina said.

"My men and I will also go now," Nedak said. "It has been a long day."

After the goodbyes were over and they had gone, Terien reclaimed his seat by the fire.

"You certainly have a way with words," Aurori observed. "I think you'll have Quatina eating out of your hand at the negotiation table."

Was that jealousy tinging her voice? Terien dismissed the notion with a casual shrug of his good shoulder. "It was only fair to return the key to her. I thought it might be important to her. Besides, I already have a key."

"This journey is certainly full of surprises," Makhani commented. He leaned forward and wrapped his arms around his upraised knees. "Tell me, do you have any idea what this business about the 'small sun' might be?"

"Not a clue," Terien admitted. "Lord Soloth never mentioned anything about it. Sounds like some sort of technology, though."

Makhani nodded absently, deep in thought. "Maybe we'll find out once we get to this 'Hidden City'."

"Something on your mind?" Duncan asked him.

"You mentioned that the other Chosen was also given a key," Makhani said. "I was just thinking that it's a pity she won't know what has taken place here and will probably avoid the city just as you were going to."

Aurori was warmed by Makhani's thoughtfulness, as unnecessary as it was. Thank the ancestors she had decided to accompany Terien. She would have hated to miss out on this.

"The other journeys alone," Terien reminded Makhani. "Personally, I'm just as happy to think that she won't be going out into the Teseni. Besides, we have no idea what we'll find. Could be a detour for nothing."

"The other Chosen doesn't follow the same path as you?" Makhani asked, surprised.

Chagrined, Terien shook his head. "I have no idea. Lord Soloth wouldn't tell me who she is, where she came from or what route she would be taking. We could walk right past her and we'd never know it."

Makhani once again nodded and seemed to be considering something else.

"Uh oh! More deep thoughts," Duncan moaned.

"I was just thinking... it's a good thing we ran into the Cohalili and the Penaro. At least Terien will gain more experience acting as mediator. After all, it was King Koren who was chief negotiator for Kaethos at the time the treaty was settled between our kingdoms," Makhani said, then gave Terien a sly smile. "I wonder if I could convince the other representatives to put you through the Trial before you negotiate for us at the Final Reunification."

Duncan and Aurori both chuckled at that notion.

"Hey, once was enough! Besides, I may still have some of these bruises left to show them," Terien complained, rubbing at his shoulder. He stifled a yawn.

"I think it's time for sleep," Duncan said. "You have a big day tomorrow."

"True."

They walked in companionable silence the short distance to their assigned huts and wished each other goodnight before retiring into them, each already making plans for the days that would follow.

Returning to the Penaro village the next morning, it soon became apparent that Terien would be stuck inside one of the huts with the two opposing factions for most of the days that followed. He would only see his people for a few minutes here and there when they would take a break or at the end of the day for a couple of hours. It was during these breaks that he would often see Aurori bustling about the village, always in the company of the Penaro physician, whose name was Keled. Annoyingly enough, for Terien at least, Makhani would invariably be following them around as well, offering to lend a hand where needed as they tended to the various needs of the villagers. As for Duncan and the rest of the men, they would wander around at will, trading stories with the warriors or tending to the animals. Terien envied them their freedom.

Although the negotiations were going well, they were also going slowly. That was to be expected, of course, but by the ninth day Terien's mood was spiraling into the abyss. He didn't let it show to the members of the negotiation teams, but it was painfully apparent to those who knew him well, especially Duncan.

Thinking to lighten Terien's mood, Duncan unleashed his most wicked grin on Terien as they sat sharing lunch. "You're watching her again," he said in an annoying sing-song voice. "Better yet, she keeps looking this way," he said of Aurori.

Terien stole a glance at Aurori who was standing by the well in the center of the courtyard, chatting with a group of women. She wasn't looking his way at all.

"Liar."

"Hey, someone has to do something to cheer you up."

Terien took a vicious bite out of the leg of fowl in his hand, glaring mutely at Duncan as he chewed.

Duncan let him glare in peace, knowing his friend couldn't stay silent for long. He caught sight of Quatina walking across the compound on her way back to the hut where the negotiations were taking place. "Tell me, what's Quatina really like?" he asked, following her progress with his eyes. "She seems really dedicated to her people. Nice, too. I've talked to her for a few minutes here and there over the last few days. She seems a little shy, though. We traded a few war stories and such, talked about our lives a bit. Seems a shame that such a vibrant young woman is alone. No husband. No family."

A wolfish grin spread across Terien's face when Duncan turned back to him.

"What?" Duncan asked.

"You like her."

Duncan's expression became pained as he realized he had divulged a bit too much. "I'm not going to be able to tease you about Aurori anymore, am I?"

"Not a peep."

Sighing, Duncan rose from the table and rapped his knuckles on it. "I'll be in the hut if you're looking for me," he told Terien, face red. "Kicking myself, in case you're interested." He stalked away, muttering under his breath.

All smiles, Terien leaned back in his chair and closed his eyes. With a little luck, this would be the last afternoon for the negotiations, then they could get under way for Brinbourne. That was what was really eating at him. Spending time with the Cohalili and the Penaro may register in someone's book as a good deed, but it wasn't getting him any further on his real mission.

"Hi, stranger. I haven't seen too much of you lately," Aurori said.

Terien's eyes snapped open. "This is a pleasant surprise. Have a seat," he invited, indicating Duncan's vacated chair. "So, have you been learning a lot from your Penaro counterpart?"

"Lots," she admitted with a smile. "He even gave me this." Aurori held up a Penaro blow stick.

Terien took the blow stick from her and turned it over in his hands. "Very nice. Have you been practicing with it, too, or is it just for show?"

"I'll have you know that I can hit a target dead center at twenty feet," she said, snatching it back from him with a laugh.

"In that case, how'd you like to aim it right over there, at Nedak," he said, aiming a finger in Nedak's direction.

"I take it he's being difficult?"

"A little, but I think we'll have everything worked out this afternoon." He sighed and stretched languidly. "I don't know about you, but I'm ready to move on."

Aurori nodded. "Definitely." She leaned her elbows on the table. "Listen, I just wanted to tell you – I really think it's nice of you, helping these people to make peace."

"And here I thought you were mad at me because of it. Typical male chest beating and all that."

Aurori stood to go. "Mad about you agreeing to take part in the Trial, yes, not about the rest. Don't forget, I was under the effects of the cactus juice at the time," she said wryly. Lightly placing a hand on his shoulder, she leaned over and kissed his cheek. "I think they're waiting for you. Good luck."

Watching her walk away, Terien put his fingers to the cheek she had kissed, suddenly feeling a whole lot better about everything, and as he made his way back to the negotiation table, he found that even his shoulder was starting to feel a good deal better.

Chapter Ten

"It smells like fish," Benem complained, wrinkling his nose.

"While there is a component of decaying aquatic animal life in the air, your olfactory senses are obviously mistaking the tangy scent of briny sea air for the less pleasing smell you're complaining about," Haren orated.

"Well, Mayquire is on the coast, too, and I don't remember it smelling like this," Benem countered.

"Every city has its downside," Makhani offered.

"Yeah, and Brinbourne smells like fish," Benem said again.

"I thought you liked fish," Haren mused.

"To eat, fool, not to smell."

"Give it a rest," Duncan chuckled. "You don't want the inhabitants to hear you bad-mouthing their city, do you?"

"I think it's a beautiful city," Aurori put in, looking around with wide-eyed wonder.

Brinbourne. Nestled in and around the rocky shore of Cosquimus Bay, the Teseni pressing on it from one side and the vibrant blue of the Sea of Cartreuse on the other, the small city of Brinbourne had a stark beauty all its own. Homes and businesses were built along the steps that had been carved into the rocky landscape, giving the city a distinctive tiered look. At the lowest step lay the harbor with its stilted shacks jutting out into the bay and jaunty fishing boats bobbing peacefully in the quiet waters. Here and there across the bay a few fishing boats could be seen, moving back and forth as their crews plied the waters for the fishing trade.

"It may be pretty to look at, my lady, but that doesn't make the smell any better," Benem said, eliciting a sour glance from Aurori.

Though he registered their banter and managed a smile, Terien's mind was still back, days ago, with the Cohalili and the Penaro. He was pleased with the successful completion of a peace treaty wherein they had settled their dispute by uniting their people into one group. Ultimately, he had little to do with that decision. He had merely pointed out that the similarities between the Cohalili and the Penaro far outweighed their differences and that they had much to gain by joining forces. In truth, both groups had been toying with the idea for years but had been unable to come forth with the proposition on their own, and it was here that he had made the greatest contribution by broaching the subject. Only the election of a new ruling body had proven problematic, for the Penaro were unhappy to abandon the Trial as a means of selecting a leader, but that issue had been sidestepped for the time being by allowing the Penaro to continue to use the Trial as a means of choosing a Penaro candidate to run for a position on the new council.

Leaving the new community he had helped create had been bittersweet for Terien, and they had insisted on holding a ceremony for him, presenting him with furs and skins in acknowledgment of his contribution. This had delayed their departure for Brinbourne by another day, but they had still managed to make good time, bypassing the small villages along the way by using a route the Cohalili often took and that cut across the desert.

During the trip, Makhani had filled them in on what little he knew about Brinbourne, including the fact that the city and its neighboring villages were governed by a ruling council of three Elders who were elected from a larger ruling body consisting of ten sub-councilors, all of whom had arrived at their position by votes cast in each district, an arrangement that was strikingly similar to the one Terien had just mediated into existence.

"Any idea where the council chambers are located?" Terien asked Makhani.

Makhani shrugged a negative response.

"I thought you'd been here before, the way you were talking," Terien said, mildly annoyed.

"My predecessor was here," Makhani admitted. "He filled me in on the details I was telling you about."

"The council chambers are on the lowest point, down by the bay," Quatina told them. When they looked at her with astonishment, she smiled. "The Cohalili come to trade from time to time," she explained. "I have never been inside their council chambers before, but I have seen the building."

Moving through Brinbourne, it became painfully obvious that something was not quite right. Very few people were out on the streets, and those that were looked wary, shying away as the entourage passed.

"Where is everybody?" Aurori wondered aloud.

"We'll find out soon enough," Terien said as they slowed to a stop before the building Quatina directed them to.

The building that housed the council chambers was average looking, built from the same rough wood as most of the houses they had passed on the way down. Its only distinguishing features were the stylized carvings of fish, anchors and other sea-related images that adorned the outer walls and support pilings.

Finding it odd that there were no guards at the doors of the building and no one to greet them, Terien dismounted and stretched to work the kinks out of his legs, then called his men into a huddle. "Same drill as in Glaybor," he told them, referring to the way they had split up, leaving half the men outside to guard the carts and animals.

"I want to come, too," Aurori said, pushing her way into the huddle.

"I wish to accompany you as well," Quatina stated, folding her arms.

"You're both more than welcome," Terien said with a smile, offering them each an arm. Aurori accepted, but Quatina chose instead to hook an arm through Duncan's, bringing a smile to Terien's face and a look of surprise to Duncan's.

"I don't like this," Duncan said as they ascended the steps that led to the doors of the building. "It's too quiet." He looked to Quatina. "Is it always like this?"

"No. This city has always been very busy when I have visited in the past." She looked over her shoulder. "This is... disquieting."

"Stay alert," Terien warned.

Pulling on the heavy wooden door, Terien found that it swung open easily and quietly, revealing a dimly lit interior. There were tables and chairs set in a semicircle along the walls at the far end of the room, presumably for the council members. Near the far wall was a raised desk at which a solitary figure sat in the middle chair of three, seemingly oblivious to their arrival.

"Hello?" Terien called out, his voice echoing in the cavernous room.

The figure looked up, startled. "Who th' hell are ye?" the man called back in a lilting accent.

"Ah… may we come in? I'd like to talk to you, if I may," Terien said. Somehow, just shouting out "Hi, I'm the Chosen" from across the room didn't seem right.

"Ye're halfway in th' bloody door, lad, so ye might as well come th' rest o' the way in."

"I like him already," Makhani said sarcastically.

Suppressing the urge to laugh, Terien led the way up to the raised desk and bowed. The man was middle-aged, gray haired with a round, ruddy face and bushy eyebrows. He was looking at them from over the top of a strange device that was perched on his nose, consisting of a pair of circular pieces of glass joined by a thin metal wire.

"What can I do for ye, then?" the man asked.

Terien straightened and made a proclamation similar to the one he'd made in Glaybor.

"I am Terien, Prince and heir to the throne of Kaethos. I come to you as the Gatherer, the Chosen of the Legend."

"Th' Chosen!" The man jumped to his feet, knocking over the chair he had been sitting on, and hurried around the bench. He grabbed Terien's hand and pumped it furiously. "Why didn't ye say so before, lad? Glad to meet ye, glad indeed. I'm Rannoch, First Councilor of Brinbourne."

Rannoch's hearty welcome took Terien by surprise. "I, uh, have proof of who I am, if you'd like to see it," he offered.

"Aw, no need, no need. What damn fool would go about claimin' to be th' Chosen if he weren't?" Rannoch asked with a laugh. His expression suddenly fell and he slapped a hand to his forehead. "What am I sayin'? Th' Chosen are supposed to be able to bring forth pictures from th' air itself. I'd like to see that, lad, if ye don't mind."

Chuckling, Terien turned to accept the cube from Duncan

and held it out for Rannoch. The image of Quayvern flickered to life, bringing a look of amazement to the old man's face.

"Bless th' ancestors!" Rannoch exclaimed, taking hold of the device on his nose and lifting it so he could peer at the image through the twin pieces of glass. "If I had nae seen it with my own eyes…" he fell silent as Lord Soloth's face appeared, announcing Terien as the Chosen. Listening with rapt attention until the cube was once more dark and silent, Rannoch took a step back and looked up at Terien. "Aye, then. Ye'll be wantin' a meeting with the council, I'm sure."

This was a refreshing change. No bowing and scraping, no formalities, just a no nonsense get-down-to-business kind of attitude. "I will, yes," Terien confirmed. "Tell me, though… it seemed awfully quiet when we arrived. Where is everyone?"

Rannoch shook his head sadly. "Ah, laddie. Brinbourne's been havin' a bad time of late. Th' fish in the bay are usually as plentiful as th' stars in the sky, and now they've up and disappeared again. Th' men have taken to going further and further out to sea, leaving home for weeks at a time." Rannoch wasn't very tall to begin with, but he seemed to shrink right before their eyes. "Those that aren't out in th' boats left to find work in some o' the villages up th' coast, leavin' naught but a few in th' city to tend the shops and work th' gardens."

"I'm sorry to hear that," Terien said sincerely.

Rannoch dismissed him with a wave. "Not the first time it's been this way. We'll survive, right enough." Taking Terien's arm, he started for the door. "Tell ye what, lad. I'll go round up th' lads for a meetin'. Why don't ye wander 'round Brinbourne in th' meantime? Show yourselves around. Poke around, maybe have some lunch. There's a fine little cafe right down th' wharf, and I'll take ye there myself, introduce ye to th' lass who runs the place."

"That would be fine," Terien told him.

"I hate to point this out, but the people didn't seem too… happy to see us," Duncan said. "They won't mind us 'poking around', will they?"

"Ah, no, lad," Rannoch assured. "We don't get many strangers through Brinbourne and they're just shy, especially with th' men bein' out like they are. Ye'll have no trouble once word spreads about who ye are, and I can assure ye that by th' time ye've had lunch there won't be a single soul who doesn't."

Rannoch had been right. By the time they had finished a delicious lunch in the quaint little cafe run by the wife of one of the council members, word had spread throughout the small city. As they wandered the streets they found themselves the center of attention. Seemingly having materialized right out of the woodwork, people were now excitedly following them around and asking all kinds of questions. The felinae were of particular interest, especially for the children who were all but climbing on the huge beasts.

At one point Aurori and Quatina separated from the men so that the Cohalili leader could take the Healer on a tour of the interesting stores, showing her all sorts of eye-catching items from the sea. For Aurori, it was a delight to nose around like this. As Princess in Eristea, she had found little time for such simple pleasures.

One store in particular caught Aurori's fancy. It was filled with all manner of items made from glass of various colors. Jars, bottles, drinking glasses, plates, and other items whose purpose was sometimes mystifying, filled the shelves, and Aurori set out on a buying spree, purchasing containers of all shapes and sizes to replace some of the clay jars she had been using to house her medicinal potions.

"I can't believe this," Aurori told the man behind the counter. "Where I come from, there are very few things made of glass. Where did you get all these?"

"Me and a few lads make 'em, lass. We have a small place out on th' beach, just outside th' city," he said, chest thrust out with pride. "Ye wouldn't be interested in seeing it, would ye?" he asked hopefully.

Aurori looked over at Quatina who was examining an etched vase. "I would like to see it, but if you're not interested, I can go alone."

Quatina gently placed the vase where she had found it. "I am always open to learning new things. I will go with you."

After the proprietor made quick arrangements to leave the

store in the care of his son, he led Aurori and Quatina to the glasshouse that was a short walk outside the city. It was simply the most amazing thing Aurori had ever seen. A handful of craftsmen were working around a furnace, handling globs of molten glass on the ends of long blowpipes. The items the skilled glass-blowers were making were all recognizable from what Aurori and Quatina had seen and purchased in the store, but there were also a couple of men they observed who were flattening their molten glass bubbles and transferring them to the iron rods they called puntys. They were then rotating the rod as fast as they could, causing the bubble to fan out into a circle.

"What are they making?" Quatina inquired.

"Windows for a new house being built," was the explanation.

Aurori's eyes lit up. "So that's how they're made!" she exclaimed, feeling more and more excited by what she was seeing. "In Eristea, we have five huge glass towers that are still intact, but some of the glass panels have broken. We were simply boarding them up as they broke, but this..." she felt lost for words and simply settled for doing a slow turn as her eyes took in the possibilities she saw.

"I'd like to see these glass towers ye're talking about, lass," one of the men said. "Too bad they're so faraway. Oh well. Maybe someday."

"Maybe someday," Aurori repeated, her mind whirring ahead to the Final Reunification. Maybe someday. The glass-blowers of Brinbourne didn't seem to have a clue that the glass they made could have applications in every kingdom and region of Primus, but she would make sure that they did when the time came. Of course it remained to be seen whether any other kingdom had this talent as well. Still, if Brinbourne could be persuaded to trade with the southern kingdoms, that alone would do much to bolster their flagging economy.

Evening was approaching by the time Aurori and Quatina rejoined the rest of the group, finding them congregated outside the council chamber building.

"Where have you two been all day? Shopping, I suppose?" Duncan asked with a wide grin. "Never mind. Tell me later.

Terien's already inside with the council, so if you want to go in and hear what they have to say, we'll have to be real quiet."

Nodding, Aurori and Quatina mounted the steps and followed Duncan into the building. The councilors were all seated at their desks and the center area was filled to capacity with the citizens of Brinbourne who had come to hear the proceedings. Duncan saw his two charges to a couple of extra chairs at the back of the room near the doors, content himself to lean against the wall.

"The Final Reunification is intended to bring together the people of Primus," Terien was saying. He stood in front of the raised bench at the head of the room, addressing Rannoch, who was once again seated in the center chair, and two other older gents who were looking down at him with an air of detached interest. "As it stands, only a few kingdoms and cities have active trade. Imagine how much better life could be for everyone if there were formalized trading agreements and well-maintained trade routes. We could have a continuous flow of goods from every part of Primus shared all across the lands, instead of sporadic bits and pieces making their way into the hands of a select few."

"That's all well and good, lad, but Brinbourne is not a rich region," one of the councilors retorted, getting to his feet. "The fishing industry has been in a slump, and always has its ups and downs. What happens then? Can ye put th' fish in the sea for us?"

A smattering of laughter accompanied the remark, and the councilor regained his seat, smirking defiantly at Terien.

Terien was determined not to let them get to him. "I've toured some of the area today, and I believe Brinbourne has more to offer than the fish in its sea. I'm told that there are large stands of trees up the coast to the north whose wood is ideal for making furniture."

"And once th' trees are gone? There's not enough wood to trade with a whole continent!" another councilor called out.

The chatter in the room was reaching an obnoxious level now as people debated matter. Rannoch banged a wooden gavel on the desk and called for order, but was ignored for the first two or three tries until the councilor on his left rose to his feet.

"All of ye! Hush!" he bellowed out.

Once everyone had been chastened into silence, he nodded to Rannoch who regained his seat, then turned his eyes on Terien. "What's th' point in sending a representative along with ye, lad? Don't get me wrong, the Prophecy has long been held in high regard in these parts, and Brinbourne would love to be a part of th' Final Reunification, but th' truth of the matter is that we're afraid we'll end up holdin' th' short end o' th' stick."

"Unless ye can come up with somethin' better than dead fish and a few trees, that is," someone said, starting a short round of laughter.

Aurori's heart went out to Terien. He looked frazzled by his inability to come up with a solution. She had planned on bringing up the issue of the glasshouse to him in private, but it looked like they might refuse him a representative. She had to act.

"I have an idea," Aurori called out, rising. Every head in the place turned to her and they fell into a stunned silence as she made her way between them until she was standing at Terien's side.

"What are you doing?" Terien whispered urgently to her, brows knit.

"Just trust me," she whispered back. She took a deep breath and prepared her speech in her mind.

She told them about her unexpected tour of the glasshouse, about Eristea's amber glass towers and their missing windows, explaining at length about how excited she had been at the prospect of seeing them repaired. She went on, telling them how valued even the simpler items such as bottles and jars could be, not just to a Healer, but to anyone who ever needed to store anything. They listened in silence, remaining that way well after she had finished.

"We'd never before considered that," Rannoch said. "I think the lass has a valid idea. We can offer fish and wood as we can, and add glass products as well. We could expand th' glasshouse, train more lads in th' trade. It might work," he mused.

The discussion that followed was much more subdued and polite than any that had gone before, and it wasn't long before the council reached its decision.

“Ye’ll be having that representative now, lad,” Rannoch beamed.

“If ye don’t mind, though, we’d like some time to consider whom we’ll be sending along,” the councilor on Rannoch’s right said.

“Not at all,” Terien said.

Taking Aurori’s elbow and leading her from the building, they emerged into the muggy night air and were immediately surrounded by Terien’s men, all asking questions at once. Holding a hand up for silence, Terien then whirled around on Aurori. For a moment she was afraid he was going to give her a reprimand for butting in as she had, but one look at his expression told her otherwise.

“That was brilliant!” Terien roared, catching her around the waist and lifting her up. He twirled her around once and set her back down, his hands moving to her shoulders. “Aurori, I owe you. You just saved my whole mission. If not for you, they never would have agreed to send a representative. Thank you.”

“It’s nothing,” Aurori said shyly. “I was happy to have been of assistance.”

“Are you kidding?” Elek laughed. “You just saved his butt!”

“I’ll never tease you again about going shopping,” Duncan swore, placing a hand over his heart and raising the other to seal the promise. “All hail the greatest shopper who ever lived!”

Aurori cuffed the side of his head and laughed. “You’re embarrassing me,” she complained.

“Seriously, though, you were amazing,” Terien told sincerely. “No diplomat I know could have done better.” That mischievous grin of his surfaced. “Are you sure you’re just a Healer? You handled that like an old pro.”

“What a talent for observation,” Elek said.

A tingle of apprehension coursed through her and her smile faltered briefly at his comment. “Just a simple Healer with a talent for shopping,” she said quickly, wishing now that they would just drop the subject.

She was saved from further comments as the members of Brinbourne’s council emerged from the building and approached Terien.

"Well, lad, we've decided on a representative for your journey," Rannoch proclaimed, the grin splitting his face giving away the identity of who it would be.

"You, Rannoch?" Terien asked in surprise, pointing a finger at the older man.

"None other! I know, I know," he said, patting his belly, "I'm a wee bit past m' prime, but I'll have ye know that I've twice the experience of anyone else on the council. Think of me as a voice of wisdom."

"Of that I have no doubt," Terien said, bowing. "It's my honor to have you along."

"How about a celebration, then?" Elek suggested. "Maybe we could share a glass or two?"

"That's our Elek, always looking for a party," Benem teased.

"Not a bad idea, though," Rannoch agreed. "Come on then. We'll go see if old Lennos hasn't got a bottle or two we can see about draining."

Chapter Eleven

The party at Lennos' establishment the night before had lasted longer than expected and had involved far more than the bottle or two promised. It had also included every one of the councilors of Brinbourne and as many of the citizens as could be squeezed into the two-storey structure. Musical instruments had appeared sometime during the evening, filling the place with joyous melodies accompanied by lilting voices, including Elek's enthusiastic baritone. Life in Brinbourne may have been full of ups and downs, but it was soon quite obvious that the people weren't about to let it get them down, and their exuberance was a joy to behold.

Unfortunately, Terien found that his men had been a little too exuberant themselves when he awoke the next morning.

Leaving the soft bed and the comfortable room he had been assigned at the inn that Rannoch had directed them to after the party, Terien stole across the hall and looked in on Duncan. Finding him still snoring softly in the middle of a rather rumpled-looking bed, arms flung over his head and one foot dangling off the side, Terien quietly closed the door and moved on to the next door. There he found Elek in much the same state as Duncan, sleeping soundly and curled up in a fetal ball.

Smiling, Terien shook his head. Suspecting that he would find the rest of the men similarly sleeping off the effects of the liquor that had flowed so freely the night before, he decided to avoid disturbing them and instead went downstairs to the small restaurant where he shared breakfast with the couple who ran the inn before heading over to the stable where the supply carts and animals had been sheltered for the night.

Finding that a stable boy was already feeding the equines, Terien went to one of the carts to procure a cloak for himself to ward off the stiff breeze that was blowing in across the bay. He took out the map Lord Soloth had given him, as well, intending to

go over it with Rannoch before they departed for the Hidden City and Pergase.

As Terien was wrapping the warm cloak around himself, the stable boy materialized at his side, standing with his hands thrust deep into the pockets of his brown trousers and head bowed so low his face was obscured by the brim of the enormous straw hat he wore.

"Excuse me, sir, but I was wondering what I should be feedin' yer cats," the stable boy said with a nervous glance at the felinae who were still curled up in the hay, their noses tucked beneath the tips of their tails.

"Just water will be fine for today," Terien told him with a smile, knowing exactly what his next question would be.

"Ah hate to ask ye, sir, but don't they… eat?"

Terien laughed. "That they do," he assured the boy, "and in great quantities. But only once every two weeks or so. Even then, they prefer to hunt for their own meal."

The boy pushed the brim of his straw hat back, revealing a thatch of red hair framing a cherubic freckled face and eyes like saucers. "Och, man! Ye'd think they'd be starvin', then!" Embarrassed by his own lack of courtesy, the boy's face flushed crimson and he averted his eyes. "Sir," he added belatedly.

Ignoring the breech of etiquette, Terien patted the boy's back. "Maybe later you can ask one of the men to explain more to you," Terien suggested.

It was evident from the way the boy was looking at the felinae that he was totally entranced by them. Terien knew how he felt. The power and grace of the felinae were very alluring, but they were also undeniably cute and cuddly looking. You just wanted to reach out and give them a good hug.

"Listen, if you'd like to, you could give them a brushing once they wake up," Terien offered.

"Could I really?" the boy asked eagerly.

Reaching into the back of the cart, Terien produced a stiff brush and gave it to the boy. "Sure, as long as you're not allergic to cats, that is."

"No sir! Not me!"

"Good. It's no different that brushing down a horse. Except

for the length of the fur, of course." He took hold of the boy's shoulder, turned him to face the felinae and pointed to each in turn. "The white one is Shangra, the cinnamon-and-cream-colored one is Tiagra, the one with the black and white patches is Miasma, that one with the ginger coat is Breti, and the other ginger one with the white paws and belly is Snowdrift."

"Snowdrift?" the boy asked.

Terien shrugged. "He was found in a snowdrift, I think. Wandered away from the litter or something. Ask Benem, it's his felinae."

"Thank ye, sir, I will!" the boy said enthusiastically.

Terien patted him on the back once and headed out of the stable, wrapping his cloak a little tighter against the breeze as he made his way up the short incline that led to the council chambers. Once inside, his eyes adjusted to the dim lighting and he found that Aurori and Quatina were already there, chatting with Rannoch as they sat around one of the tables.

"And here I thought I was the only one who had managed to crawl out of bed this morning," he said as he removed his cloak and hung it on a hook on the back wall.

"Perhaps the men over-indulged last night, but we ladies prefer to sip our drinks," Aurori said when she looked up and smiled. "Present company excepted, of course. Good morning, by the way."

"Oy, lass! Were that true, I'd nay be sittin' here with a headache!" Rannoch laughed.

"Well, why didn't you say so? I could get you something for it," Aurori offered, already rising from her chair.

"Nay, no need. Sit," Rannoch told her, motioning her back to her chair. "A lad as old as I should know better. If I suffer the headache, I'll be knowin' better fer next time."

Terien took a chair and turned it around, straddling it backwards and resting his elbows on its back, the rolled map hanging in one hand. "If that were true, none of us would ever drink again," he laughed.

"What have ye got there, lad?" Rannoch asked, nodding at Terien's hand.

"This," Terien said, unfurling the paper and laying it out on the table between them, "is the map I was given."

Rannoch reached out and ran his fingertips over the smooth surface of the colorful map. "Very interesting parchment. Smoother than any I've seen before," he said, squinting at it and leaning closer for a better look. "Feels like… flexible glass. Or the inside of a seashell."

Quatina cleared her throat and gently elbowed Rannoch's side. "I'm sure this is very interesting for you, but I would prefer to hear what the Chosen has to say."

Rannoch harrumphed and leaned back, but kept one hand lightly on one corner of the map, ostensibly to hold it down.

"I thought you might like to know what you're getting yourself into, Rannoch. This is the route we'll be taking to Pergase," Terien informed him, tracing a finger from Brinbourne up and to the west, through the Teseni Desert to the Alatesh canyons at its center, then to the north-west where Pergase lay.

Rannoch blinked twice. "Are ye daft lad? Travelin' the desert that way is beggin' for trouble! Sure, it's a shorter route, but nobody's fool enough to cross a desert without knowin' where the water is. Whenever we've had call to make the journey to Pergase, we've always gone this way," he said, his finger moving from Brinbourne to the towns that lay to the north, then along the coast until he reached the Smokasen river, then west to Pergase. "It's safer, to be sure."

Terien stabbed a finger down on three spots that were marked in blue along the route he had indicated through the heart of the Teseni. "Lord Soloth marked these spots on the map as being oases with freshwater springs. Moreover, if we follow this path we will come to the Alatesh canyon, the site of the Hidden City."

A brief explanation about that brought understanding to Rannoch's face and he nodded. "Aye, then. If we're to cross th' Teseni, I'd best get the lads busy making some more lanterns and such."

"Lanterns? What for?" Quatina asked.

Giving her a patient look, Rannoch said, "So we can travel at night, of course." Getting only a blank stare in return, he exhaled heavily and rubbed a hand across his face in a gesture of total exasperation. "For a lass who lives on th' edge of the blinkin' desert…" his voice trailed off and he gave his head a shake. "Th' Teseni will bake yer brains fer certain if ye travel during th' day. Best to travel at night when it's cooler," he said.

Quatina shook her head violently, frowning. "The predators come out at night, fisherman. It is best to travel in the day when they sleep. It is easier to guard a camp at night than to fend them off as you journey." Standing, she folded her muscular arms in silent challenge.

"Donna be tellin' me, girl!" Rannoch insisted, slapping a hand on the table. He stuck a finger out and jabbed it in the air at her. "Th' lanterns will keep the predators away!"

The two stood facing each other, silently fuming for a moment, then both looked to Terien at exactly the same time, each with a look of expectation.

Aurori and Terien traded an amused glance.

"I'll tell you what," Terien said, reaching for the map and rolling it up. "We'll try a little of both. Quatina, tell Rannoch what we would need to travel during the day without baking ourselves, and Rannoch, you will see to it that we have enough lanterns to travel at night." He looked to each in turn with eyebrows upraised. "Fair enough?"

Quatina backed down first, unfolding her arms and letting them hang at her sides. She glared at Rannoch for a moment, then turned to Terien and nodded.

"If that's what ye want, then so be it," Rannoch said, obviously not quite satisfied but unwilling to challenge Terien on the matter.

"Good. We'll leave you to it, then. Any idea when we'll be ready to leave?"

Rannoch offered a shrug and pushed his glasses further back on his nose. "Right after lunch, I'd think, if ye're hell bent on leavin' in such a bloody hurry."

Aurori noticed that Terien seemed taken aback by the comment. He managed to hide it fairly well, but the firm set of his mouth told her that Rannoch had just hit a raw nerve, and she was determined to find out what was going on.

"After lunch would be fine," Terien told Rannoch, already striding towards the doors of the council chambers. He stopped only long enough to put his cloak on and was out of the door.

"I'll see you later," Aurori said to Quatina as she rose from the table and quickly gathered up her own cloak.

"Aren't you going to stay and discuss this with us?" Quatina asked, puzzled.

Whirling her cloak onto her shoulders, Aurori shook her head. "I'll be back. I forgot to ask Terien something," she said over her shoulder as she hurried out of the door. Hesitating on the step, she looked up and down the street for Terien. She finally caught sight of him heading away from her along the windswept beach, his long legs carrying him at a pace she had little chance of matching without running.

"Terien!" she called after him, cursing the soft sand that was hindering her every step. "Terien! Slow down!"

Terien stopped and spun around, waiting for her to catch up with him. She was breathless by the time she reached him.

"Are you okay?" Terien asked, placing a steadying hand on her elbow.

"I was… going to… ask you… the same thing," she gasped out. Taking a deep breath, she plunged ahead. "What Rannoch said… about you being in a hurry. It looked like it bothered you. I thought you might want to talk about it," she offered.

The wry smile Aurori had come to know so well once again graced Terien's lips. "You really are very observant. No wonder you noticed that little detail about the glasshouse and I didn't," he complimented, tucking her hand into the crook of his elbow. He turned them around so the wind was now at their back and they were heading once more in the direction of the council chambers, but at a much more leisurely pace.

Aurori assumed this was a feeble attempt to change the subject and pressed on. "Never mind that right now. Something is bothering you and I'd like to help, if I can."

Terien's sigh was caught on the wind and swept away before Aurori could hear it, but there was no mistaking the look that came across his face. Regret.

"I'm an impatient man," Terien said, his tone making it seem as though he were divulging a deep, dark secret. "Not that I act on impulse, mind you. I do think things through, sometimes until

I'm all tied up in knots. But once I've determined a course of action, I tend to stick to it no matter what crops up in the meantime. I just hate interruptions and can't seem to tear my attention away until I've completed whatever I set out to do."

"That's a good thing, isn't it? It's worse when someone starts doing several things and never completes any of them," she pointed out.

"Maybe, but I miss out on a lot because I'm too busy pushing ahead, trying to reach the finish line."

Aurori looked up at him, realizing that this had everything to do with his comment about her being observant. "You're upset about not seeing the potential of the glasshouse, aren't you? I'm sorry if I overstepped my authority, but..."

"No. Don't you dare be sorry," Terien said sincerely, looking sideways at her. "Don't you see? I'm in such a hurry to go from city to city and collect the representatives that I'm not spending enough time looking around. I see without really seeing." He shook his head. "Rannoch was right. I'm doing it again. We spent only one day in Brinbourne and already I'm impatient to be under way. It leaves me wondering – what else am I missing here in Brinbourne? And if I did stay longer, would I really be able to see what's here, or would my impatience just... blind me? I don't know."

"You seemed to have little trouble keeping your mind focused when we were with the Cohalili and the Penaro."

"That was different. I had something to occupy my mind. Something more than nice scenery, at any rate," he said, indicating the ocean and the city with a sweep of one hand.

"At least you've noticed that Brinbourne is a nice place," she teased, giving his arm a squeeze. "Seriously, though, only you can decide how much time you need to spend in any one place, and maybe you could spend more than a single day, but I think you're also being too hard on yourself. Don't forget, you have many, many miles of journey to go, giving you a great deal of time to talk to the representatives about their lands. That should be more than enough for you to get an idea what each one has to offer for the Final Reunification."

Feeling a little better about it, Terien's lips started to curve up

into a small smile. “True. Just as long as I don’t come across another Brinbourne where they won’t even send a representative until I come up with a good reason for them to do so.”

“If you do, just remember to ask the rest of us what we found when we were out touring.” Aurori laughed and tugged on Terien’s arm, bringing him to a stop. She wriggled her hand from his arm and slipped it around his waist. “Don’t forget that you have twenty-four pairs of eyes you can count on for help. You may be the Chosen, but that doesn’t mean you’re all alone in this. You can count on all of us to help wherever and whenever we can.”

“And with those sharp eyes of yours, I’m sure you’ll be able to spot anything the rest of us miss,” he laughed, draping an arm over her shoulder.

“Hey, that’s why I’m called the…” Aurori cut herself off abruptly before she could finish the thought and the word “observer” could slip out. Terien was looking at her. She had to say something, and fast. “What did Duncan call me last night? Oh yes. The greatest shopper who ever lived. I can spot a bargain a mile away.” Her palms were suddenly sweaty despite the chill breeze.

“Just keep it up,” Terien said. “And thank you. Again. For coming with me – with us,” he corrected.

“You’re welcome. Again.” Aurori smiled mischievously and applied a little pressure to Terien’s back, getting him moving once more. “Come on, Chosen. I think it’s time we got your little group together and got under way. I think the salty sea air is starting to wrinkle your brain. You sounded like Duncan back there, all serious and full of introspection.”

Terien’s eyebrows shot up. “Whoa. There’s a scary thought,” he intoned.

Laughing, they made their way back to the inn where preparations for their departure were already under way.

Chapter Twelve

As it turned out, the Teseni Desert was not quite as desolate as one might have thought. Though it was well known that the edges of the Teseni were filled with rocky bluffs, rock pillars and outcroppings as well as various types of cactus and hardy plants, it had long been thought that the interior was little more than a wasteland of endless sand dunes, devoid of any kind of life. Not so. As they journeyed towards the first oasis marked on Terien's map, it soon became apparent that the Teseni was actually teeming with life, though not all of it was of a benevolent nature.

The sentati, which they had heard howling on the night of their abduction by the Cohalili and the Penaro, were a particular annoyance. More of a nuisance than a danger, their nightly presence at the fringes of the camp disturbed the animals and set everyone's nerves on edge until the time came for the felinae to be let loose to hunt for themselves. After that, the instance of sentati following them became a little more sporadic.

Of more concern were the smaller but more perilous creatures. Snapping and stinging insects became a concern soon after one of the felinae inadvertently stepped on a bug that put a nasty gash into its paw. About three inches long with long articulated legs, the insect was a shade darker than the sand and had a hard carapace that made it tough to squash. Its sharp pincers had clamped shut on the side of Snowdrift's paw, scissoring right through fur and flesh with frightening ease. It was only Aurori's swift ministrations that allowed them to continue with little delay, a shaved patch of fur and a raised scar on Snowdrift's paw the only thing to show for the mishap.

Snakes, bugs and sentati aside, the most difficult thing to deal with was the heat, just as Rannoch had warned. The white robes and headgear Quatina had suggested went a long way towards staving off that problem, proving that Quatina's desert smarts were not to be taken lightly. They had tried traveling at night as Rannoch had suggested and soon found that idea lacking. In point of fact, this world had two suns but no moon. Night was always as dark as pitch and the light from the lanterns wasn't nearly enough to light their way across the rocky terrain without risking a possibly fatal misstep. Fortunately, the Teseni was also cooler than advertised, perhaps owing to the fact that it was still only spring.

For all the dangers of the desert, there was also great beauty in its variegated shades of sienna and umber, in the rise and fall of the dunes and in the wind-sculpted spires and buttes. There was also beauty to be found in the creatures of the desert. Small furry creatures would poke out of the nooks and crannies of the rocks they passed, some hopping, some scuttling about as they scratched a living out of the land. Some would quickly hide while others, out of curiosity, would creep closer, sniffing at the newcomers.

Using a standard compass and the map in Terien's possession they had managed to come across the first two oases and had spent a day and night luxuriating in the respite they offered from what was otherwise a long and ultimately boring trek. Each had consisted of a large freshwater pool fed by a spring that burbled up from the rocks, surrounded by a veritable miniature jungle of plant life whose rich green color offered a pleasant break from the more somber colors of the desert.

Leaving the first oasis had been hard, but taking leave of the second had brought with it the promise of soon reaching the Hidden City of Alatesh, putting everyone into a bright mood of expectation. Now, with their first objective no more than a day or two away, they picked their way through the outer edges of the network of canyons that were etched on the map like the interconnected strands of a spider's web, and the conversation turned to speculation about what they would find, what could be expected.

Laughing and talking amongst themselves, it wasn't until the ears of the felinae pricked up and they began to growl that they had their first inkling that something was amiss.

"What is it, boy?" Terien murmured, patting Shangra's neck in an attempt to quiet him.

Their ears now flattening back, Shangra and the other felinae suddenly ceased growling and slowed almost to a stop, their huge heads raised up, nostrils flaring as they sniffed the air. Tails slung low, the five cats were assuming postures that could only be described as cautious while they cocked their heads to the side, scanning the shadowed crevices of the canyon walls. All around them the entourage had also slowed to a near halt as everyone took a cue from the cats and began looking around, nervous and silent.

"What are they doing?" Makhani asked in a loud whisper directed at Terien.

Terien held up a hand to shade his eyes from the sun and studied the area, twisting left and right. "They must be smelling something."

"Oh, well, tell me something I don't know," Makhani remarked sarcastically, heeling his equine closer to Terien. "I mean – why are they acting so strange? Even the sentati never made them this nervous."

Terien looked over at the other felinae. Eyes dilated, ears flattened, crouching lower to the ground, backs starting to arch, the fur of their tails was standing on end. He'd seen this behavior before, and it was cause for alarm.

"Ready your weapons," Terien said, unsheathing his own sword.

"I don't see anything," Duncan muttered. Trying to balance himself on a felinae whose back was arching higher and higher was becoming problematic, making him fumble as he reached to draw his sword.

The equines, who had been calm up to this point, also began to snort and whinny, prancing around and tossing their heads.

"Whatever it is, I wish it would hurry up and show itself," Benem complained.

"It won't be other people, I can tell you that," Elek said. "Otherwise the felinae and equines wouldn't be reacting like this."

"Do we wait around or keep moving?" Makhani asked.

"Keep moving," Terien told him, digging his heels into

Shangra's sides. All he got for a response was a low growl and a soft hiss that made his eyebrows shoot up. "Or not."

Makhani chuckled and was about to make a snide comment, but fell silent as a familiar yowling sound echoed through the canyon.

"Felinae!" someone shouted.

Then all hell broke loose.

A blur of mottled orange, black, and white fur shot from a notch in the canyon wall high above, landing directly in front of the group. Letting out a primal roar, the felinae set baleful eyes on the felinae of Terien's group, its mouth contorting into a vicious hiss as it squared off against Shangra whom it perceived as the leader of the offending pack that had wandered into its territory.

The equines went wild, rearing and breaking away as several more felinae dropped into view, all hissing a challenge. Amid shouts and cries of alarm, several riders were thrown to the ground while others managed to hold their seats but were carried away in all directions as they made vain attempts to get their animals under control. The supply carts, sturdy as they were, were taking a pounding, their wheels crashing over rocks and their contents and drivers bouncing around as their equines, too, made a mad dash for safety.

The felinae riders were spared the rough ride, but were in far more danger. Terien had managed to dive off Shangra's back and roll away into the rocks just as the mottled felinae had sprung at them. Shangra and the wild cat circled and batted at each other, then fell to fighting belly to belly, fore claws sunk into each others backs as their hind legs ripped into each other with piston-like kicks. Tiagra stared down a pair of smaller white and gray felinae, engaging in a slow dance of nerves. Breti and Miasma were each engaged in combat as well, moving through every fighting stance a cat could use, as they rolled, scratched, bit and howled in a free-for-all that sent sand and fur flying. Snowdrift, however, the most timid of the group, was running flat out down the canyon with three of the wild cats literally nipping at his heels.

Blood oozing from a cut he had received on his forehead when he had rolled to a stop amongst the rocks, Terien dazedly got to his feet and helplessly surveyed the scene, his sword useless in his hand. Benem and Haren were on the other side of the canyon, crouching behind rocks. They looked shaken but seemed unharmed as they, too, watched with wide, fearful eyes. Searching for Duncan, he quickly spotted his best friend a short way down the canyon, just now getting to his feet. Only Miasma's rider was missing, a young fellow by the name of Rioto, but it looked like Duncan was already starting to look for him amongst the rocks.

Turning his attention outward for a moment, Terien could see that Elek and a handful of riders were hot on the heels of Snowdrift and his pursuers, weapons out. In the other direction, his men were just now getting their animals under control, herding them together into groups well out of the way of the cat fight that was still taking place. He noted that some men were slow to rise after having been thrown from their mounts, and that set him to scanning for a certain set of familiar colors. Terien's heart lurched when he couldn't see either Aurori or her Appaloosa, but he resolutely pushed away the unwanted image of her lying injured somewhere and forced his eyes back to the felinae, relieved to know that at least the wild felinae were leaving the men and equines alone.

Regretting the necessity of it, Terien upholstered the ancient weapon that was strapped to his right thigh, unlocked its safety and sighted down the barrel. Shangra and the wild cat were rolling around too close together to risk a shot, as were Tiagra and his counterpart. But Breti's assailant had just bounded out of reach of a wicked swipe from his paw, giving Terien a clear shot. The report of the weapon rang out, reverberating throughout the canyon and sending a renewed jolt of electric nervousness into the equines. Breti's counterpart spasmed once and lay still. Startled by the unexpected sound, two of the attacking felinae sprang high and darted away, leaving Miasma free and clear. One managed to leap away into the safety of the rocks, but the other somersaulted in mid-air as another shot barked out, this time from Duncan's weapon. It thumped to the ground and lay still.

His heart beating furiously, Terien sighted again for the cat battling Shangra but still couldn't get a clear shot. Patches of blood stood out in stark relief against the white fur of the felinae Terien had raised from a cub, and he felt utterly heartsick and infuriated at the prospect of losing Shangra to this chance encounter. The two were evenly matched and the fight could go either way. He had to act.

Lips curled back in fury, Terien held his breath and felt the world drop away as he concentrated on the grim task he had set. Duncan's weapon sang out once more, but Terien barely heard. His finger squeezing in on the trigger, his vision became a tunnel until all he could see was the massive head of the wild cat thrashing and biting at Shangra. Later he wouldn't be able to recall the precise moment he had known it was time to take the shot. All he would remember was the unerring flight of the bullet as it pierced the side of the wild cat's head, finally ending the fierce battle for territorial supremacy.

Gasping for breath, his hands shaking, Terien staggered on shaky legs to Shangra's side and fell to his knees beside the great cat who now lay on his side, panting as hard as his master. He raised his massive head at Terien's touch and let out a mournful mewing sound.

"It's all right. You're going to be fine," Terien whispered as he carefully ran his hands through the matted fur around Shangra's wounds. Although the bites and scratches were deep and bleeding freely, they didn't seem to be life-threatening as far as he could tell.

Duncan squatted beside Terien and put a hand on his back. "Tiagra's pretty beat up, but I think he'll be okay. Same with Breti and Miasma. Still no sign of Elek, though," he said, looking off in the direction Snowdrift had been chased. "I'd hate to see Benem lose his felinae. It would break his heart."

Terien and Duncan both looked up at the sound of booted feet running over sand and rock.

"Terien, Duncan, come quick! Jeret's had an accident!" Quatina called out urgently, motioning for them to follow her.

Springing to their feet they sprinted after her, following her around a bend in the canyon and in-between a large stand of rocks. The men were clustered around the prostrate form of Jeret, obscuring Terien's view of the man, but a rock settled in the pit of his stomach when he caught sight of Aurori standing there in Makhani's arms, the tears streaming down her cheeks telling

Terien what he could expect to find.

Pushing between the men and falling to his knees beside Jeret, Terien studied the dead man's peaceful face. He reached out and put a hand on Jeret's chest. Eyes closed as though in peaceful slumber, there wasn't a mark on him to indicate an injury, but the way his head was canted to the side at an odd angle made the diagnosis of a broken neck all too clear.

Only the sound of the wind moaning through the canyon and Aurori's ragged sobs filled the air as Terien squeezed his eyes shut. Jeret. He hadn't known the man well, but knew that he had a family back in Kaethos, a wife and two girls. How tragic that an accident such as this would leave them without husband and father. Worse, they wouldn't even know for a long, long time to come.

"What happened?" Terien asked quietly, opening his eyes and withdrawing his hand, letting it fall slack into his lap.

"He was thrown from his equine when the felinae attacked," one of the men told him, his voice tight with emotion. "We called Aurori over right away, but..." his voice broke and he shook his head, indicating that there had been nothing they could do.

Aurori now appeared at Terien's side, falling to her knees in the sand. Although her hand fluttered momentarily towards the cut on his forehead, it ended up closing into a tight fist that she held against her chest as she looked at him with eyes full of heartache and regret. "Terien, I'm so sorry."

"He didn't suffer," Makhani commented quietly. "Not that there's any good way to go."

Terien took a deep breath. Knowing that his men would look to him for direction, he would have to balance their grief and his own against their need to get matters settled and move on. Terien looked at each of the men before him. He looked back to Duncan, saw the look of misery shared and managed a small nod.

"Duncan, take charge of seeing to the felinae," he said, getting to his feet. "You boys assemble the supply carts. Get them sorted out and get a camp set up. We'll have to spend the night here. And keep watch for Elek and the others. If they're not back in half an hour we'll send out a search party. Makhani, you and I will see to

Jeret."

As everyone silently dispersed to their assigned tasks, Terien gently took hold of Aurori's arm and pulled her to her feet. "Aurori, I would appreciate anything you can do to help Duncan with the felinae," he said softly. She wasn't even looking at him, just staring down at Jeret. Cupping her chin in his palm, he turned her face towards him. "There was nothing you could have done for him," he told her.

"I know," she whispered, closing her eyes on the fresh tears welling in her eyes. "That's why it's so hard. What if it had been…" she sobbed, unable to finish the thought.

"It wasn't," he whispered softly, drawing her into his arms and stroking her back as she cried into his shoulder. He was uncertain if she was talking about him specifically, but still felt a warm rush at the thought.

She pulled away from him after a minute and hastily swiped at her tear-streaked cheeks, suddenly embarrassed. "It's okay. I'll be fine. I'll go find my pack and see what I can do for the felinae," she said before hurriedly moving off towards where the supply carts stood.

Terien watched her for a moment, then turned to Makhani who had been standing silently to the side, looking more grim than was usual, even for him.

"We can't bury him here. The sand's too shallow. Besides, some of those felinae survived. They could come back and…" Makhani said, trusting that his implication was clear.

Terien nodded agreement. "Get some cloaks from the cart to serve as a makeshift shroud, then we'll scout the area. There are a lot of small caves in these canyons. Hopefully we'll find one that we can use as a tomb."

As Makhani went for the cloaks, Terien looked down at Jeret and made a silent vow to make sure that the first casualty of their journey would also be the last.

Chapter Thirteen

Although the felinae had already regained some of their strength and had started licking their own wounds by the time Aurori arrived, she had still insisted on healing every one of their injuries. The process had taken hours, during which time Elek and the others had returned with Snowdrift in tow, unharmed but tired from his mad dash through the canyon. Unfortunately, Elek had to report that they had only managed to chase the wild cats away, leaving the possibility of their return.

As could be expected, Elek's group had reacted with shock and grief over the unexpected loss of Jeret, and a pall had fallen over the entire camp. Everyone went about the business of getting settled in for the night without their usual cheerful exchange of banter, including Rannoch who had previously kept up a perpetual stream of conversation.

Makhani and Terien had managed to find a suitable cave a short distance back in the direction they had come from and the first order of business after the camp had been set up was to hold a funeral for Jeret.

With the last rays of the setting suns casting long shadows across the canyon floor, Benem had eulogized the young man who had been one of the more quiet members of their group and a fairly close personal friend of his. Terien had also said a few words, as was required of him, but there was no mistaking the sincerity of the grief he expressed at the loss of a member of his entourage. He had then removed the wedding band from Jeret's finger and given it to Benem, promising that together they would return it to the man's widow when the time came.

After reciting the prayer for the dead together and observing a minute of silence, they had laid their friend to rest inside the small cave, wedging rocks into the small opening to seal it for all time.

The events of the day had taken an especially terrible toll on

Aurori. Her emotional reaction to Jeret's accidental death, coupled with having spent most of the afternoon and evening tending the wounded felinae, had left her exhausted and in a particularly morose frame of mind. She had barely touched her dinner and had almost immediately fallen into a fitful slumber while still propped up by one of the fires, leaving Terien with no choice but to carry her to the lean-to she and Quatina would share for the night.

Even with extra guards posted throughout the night, sleep did not come easily for anyone as images of the surviving felinae stalking through the rocks of the canyon filled everyone with unvoiced dread, and it was only with the first golden rays of the morning suns that a sense of peace finally settled over the camp.

They were able to resume their journey the next morning, thanks to Aurori's expert care of the felinae, but would have to allow the great cats to remain riderless for a few days to give them time to make a full recovery. Despite the inconvenience, they pressed on towards the Alatesh canyon, the general mood of the group improving over the next day and night as quiet conversations began to spring up once again.

By the time Terien announced that they had arrived at the mouth of the Alatesh canyon late morning on the second day after the attack, things were pretty much back to normal, and although there was still a somewhat somber tone to their banter, he knew that the passage of time would resolve the matter.

"So this is where your people came from," Duncan said to Quatina, craning his neck to look around.

Quatina didn't reply, but instead dismounted from her equine and stood looking around at the place. It was really quite unremarkable. The canyon walls were the same banded, sienna-colored sandstone as the rest of the canyons they had traversed to get to Alatesh, except that these walls were sheer and wholly vertical, giving the impression that they had been sculpted that way. Wider across here than at any other point, every man and animal of the entourage could stand side by side single file and still not reach from wall to wall. In the distance the canyon broadened out, giving access once more to the desert beyond.

"It is... not what I expected," Quatina said finally, her

shoulders sagging a bit. "You are certain this is the place?"

Terien checked the map again to confirm, but was nodding even as he did. "This is the place, all right. Lord Soloth said that the locks for the cities were usually hidden in such a way as to blend in with the surrounding, so we'll have to fan out and search."

"What are we looking for, exactly?" Makhani queried.

Terien jumped down from the cart he had been riding on and tucked the map under his arm. "A hole in the wall that's about one inch in diameter. It should be set inside a cube-shaped elevation set at about waist height. That will be the receptacle for Quatina's key."

"I guess we do this the hard way, then," Duncan sighed. He pointed to ten of the men and waved for them to follow him, heading for the rock cliffs to the west, Quatina one step behind him, while Terien and the others spread out along the east wall.

Searching both by sight and by touch, they scoured the sides of the canyon in silence for what seemed like hours, the hot suns beating down from overhead until Rannoch's lilting shout sent them all scurrying towards where he had been searching at the far end of the eastern wall.

"I think I found it!" Rannoch yelled out. He gingerly poked a finger into the crevice, as he waited for everyone to reach his position, half expecting it to be bitten off.

The moment they had been waiting for, once arrived, seemed anticlimactic. The hole Rannoch had found was the right dimension and set in a raised cube of rock protruding from the cliff wall as predicted, but there was no door evident anywhere on the sandstone surface before them.

"Where's the door?" Benem muttered aloud, giving voice to what everyone else had noticed.

Poking a finger into the hole as Rannoch did, Quatina turned to Terien and gave him a questioning look.

"Just try your key," Terien suggested, but as she pulled the cylinder from her tunic, he grabbed her hand. "Wait a minute." He went to the stonewall and ran his hand inward towards the center of the cliff face, away from the cube-shaped protrusion, feeling with his fingertips for a door edge. Finding nothing, he stepped back and let out a heavy breath.

"What now?" Makhani asked, hands on hips.

"Everyone move away from the wall, just in case," Terien said.

"Are ye expectin' trouble, lad?" Rannoch asked, shuffling a few feet back along with everyone else.

Terien had no real answer for that. Maybe he was just being overcautious after what had happened to Jeret, but he had to consider the matter of everyone's safety. "Not really, but we have no idea what to expect. Just be ready to run."

Aurori wedged herself between him and Duncan, and Terien smiled at the wide-eyed look of expectation on her face, a look that was mirrored on every face around him. Nodding for Quatina to proceed, he held his breath.

Quatina slowly inserted the cylinder into the hole, its glass housing making a soft scraping sound against the stone until it came to a stop, settling into place with a faint click.

The reaction was immediate. The sound that came from somewhere inside the cliff wall wasn't all that loud, but it was deep and rumbling and sent a vibration through the ground under their feet. Then the most amazing thing happened. Half the side of the cliff face began to recede into the cliff, making a grinding, grating sound as it did. When the wall came to a stop at about a foot into the cliff face, a new noise sounded from inside and everyone took a few hasty steps back. Akin to the whistling whine of the Sky Lord's aircraft, it set everyone's teeth on edge as the wall now began to lift from the canyon floor, sending a gust of warm air rushing out from somewhere inside. The wall continued to rise up until its bottom edge was a good twenty feet up, then it finally stopped, as did all other noise from inside.

A yawning cavern awaited them. Dark and silent, its depths holding untold mystery, it seemed to speak of great age and unimaginable power. The air wafting out from the opening in the cliff held an odd tangy scent that seemed at once alien and familiar. Blocky shapes were shrouded within the shadows, barely discernible but tantalizing in their invitation to come and explore the world that had once been.

With great reverence, Quatina took the first hesitant step inside the place that had once been home to her people. Her dark eyes glittered in the light streaming from outside as she turned and looked back at Terien. “At last we have found the Hidden Home,” she breathed, a smile lighting her face. Cautiously moving further into the depths of the cavern, she beckoned over her shoulder for the others to follow her.

Terien slowly took a few steps inside, keeping close to the wall as he let his eyes adjust to the dim interior. The wall beneath his hand was made of the same flat gray metal as Lord Soloth’s aircraft, that much was apparent, but without more light there would be no way to explore more than a few yards from the door.

“Rannoch, I think now would be a good time to put those lanterns of yours to work,” Terien said.

“Aye! I’ll fetch ye some,” Rannoch replied, hurrying off.

“I don’t like this,” Duncan said loudly, craning his neck to look up at the door suspended high overhead. “What if that door decides it doesn’t like staying open? The whole place is hundreds of years old, you know.”

Terien blew a breath out and strode back outside. “Have a little faith, Duncan. It opened once, so I’m sure it would open again, even if it did happen to close.”

“Did you hear all that grinding?” Duncan shivered. “I’m not so sure I want to go in there.”

Clapping a hand on Duncan’s shoulder and giving him a grin, Terien looked over at Aurori who was standing at the edge of the opening, peering inside and trying to follow Quatina’s progress in the dark room.

“What about you, Aurori? Planning on joining me for a little spelunking?” he asked.

“Maybe,” she said uncertainly.

Once Rannoch arrived with several men carrying lit lanterns, Terien took one for himself and a spare for Quatina and moved into the ancient bunker, accompanied by Aurori and Makhani who walked on either side of him, as well as several of the men who couldn’t wait to go exploring. Duncan remained outside, however, steadfastly refusing to venture inside. He had company, though, for several others made excuses about needing to tend the animals and remained on the outside.

With the lanterns dispelling the gloom, the true dimensions

and contents of the place were revealed. Cavernous was the only way to describe the room. Its walls and ceilings were all made of the same metal, as was the floor. The blocky objects that had been visible only as shadowy shapes were now exposed as being some sort of consoles and machines with buttons and depressions on their surfaces. No one could even guess at their purpose, but some had writing etched into their smooth surfaces, and though the text was ancient, some of it was still decipherable. Words like OUTSIDE EXHAUST AUTO ON, or TEMPERATURE CONTROL VALVE POD ONE were readable but meaningless. Dust was everywhere, as were cobwebs and the same stale and tangy scent of ancient disuse.

The most interesting discoveries lay to the back of the room, however. There, several doors led further into the interior, revealing stairways that led up and down. Ordering everyone to split up into pairs, Terien sent them out to explore further through the complex while he and Makhani remained in the main entry chamber to examine its contents more closely.

It was soon discovered that the lower floor held vast rooms filled with bank upon bank of massive machines, while the upper floors held what had obviously been the living quarters where Quatina's ancestors had ate and slept and lived. Rooms within rooms had been built into three levels, all clustered around a central open area that looked like it had once been made to simulate a small park complete with winding walkways and a small artificial waterfall structure. The vaulted ceiling had huge panels set into it, not unlike those of a skylight, except that so deep into the canyon there was no way for sunlight to reach down.

Standing at the top of the stairs on the second floor, Quatina ran her hand over the protective railing and looked down at the open area below. Sighing in satisfaction, she turned to Aurori who had automatically paired off with her to go exploring. "It is good to have seen the place my ancestors came from, even if I have little hope of ever understanding how they lived." She closed her eyes and cocked her head to the side. "When I close my eyes I can almost see them here, can almost hear their voices as they laugh and talk, but I cannot picture what this place looked like then. It is so empty now. So sad. As they must have been when they had to leave their home."

"That may be, but look at what became of them," Aurori told her. "Your people are all healthy and have a good life out in the desert. The legacy of who they were survives in you and in your people." Holding her lantern a little higher, she leaned one hip against the railing and looked up at the dark ceiling. She knew that it once must have been very bright, but still thought it was a poor replacement for open sky and natural sunlight. "I'd say that the Cohalili got the better end of the bargain, anyway. I don't think I'd want to live underground like this."

"It has been an interesting place to see, but there is not very much left behind," Quatina said. "I am uncertain what I expected to see, however."

"More small technological devices," Aurori said instantly. "Like the recording cube Terien has. Or the keys. Something, anyway. The big machines we've seen so far all seem to be fixed in place and I doubt they'll ever work again."

A whine suddenly issued from somewhere back towards the great cavern, interrupting their conversation. They exchanged puzzled glances and listened for a minute as the whine rose and fell a few times before leveling off in intensity. That was when they heard what sounded like startled shouts.

"Something is wrong!" Quatina cried.

Aurori spun around and took off down the stairs, fearing what they would find. With Quatina close behind, she ran full tilt through the maze of corridors that led back to the cavern entrance. As they wound their way back towards the doors to the cavern they were joined by others who had also been out exploring on the various levels. Bursting through the doors and into the main entry chamber, they were assaulted by the full force of the high-pitched whine. The first thing Aurori noted was that the giant door was still wide open, laying to rest the fear that Duncan had been right and they had somehow been closed inside.

Skidding to a stop as she rounded the corner of a massive machine that lay near the back of the room, Aurori's jaw dropped open. In a domino effect, Quatina bumped into Aurori and was in turn bumped into by the man directly on her heels until everyone who had come running from the inner chambers was standing and staring in mute disbelief at the sight before them.

Terien, Duncan and Makhani were standing atop a huge machine that was hovering a few feet in mid-air directly in front of the aperture in the cliff side. The machine was rectangular-shaped and simply immense, consisting of a thick, flat deck with metal rails for sides and had a raised console at one of the narrower ends at which Terien and Makhani stood jockeying for position around the controls. Duncan, meanwhile, was running from side to side across the deck, leaning over the edges and yelling out orders. The whine coming from the machine rose and fell as Makhani worked a slide bar set into the console, while Terien had both hands wrapped around a black stick protruding from it which he was bending from side to side. The machine skittered first to the left, then to the right, then back a little more to the left again.

"That's it! You've got it!" Duncan called out, holding up a triumphant thumb and flashing a huge grin.

"Okay! Here we go!" Terien called out, bending the stick towards himself.

The machine lurched backwards a few feet.

"The other way! The other way!" Makhani yelled, cuffing Terien's shoulder with the back of his hand.

"I got it!" Terien yelled back in irritation, now pushing the stick in the opposite direction.

The machine lurched forward a little faster than they expected, making both Terien and Makhani do a little dance before they managed to plant their feet more firmly, while Duncan let out a startled whoop and tumbled to the deck.

Easing back on the slide bar, Makhani nodded at Terien who now shifted the stick forward a little more slowly. The machine glided forward through the open doors, clearing the sides of the entryway with only a foot or two to spare, and emerged into the light of the midday suns amidst the wild cheers of the men gathered outside.

Climbing to his feet, Duncan joined them at the console and they exchanged a few shouted words before Duncan reached out to flip a switch set on the side of the console. The machine settled slowly to the ground, the whine dying into silence.

The men who had been standing a safe distance back now rushed to the machine, all talking and gesturing excitedly. Aurori and Quatina came running from inside and pushed their way past them until they were standing shoulder to shoulder at the side of the machine, both glaring up at the three standing on the deck.

"What were you thinking?" Aurori demanded, aiming her anger at Terien. "You don't know anything about this old technology! Who knows what could have happened!"

"Hey, it wasn't my fault," Terien said with wide-eyed innocence, putting a hand over his heart.

Looking sheepish, Duncan chuckled and said, "I kind of… accidentally leaned against the switch that turns it on."

Braids swinging as she whipped around to scowl at Duncan, Quatina gripped the lowest rail and hauled herself up and over the guard rail. Three steps later she was toe to toe with him, hands on hips.

"You are the last person I would expect to see going along with this foolishness," she told him angrily. "Yet here you are, risking injury without purpose."

"Now, wait a minute…" Duncan began, frowning and holding up a finger.

"It was an accident," Terien said again, coming to Duncan's defense. "Besides, we had already figured out what most of the controls were for before Duncan leaned against that switch. We didn't know it would be so loud, and I'll admit to being a bit startled by it, but we were never in any real danger."

Brows unknitting, Aurori chuckled. "Well, it was pretty amazing to watch this thing fly out of the door. I can't believe it still works, though. It's hundreds of years old."

"Your ancestors knew how to build things that last," Makhani told Quatina.

That comment seemed to mollify her a bit and her anger seeped away.

"I suppose it is exciting to find something that still works," she said finally, taking a step back from Duncan. She bowed her head and clasped her hands in front of her, avoiding his eyes. "I am sorry I was angry with you. You… frightened me when you fell to the deck," she whispered softly enough for his ears only.

Surprised by her admission, Duncan hesitated before reaching out and stroking his hand against her bare upper arm. "I appreciate your concern," he whispered back, feeling his cheeks start to burn. Good thing Terien hadn't heard or he'd never hear the end of it.

"I think we should be able to fit everyone on it, carts and animals included," Terien was saying as he climbed down from the machine. He dusted his hands off on his white robe, leaving dark smudges behind. "We'll have to experiment with it first, but we believe that this machine is capable of traveling faster than we're able to walk. If that's true, we can save a good deal of time and energy getting to Pergase."

"So this wasn't just some hot-headed joy ride, then?" Aurori asked, tongue-in-cheek.

Terien smiled and swiped a dirty finger on the tip of her nose, leaving a black mark behind. "As if," he intoned, turning on his heel and heading for the back of the machine.

Snickering at Aurori, the men followed Terien away.

"What?" Aurori asked, shrugging her shoulders and spreading her hands.

Quatina leaned over the side of the rail, took one look at Aurori's smudged nose and burst out laughing.

"Aw, come on, you guys! What's so funny?"

Makhani raised a dubious eyebrow and shook his head, walking away without comment.

While most of the group had opted to stay outside and see to setting up camp for the night, some had chosen to continue exploring the interior of the Hidden City. Although they did come across a couple of more machines that started up when their switches were thrown, these had no discernible purpose besides making horrendous noises.

As for Terien, Duncan and Makhani, they had passed the rest of the day by familiarizing themselves with the fantastic floating machine they had discovered, taking it outside the confines of the canyon and giving it a thorough testing. They soon discovered that its top speed put a sprinting felinae to shame. They also discovered the purpose of the clear piece of glass that was mounted directly above the operating console, ducking out of reflex the first time a bug splattered against it as they zipped across the desert.

"This is great!" Terien crowed, relishing the feel of speed.

Even with the glass barrier, the wind was whipping Makhani's long blond hair in every direction, giving him a wild look that suited the unrestrained glee painted on his normally somber face.

"Don't you dare tell the girls how much fun this was!" Makhani admonished, only half-jesting. "They'd have a fit!"

"Women!" Duncan shouted above the whine of both wind and machine. "And everyone keeps telling me *I'm* too serious!"

"They only get upset because they care," Terien shouted back, his lopsided smile telling them he was pleased with the thought. Then his expression darkened as he remembered the minor tongue-lashing they'd received just for tinkering around with the machine in the first place. "Even so, if either one of you tells them we were actually having fun out here, I'll personally tie your tongue in knots!"

When they had finally arrived back in the canyon and shut down the machine, both Aurori and Quatina were there to question them about the machine's performance out in the desert.

"So, how was it?" Aurori asked excitedly.

Terien shrugged non-committally. "Good. It handles very well. Wouldn't you agree, Duncan?"

"Oh, Yes. Very fast, too," Duncan replied, adopting an air of detached interest. "We'll be in Pergase in no time at all."

"A very smooth, comfortable ride, as well," Makhani added soberly as he ran his fingers through his hair, trying to untangle the knots. "Somewhat windy, however, but I'm sure we'll manage."

Aurori and Quatina looked at each other, the smiles fading from their faces.

"That's it?" Aurori prompted, brows raising into question marks.

The three men exchanged glances, shrugged, then nodded.

"Oh well. I suppose we shall find out for ourselves soon

enough," Quatina said, disappointed with their lackluster responses.

"Come on. Let's go get something to eat," Duncan said a little too quickly, hoping to change the subject.

"Sounds good to us," Aurori responded, indicating that they should lead the way by waving a hand towards the campfires that were a short distance away.

Following behind the men at a short distance, Quatina leaned in close to Aurori.

"They are terrible liars."

"Pathetic," Aurori agreed, allowing a small smile. "They had so much fun they're practically bursting at the seams."

"Should we tell them that we are on to them?"

Aurori shook her head. "Nah. Let them think they got away with one. I haven't the heart to spoil their day."

Chapter Fourteen

"Yeehaw!"

Arm pumping the air over his head, Elek was standing near the front of the floater, legs braced wide apart as the hovercraft tore across the open desert, kicking up sand and setting the hot air swirling in its wake.

"Amen to that, laddie! Sure as shootin' beats th' hell out o' sittin' atop a fussy ol' equine all day," Rannoch observed from where he sat on the metal deck, his back leaning comfortably against the lower rail. "Does me rheumatism good to be able to stretch out," he said with a grin and a sigh, massaging the low of his back.

Makhani stood with one hand on the rail, feet braced wide apart. "I just keep wondering how this hovering craft works. And why. Has anyone considered what happens if it suddenly shuts down?"

Rannoch dismissed the comment by putting his arms behind his head and closing his eyes. "Ye think too much, laddie. Who cares about th' how and why? And if this beastie stops working we just go back to walkin' is all. Just be happy we got everythin' aboard with as little fuss as we did," he said, putting an end to Makhani's ruminations.

Getting the carts secured on the deck of the hovercraft had been easy enough, but the equine had been another matter. Some of them had placidly ascended the metal ramp and were content to stand shoulder to shoulder on the deck, while others had bucked and fussed at the unfamiliar feel of the metal deck underfoot, prompting the men to fashion blinders for them out of spare bits of leather from a few discarded pair of boots. Getting under way had also been tedious at first when the new sensation of speed had caused a few to whinny and prance a bit, forcing them to stop and hastily add blinders to a few more.

The felinae, however, had taken to the experience with

obvious relish. Standing on the outmost edges against the guard rails, they were hanging their heads over the sides and facing into the wind, their tongues lolling out and mouths hanging wide open in happy cat grins.

A journey that would have taken many long, hot days on foot was shortened considerably thanks to the awesome speed of the hovercraft. Although they still had to stop for breaks during the day and make camp for the night, they were also finding that they were far less fatigued than they had been at any other time during their trek, leaving them plenty of energy to resume the practice of keeping up their self-defense skills. As a matter of course, Aurori and Terien had picked up where they left off with her quarterstaff lessons, and her skills improved until she was at last able to make good on Terien's promise that she would have the opportunity to dump him on his rear once more.

Taking a cue from the pair, Quatina had challenged Duncan to act as her sparring partner and it soon became apparent that she was an accomplished warrior herself, besting Duncan in hand-to-hand combat, a fact which did not go unnoticed by the group.

Backlit by the light of the fire, Quatina also practiced alone with the ornamental dagger she kept in her boot. She faced off against an invisible enemy as she moved sinuously through several moves, thrusting, feinting, then thrusting again from a different angle. Executing a backflip that would have taken her high over the head of her imaginary foe, she landed lightly and spun around, slashing out with the dagger. One could almost picture her opponent falling under the force of her attack.

"Remind me never to get on Quatina's bad side," Makhani remarked as he watched her.

Terien and Duncan both nodded sagely at that.

The only tricky part came when the group reached the banks of the Smokasen river that wound its way between them and the empire of Pergase. Uncertain how well the hovercraft would traverse the wide expanse of moving water, they had offloaded everything before making an attempt to cross. Choosing a point at which the river was at its narrowest, Terien, Duncan and Makhani had slowly guided the hovercraft out over the water at a point where it was more tranquil, ready to leap away to safety at the first sign of trouble. They needn't have worried. The hovercraft traversed the river with ease, and they returned once more to load the carts and animals for the trip across.

Making it to the other bank without incident, they trundled up to the outskirts of the city of Pergase a half day later, finding that they faced a new problem.

"This contraption is too wide to make it through the streets of the city. We'll have to leave it here under guard until we're ready to move on," Terien observed as they maneuvered the hovercraft to a stop.

Already there were people flowing out from the city, coming for a first-hand look at the fantastic device that had arrived. Hastily shedding their white robes and getting themselves back into their black dress uniforms, Terien and his group were soon assailed by question after question from the people who knew without doubt that he was the Chosen.

"Nothing says VIP like an ancient piece of technology," Duncan joked.

Pushing through the crowd, six men dressed in colorful purple and green uniforms consisting of balloon-legged pants and short-sleeved vests approached a short time later. Carrying long spears decorated with tassels hanging from their shafts, they cautioned the people to move back out of their way as they strode up to Terien and immediately went down on one knee before him.

"The Empress Sahala sends her welcome, Chosen, and bids you come to the palace," one of the guards said, then rose to his feet. "We will escort you immediately."

Terien turned to give orders to his men, but was forestalled by Elek who raised a hand.

"I know, I know. Stay here on guard, same as usual," Elek said with a small smile.

"Mind-reader," Terien accused, laughing.

Accompanied once more by half his men, along with the representatives of Glaybor and Brinbourne and the ever present Duncan, Aurori and Quatina, Terien followed the six guards through the streets of Pergase.

A city on the edge of the desert, Pergase boasted squat buildings made from quarried stone and mortar. The streets were narrow and winding but not untidy. Taking a route through the business district, they passed small open-air shops and outdoor stalls with an inviting variety of goods displayed on tables around which people were congregated, doing a brisk business in the late morning light. Duncan tapped Aurori and Quatina on their shoulders and indicated the shops with a smile, receiving laughs and playful smacks from each of them for his effort.

As they moved deeper into the heart of Pergase, the palace came into view. A sprawling single-storey structure made of huge interlocking slabs of marble, it had several minarets, arched doors and open windows, and was flanked by sculpted support columns that were painted with intricate geometrical designs. The wide courtyard they passed across held a circular garden at its center and was also paved with smaller interlocking marble pieces that were shiny and smooth from years of use.

Entering the cool interior of the structure, they were greeted by the sight of colorful tapestries hanging from the high walls and more support pillars, all etched in the same geometrical designs as the outer columns. Elegant statuary and hand-carved furniture items were dotted throughout, giving the interior of the palace a cozy, if somewhat sumptuous, feel.

Moving through a pair of gilded golden doors, they were now ushered into what was obviously the throne room of the Empress. There were four columns in the center of the room, draped in a shimmering translucent fabric in a pale mauve. On a raised platform in the center of the columns stood a lounge chair whose legs and arms were plated in gold leaf and was upholstered in the same pale mauve as the drapes. Reclining on the chair was the Empress Sahala, sitting with one leg tucked beneath herself and an elbow propped casually on the arm of the chair.

Rising as they entered, the Empress rose and sashayed to the edge of the platform, looking down at them with luminous brown eyes. She was utterly breathtaking. Slim and curvaceous, she seemed to exude sensuality. The floor-length pale mauve gown she wore was sleeveless and dipped low away from her neck. Its shimmering folds revealed shapely legs through their slitted sides.

Jewels and gold chains graced her neck and fingers and sparkled in the tiara she wore in her thick, free-flowing brown hair. Her skin was alabaster smooth and her lips were full, painted in a deep shade of red.

"I welcome you to Pergase," she said in a sultry tone, stepping down from the platform and approaching Terien.

"Thank you," Terien said, swallowing hard as she lifted a bejeweled hand and traced one finger along his jaw line.

Aurori forced her face to remain neutral, but the urge to laugh was almost overwhelming. Empress or not, she seemed rather full of herself.

"You are even more handsome than I imagined," the Empress told him.

Terien cleared his throat uncomfortably. "I would like to introduce the representatives of the other... lands," he said, hesitating over a descriptive word for the places he had encountered. He had grown up thinking that every land was a kingdom, but had now found that wasn't accurate. Glaybor fit the bill, but Brinbourne had a democratic government and Pergase was an empire with a female leader.

"This is Makhani of Glaybor, Rannoch of Brinbourne, Aurori of Eristea and Quatina of the Cohalili," he said, indicating each as he went. "And this is Duncan, Captain of my guard."

The Empress barely gave them a glance, even when Aurori and Quatina exchanged startled looks at having been included as representatives.

"A pleasure, I'm sure," she said, her tone making it clear that she considered most of them beneath her, but she did pay closer attention to Duncan, flashing him a shy smile that froze him in place.

Terien nudged Duncan in the ribs, giving him the sign to produce the Sky Lord's cube. Getting no response, he surreptitiously pinched his friend's thigh. Duncan jumped a bit and hastily handed the cube to Terien who activated it and let the Empress view its message.

"When I saw you approach Pergase in your floating ship I knew you were the Chosen," she said, dismissing the cube with a wave of her manicured hand.

"We've been calling it a hovercraft," Duncan helpfully supplied.

She smiled at him and turned to Terien. "You should know that there have been rumors in Pergase of late. Some have said that the other Chosen is here," she told them.

Shock coursing through her, Aurori blinked in surprise. "What… what makes them think so?" she asked.

The Empress gave her a look of disdain but still chose to answer. "There has been a strange woman spotted on the streets. She is said to carry herself well and ask many questions of the people. Some speculate that she is the Observer, but I do not put much stock in the mutterings of the rumormongers. I tell you this only because I thought it might interest the Gatherer," she said sweetly, taking Terien's arm and giving him a warm smile.

His interest definitely sparked, Terien was about to ask more when the Empress suddenly clapped her hands together. Servants appeared from nowhere, bowing as they stepped from behind curtains that artfully hid several doorways in the room.

"See to it that Terien's people are shown to comfortable rooms," she ordered, already using a more familiar form of address for the Chosen. "And bring a comfortable chair for Duncan. Set it there," she said, pointing to a spot just to the left of her lounger.

It was obvious that she meant to exclude everyone else from her meeting with Terien, and he looked helplessly at them. He would have preferred to have at least Makhani and Rannoch present, and he was wondering how best to address the topic when Makhani spoke up.

"Rannoch and I would be interested in a tour of your fair city," he said, bowing slightly from the waist.

"We would?" Rannoch asked, hooking a finger on his glasses and pulling them down a bit so he could look over them at Makhani, who gave him a meaningful look. Catching on, his lips puckered. "Oh. Aye. A tour would be a delight."

"Then I shall assign two guards to attend you," Sahala said. She thrust a finger at two of the young men hanging back in the shadows and they immediately hurried over to Makhani and Rannoch.

"Aurori and I shall likewise be out in the city for a time, exploring the market we passed on the way here," Quatina announced. "I doubt that an escort will be necessary, however," she said quickly.

"As you wish," Sahala said. She took firm hold of Terien's hand and began to lead him towards her lounger. "Come, Terien. There is much we have to discuss.

Following Quatina from the room, the last thing Aurori saw was that Sahala had seated Terien on her lounger and was taking a place next to him, close enough to send a little shiver through Aurori as the image of a spider and a fly danced through her mind.

⋆

After hurriedly packing her belongings, Idona sought out the innkeeper of the establishment she had rented a room in, for the last few weeks while waiting for the Chosen to show up in Pergase and paid the large man what she owed. Without sparing so much as a glance backwards, she strode out of the dingy building and turned on to the main street, following it until it took her out of the city. She had to hike for almost two hours through the hilly terrain, scrabbling over rocks and around boulders until she came to the place her aircraft had been hidden.

Nestled between two small hillocks and draped in a tan camouflage tarp, the aircraft was a welcome sight after having had to live in the city all this time, and Idona wasted no time in removing the tarp and climbing into the soft operator's chair. She sighed heavily. As Soloth's trusted aide, the task of finding out whether the Chosen had survived the journey to Pergase had fallen to her. Despite having voted to leave the Chosen to their journey unmonitored, Soloth's curiosity had been such that he approached the council for permission to send Idona to Pergase to ascertain whether they had survived the journey thus far. It didn't help Idona's mood at all when Leander had enthusiastically agreed with the council that she was the perfect choice for the job, but she could see the logic of his thinking.

Idona had hoped that she would arrive in Pergase and find out that the Chosen had already passed through, but such was not the case. She had returned to the aircraft once earlier and radioed Soloth who had then asked her to stay on another few weeks and await their arrival, refusing her request to fly out over the desert in search of them, citing that he didn't want to risk them to spotting her aircraft when he had already told them that the Sky Lords would not be monitoring their progress.

Cursing every minute of her stay in a city without the amenities afforded by the technology she was accustomed to, she had passed the last three weeks by wandering the streets of Pergase and talking with the people. In spite of herself, she had actually enjoyed both the experience and the people and had been delighted when rumors began to circulate that she might be the second Chosen.

Pushing aside her thoughts on the matter, Idona activated the communications panel.

"Idona to Primary Soloth," she said, putting as much excitement as she could muster into her voice.

"*Soloth here*," came the response after a moment.

"It's confirmed. The Chosen is in Pergase. Both of them, I think. The Gatherer has a Healer in his group who matches your description of the Princess."

There was a pause on the other end, then a low chuckle. "*Unexpected, but not surprising. And they have the representatives of Glaybor and Brinbourne with them? They appear to be in good condition?*"

"Yes to both questions. Here's a surprise, though. They arrived in Pergase on a flat deck cargo carrier."

"*A… cargo carrier?*"

Idona shrugged even though Soloth couldn't see it. "They must have stopped at Alatesh despite being told there was no need."

His voice filled with wonder and pride, Soloth said, "*It seems I underestimated Prince Terien's intelligence and ingenuity – not to mention his curiosity. I can see that there is real hope for the success of the Final Reunification.*"

"Oh, certainly," Idona agreed readily, putting a smile in her voice.

"I thank you for being so patient in staying on in Pergase, Idona. I know it must have been difficult for you and that you're looking forward to coming home, so I won't keep you any longer."

So, the old fox knew she hadn't liked being in Pergase. How insightful of him. "Not a problem, Primary. I should be back in a few hours."

"I look forward to having you back on Quayvern. I must admit that I've missed your wise counsel these last few weeks."

Wouldn't he be surprised to find out just who's counsel she was passing on, Idona thought.

"Thank you, Primary."

"Soloth out."

Idona immediately readjusted the frequency on the communication panel and stabbed down on the button.

"Idona to Leander."

The communication panel crackled with static for a moment. The frequency was low band and unlikely to be detected or traced, but that also meant that it was low power and that conversation would be filled with static.

"What news have you?" Leander's crackling voice asked.

"The Chosen is alive and well," she stated simply. They had agreed to keep their comments vague in the unlikely event that their communication was intercepted. The system on the aircraft weren't as secure as the ones in the offices.

"I see. Then I shall immediately contact my associate and have him prepare a warm welcome. When will you be returning?"

Idona smiled to herself. "A few hours. I need to avoid the populated areas on my way back."

"Excellent. I shall have a warm welcome prepared for you as well. Leander out."

Grinning now, Idona set about preparing for take-off.

★

Walking side by side through the crowded market, Aurori and Quatina shared a companionable silence as they drank in the sights and sounds of the market in the late afternoon. The people were fascinating. The dress code in Pergase was as varied as the

people themselves, although most wore loose-fitting robes or billowy shirts and pants in pastel colors as was appropriate for the desert heat. Every skin tone created was represented, as was every hair and eye color imaginable.

Passing by one particularly dim-looking establishment with a pair of stern-looking guards standing on either side of the open door, they slowed down and nonchalantly glanced inside, trying to catch sight of what lay beyond. There in the dimness they could see a bar set along the far wall and tables around which several tough-looking men and women were sitting, talking and gesturing as they nursed frothy drinks amid a smoky atmosphere.

One of the guards gave them a broad, toothy smile.

"The first drink is always free for a lady," he told them, extending an open hand in invitation.

"Maybe later," Aurori said with a smile, increasing her pace and forcing her eyes away.

When they had advanced further up the street, Quatina finally broke the silence. "There is much to observe in this city. Perhaps we should take the gentleman up on his offer. One never knows what useful information could be overheard."

"Like rumors about the other Chosen?" Aurori asked with a laugh. "No thanks."

Quatina looked at her askance and then stared straight ahead as they walked.

"I know that rumor is in error."

Aurori plastered a benign expression on her face and looked over at her friend. "What makes you say so?"

Quatina shrugged. "Considering that you are the other Chosen, the Observer, the rumor is obviously false."

Aurori stopped short and was about to deny the allegation, but one look at the firm set of Quatina's jaw told her not to bother.

"How long have you known?" she asked, leaning her cheek against the quarterstaff she had been using as a walking stick.

"A week," Quatina said with a small smile. Seeing Aurori's questioning look, she continued. "We have shared shelter nightly for a long time, now. The key you wear fell out from beneath your tunic while you slept."

"Why didn't you say something before now?"

Quatina finally met Aurori's eyes. "I did not feel it was my place," she said simply.

"What changed your mind?"

Looking uncomfortable, Quatina scuffed the toe of her boot on the ground, hesitating over her response. "The Empress is very beautiful. It seemed that she may turn Terien's head. It is obvious that you care for him deeply, yet you keep him at a distance. I was perplexed. You have not told him who you are." She shrugged. "I was curious to know why."

Now it was Aurori's turn to feel uncomfortable. She looked away, embarrassed. Were her feelings for Terien that transparent? "It's... complicated," she said with finality, making it clear that she didn't want to talk about it.

Quatina sighed in exasperation. "I understand better than you may think. I care a great deal about Duncan but have been afraid to let him know. I wonder if pursuing a romance is a wise idea considering the magnitude of his responsibilities on this journey. I am certain you feel the same way. Still, I cannot help but wonder why you do not at least tell him who you are. I fail to see the harm in it."

Speechless, Aurori rubbed the back of her neck, trying to decide what to say. It was actually a relief to finally have someone to share the burden of her secret with, and Quatina was certainly trustworthy; but having someone else give voice to the feelings she had for Terien was a shock. She and Quatina had developed a fairly close friendship over the weeks they had spent together, though, and Aurori realized she was actually looking forward to sharing more.

"All right. Why don't we discuss this over a drink?" she suggested.

Quatina smiled broadly. "I was hoping you would say so. I must confess, I have missed having a friend to talk to."

Heading back to the bar they had just passed, they gave the two guards a smile and stepped into the darkened interior. The place was more crowded than it had looked from the outside and they had to excuse themselves several times as they wended their way towards the bar. The air was thick with an acrid haze that was coming from smoking pots set in the middle of each table, most likely in the hopes of warding off the ever present flying insects. If so, they were failing.

Squeezing their way between two burly gents at the bar, the pair had to shout to have the barkeep hear their orders above the din of voices. Picking up their free drinks, they turned and scanned for a place to sit. Spotting an open booth near the door, Quatina motioned for Aurori to follow her.

Balancing her drink in one hand and clutching the quarterstaff in the other, Aurori almost had to dance to get around the crush of bodies. She had almost made it to the booth unscathed when a woman with a series of tattoos on her forehead pushed her chair back directly in her path, forcing Aurori to jerk to a halt. Unfortunately, the contents of her drink sloshed over the side as she did, splashing onto the woman's light-colored blouse.

"Sorry about that," Aurori apologized immediately.

The woman scrambled from her chair and brushed angrily at the dark wet spot. "Clumsy idiot! Watch where you're going!"

Aurori saw red but did her best to remain calm. "I am very sorry," she repeated evenly.

"I just bought this blouse yesterday!" the woman shouted. She snatched Aurori's drink from her hand and threw the remaining contents of the glass at her, drenching the front of her white cloak in the frothy brown liquid. "How dare you spill your drink on me?"

Quatina was between the two in an instant. "It was an accident, my friend. Come. We will pay for a new blouse and buy you a drink."

Only Quatina's lightning reflexes saved her from the full force of the left hook the woman aimed at her jaw. Even so, she caught a piece of it and went stumbling back, eyes smarting.

Horrified, Aurori stood dumbstruck for half a second, just long enough for the woman's partner to knock back her chair and throw a wicked punch that caught Aurori on her upper left cheek and sent her reeling into the table behind her.

"Lousy foreigners! Get out of here!" the second woman screamed, advancing on Aurori with murderous rage in her eyes.

Without conscious thought, Aurori whipped her quarterstaff up and twirled it, striking the side of the woman's head and spinning her around. She went sailing into a table where she landed flat on her stomach, sending drinks flying and patrons diving for cover.

Quatina, meantime, was wrestling with the woman whose blouse had had a taste of Aurori's drink. They were careening into tables and people, leaving a path of destruction in their wake.

"Fight!" Someone shouted, and the whole place erupted into chaos.

Scared to death, heart pounding, Aurori ducked as a glass flew past her head and shattered against the wall behind her. Unable to determine who was fighting whom and why, she took to wielding her quarterstaff on anyone who came within range, moving with expert ease and grace as she fended off numerous attacks. At one point she found herself hip to hip with Quatina and they exchanged rueful looks.

"That's an impressive bruise you have on your cheek," Quatina shouted, teeth bared in a feral grin as she drove her shoulder into the gut of an onrushing opponent and tossed him over her back.

"You don't look so good yourself," Aurori shot back, side-stepping the guy who had been making a grab for her. She brought the quarterstaff down on his back, driving him to the floor.

"We have to get out of here!" Aurori yelled urgently, catching Quatina's arm and dragging her in the direction of the door.

They were only a few steps from freedom when a group of guards rushed through the door, two of whom they would have recognized as the pair who had been assigned to accompany Makhani and Rannoch on their tour of the city if they hadn't been so intent on escaping the bar.

Rushing outside, Aurori and Quatina skidded to a halt as they almost ran directly into the arms of Makhani and Rannoch.

"Oh no," Aurori moaned.

"Aurori? Quatina?" Makhani was so surprised he stumbled backwards, bumping into Rannoch so hard that the older man almost fell over.

The two women were a mess. Aurori's white cloak had a huge brown stain on the front and had spatters of blood on the shoulder. Her hair had completely come out of the braid she usually wore and her left eye was puffing closed from the angry blue bruise spreading across her cheekbone. Quatina wasn't in much better shape. She had a cut and bruise on her forehead where a bottle had connected and blood smeared on her tunic. They both smelled like fermented grain.

"Oy! Poor wee lasses! What happened to ye?" Rannoch cried, his hand flying to the top of his head in a gesture of surprise.

Concern marking his features, Makhani went first to Aurori and examined the bruise on her cheek, then turned to Quatina. Searching around his pockets, he pulled out a handkerchief and pressed it to the cut on her forehead to staunch the flow of blood.

"What were you two doing in a place like this?" Makhani asked angrily.

Before either could answer, the guards came out of the bar, dragging several people in their wake, two of whom were the women who had been responsible for the altercation in the first place. They were in terrible shape. Each was bleeding from various wounds and their clothes had been ripped in several places.

The woman with the tattooed forehead caught sight of Aurori and pointed at her, trying to wrench free of the guard's grip. "That's them! They started it!" she screamed.

"It was your fault that she spilled her drink on you!" Quatina yelled back. "You bumped into her!"

"We tried to apologize. Even offered to pay for a new blouse," Aurori confirmed in a more reasonable tone. "Then they just... attacked. And the whole place went crazy."

Makhani couldn't believe his ears. Aurori and Quatina had somehow instigated the fight.

"Hey, aren't these two members of the Chosen's group?" One of the guards asked Makhani, nodding at Aurori and Quatina.

Makhani scowled in order to keep from laughing. "Sadly, yes." He turned smiling eyes on Aurori and Quatina, then sobered and looked back at the guard. "I will personally see to it that the Chosen is apprised of what has happened. I'm sure he will be more than happy to take disciplinary action against them."

The guard considered for a long moment, then nodded. "Very

well. I leave them in your custody. See to it that they do not cause anymore trouble. You will have to see yourselves to the palace, though."

"Not a problem," Makhani responded.

Once the guards had left with their prisoners in tow, Makhani was free to finally let out the laugh he had been holding back. He pointed at the quarterstaff Aurori still had clutched in her hand.

"Well. Won't Terien be happy to know that at least all those quarterstaff lessons didn't go to waste."

Aurori and Quatina moaned in unison, though not in pain.

"We are so dead," Aurori intoned.

"Absolutely," Quatina sighed.

The walk back to the palace wasn't very long and they made it in silence, although both Makhani and Rannoch would chuckle to themselves from time to time, presumably as they envisioned the reaction the two women would receive once everyone knew what had happened.

Entering the palace, Makhani asked one of the footmen where he could find Terien and was directed to the library.

Pausing outside the door, Aurori grabbed Makhani's arm. "Terien's probably busy. Couldn't we tell him later?"

"Much later," Quatina added hopefully.

"No way. We tell them now. I won't risk the wrath of both Duncan and Terien, not even for you two," Makhani said, snatching the quarterstaff from Aurori's hand. "Now get in there," he ordered in a tone that showed he would not entertain a debate.

They marched inside and received a predictable reaction.

Terien was seated on a couch beside Sahala with Duncan sitting across from them on another. They looked up in unison as the door opened and the blood drained from Duncan's face while Terien shot to his feet.

"What happened!" Terien cried.

"Bar room brawl," Rannoch drawled, grinning from ear to ear.

"What?" Duncan shouted incredulously.

Duncan and Terien crossed the distance between where they had been sitting and where the two women contritely stood in a matter of a few strides. Terien touched a gentle finger to Aurori's swollen cheek and she winced away.

"It's true," Makhani confirmed. "They claim they didn't actually start it, however."

Quatina shot him a defiant look. "It was *not* our fault," she asserted unrepentantly.

Describing what had taken place, Aurori and Quatina tried to downplay the danger they had been in, but Duncan and Terien weren't buying it. Being in the middle of a bar fight was the last place they would have pictured the two.

"If I had known that you were traveling in the company of such ruffians, I would have insisted on an escort for them," Sahala said from across the room.

Sparing her a withering glance, Aurori sighed and folded her arms.

"What were you thinking, going into a bar like that?" Terien chided. "You two should know better than that."

"How were we supposed to know?" Aurori shot back. "I've never even seen a place like that before, and I know there sure weren't any bars in the Cohalili village."

Terien held up an accusing finger and was about to rebut her argument when he realized they had an audience. He turned and gave the Empress a small bow.

"If you'll excuse us, I would like to accompany these two to their quarters."

"Of course," Sahala replied, rising. "Will they be joining us for dinner or shall I have it sent to their rooms?"

Casting a wicked look at the two women, Terien said, "I don't know yet. I'll let you know."

Ushering everyone from the room, Terien led the way through the decorated halls, ignoring the curious looks they were getting from the servants they passed along the way. When they arrived outside the doors to the separate set of suites that had been assigned to the two women, Rannoch and Makhani made hasty excuses and departed for their own rooms.

The minute they were inside, Terien closed the door and heaved a heavy sigh.

"What are we going to do with you two?"

"Come on," Duncan said to Quatina, taking her arm and

heading for the adjoining washroom. "Let's get you cleaned up."

She followed him mutely, her head bowed. Only the slight smile on Quatina's lips betrayed the fact that she was all too happy to submit to Duncan's ministrations.

Alone now, Terien leaned against the door and watched as Aurori removed her cloak and flung it into a corner, reminding him of the last time she had tossed aside a ruined white cloak. At least her tunic and slacks had once again been spared.

Aurori sat heavily on the edge of the bed, letting her shoulders slump and her hands fall into her lap as she looked back at him with her one open eye.

"So, who heals the Healer?" he asked.

She smirked at his attempt to lighten her mood. "Very funny." She caught sight of herself in the mirror set in the wall and she shook her head, tears welling in her eyes as she compared the image in her mind of the perfectly coifed and manicured Empress with what she saw reflected back at her.

"I'm so sorry, Terien. What you must think of me right now..."

Terien pushed away from the door and came to kneel at her feet. He took her face gently in his hands and turned her towards him. "Hey, why the tears? Did you go into the bar looking for a fight?"

"No."

"And you didn't spill that drink on purpose, did you?"

"Of course not."

"And you did everything you could to resolve the situation, didn't you?"

"Yes," Aurori said, sniffling.

"Then you have nothing to be sorry about." He smiled at her and wiped away her tears with his thumbs. "We all make mistakes. Besides, you were right. If you've never been in a bar like that before, then you had no idea how careful you had to be." His smile widened. "I hope you'll never be in a situation like that ever again, but it would have been something to see you handling that quarterstaff. I bet you gave everyone a thorough trouncing."

Laughing through her tears, Aurori nodded.

Terien was looking at her with so much concern and

compassion that she just knew he was going to kiss her. Her heart pounded at the thought. He would kiss her, then she would tell him who she really was. Tell him everything. Quatina was right. She'd been stupid to hold back from telling him.

As his face moved closer to hers, she held her breath and closed her eyes.

Then he kissed her forehead and patted her cheek.

"By the way, I have some good news," he told her as he rose to his feet. "Sahala has agreed to send a representative along and I didn't even have to come up with a reason for her to do so," he said with a broad smile, alluding to what had happened in Brinbourne.

Aurori blinked a couple of times, stunned. "That... that's great," she managed to say. "At least something good happened today."

Terien grinned down at her. "The most amazing part is that it's Sahala herself who will be coming with us. Isn't that great?"

"Wonderful," Aurori said between clenched teeth, a false smile painted on her lips to hide the bitter disappointment and astonishment she truly felt.

"I'll see you downstairs for dinner," Terien tossed over his shoulder as he headed for the door. "Tell Duncan I'll see him back in the library."

He was gone out of the door before she could even think to breathe again.

Flopping back on the bed, Aurori stared up at the mauve material swathing the canopy of the bed and felt sick to her stomach.

"I take it back. This has been the worst day of my life."

Chapter Fifteen

"I still have to go out into the city, but after what happened yesterday I'm afraid he'll insist on sending an escort with us. That was the real reason I didn't want to tell Terien that I was the Observer. I couldn't accomplish my mission if I had a couple of bodyguards trailing behind me," Aurori said as she sat cross-legged in the middle of her bed, holding a silky pink blouse up to the light streaming through the window. Sometime during the night her soiled cloak had disappeared and been replaced by the blouse and a matching skirt, most likely compliments of the Empress who had, at dinner the night before, reasoned that the two women would not have encountered such resistance if they had not stood out as foreigners. Accessories such as bangles, earrings and a pair of comfortable slippers had also been supplied. It was a thoughtful gesture on the part of Sahala, which only made Aurori suspicious of the woman's intentions and she assumed that the magnanimous gift was calculated to endear her to Terien.

"You do not know for a fact that Terien would impose such a restriction," Quatina said as she stepped into the pale blue skirt she had found on the dresser beside her bed and then struggled into the matching sleeveless blouse. She twirled, sending the skirt's voluminous folds flaring out in a circle. "However, if it becomes necessary, I am not above engaging in a bit of subterfuge. We will find a way for you to sneak out if need be," she said with a conspiratorial smile, admiring her image in the mirror.

Sliding to the edge of the bed, Aurori stood and also wriggled into the clothes she had been provided. The material was soft and felt as light as a feather against her skin. Slipping on the bangles and earrings, she twisted and turned to get a good look in the mirror, then bent close and touched a finger to her cheekbone. The concoction she had applied the night before had taken away the swelling and reduced the bruising until there was only a faint blue cast to the skin. Satisfied, she turned and regarded Quatina with a critical eye. The gash on her forehead was little more than a bad memory, with only a slightly pink raised line to indicate where the bottle had struck.

"I am more concerned with the fact that you didn't tell Terien who you are when you had the opportunity," Quatina said with a frown.

Aurori rolled her eyes. "Some opportunity. I think I forgot my own name when he told me that Sahala was coming along as the representative of Pergase. He was so excited about it." She ruefully shook her head.

"At least you got a kiss. All I got from Duncan was a pat on the shoulder."

Twisting her fingers through her thick auburn hair, Aurori set about braiding it back into the style she had adopted since leaving home. "Oh sure," she laughed derisively. "My father kissed my forehead every night before I went to bed, too."

Quatina sighed. "Do not confuse love with physical attraction. The two are not mutually exclusive, but neither are they inseparably linked. It is obvious that Terien cares about you very deeply. Perhaps he is simply as reticent about pursuing a romance as you have been," she said with the patience of someone having to explain the facts of life to a child.

Tying off the end of her braid, Aurori angrily flipped it over her shoulder. "Let's just drop the subject, okay?"

"Acceptable. As long as you promise to tell him who you are at the next opportunity," Quatina admonished as she headed for the door.

"I will. I just need to wait for the right moment," Aurori told her, shouldering her pack in case it was needed for their tour of the city. "Like the ones I missed in Glaybor and Brinbourne," she muttered to herself, her mind going back to the night of the ball when she had agreed to accompany Terien on his journey beneath the equine fountain, and to their walk on the beach in Brinbourne.

Closing the door behind them with more force than was necessary, she followed Quatina down the hall and tried to keep from thinking about how stupid she had been.

★

Sitting once more in the library at a large wooden table that featured a dragon carved into its surface, Terien and Duncan were regaling Sahala with the tale of their journey and what they had encountered thus far when Aurori and Quatina walked in.

Noting that the pair looked clean and refreshed, Terien gave them an impish smile. "I see that the Healer was busy last night."

Aurori fingered her cheek and smiled.

"You two look very nice this morning," Duncan told them. "Let me guess. All dressed up for a day of shopping?"

Quatina laughed. "Perhaps." She turned to the Empress and bowed. "You have our gratitude for the new clothes you have so thoughtfully supplied for us."

Sahala dismissed her gratitude with a hand. "The maid will return your own clothes to you after they have been cleaned, but you are welcome to keep the outfits. They are my gift to you," she said, inclining her head.

"Well, if you're going out into the city, just remember to avoid dark bars," Terien warned with a mock frown. "I see you have your pack full of potions with you. Is that just in case?"

Aurori shot him a withering glance. "Very funny."

"Do you need any currency?" Sahala asked solicitously before Terien could comment further.

"No. Thank you," Aurori replied flatly, quietly fuming. How dare she ask such a thing!

"The cook has prepared breakfast for you in the dining room. My servant will show you the way," Sahala said.

The clap of her hands brought a young woman running from behind a curtain. She bowed to the Empress, then to Aurori and Quatina before beckoning them to follow her.

"See you later," Terien called out after the two as they disappeared from the room.

"You were telling me about the Hidden City before we were interrupted," Sahala reminded Duncan, pointing to the squiggles that marked the Alatesh canyon on the map that was spread out on the table before them.

"Yes. Of course," Duncan said.

Terien was aware of Duncan's lips moving and he could hear him telling Sahala all about what had happened at Alatesh, but his mind was elsewhere. More specifically, his thoughts were back at the dinner the night before. It had been a sumptuous feast with many new and delectable dishes he had never tasted before and he had thoroughly enjoyed the experience, yet there was something that niggled at the back of his brain.

The fact that Sahala had insisted on accompanying them herself, acting as representative for her own empire, had been an exciting prospect at first. She possessed undeniable beauty and a sensuality that made his head spin, and while her explicit attraction to him was flattering, he now found her attitude and method of dealing with people appalling. All during dinner the evening before, he had watched as she had ordered her servants about with a total disregard for them and had seemed to delight in making high-handed comments to her guests. Even Aurori had been uncharacteristically acid in her responses to Sahala's most innocuous questions about her home kingdom and life as a Healer, perhaps owing in part to her injuries and the embarrassment of having been involved in a brawl in the bar, but he was still certain there was more to it than that. He couldn't help but think that having Sahala along would simply be a burden. She would most likely demand much of both him and his men. He would have to try and dissuade her from coming, or at least impose a few restrictions.

"Anyway, we're just happy to have made this far with as few casualties as we have," Duncan was saying when Terien finally snapped out of his deep thoughts.

Leaning forward and planting his elbows on the table, Terien rested his chin on his fists and fixed his gaze on Sahala. "Actually, I've been thinking about just that. The journey hasn't been wholly unpleasant, but it has been a hard one and we're barely halfway through. Are you sure you want to come with us? It would be safer if you assigned someone else to the task."

She smiled coyly and placed her hand on his arm, giving his bicep an appreciative squeeze. "I'm sure that you're more than capable of seeing to my safety."

More flattery. Maybe a different tactic was in order. "You said yesterday that you didn't trust anyone else to act as representative on behalf of Pergase. If that's true, then who will run the empire in your absence?"

Her delicate brows knit into a frown and she withdrew her hand, shifting in her chair until she had one leg curled underneath herself and her hands were resting on the arms in an imperious pose. "My viziers are more than capable of seeing to the day-to-day affairs of my empire, but they would be incapable of conducting themselves to my satisfaction during delicate negotiations." She tilted her chin up. "I will hear no more on the subject. I am coming with you," she said petulantly.

Terien resisted the urge to sigh in frustration and instead inclined his head, striking an imperious pose of his own as he straightened. "As you wish, but it is only fair to warn you that I will not afford you any special considerations on this journey. You can expect to sleep on the ground and see to your own needs. We will be traveling by hovercraft as far as possible, but it may become necessary to abandon the craft and take to riding equines once more. And you'll have to travel light. We haven't that much room on the hovercraft." He lowered his head and gave her a meaningful look. "No porters, no servants, no handmaidens," he stated, making his expectations clear.

Though her lower lip quivered slightly, she kept her head high and met his eyes with a fiery look of her own. "You ask much," she said finally, but dipped her head slightly as a sign of her acquiescence. "However, I am an accomplished rider and am well versed in the rigors of travel. Although I have rarely left Pergase without an entourage of my own, I will submit myself to your restrictions on one condition – you will assign one of your men as my personal bodyguard." Her eyes narrowed as though challenging him to refuse.

"I would be pleased to ask for a volunteer for you," Duncan said.

Sahala's lips pouted. "I was hoping you would volunteer, Duncan."

He gave her a small smile and his eyes flicked to Terien,

finding an amused smile playing on his lips. "My duties as Captain of the Guard would not permit that. However, there are several young men in our group who would be honored to be afforded the opportunity to act as bodyguard for someone as distinguished as yourself," Duncan said diplomatically. "Terien and I had planned on leaving shortly to check on them. I will present them with your request."

"Excellent. Then I will have two of my guards escort you on a tour of Pergase while I make arrangements to leave. I assume you wish to leave at first light tomorrow morning?"

"That would be acceptable," Terien said as he pushed his chair back and rolled up the map, tucking it under his arm.

Sahala rose as Terien did and stepped close to him. She put her hands on his chest and stood on tiptoe to kiss his cheek. "I'm glad that that unpleasantness is over. I look forward to getting to know you better as we travel," she whispered in his ear, then pulled back and gave him a coquettish smile as she sauntered away.

"She sure likes you," Duncan said, grinning wolfishly once she was gone.

"Don't even go there," Terien growled.

Duncan laughed and gave Terien's back a slap. "Just teasing. Don't worry, I can see she's not your type. Personally, I find her too self-absorbed and bossy."

"You're being too polite. I think she's abrasive, rude and vain. And that's just for starters," Terien said in a low voice.

"Yeah. Too bad all that beauty is wasted on a personality like hers."

As their two escorts appeared in the doorway across the room Terien smiled and whispered, "I've seen more beautiful women than her. Like the two we already have in our company."

Duncan returned his smile. "You know, I think you might be right."

*

Giving themselves an unofficial tour, Aurori and Quatina found they could move through the streets of Pergase without getting so much as a sideways glance thanks to the fact that they now blended in with the rest of the citizenry because of a simple change of clothes.

"This is much better than yesterday," Aurori commented as they walked. "I have to admit I was a little surprised when Terien just joked about us getting into trouble, though."

"I was not. He trusts you."

Aurori looked to Quatina, then sighed and shifted her gaze to the ground. "I see that now, and it makes me feel even worse about not telling him who I am. Now I'm afraid to tell him. He's going to be so mad at me."

Quatina nodded sympathetically. "He may even feel betrayed, but I am confident he will not hold it against you. Everyone knows that the Observer's identity is secret." Placing a hand on Aurori's slumped shoulder, she smiled and indicated the market with a sweep of her hand. "For now, however, you should simply enjoy the day and carry on with your duty. The past cannot be changed and the future has not yet arrived. Dwelling on this subject will not change that."

"You're right," Aurori said, brightening a little. "Come on. Maybe I'll feel better if I do what I was chosen for."

They started out by doing some serious shopping in the market, acquiring a few more pieces of clothing that were made of the same luxurious material as the articles they had been given by Sahala. Upon finding out that the material was produced right here, within the empire of Pergase, they asked how it was made and were astonished to learn that it came from the cocoon of an insect. They hesitated over being given a tour of the orchards and the small factory that produced the amazing fabric, but decided in the end that they had learned enough from the shopkeeper's detailed explanation and would instead carry on with exploring the city further.

Packages slung over their shoulders in colorfully embroidered cloth bags they had purchased for that purpose, they walked slowly and listened intently to the chatter of the people on the street. Word had already spread that the Chosen had arrived (no surprise considering that the hovercraft was parked on the outskirts of the city and was apparently drawing crowds of curious viewers), and the topic of choice revolved around the Empress Sahala and her announcement that she would personally accompany the Chosen to the Final Reunification.

Unsurprisingly, most folks had few nice things to say about their Empress beyond a brief mention of the fact that at least the city prospered under her rule. When asked, most would heave a sigh and happily recall the rule of Sahala's mother who had passed on several years ago, quietly saying that the current Empress must have taken after her father. When pressed for information about him, however, all that Aurori and Quatina would receive were shrugs and muttered excuses before they were suddenly left standing alone.

"I'm so curious about Sahala's father that I can't stand it!" Aurori whispered to Quatina as they strolled through a residential district.

"I, too, am curious to know the truth," Quatina whispered back.

Sidestepping as a group of children ran laughing past them, Aurori glanced around. The dwellings they were passing by were becoming increasingly dingy looking and the street had narrowed to the point where they could almost have touched the buildings on either side by merely stretching their arms out to the sides. Overhead, laundry hung on lines strung between the houses and women were sitting outside in the afternoon heat, cooking over open fires and doing laundry in huge basins full of dirty water.

"Is it my imagination, or have we just entered the poorer district of Pergase?" Aurori said in a low voice, trying to get a good look around without making it seem she was staring.

"It is not your imagination," Quatina confirmed, answering the rhetorical question.

The wrinkled faces of the aged and infirm peered out at them from the shadowed alleyways between the homes as they passed by, giving them curious looks. Spotting one elderly man sitting in a rickety chair that had been moved out into the light, Aurori's heart went out to him when she noticed that there was an oozing lesion on the leg he had propped on another chair. She hesitated over approaching him, but he noticed her looking his way and gave her a toothless smile as he beckoned her over.

"Hello, pretty ones. What brings you so far into the city? Ladies such as yourselves don't often venture here," he said, squinting as he tilted his pale, wrinkled face up at them.

"We're… new to Pergase," Aurori admitted. "We thought we'd take a tour and ended up here."

"Fancy that. Well, stay for a minute, won't you, and keep an old man company?"

Aurori settled her pack to the ground and squatted beside the man. "Actually, I'm a Healer. Would you mind?" she asked, indicating his leg with her eyes.

Feeble as he appeared, the old man bolted upright from the slumped position he had been in and grabbed Aurori's wrist, tears suddenly brimming in his eyes.

"A Healer! Oh…" he moaned, settling back into his chair and rubbing the knuckles of one hand into each eye. "Bless you, child, but I have nothing to offer in return."

"I don't require payment," Aurori assured him, gently removing her wrist from his weak grip so she could better rummage in her pack for an appropriate salve.

"Bless you, child," he said again, knuckling his eyes once more.

"I take it there's no physician to attend you, then?" Quatina inquired.

The man shook his head slightly. "There are physicians in Pergase, but I have no way to pay for their services. My daughter has a little stall in the market where she sells vegetables she grows just outside the city, but she makes barely enough to keep herself and her children. I can hardly ask her to burden herself further by paying for a physician. Although there are a couple of physicians who work for free in this part of the town from time to time, they're so busy with the more seriously ill that I feel ashamed asking them for their help."

Aurori slathered the salve over the man's wound and wrapped it with a bandage. She then produced a spare glass jar from her pack and transferred a small portion of the salve into it and handed it to the man. "Apply this to your leg once a day. You don't need much. And keep that leg elevated like you have been. Make sure you eat plenty of fresh vegetables and fruits as you can, and avoid sweets."

"How can I ever thank you? Are you sure there's not something I can do for you?"

Quatina leapt at the offer before Aurori even had a chance to think about it. "Would you be willing to answer a couple of questions for us? Most people have been unwilling to speak to us on certain topics."

"Anything!" The old man said. "Answering a few questions is hardly payment enough for your kindness, though."

Kindly refusing the man's offer to go and get a couple of chairs for them, Aurori and Quatina chose instead to settle themselves on the ground at his side and asked him about the political climate of the region.

Pergase was a city of marked economic disparity with the rich and the poor living vastly different lives. The people paid high taxes that went to support both the Empress and an army that was currently deployed to the south-east where several towns had risen up against each other over the matter of religious beliefs. Undertaking a peacekeeping effort, the Pergasian army had been called away several times over the years. It seemed that they would no sooner quell the fighting and return home for a few brief months when the tensions would rise again and they would have to return to the area once again. Aurori found this information most disheartening, for the people of Pergase were being made to suffer because of the hatred of others.

On a lighter note, they also discovered why people had been unwilling to talk about Sahala's father. It seemed that Sahala's mother had been accustomed to travel often throughout her empire and had returned from one such sojourn already with child. Choosing to remain single and keep the identity of the father a secret, she had doted on her daughter to the point where Sahala had grown up pampered and spoiled, expecting everyone to bow to her slightest wish. People were unwilling to speak about it because Sahala herself had forbidden it even though most people certainly didn't regard her origins as a detriment, only her attitude.

After thanking the man for his forthright answers to their questions, Aurori and Quatina continued on their tour of Pergase and soon found that they had a small following. Word had spread quickly that Aurori was a Healer and she soon found herself inundated with pleas for help. Loath to send them away, she spent the rest of the afternoon tending wounds and dispensing advice. In payment, the people opened their hearts and homes to her and Quatina, offering them food and drink and answering questions as they occurred to the pair.

By the time the long shadows of approaching evening were being cast across the city, Aurori was thoroughly exhausted and was almost dragging her feet by the time she and Quatina finally trudged into the courtyard of the palace.

"I am proud of what you did for those people today," Quatina told her softly.

Aurori gave a tired laugh and patted her friend's arm. "Thanks."

"You look exhausted. Would you prefer that I ask to have your dinner sent to the room so you can relax for the rest of the evening?"

"Trying to spare me another round of Sahala's barbed remarks?" Aurori asked with a chuckle.

"Actually… yes," Quatina admitted as they stepped inside the room they shared and closed the door.

"I appreciate the thought," Aurori said sincerely, dropping her pack to the floor and flinging her bag of purchases on her bed, "but she's going to be with us a for a long time. I'd better get used to it."

"Speaking of which, since we females are far outnumbered, I would assume that you and I may be expected to share accommodations with her along the way. Won't that be interesting?"

Her mouth forming a silent scream, Aurori smacked a hand to her forehead and toppled over on her bed, clutching at her chest as though she'd been shot.

Chapter Sixteen

There had been quite a commotion the morning they left Pergase. The Empress had run all over the palace, giving last-minute orders to her servants and viziers, driving them mad with various demands. She had also insisted that room be found on the supply carts for various foodstuffs she simply refused to do without and Terien had no choice in the end but to give in, if only to speed up their departure. Grumbling as they reshuffled a few things, Benem and Haren found room for the assorted boxes that were brought out by the suffering servants, but balked at stowing one particularly smelly box of cheese. Fuming, Sahala had stamped her foot and tried to overrule them by appealing to Terien who took one whiff of the box and sided with his men. The cheese stayed in Pergase.

Amazingly enough, Sahala was actually appropriately dressed for the long journey. In place of her billowy dress she now wore pants and a tunic. Although these, too, were made from silk, they weren't at all diaphanous and were of a practical and utilitarian cut. Also missing was her make-up, which was most surprising of all as the lack of artificial color revealed a rather plain and pale face. Only her hair was done up in a fancy style, piled high on her head and held in place with a pin bearing an unusual logo; set inside a stylized circle was a bird in flight with a torch and a sword crossed over its breast. When Aurori commented on it, Sahala had replied that it had been her mother's.

With everyone settled into place on the deck of the hovercraft, they made a slow departure away from the city. Clutching on to Haren's arm, who had grudgingly volunteered to act as her bodyguard even after being warned about her despotic tendencies, Sahala waved and smiled to the people who had congregated to see her off. Once the city of Pergase had receded into the distance behind them, Terien advanced the throttle to maximum and they sped across the desert on a direct course for the Merani Ocean and their next destination.

Much to the delight of Aurori and Quatina, Sahala had brought her own tent and did not have to share space with them. Much to Haren's discomfiture, however, she insisted that he sleep outside at the foot of her tent, making him the butt of several jokes that circulated through the camp. He weathered these with his customary good-natured gentleness, but it was plain to see that he was wondering what he had gotten himself into when she started ordering him around, asking him to fetch her a drink or bring her supper or some such thing.

The strain of dealing with the woman's constant presence was beginning to show in the tense and irritable moods she inspired in Haren, Terien and Aurori. When she wasn't pestering Haren, Sahala was hanging off Terien's arm, getting in his way when he was navigating the hovercraft or engaging him in pointless and trivial conversation until he was ready to toss her over the side. Without knowing it, he had company. Aurori had been hoping that the right moment might present itself for her to have a quiet conversation with Terien so that she might finally reveal her identity to him, but Sahala's constant demands on his attention precluded that.

Upon reaching the shores of the Merani Ocean a few days later, however, their moods underwent a miraculous transformation. Excitement and expectation motivated everyone as they undertook the task of looking for the lock that would gain them access to the city under the ocean. Unlike the stepped shores of the Cosquimus Bay at Brinbourne, here the beach was wide and flat with mammoth towers of rock jutting up from the sand at irregular intervals, and it was for one of these outcrops, supposedly shaped like the crook of a shepherd's staff, that they searched.

Terien had already recounted Lord Soloth's somewhat vague description of the city for everyone as they had journeyed, giving an account of a domed city situated on the floor of the Merani Ocean, filled with people all living in a technological marvel left over from the past. Filling in the details with what they remembered from Alatesh, everyone was speculating about what it would be like to live under-water, debating whether or not they would be comfortable in the confines of such a place, when they finally spotted the rock formation they were looking for.

Excitement building, Terien brought the hovercraft alongside the rock tower and quickly shut it down. Within seconds they were spilling off the deck and fanning out to find the lock.

"I've been looking forward to this since we left Kaethos," Terien said, feeling a little giddy as he ran a hand over the rough texture of the rock. "Of all the cities and lands Lord Soloth told me about, this is the one place that really caught my attention. Just imagine! A city under the ocean, filled with technologies that still work. I can hardly wait to see it!"

Duncan laughed. "You and me both! Even Quayvern doesn't sound as exciting as this place. Of course, after having seen that same image of Quayvern over and over on that cube of yours, I suppose I've gotten used to the idea of a floating city. But this... well, it's hard to even imagine."

With twenty-six people searching for the raised cube shape that held the circular opening for Terien's key, it wasn't long before it was found. Placed chest high on the side of the rock that was sheltered by the massive overhang, it was well hidden amongst the natural bumps and depressions on the rock's surface. Calling out that he had found it, Makhani was quickly surrounded as everyone came running.

"I hope you know how to use the device you were talking about," Makhani said, taking a step back to allow Terien room to get at the lock.

"It sounded like it was pretty much foolproof," Terien said, removing the key from around his neck.

"Great. Then you shouldn't have a problem at all," Makhani jibed, smirking at Terien's sour glance.

With everyone watching, Terien held up the key then slowly inserted it into the hole until it made a faint click. Withdrawing his hand, he held his breath and glanced over at Aurori who was standing on the other side of Makhani, eyes intent on the rock cube. For a long moment there was only the sound of the ocean pounding on the shore, then a faint whine issued from somewhere inside the rock and a one-foot square section of the rock receded back a bit and slid up, revealing a metal panel with a circular grill and a button.

A cheer went up but quickly died as the panel started beeping loudly at regular intervals.

Waiting patiently for something else to happen, Terien exchanged a nervous glance with Duncan and shrugged his shoulders. "Lord Soloth said it would call the people in the city by itself once it was activated."

"Maybe it's not working anymore," Makhani said.

"Or maybe the people left, like in Alatesh," Rannoch speculated.

Terien shook his head. "No. Lord Soloth said he had visited them a few months ago. Unless something drastic happened between then and now, I think it's more likely that they just haven't yet heard the signal it's sending."

A crackling sound issued from the panel suddenly, making everyone jump.

"*This is Merani Base. Whom am I addressing*?" a male voice asked from the grill in the panel.

Another cheer went up, but Terien quickly shushed them.

Terien stabbed a finger down on the button beside the grill and leaned close to it. "This is Prince Terien of Kaethos. The Chosen. I have come with my entourage to collect a representative from your city for the Final Reunification."

"*Ah. The Chosen at last*," the voice said, sounding a touch sarcastic. "*I am Director Maxen. Welcome to Merani Base, Terien. I'm sure you're quite impatient to come down for a visit, so I'll have one of my men come for you in our minisub. How many are in your entourage?*"

"Twenty-six," Terien told him.

"*Hmm! That presents a problem. The minisub can only hold eight, including the pilot. You'll have to restrict yourselves to sending only seven. I hope that's not an inconvenience*," Director Maxen said.

"Not at all. We're already accustomed to splitting up when we reach a city," Terien explained.

"*Excellent. The minisub can make the trip to your position in about an hour. I look forward to meeting you when you arrive. In the meantime, I'll make the arrangements for your stay. I would expect that you'll be here a couple of days, perhaps three.*"

"I look forward to it," Terien said, a broad smile spreading across his face.

"Maxen out."

The communication panel fell silent and the cover once more activated, sliding down and resuming its closed position and the key popped back a bit, indicating it was no longer needed. Terien removed the key and turned to his people.

"Only seven people can go. How unfortunate. Well, we'd better decide who's going before the minisub arrives," Terien said with a sigh of disappointment.

"I have a question fer ye," Rannoch announced, holding up a hand.

"What is it?"

"What's a 'minisub'?"

Everyone laughed, dispelling the nervous tension they had all been feeling.

"I think we'll find out when it gets here," Terien chuckled. "Now, how do we decide who're going?"

"It only makes sense for the representatives to go," Elek said.

Terien looked around. The faces of his men held no disappointment at the prospect of being left behind and he was proud of them for it.

"Duncan and myself, then. Makhani, Rannoch and Sahala. Quatina and Aurori. That's seven," Terien counted out.

"I am not truly a representative for the Final Reunification," Quatina pointed out, ignoring Aurori's wide-eyed stare.

Folding his arms, Terien considered that. "Actually, you are. With the joining of the Cohalili and the Penaro into one group, they easily comprise a large enough population to be considered a people unto themselves."

"Oh!" Quatina said, taken aback. "In that case, I would be honored to accompany you to this Merani Base," she said, a slow smile spreading on her face as she considered the wonders she would see.

"Well, I don't want to go," Sahala said suddenly, pushing between the men until she was standing toe to toe with Terien. She folded her arms in a pose that mirrored his. "I hate confined spaces, and from your description of Alatesh I will not subject myself to such a place."

"You're sure about this?" Terien asked solemnly. "If you don't want to come, I'll ask someone to come in your place, and I won't have you change your mind at the last minute."

Her face fell into a sulk. "I resent that."

Terien raised an eyebrow and stared at her, waiting for an answer.

Blowing out an angry breath, Sahala's arms fell to her sides and she looked away. "Very well. If you must know, I'm claustrophobic. I certainly won't be changing my mind."

With nothing to say to that, Terien now looked out over the sea of faces before him. Whom to choose? "Okay, then. How about casting lots to choose a replacement for Sahala?"

The men started whispering amongst themselves, slowly congregating into a group as they discussed the idea. Every now and then they would glance furtively around.

"Bad idea?" Terien whispered to Duncan, who only shrugged.

"I didn't think so," Elek whispered from where he stood on Terien's left.

Breaking from their huddle, Benem approached Terien and cleared his throat. "With all due respect, we've decided that we'd rather not take part in a lottery. We've discussed it and decided that there's only one real choice for a replacement for the Empress. One man has consistently shown diligence in his duties and remained behind to guard the animals in every city we've encountered, even while the rest of us rotated through the honor of accompanying you as you presented yourself as the Chosen." Turning his gaze to Terien's left, Benem smiled broadly. "Elek."

His jaw falling slack, Elek took an involuntary step back, stunned by the looks of happy approval on the faces before him.

"I… I don't know what to say," Elek stammered, his eyes misting.

"Just tell me you're not claustrophobic," Benem laughed, clapping him on the shoulder.

Elek laughed and dabbed at his eyes. "Hell no!"

Clamping a hand down on Elek's shoulder, Terien said, "Welcome aboard, Elek." He smiled and indicated the hovercraft with a toss of his head. "Sorry to put you to work before we go, but I think we'd better offload and get a camp set up before that minisub gets here."

"No problem!" Elek replied, then waded into the midst of the men and started giving orders, smiling all the while as he received pats on the back and words of congratulations.

Catching Benem before he could hurry off to help out, Terien pressed his key into Benem's hand. "I'm leaving this with you in case you need to contact me while we're down there. Do you remember what to do?"

Benem nodded. "Sure. I was watching pretty closely. Insert the key, wait for the panel to open and for someone to answer, then press the button down when I want to talk. Easy as falling off a felinae," he assured Terien. "Don't worry. A couple or three days ain't all that long. We'll take care of things here."

"Of that I have no doubt," Terien told him with a confident smile.

"I don't envy you, though. It was fine going inside Alatesh, knowing the door was open and we could walk out whenever we wanted, but this makes me nervous. All that water. No way out," he said with a shudder. "I'm with the Empress on this one."

Terien laughed. "Speaking of her, I think I'm getting the better part of the deal, leaving her here with you and Haren," he said with a wink. "Besides, Merani base has been functioning for centuries. Why should anything go wrong now?"

Chapter Seventeen

An hour was barely enough time for them to unload the hovercraft, and they had just finished setting up camp when the minisub surfaced just offshore, bringing everyone running to the beachhead to watch as the oblong vessel coasted towards them, borne along with the breaking waves. They surrounded the craft the instant it had pushed up onto the beach, everyone talking at once and running their hands over its metal hull as they examined it and peered into the glass viewports.

A hatch on its side irised open and a short ramp descended, down which a young man stepped out, smiling from ear to ear at their excitement. Of medium height and pencil thin, he was dressed in a one piece jumpsuit that was a pleasing shade of deep green and had white piping on its seams. A high white collar peaked out from underneath the lapels at his neck. His dark brown hair ruffled in the breeze off the ocean and he shivered as he shaded his eyes from the light, squinting at them.

"Hiya folks! I'm Garel. Director Maxen sends his regards," he said. "Which one of you is the Chosen?"

Terien stepped forward. "I am," he said, offering Garel his hand. "Call me Terien."

"Sure. So, are you all ready for the trip down to Merani Base?"

Glancing around, Terien had to laugh. All those who would be going down to the city already had small travel packs slung over their shoulders and were standing in a tight group, wide-eyed and grinning at him.

"I'd say we're all set," said Terien, picking up his own pack.

"Great! Let's get your gear stowed first, and I'll give everyone a quick tour of the minisub before we go," Garel said. He strode back up the ramp and stood at the top, gesturing for them to hand him their packs.

Once he had all their things safely stowed within a compartment inside, Garel hopped out again and started to walk slowly around the outside of the minisub, keeping one hand at his brow to shade his eyes as he pointed out the twin propellers mounted on the sides of the oblong craft, briefly explaining how they used battery-powered electric motors to drive the minisub underwater, then moved on to giving everyone a look inside. There were two operator chairs at the front of the craft, situated before a complex panel with switches, dials and displays that were backlit by pale green light. There were six more upholstered seats in the cabin, arranged with two each behind the operator chairs and one behind each of the pairs. The rest of the interior was a jumble of panels and protruding parts, making it a cramped place.

With the short tour at its end, Garel gave them all a big smile and clapped his hands together. "Time to shove off, I'd say."

After a few last farewells and back slaps, Terien was the first to board the minisub. Choosing a spot beside one of the small viewports in the paired seats behind the operator chairs, he patted the seat beside him, inviting Aurori to sit next to him.

"Good thing there are seats in this beastie," Rannoch commented as he took the seat directly behind Terien and Aurori. "It's so cramped in here that even I have to stoop over."

"You're just happy that the seats are padded, and don't you deny it," Makhani teased, taking the seat opposite.

"Aye, lad. An' me poor bones are glad of it after sittin' on a metal deck all day!"

Taking Quatina's hand, Duncan led her over to the other set of paired seats, leaving the two operator chairs the only ones vacant.

Elek shrugged and turned to Garel. "Damned if I plan on driving this thing. Which seat is mine?"

Garel hit a button on the panel beside the hatch. The ramp retracted and the opening irised shut. He squeezed past Elek and dropped into the left hand operator seat, indicating that Elek should take the other. "I'll do the piloting, if you don't mind," Garel laughed as Elek swallowed hard and gingerly settled into the other chair, trying hard to avoid touching any of the controls before him. "Everyone strap in. The ride through the surface waves can be bumpy."

Scrambling to figure out how the seat restraints worked, they were soon belted in and ready to go.

Engaging the engine, the minisub slowly crawled away from the shore on a set of caterpillar treads on its bottom until it was floating free, bobbing with the action of the waves. Garel then retracted the treads and engaged the propellers.

As they started to turn, Terien and his group leaned close to the windows and waved to the men standing on the shore, receiving wild waves and smiles in return. The sound of water rushing into metal containment tanks now filled the compartment, raising eyebrows.

"Don't worry. Just taking on ballast so we can dive," Garel explained. "All perfectly normal."

Cutting off their view of the topside world, the minisub submerged and began to skim through the water on a shallow descent. The cabin lights switched to a lurid red that was easier on the eyes but made the experience seem a little spooky until Garel turned on the outboard lights, illuminating a new and fascinating world they had never before had the opportunity to see. Strange formations of coral, schools of brightly colored fish and scores of different kinds of plant life kept them glued to the viewports.

Glancing at Aurori, Terien noticed that she was nervously wringing a piece of her cloak in her hands. "You're not afraid, are you?" he whispered.

Aurori looked over at him and smiled weakly. "Not afraid of the trip, no."

"Then what is it?" he asked softly, taking her hand and intertwining his fingers with hers.

An electric thrill shivered through her at his touch. She really wasn't afraid of the trip at all. Her nervousness was due to the fact that she had realized that she would most likely find the right moment for a heart-to-heart talk with him at some point on this particular trip, especially without the Empress along to hog all his attention, and the prospect filled her with uncertainty. What would she say? How would he react?

"Just excited, I guess," Aurori lied, casting her eyes to the side. Now was not a good time with everyone sitting so close. Later. She would tell him later, she promised herself.

It was surprising just how fast the hour-long trip passed and it wasn't long before the five domes of Merani Base came into view directly ahead and everyone let out inarticulate sounds of awe. Immense in size and arranged in the shape of a flower with open petals, the city had a large central dome surrounded by four smaller ones that were connected by short walkways. Only the central building had a clear dome with buildings visible inside, however, while the other four were opaque and had lighted windows dotting their sides.

"If you think it's pretty impressive from the outside, you'll just die when you see the inside," Garel told them proudly. "Merani's central dome houses the living quarters and such, while another two have all the gardens in them. The smaller one over there is full of old laboratories and such, while the fourth one is where all the equipment for running the base is kept."

"It's a lot bigger than I expected," Makhani said, leaning around Duncan's chair to get a better view through the forward window as they neared the fourth dome Garel had indicated as being the one with all the equipment.

"I think it feels smaller once you're inside," Garel told them with a shrug. "Anyway, you're about to find out. Here we go."

The domes did not actually rest on the ocean floor but were mounted on thick pilings, a fact which became clear when Garel maneuvered the minisub under the dome, then took it straight up through an opening in the bottom, the swooshing sound of water rushing back out of the ballast tanks echoing in the cabin. Popping out into open-air in the middle of a large pool that was centered inside a well-lit room, the minisub's interior lights brightened, forcing everyone to blink furiously until their eyes adjusted. Garel then guided the sub over to the side and shut it down. Outside, they could hear someone moving around and the sub jerked a bit as it snugged in close to the edge of the pool, the sound of its hull hitting the side making a low resonant sound.

"Okay, you can unstrap yourselves now," Garel told them as he unfastened his own restraints and went to the hatch controls. He hit the button with the heel of his hand, waiting until the door had irised open and the ramp had descended before looking over at them with a dazzling smile. "Welcome to Merani Base. Watch your step on the way out, now."

Aurori stood aside and let Terien lead the way to the hatch where he shook hands with Garel again, then stepped down the ramp to be greeted by a small complement of men who were all dressed in jumpsuits of a design and color similar to Garel's. They stood at attention with their eyes fixed straight ahead and their hands clasped behind their backs. One couldn't help but notice the sidearms they wore strapped to their hips, and Terien wondered briefly what they could be possibly armed against when his eyes took note of the man standing at their center and the thought fled altogether.

Dressed in dark blue pants and a waistcoat with a white turtleneck undershirt, he was tall and thin with intense brown eyes and angular features marked by a strong chin. Old enough to have been Terien's father, the man's dark hair was graying at the temples and was slicked back. He smiled pleasantly and stepped forward, extending his hand.

"I'm Director Maxen," he said, shaking Terien's hand firmly. "You must be Terien. It's a pleasure to finally meet the Chosen." His appraising glance raked Terien from head to toe, taking in the sidearm and sword without comment.

"Thank you. I confess that I've been looking forward to meeting you, as well."

Maxen laughed. "I would say, rather, that you've been looking forward to seeing Merani Base, no doubt."

Terien smiled. "No offense intended."

"None taken."

"I'd like to introduce my associates," Terien said, turning to indicate his entourage.

He started to name them one by one, stating their place of origin as he did. Director Maxen politely shook hands with each in turn, but gave a slight start when introduced to Aurori, his expression flickering momentarily.

"I have heard of Eristea. It's the Healer's kingdom, isn't it?" Maxen asked her.

"Yes, it is," Aurori answered, feeling a little confused by the restrained excitement she heard in his tone. For some reason, something about his eyes and the way he was smiling made him seem vaguely familiar.

"You are a Healer, then?"

"I am, but I'm curious to know how you've heard about us. I thought this city had been hidden away all this time," Aurori told him honestly.

"Hidden away from the eyes of outsiders, yes, but we have often traveled to the surface and know all about the lands above," Maxen said with a chuckle. "We've had contact with several kingdoms in the past. They just didn't know it," he said with a sly smile that made the hair on Aurori's arms stand on end.

Finally releasing Aurori's hand, Maxen went on to greet the rest of Terien's entourage and then held his arms wide. "I'm sure that you're quite anxious to see what Merani Base has to offer. Come. We'll start with a tour of the main dome. I think you'll find the view unique. Don't worry about your luggage; Garel will see that it's brought to your rooms."

Aurori looked over to Garel and realized why Maxen had looked so familiar. He and the younger man shared the same dark hair, brown eyes and slender build. Were they related in some way? Aurori gave a mental shrug and turned her attention back to taking in the sights.

Leading them through a network of tunnel-like corridors, Maxen brought them into the central dome of Merani Base. It had buildings and streets like any other city, except that here the design of the buildings included fluid lines and sweeping arches, and they were made of a strange material that was shiny and smooth, while the streets were paved with a hard, uniform gray substance no one in Terien's group had seen before. The central area of the dome was a huge open area filled with trees, plants, and benches and had a man-made stream coursing through it, making it an inviting substitute for the world above. People walked past, smiling slightly and offering a wave as they passed, but they didn't slow down or stop, which Terien found unusual. They simply went about their business, casting the occasional wary glance in the direction of the armed men who were trailing behind the group. It was too soon to make any kind of mention about that, though, and Terien contented himself with taking in his amazing surroundings.

The most awesome sight was directly overhead. Large panels were set into the dome a third of the way up and the light they cast down on to the buildings rivaled the intensity of the suns. Above those, the clear dome gave them a spectacular view of the ocean beyond. Lit from floodlights set on the outside, the ocean depths were illuminated in all their glory. Schools of fish meandered past, along with many other creatures too bizarre to describe.

"I've spent all me life either beside th' sea or out on it, and I've never seen th' likes of this," Rannoch breathed, doing a slow turn as he craned his neck back and stared up at the view.

"Careful, Rannoch, or next you'll be complaining about a sore neck," Makhani warned, planting a hand on the back of Rannoch's head and tilting it forward.

"Leave me alone, lad," Rannoch complained without anger, batting Makhani's hand away. "'Tis worth th' pain to see this."

Clearly enjoying their reaction to the spectacle, Maxen chuckled. "Your wonderment is refreshing. We've long since grown accustomed to the sights Merani Base has to offer, and I'm afraid we take it for granted."

"I can't imagine that ever happening," Quatina spoke up. "Alatesh was a pale shadow compared to the wonder of this place."

"A pity about Alatesh," Maxen said, shaking his head sadly. "My ancestors made mention in their logs that they had lost contact, and I often wondered what had happened. It's nice to know that they didn't just die out." He brightened and clapped his hands together almost immediately, showing just how false the sentiment of his words had been. "Let's continue our tour, shall we?"

Taking them to the another dome, Maxen led them up a series of stairs until they were walking along catwalks that were suspended high above the floor. Far below, the dome was filled with row upon row of green growing things. Vegetables, plants, and trees in every shade of green imaginable were being tended by a small army of workers all dressed in yellow jumpsuits.

"This dome and the one next to it are both filled with gardens like this. We grow our own food here and supplement it with fish and other sea creatures we catch outside the dome in a series of nets and traps," Maxen told them. "We also have many species of plants and trees growing here that can't be found anywhere else on Primus," he said with pride, then turned his head and coughed into his hand for a moment.

"How is that possible?" Duncan asked.

Maxen leaned on the rail of the catwalk and looked down over the edge. "Merani Base was originally an underwater research station before the Great Division. Scientists studied the Merani Ocean from here, but they also conducted experiments in the labs that are in another dome. They had brought samples of many different types of plants for purposes of scientific research, intending to find ways to create varieties that were hardier or better able to resist disease and insects. When the comets fell, the resulting firestorms destroyed large tracts of land, rendering many species instantly extinct. Only the specimens kept here survived." Maxen shifted position to look over at Terien. Another coughing spell caught him, however, and it was a few moments before he continued.

"That's one of the things Merani Base has to offer for the Final Reunification. We have many plant specimens that can be reintroduced to the lands they once grew in. In particular, there are several fruits and vegetables that are quite simply delicious and exist nowhere else. You'll have to try them for yourselves."

"I look forward to it," Terien said, his gaze falling on the workers below as he leaned against the railing.

By looking directly down, Terien could just make out the forms of several guards standing by the main floor entrance to the dome. They, too, were armed. Duncan joined Terien at the rail and looked down as well. Taking note of the guards as Terien had, he looked sideways at his friend and raised his eyebrows in silent question.

"We won't bother with a tour of the other garden today. Perhaps tomorrow. But I would like to show you the labs," Maxen said, indicating that they should follow him back down the stairs. He looked over his shoulder as they descended in his wake and smiled. "You might say I have a bit of a surprise for you."

Reaching the central dome once more, they skirted the edges of it until they came to another short connector tunnel. Moving through it, they emerged into the dome that obviously held the laboratories Maxen had mentioned. They passed a series of closed doors, finally arriving before one that had a picture of a man posed with arms and legs outstretched engraved into it.

"This is our medical bay," Maxen told them, opening the door by passing his hand over a sensor pad set in the wall by its side.

The lights came on as they entered. Raised beds with banks of darkened machines behind them lined one wall, while the wall opposite had rows of shelves that were filled with bottles and jars whose contents were a mystery. Directly below the shelves was a counter that ran the length of the wall and had a few chairs parked against it. Dried plants hung from hooks in the ceiling, filling the room with their pungent aroma, and a large desk stood at the far end of the room, covered with papers and books.

"This is fantastic," Aurori breathed, taking a few tentative steps towards the shelves.

"Go ahead and look around," Maxen told her with a laugh.

Delighted with the invitation, Aurori now walked over to the shelves and began inspecting the bottles, sliding her fingertips along the edge of one shelf as she slowly moved along, scanning the labels on the bottles. Moving to the cluttered desk, she studied the papers laid there and felt her blood run cold. Most of the writing was in basic script, but there were notations in the margins that were in another script she knew all too well.

"There was a Healer here," she said flatly, turning to stare wide-eyed at Maxen.

Every head swiveled to look at Maxen with astonishment at Aurori's pronouncement, but Maxen simply clasped his hands behind his back and nodded, a smile playing at the corners of his mouth.

"The surprise I told you about," he announced, unperturbed by Aurori's shocked expression. He advanced towards her and gestured at the shelves she had just been studying. "Merani Base had a Healer attending the needs of the inhabitants for nearly twenty-nine years. A fellow by the name of Brennai. All this was his."

"Brennai? I... I've heard of him. He never returned from his Healer's journey," Aurori said, her heart lurching. "How did he end up here?"

Maxen chortled softly and leaned a hip against the counter, folding his arms. "We met when I was in the city of Pergase. Merani Base had been without a physician for many years and I was assigned to see if I could find a suitable person to fill the position. I observed Brennai for several days as he tended the people in Pergase and became convinced that he would be perfect for the job. So I invited him to see Merani Base."

"An' he came down here with ye, just like that," Rannoch said, snapping his fingers.

"Basically, yes. Once he saw Merani Base and this medical bay, he agreed to stay on. It took him a long time to learn how some of the equipment works, but he managed to become quite proficient in its use. With his own talents for healing and his knowledge of natural medicine, he became a well-respected member of the community," Maxen said. He pushed away from the counter and coughed a little, then took a few steps closer to Aurori. "Brennai passed away almost a year ago. We've been trying to find another Healer to take his place, but have been unable to." He smiled and placed a hand on her shoulder. "Until now."

It took a minute for the implication to sink in.

"You... want me to stay?" Aurori stumbled back a step until she was pressed up against the desk.

"Yes, I do." Maxen stepped away from her, his hand motioning through the air to encompass the whole room. "Think of all the good you could do for the people of Merani Base. Of all you could learn. Brennai left detailed notes. It wouldn't take you long to master the equipment here."

Aurori was speechless as she looked around the room. It was a tempting offer. After all, how often was a Healer offered the opportunity to relearn the old techniques of medicine that the ancestors had known? Tempting, indeed. But not enough. She had other duties to consider, and her own hopes and dreams to fulfill. They couldn't be accomplished here under the ocean.

Her eyes found Terien and noted the stricken look on his face, then shifted to Quatina and took in the small shake of her head. Nice to know that she would be missed if she were to accept the offer.

"I appreciate your generous offer, Director Maxen, but I can't accept. I'm sorry," Aurori apologized. "As exciting as it would be to stay here and learn about the old technologies, I have other commitments that I intend to see through." She was speaking to Maxen, but her eyes were on Terien. His look of relief was heart-warming.

Maxen's smile faded instantly. "I see. Well, at least keep the offer in mind, won't you?"

Aurori shook her head. "I doubt that I'll change my mind. However, when I return to Eristea, I'm sure I could find another Healer who would jump at the chance to come here."

Forcing a smile, Maxen nodded. "Yes. Yes, that would be wonderful."

"You realize, of course, that Aurori won't be returning home for some time," Terien informed Maxen.

"We've managed this long. I'm sure a few more months won't make a difference," Maxen replied, though it was plain to see that he was deeply disappointed. He sighed heavily, which brought on another fit of coughing. He leaned heavily with one hand braced against the counter.

"You seem to be having respiratory difficulties," Aurori observed. "Perhaps there is something I can do for you?"

Maxen waved her offer away. "No, I'm fine, thank you. Just a passing virus of some sort." He straightened and took a shaky breath. "You must be tired after your long trip and the tour. Why don't I have my men show you to your rooms? After you've rested and refreshed yourselves, you can join me for dinner." His oily smile returned as he moved towards the door and clapped a hand on Terien's shoulder. "After that, you and I can further discuss the Final Reunification."

"An excellent idea," Terien agreed.

Maxen offered them a small bow and hurried off, leaving the guards who had been waiting outside to see to Terien's group.

"Follow us, please," the lead guard said, and started away.

As they filed out of the room, Aurori cast a final glance back and shuddered. Maxen had been lying when he said his cough was just a simple virus. She had seen him surreptitiously wipe away the bloody sputum from his hand, and his fingers were clubbed, which was a peculiar deformity that accompanied a chronic form of lung disease. It was treatable with certain herbs, but only a Healer would know which ones and how to prepare them. Maxen obviously knew this or he wouldn't have been looking for another Healer to replace Brennai.

A feeling of dread settled over Aurori as she wondered what else Maxen was hiding from them.

Chapter Eighteen

Coughing and holding his chest, Maxen hurried into his office, cast a frown at the young man seated in the chair at his desk, then rushed over to a cabinet that stood against the wall and pulled out a flask full of an amber-colored liquid. Pouring a small amount into a glass, he downed it in one gulp and braced himself against the cabinet as another coughing spasm racked his body.

"I see you were a little late taking your next dose," Garel said, swiveling the chair around and rising.

When the coughing fit had passed, Maxen swiped a hand across his mouth and set the glass down hard. "Damn this!" he spat, fury twisting his saturnine features into a grotesque mask.

"Calm down. Now that we'll have a Healer again everything will be fine."

Maxen leaned with both hands on the cabinet, back bowed and head hanging down. "How ironic. We've had our operatives searching for a Healer for months. Unsuccessfully, I might add, despite the handsome price I've offered. Then we're practically handed one by Councilor Leander."

"None too soon, either. There are at least another five people who have started complaining about muscular cramps, pains in their bones and stiffness. No one knows what's causing it or how to treat it, but I'm sure the Healer will be able to figure it out," Garel said with confidence as he crossed to the front of the desk and leaned against it, arms folded.

Maxen pushed himself upright with effort and straightened his waistcoat. He took a calming breath and turned to face his son. "Leander has been most generous in allowing us to retain the Healer. I only hope he will be able to deliver the shipment of weapons he promised. With all the malfunctions in recent months, we've had to dispose of far too many for comfort. Without those weapons to keep the people in line, we could be facing another coup attempt."

Garel shrugged. "Our weapon supply may be seriously depleted, but the guards are the only ones with access to them. The citizens would be foolish to make another attempt after what happened last time."

Maxen nodded absently. "Perhaps, but I will feel better when this is all over and our guards have weapons that aren't likely to malfunction unexpectedly." Crossing to the communications panel, Maxen hesitated before activating it and turned questioning eyes on Garel. "The guards have their instructions and the minisub has been prepared?"

Garel nodded. "Everything's ready."

Maxen dialed the frequency indicator to the appropriate setting and held his finger on the call button, sending a crackle of static over the system. If anyone were in Leander's office right now, the static could be explained away as a minor malfunction. Instead of a long wait, however, Leander's voice immediately came over the speakers, tinny and garbled as usual.

"*Greetings, Merani base. I would assume that the Chosen has arrived.*"

"He's here," Maxen confirmed. "I limited him to bringing only six people with him. A respectable complement of people without being too many to handle. As a matter of fact, however, he brought the representatives with him and I've just finished giving them a brief tour of our facility. I'll be having dinner with them shortly."

Leander laughed with delight. "*Excellent*! *And he suspects nothing*?"

"How could he? I've made sure to avoid having him come into contact with the people and have been nothing but courteous," Maxen replied indignantly. "Everything is in place and has been since we last spoke."

There was a thoughtful pause on the other end. "*Indulge me. What are the planned sequence of events*?"

Impatient now, Maxen blew out a wheezy breath. "I have already invited the Healer to stay on and she has refused, as predicted. At dinner tonight I will make a show of insisting that she stay and the guards will storm the banquet room at that time. I will assure everyone that I fully support the Chosen's mission and am only returning them to the surface while I keep the Healer here. The Chosen's entourage will be held until morning and then transported to the surface. On the way they will meet with an accident – a catastrophic failure of the minisub's fusion engine. All hands will be lost, of course, and I will contact Primary Soloth to express my deepest regrets and sympathies. If possible, we will recover a few bodies for presentation. Not all, mind you, lest the Healer be missed."

"*And I will make certain that questions are raised about the management of the Chosen's journey, inciting a debate about the wisdom of tampering with the affairs of the people of Primus. Excellent. You will have your Healer and new weapons, and I will have the means to remove Soloth from office.*"

Maxen glanced at Garel as he spoke. "Keeping order in Merani will become difficult once the citizens learn about what has happened, and I have no doubt that they will find out. I will need those weapons as soon as possible. How are you planning on delivering them?"

Leander chuckled. "*I'm sure that Soloth will want to go to Merani Base when he learns about the accident, and I will insist on accompanying him, as will several other councilors. A confederate of mine will have your weapons on board his flyer and will break off from the rest of us, claiming engine trouble. Arrange to have a minisub meet with him at the rendezvous you maintain for your topside operatives. We'll discuss the details and timing after the accident.*"

"This had better work, Councilor Leander. Are you certain that Soloth won't suspect foul play?" Maxen asked, frowning despite Leander's inability to see the expression.

Leander snorted derisively. "*I have been a vocal supporter of the Chosen and the mission from the start. My only public reservations have been regarding the decision not to monitor the journey. Soloth and his supporters will have no reason to suspect either of us.*"

Maxen scrubbed a hand across his face. "Very well. I'll contact you after the accident, then."

"*No. My office may be a little busy after your call to Soloth. I will contact you. Leander out.*"

Smiling, Maxen leaned against the communications panel and turned to his son. "I hope you've had the cooks prepare a splendid

feast for tonight. I'm in the mood for a celebration."

Garel pushed away from the desk, grinning. "Sure. Nothing but the best." He raised an eyebrow. "One thing, though. The Chosen and his group are all armed. That might present a problem."

"Not at all," Maxen assured, waving a dismissive hand. "It's considered impolite to wear weapons at a social occasion. They'll be as helpless as fish in a net." He moved away from the panel and took a seat at his desk. He leaned back and closed his eyes, suddenly feeling very tired. "Go see to the last-minute details, would you, Garel? I think I need a short nap before dinner."

Tossing off a salute, Garel smiled and left his father to rest.

★

"Something is terribly wrong in Merani Base," Duncan was saying, pacing around the sitting room while Terien dressed for dinner in the adjoining bedroom.

"I noticed," Terien called out, toweling off after having just enjoyed a wonderful device called a shower. "Armed escorts, people who won't even stop to talk and workers toiling under guard."

"This place is a police state," Elek declared.

There was a knock at the door and Duncan jumped slightly. Chagrined, he went to the door and opened it to find Makhani and Rannoch standing there. Both had wet hair, indicating they, too, had taken advantage of the facilities in their rooms. Both were dressed for the occasion in their finest.

"We have to talk to Terien. We're concerned that there's something not quite right in Merani Base," Makhani said, striding inside with Rannoch two steps behind.

"That's the topic of choice at the moment," Elek laughed, shifting over to make room on the small couch for Rannoch who plopped his bulk down beside him.

"Good. Then ye've seen it, too," Rannoch said.

"The question is, what are we going to do about it?" Makhani asked, perching himself on the arm of the couch.

Another knock sounded at the door and Duncan sighed as he

went to answer it. This time it was Aurori and Quatina standing there, making the group complete. They were also dressed for dinner, with both wearing the silk skirts and blouses Sahala had given them. Aurori had chosen to wear her Healer's cloak over her ensemble, though, and had the front open and pinned back over her shoulders, turning it into a flowing cape that made her look quite regal. Quatina also looked very nice, but had on her own pair of lizard skin boots instead of the delicate slippers that had been provided with the outfit.

"We need to talk. Something's not..." Aurori started to say, but Duncan held up a staying hand.

"Take a number," he said with a laugh, ushering them in and closing the door behind them.

Terien emerged from the other room dressed in a fresh dress uniform, running his hands through his damp hair. "I share your concerns, but I don't see what I can do about them." He pulled out the chair parked in front of the small desk that stood in one corner of the room and sat heavily, crossing one leg over the other. "Until we have a chance to talk to some of the people, we don't know for certain that anything is wrong, and so far the opportunity hasn't presented itself. Maybe if we stay a few more days we'll be able to learn a little more. Who knows? Maybe we're jumping to the wrong conclusions."

"We're not," Aurori told him firmly. "Maxen lied to me about his cough. It's not just some passing virus. He's seriously ill."

Terien raised an eyebrow. "No wonder he would like to have a Healer in residence. I wonder if it's only him or whether there are others who are sick."

"There are others," Aurori assured him. "Garel is photophobic for starters, and I've noticed that several people walk with an uneven gait, as though they're in pain. I'd need to examine them to be certain, but I have my suspicions about a diagnosis."

Makhani shook his head. "I say we find a way to make an excuse to get out of here. Get the representative and get out. Assuming that Maxen even intends to send one."

They started debating the matter, batting their opinions around until Terien held up a hand for silence.

"I don't like what I've seen so far, either, but there's really very little we can do at the moment. Unless one of you thinks he or she can pilot a minisub?" he asked, reminding them how stranded they were. "We have no choice but to sit back and see how this plays out. We go to dinner, I have a little talk with Director Maxen, see what I can find out, and then we decide what to do from there. Agreed?"

Reluctantly agreeing that there was truly little else to do, they fell silent just as another knock sounded at the door.

"Our escort, no doubt," Duncan said, rolling his eyes as he went to the door.

Garel stood there, smiling that pleasant smile of his. "Hiya! I see you're all ready for dinner," he said, peering into the room. He now wore a dark blue outfit similar to the one Maxen wore. "I hope you're hungry. The cook prepared several samples of the vegetables we grow here."

Terien stood and returned a pleasant smile of his own. "Tasting them is something I definitely look forward to."

Chapter Nineteen

The banquet room was small but well appointed. The walls were finished in the same strange, smooth material as in the guest rooms, but were a subtle shade of blue instead of white. Paintings depicting various scenes from the world above adorned the walls and there was an elegant wooden oblong table with chairs in the center of the room upon which a sumptuous feast awaited them. They found that Maxen had not been exaggerating when he had said that the fruits and vegetables grown in Merani Base were truly unique and delicious as they set about tasting a little of everything. Several different kinds of fish and unfamiliar sea creatures were also on the menu, and they tried them all.

Conversation had been stilted at first with everyone casting wary glances around the room, but it wasn't long before they had started to relax and enjoy the evening. The armed guards were nowhere in sight and there were several servers in attendance who seemed utterly relaxed and genuinely happy as they answered a few innocent questions about Merani Base.

Director Maxen, who was seated at the head of the table, also seemed to be in fine spirits as he chatted with Terien and Aurori who had been seated on either side of him. He explained at length about how the underwater city functioned and in turn listened as they described the journey they had made thus far. He had even finally introduced Garel as his son, expressing pride in the young man's indispensability as his aide.

It wasn't until dinner was long since over and conversation had began to falter that Maxen asked Aurori if she would reconsider his proposal to stay behind on Merani Base.

"I appreciate the confidence you show in my abilities as a Healer, considering they haven't yet been demonstrated, but I really must refuse," Aurori said demurely. "However, I would be happy to make sure that your medical supplies are put in order and would be more than willing to see anyone who has a medical condition before I leave. If necessary, I can make sure that medications are left behind."

Frowning, Maxen laid his palms flat on the table and pushed his chair away. He rose and began to pace around the table. "We've been making do in just such a manner," he said, "we need more than that."

"I really am very sorry," Aurori told him, feeling apprehension starting to gnaw in her gut. "As I said, I will certainly see to it that another Healer be asked to attend Merani base."

"Not good enough," Garel said angrily. He rose from his seat and moved to the wall by the door where a communications panel was inlaid, pressing a button before he continued. "We need someone now, not months from now."

Terien stood, locking eyes with Maxen. "Aurori is unwilling to stay. I ask you to leave it at that."

"I'm afraid you have no say in the matter," Maxen told him coldly as six armed guards rushed into the room, their weapons already drawn as they took up positions behind every one of Terien's people.

A ripple of disbelief and betrayal stirred the room, but no one moved, frozen in place by the threatening stance of the guards.

"I won't let you keep Aurori here against her will," Terien snarled, his hands closing into fists.

The guard standing behind Terien pressed the barrel of his weapon into his back. "Shut up and don't move," he warned in a low growl.

"That's enough!" Garel barked at the guard.

Heart pounding so hard she felt dizzy, Aurori locked eyes with Maxen. "You don't have to do this. I know about your illness. I can make all the medicine you need. You don't need me to stay here just for that," she appealed to him.

Maxen sighed and rubbed at his forehead. "If it were just me, I would have been willing to do as you suggest, but it's not." He walked around to where Aurori sat and crouched beside her. "There were once 10,000 people in Merani Base. Now there are less than 3,000 and many of them are becoming ill. Without a full-time Healer, I'm afraid our numbers will continue to dwindle." Maxen laid a hand on Aurori's arm. "We need you desperately. I'm sorry, but I have to do what's best for my people. You must stay."

Aurori pulled her arm away from his touch as she looked around at her friends and the guards standing over them. "If you hurt any of them, you can forget about me doing anything to help you!" she said angrily.

Maxen chuckled at her bravado and stood. "You misunderstand. I have no intention of harming anyone. I have nothing but respect for the Chosen and his mission as Gatherer. A pity I won't be able to send a representative, but under the circumstances I'm sure you understand," he said to Terien, bowing slightly. "You will be transferred back to the surface in our minisubs. Under guard, of course."

"While Aurori remains here as your prisoner for the rest of her life. Just like Brennai, no doubt," Duncan said hotly.

"No doubt," Maxen conceded. "She will be well looked after and want for nothing. I promise you that." He motioned for the guards to remove them from the room, but resistance was encountered from Quatina.

"I will not go! If Aurori must stay, then I will stay as well," she cried. She looked to Aurori and gave a her a tight smile. "You should not have to remain here alone," Quatina said softly.

From where he sat across the table, Duncan gave Quatina a gentle kick on her right ankle, striking the dagger hidden there. He raised an eyebrow when she looked at him, hoping she would catch on. She was the only one who had a weapon and it might come in handy.

Aurori caught Duncan's meaningful look and she raised her eyes to Terien. The way he was looking at her spoke volumes. He wasn't about to abandon her. They were warriors. Even unarmed and under guard they were hardly helpless.

"No. Go with them," Aurori quickly said to Quatina. "I'll be fine, but Terien and Duncan need you."

Quatina blinked, stunned by what Aurori was telling her, but caught on quickly and nodded her head, relaxing a bit as she made a show of giving up. "Yes. Yes, I see your point." She looked to Rannoch and held his eyes. "I suppose I must look after Rannoch for you now. He is rather old and feeble."

Rannoch gulped, suddenly looking a little pale as he caught on to Quatina's hint. "Och! All this fuss is givin' me a bellyache," he muttered, rubbing a hand across his ample gut.

"Enough. Take them to the docking bay," Garel ordered.

As everyone slowly got to their feet and started to file out of the room, Aurori locked eyes with Terien across the table that separated them. "I'm so sorry," she told him, tears now flowing freely down her cheeks.

"Don't be. We'll be fine. So will you," he promised, then gave in to the guard's insistent nudging and walked meekly through the door.

"I truly am sorry," Maxen told Aurori, taking hold of her arm. "Come. I will take you back to your room."

Aurori yanked her arm free from his grip and glared at him through her tears. "You are a monster. The only reason I will help you is because I made an oath as a Healer, but don't you think for a second that I hold anything but contempt for you," she said coldly.

"So be it," Maxen said, stubbornly taking her arm once more and leading her from the room.

⋆

As they were herded down the corridors that led to the docking bay, Terien glanced at each of his men, giving them silent signals with his eyes. Warriors all, except Rannoch, they knew what he had planned and gave him covert nods in the affirmative. There were six of them and seven guards if he included Garel, but the Director's son wasn't armed. The weapons presented a minor problem, but if they all made their moves at the same time the odds were in their favor. Only Rannoch concerned him. The older man was a fisherman, not a warrior. Would he understand what to do and be able to do it? Considering that their options were limited, Terien decided there was no choice but to go ahead and hope for the best.

Passing into the narrow connector tunnel that led to the docking bay, Terien was about to give the order to strike when Rannoch suddenly doubled over and began to retch.

"What the hell!" one of the guards exclaimed.

"Get up, old man!" the guard responsible for Rannoch shouted at him. "You're not fooling anyone with that old trick!"

With the whole procession coming to a halt, Quatina squatted in front of Rannoch and put one hand on his shoulder while the other slipped inside her boot, the movement hidden by the folds of her skirt. "This is pointless, my friend. Get up. They are not so stupid that they will fall for your feeble attempt."

Rannoch sighed theatrically. "Ah, well. They're too smart fer the likes of me, I guess."

A more perfect distraction couldn't have been pre-planned. The guards were so busy patting themselves on the back for not being taken in by the old trick that they were distracted by it anyway.

Everyone in Terien's group moved at once, as though reading each other's thoughts, and everything happened at the same time.

Driving an elbow into his guard's face, Terien was rewarded by the man's howl of pain as he slammed back into the wall and dropped his weapon in favor of clutching at his bleeding nose, while Terien dove for the fallen weapon as it skittered away. Once he had it in hand, he rolled onto his back and fired it at his guard, who jittered and shook before sliding down the wall, ending up in an unconscious heap on the floor.

Duncan whirled on his guard, landing a kick that swept the weapon from his hand and continued up, driving into the side of his head and snapping him around. With reflexes honed by years of training, Duncan snatched up the fallen weapon and used it as a bludgeon, bringing it down on the back of the man's head with just enough force to knock him insensate without killing him.

Relying on the power of his build and superior height, Elek slashed down on his guard's weapon arm and heard the bones of the man's forearm snap under his assault as he simply extended his other hand to catch the weapon as it fell from his limp fingers. Cradling his broken arm, the guard whimpered as Elek caught his throat in one hand and slammed him back against the wall, smiling menacingly as he buried the weapon's muzzle in his belly.

Makhani wasn't quite the warrior the others were after so many years of attending to matters of state, but had recently been practicing with the men and was pleased to find that he still had a bit of the old spirit left in him. His guard was about the same height as he and was standing directly behind him, presenting a bit of a dilemma. Makhani mentally crossed his fingers and took a sudden step back, planting one foot between the guard's legs as he ducked his upper body to the side and out of the weapon's line of fire just in time. A shot of energy erupted from the weapon, barely missing Makhani but striking one of the guards standing over Rannoch who was still crouched on the floor. The energy blast caught the guard square in the stomach and he began to shiver and shake, then fell over on his side. Makhani barely took note of this, though, as he clamped his hand on the guard's wrist and wrestled the weapon out of his hand.

Unsurprisingly, Quatina made short work of her guard who had come to stand over her when she went to attend to Rannoch. Sweeping her dagger up and out in an arc, she slashed unerringly at her guard's wrist, forcing him to drop the weapon and clamp his other hand around the vicious cut to stop the bleeding. Springing to her feet, she drove him into the wall and held her dagger at his throat, baring her teeth at him in challenge.

Garel was standing off to one side by the door to the docking bay, his mouth hanging open in disbelief, and Terien was just spinning around to get him in his sights when the door to the docking bay suddenly swung open as though kicked from inside and a man dressed in a dark blue suit jumped out holding a weapon. Garel's reaction was immediate and left little doubt as to the true intentions of the newcomer.

"Jos!" Garel hissed contemptuously. "You son of a bitch! I knew I should have had you eliminated a long time ago!"

Garel threw himself at the man but ended up on the receiving end of a punch that drove him back into the wall where he slithered to the floor, his eyes fluttering closed.

Jos shook his hand out and grinned down at Garel's unconscious form. "Looks like daddy's boy has a glass jaw." He then turned his eyes to Terien and smiled. "And here we thought you needed rescuing," he said, shaking his head.

"Who are you?" Terien asked, still holding the weapon out. He could hear his people still scuffling around behind him, but knew they'd call out if they were having trouble.

"The name's Jos. It's a long story, but when we heard what the Director had planned for you and the Healer, we knew it was time to take action. We didn't count on this, though," he said sheepishly, indicating Terien's group with a nod.

Lowering the weapon, Terien got to his feet and turned around to survey the scene. Everyone but Rannoch held a guard at bay. Beyond the corridor the sounds of shouting and firing of weapons fire could be heard. Something big was happening.

"We have to move quickly," Jos said urgently to Terien. "Bring them into the docking bay."

Without waiting for further explanation, Terien helped move the subdued guards into the docking bay where Jos's men took custody of them, tying them up and placing them in a corner of the room with the crew and guards they had already taken out beforehand.

"What's going on?" Terien asked Jos. "How did you know what Maxen had planned?"

"We've had spies in Maxen's police force for a long time," Jos explained. "Almost two weeks ago we found out that he was planning on staging an accident with the minisub on your return trip. You weren't going to make it back to the surface," he told them gravely.

"So much for all Maxen's good intentions," Makhani muttered.

"If he intended to kill us all along, why the elaborate tale about only wanting a Healer?" Terien asked.

Jos shook his head. "No one knows. Maybe he just wanted to ensure her compliance. Anyway, we had been planning the rebellion for a long time. It wasn't until Lady Idona arrived and announced that the Chosen would be coming to Merani Base that we seriously started to prepare, though. We had hoped to have everything over with by the time you arrived, but getting ready took longer than we expected."

His hands gesturing as he spoke, Jos started to pace the bay with nervous energy as he warmed to the subject. "At first we had planned on finding a way to get to you so we could tell you what was going on in Merani, but when our men on the police force told us what Maxen was going to do, we knew we had to mobilize." Jos stopped pacing and looked Terien in the eye. "I'm sorry to put you in the middle of all this, but we had no choice."

"Under the circumstances, I'm certainly not going to hold it against you," Terien said with a laugh, placing a hand on Jos's shoulder, then sobered. "I need to know what's happening. Is Aurori in danger?"

Jos shook his head. "No. Maxen needs her alive, and all our people know to keep her out of their sights."

"We must go after her," Quatina urged, digging her fingers into Terien's arm.

"I know where he'll take her," Jos said of Maxen. "Same place he went during the last coup attempt three years ago. The gardens in bay two are especially dense and offer the perfect hiding place. And the bay can be locked from inside."

"Your people have attempted a takeover once before?" Makhani asked, his eyebrows shooting up.

"The citizens of Merani are as much prisoners here as the workers in the gardens," Jos said. Seeing their looks of astonishment, he pressed on, giving them a hurried history of Merani Base.

Director Maxen had been elected to his position as a young man and his ambition and love of power had spurred him to go to great lengths to ensure his continued rule over Merani Base. With the population dwindling to the point where it was a struggle just to tend the gardens, Maxen had ventured out and recruited a workforce from amongst the nearest lands, promising the workers a high lifestyle in exchange for their silence about the existence of Merani Base. It was during this period that he also recruited the Healer, Brennai, who was all too happy to rediscover the old medical technologies. At the same time, Maxen was secretly hiring a private police force made up of thugs and bandits whose only qualifications were their amoral attitudes and a willingness to hold a population at bay for money. Passing them off at first as being more workers for the gardens, Maxen soon had everything required to stage his permanent takeover of Merani Base.

With his mercenaries in place, Maxen's true intentions were made known. The workers to whom he had promised a better life essentially became slave labor, and to seal control over Merani Base, the citizens, who had previously been free to venture outside at will, were now forbidden from leaving, as was Brennai. With an army of highly paid guards whom he kept happy by allowing them leave to commute freely between Merani and the lands above, Maxen was able to dictate every aspect of life on Merani. Demanding that the citizens live up to his vision of a utopian world, he ordered them to pursue purely academic ventures.

As time passed, however, people began to become ill. Merani had never been intended to function as a permanent home, and despite the best air scrubbers and water filtration systems the old world could build, people still needed to be able to get out from time to time and reap the benefits of a simple walk under the suns. An ill-conceived coup was attempted three years ago but failed due to a lack of proper planning and weapons.

Injured during the attempt, Brennai had barely recovered from his wounds, but never fully, due in part to his advanced years. He had managed to hang on for a while, but with his passing, the health of the people had begun to deteriorate to the point where another attempt to free themselves from Maxen's despotic rule became necessary.

"We have to help them," Duncan said when Jos had finished.

"That won't be necessary," Jos assured him. "This time we have the garden workers on our side and have managed to arm ourselves. We have enough resistance cells to cover every area of Merani, and the children and other non-combatants are being moved to the safety of the laboratory dome even as we speak."

"How many mercenaries does Maxen have?" Elek asked.

"Two hundred, but they rely on their weapons to keep everyone under control and we've seen to it that those weapons tend to seize up unexpectedly." Jos smiled. "I'll explain about that later, but as you found out, they have no skills in hand-to-hand combat. That and our superior numbers are our advantage."

"Fine. We'll leave you to your revolution," Terien told Jos. "But I'm going after Aurori. If it comes to it, I'm sure Maxen isn't above using her as a hostage if his back's against the wall."

Jos nodded. "I'll let our leader know that you're going after the

Director, then. That'll free up a few more people to help out with protecting the lab dome." He motioned for his men to hand over some of their weapons to Terien and his people. "They have two settings. The first one fires an electrical charge that will knock a person out. The second one fires enough of a charge to kill. These ones aren't rigged to malfunction, either. We're expecting Maxen to order his men to use setting one. We doubt he'll be willing to kill the people he wants to rule over."

Making sure the weapons were adjusted to their lower setting, Terien and his people moved back into the corridor and carefully peered out into the main dome where a firefight was under way.

It would be difficult, but they had to find Aurori.

Chapter Twenty

Maxen had just brought Aurori to her quarters when the first sounds of rebellion echoed through the main dome. Shoving her inside her room, he stepped in after her and shut the door. He went directly to the communications panel on the wall and pressed a button while Aurori sat nervously on the edge of the room's small couch, hugging her arms around herself.

"This is Maxen. What's going on?" he demanded to know.

There was no reply for a second, then a breathless voice came on. "*This is team nine, bay one. We're under attack, sir! Some of the workers somehow got hold of a couple of weapons! I've called for back-up.*"

"Keep me apprised," Maxen ordered, releasing the first button and angrily stabbing down on another. "Garel, have you gotten the Chosen to the docking bay yet?" He released the button and waited. No reply. "Garel, answer me." He waited another few seconds and blew out a frustrated breath before pressing a third button. "This is Director Maxen to team three, bay two. What's your status?"

"*All clear, sir. The workers have all left for the night. What's going on out there?*"

"Trouble in bay one. Stay where you are and secure the area. Expect armed workers."

"*Armed?*" was the astonished echo.

"Yes, I said armed! Now get to work and sweep the bay. Make sure it's clear. Move!"

Aurori now sat back on the couch and suppressed a smile, encouraged by the fact that Maxen had been unable to raise Garel on the communications device. She was still horribly worried about Terien and the others and knew that Garel's lack of reply could mean many things, but at least there was hope for a positive outcome.

Maxen tapped an impatient finger against the communications panel and waited a minute before trying to reach Garel again.

With no reply forthcoming, he wiped his hand across his face and coughed into his hand.

"Problems?" Aurori asked innocently.

Maxen shot her a glance, but whatever he was about to say died on his lips when the panel came to life.

"*Team one, main dome to Director Maxen*!"

"Maxen here!"

"*Sir*! *We're under attack*! *It's the citizens – they're all armed*! *I repeat*! *They're all armed*!"

"Damn it!" Maxen pressed the button. "Deploy all available forces! Use setting one only! I repeat, setting one only. Do not shoot to kill! Just get them under control!"

"*Sir, recommend you find a safe haven. They're closing on your position*!"

Abandoning the communications panel, Maxen strode over to Aurori and grabbed her arm, roughly hauling her to her feet.

"Where are we going?" she demanded to know.

"Somewhere safe," he replied evenly.

Once out of the door, the sounds of shouting and the whine of weapons discharging became clear. Pulling Aurori along behind him, Maxen wove his way towards the dome that housed the larger trees and shrubs, the one he hadn't yet shown Terien and his entourage. He was met outside by six guards who all had their weapons out and were hiding behind several metal tables they had overturned in front of the bay doors.

"You three stay here. You three come with me," Maxen told them. "I won't open the doors again until the rebellion is over. Do you understand me?"

"Perfectly," one guard replied.

Once inside, Maxen appropriated a weapon from one of the guards and ordered the three to spread out but remain close to the doors while he led Aurori deeper into the magnificent gardens where they could hide until it was all over.

★

Once outside the safety of the corridor, Terien and his group kept low as they moved out into the main dome, using the buildings for cover. With the giant lights of the dome now dimmed to simulate night, the firefight around them was intensified as energy bursts flashed everywhere in strobe effect. Citizens and workers alike shouted and exchanged volleys with the guards and there were several bodies littering the streets. It was unclear, however, whether they were dead or merely unconscious and they had no time to stop and check.

As they moved along the walkway that ran past the rooms they had been given, Quatina suddenly disappeared from their midst.

"Where'd she go?" Duncan shouted. "She was right behind me!"

"I'm right here," Quatina yelled in his ear, emerging in a crouch from the room Aurori had been assigned. She held up the blow stick and darts Aurori had been given by the Penaro physician, smiling broadly. "I wondered whether they had thought to transfer our belongings to the minisub. They did not," she said, handing her energy weapon to Duncan. "I am uncomfortable with these weapons," she explained when he looked at her questioningly.

Terien flashed her a smile and they all disappeared into their rooms to collect their own weapons. Now armed with both the new and unfamiliar energy weapons and the ones they were more comfortable with, they continued towards their objective.

Getting to the corridor that led to bay two was easy enough since the citizens of Merani Base were all too happy to lay down cover fire for them as they went, but once they reached the corridor itself they were forced onto their bellies by the fire coming from the three guards Maxen had posted outside the doors.

"I'd say Jos was right!" Makhani yelled. "Those guards aren't there to protect an empty dome!"

Elek and Terien returned fire, but the energy splashed harmlessly against the protective barrier of the metal tables.

"We'll never get in this way!" Terien fumed, rolling back outside the corridor with the others close behind. He propped his back against the wall and squeezed his eyes shut. Visions of Aurori being held under guard by that madman made his heart skip a beat.

"Lad! Remember the catwalks in th' other dome we were at?" Rannoch suddenly asked.

Terien's eyes flew open. "Of course! This dome must have them, too!"

Duncan grinned at Terien. "You think they might have forgotten about their own back door?"

"Let's hope so. Duncan, I want you, Quatina and Rannoch to stay here. Keep firing on those guards. Keep them from thinking too much. Makhani, Elek and I will see if we can find the stairway to the catwalk," Terien said.

Moving off with Elek and Makhani, Terien followed the convex curve of the dome until the door to the stairway was in view. It was unguarded but locked. Shooing the other two men a safe distance back, Terien advanced the setting on the energy weapon to maximum and shaded his eyes as he fired on the panel. The energy burst left the panel scorched and smoking, but the door was still locked. Grumbling to himself, he switched the energy weapon to his left hand and drew his own projectile weapon. One shot was all it took. The panel sparked and frizzled and the door slid open, squealing in protest as it did.

Taking the stairs two at a time, the three men bounded up the stairs. Emerging onto the catwalk, they lay down on their stomachs and moved cautiously to the edge to peer down into the dimly lit dome. From their lofty vantage point they could easily make out the forms of three guards who prowled the edges of the man-made forest near the main doors.

"One shot and they'll know we're here," Elek whispered.

"Not good. We're sitting ducks up here," Makhani whispered back.

"Either of you see Aurori or Maxen?" Terien asked in a murmur.

They shook their heads in unison.

"We have to get down there. Any ideas?" Terien asked.

Makhani smiled mischievously. "You really aren't very observant, are you?" he whispered, jerking a thumb over his shoulder. Set at the far end of the catwalk, a metal stairway descended along the wall, coming out faraway from the main doors. It was shielded by several tall trees.

Terien rolled his eyes and started to crawl towards the stairs, being careful to keep as quiet as possible.

★

Frustrated by their inability to take out the three guards at the bay doors, Duncan and Rannoch took turns firing off random shots down the corridor. Sitting with their backs to the wall on either side of the doorway, they would lean around the corner, pop off a shot and duck back again. This went on for some time until Quatina, impatient with the whole farce, pulled Duncan away from the doorway and took his place.

Lowering herself onto her stomach, she pulled out the blow stick and loaded it with a dart.

"What are you planning to do with that?" Duncan asked, bewildered.

"You have tried energy weapons and your projectile weapon, all to no avail," she explained. "I have noticed that the guards have simply been raising their hands above the table and firing their shots blindly. The blow stick and darts can hit a small target, such as a hand, and still be effective."

Rannoch pushed his glasses up his nose and shrugged. "Worth a try, lad."

Without waiting for Duncan's approval, Quatina rolled into the doorway and raised the blow stick to her lips. Bracing herself with one forearm pressed to the floor, she raised her head and upper body just high enough to get herself set at a good angle. The instant a hand appeared over the top of the table, she puffed a breath into the blow stick, sending the dart on its way.

Before the hand even had time to squeeze off a shot, the dart imbedded itself between the third and fourth knuckles. A yelp of surprise sounded from the hand's owner and he jerked it out of sight. Three heartbeats later the other two guards were shouting at their comrade, their voices high with shock and dismay.

Quatina rolled back to Duncan's side, grinning from ear to ear.

"You're brilliant!" Duncan enthused, giving her a quick hug as she sat up.

Reaching for another dart, Quatina laughed and averted her eyes, embarrassed by his praise. "When I was a little girl, my father insisted that I learn how to use the blow stick. My mother protested, saying that she didn't want her daughter joining the warrior faction of the Cohalili, but my father would not give in." She looked up at Duncan and gave him a radiant smile. "Today is the first time I have truly appreciated the gift he gave me by teaching me despite my mother's protests."

A renewed round of fire erupted from down the corridor. Apparently the guards had discovered that their comrade wasn't dead and were looking to retaliate on his behalf.

"He'd certainly be proud of you," Duncan told her quietly. "As I am."

Quatina reached out and stroked the side of his face, her eyes smiling their thanks for his saying so, then she rolled back into the doorway and set herself up for another shot. It took a few seconds of patient waiting, but her opportunity finally presented itself and she sent the dart flying unerringly into the hand of another guard.

Another yelp, another shout, another man down.

As Quatina rolled away once more, Rannoch laughed so hard that his belly shook. "Lass, I could kiss ye!" he blurted out, excited by her success. His face fell just as suddenly. "Not that I would, mind ye," he added quickly, eliciting a laugh from both Duncan and Quatina.

"Hey! Hey! You down there!"

All three fell silent at the call from the third and final guard remaining down the corridor.

"Don't shoot! I surrender!"

The sound of something landing hard and sliding across the floor caught their attention, and Duncan leaned around Quatina to see what it was just as two more objects hit the floor and slid down the corridor.

There in the middle of the corridor were the weapons the three guards had been using.

Duncan leaned back and smiled at Quatina and Rannoch.

"Hey! Can you hear me? I surrender!" the lone guard called again.

Sliding an eye around the corner, Duncan noted that the guard had moved in front of the overturned tables and had his hands on top of his head.

Tossing his extra energy weapon to Rannoch, Duncan stood up and moved into the corridor, keeping his weapon trained on the guard as he walked over to the discarded weapons and kicked them back to Rannoch.

"What did you do to them?" the guard asked as Duncan approached. "They're out cold!"

Duncan smiled and remained mute on the subject. Instead, he said, "Decided to give up, eh? Smart move."

"I don't get paid enough to risk my neck like this," the guard said. "I figure if I surrender now I might have a better chance of staying alive."

Clamping a hand on the man's shoulder, Duncan turned him around and had him stand spreadeagled against the upturned table.

"I don't have anything to tie him up with," Duncan called over his shoulder.

"That's not a problem," Quatina replied, coming to her feet.

Standing at the entrance to the corridor, she suppressed a smile as she raised the blow stick to her lips and let fly another dart. It missed Duncan's hip by a hand's width, hitting dead center of the guard's right buttock. He jerked, cursed once and only had time to turn accusing eyes on Duncan before they rolled back and he toppled over into Duncan's arms.

Setting him down as gently as he could, Duncan turned to face Quatina.

"You're one wicked lady," he laughed.

Smiling, Quatina took one step towards him, then screamed as her body was bathed in the glow of energy from a weapon's discharge. Her back arching, her limbs shook and she crumpled to the floor.

"Quatina!"

Duncan's world shattered and the pieces fell in slow motion. Fear, grief and utter disbelief pounding through his veins, he had just started to run down the corridor when Rannoch shot to his feet with surprising speed, bellowing like a stuck bovine as he raised a weapon in each hand and started to squeeze off round after round, alternating left and right, as he charged after the squad of six guards who had fired on Quatina.

Completely caught off guard at the unexpected turn of events, the six men turned and hightailed away, following the curve of the dome in the hope of using it as means of blocking Rannoch's attempts at mowing them down. It was no use. Despite his rotund bulk and painful joints, Rannoch was driven by righteous outrage. His rapid-fire shots were random and splashed everywhere, but the law of odds dictated that the sheer magnitude of their numbers couldn't help but hit home and it wasn't long before all six men were sprawled unconscious on the ground.

Trotting back to the corridor on shaky legs, Rannoch arrived huffing and puffing, his face red from exertion. Duncan was sitting on the floor with Quatina held in his arms, tears streaming down his face.

"Th'… lass… is… she…?" Rannoch gasped out, sinking to his knees beside them, feeling heartsick.

Duncan shook his head. "She's alive," he managed to say, his voice tight with emotion.

Rannoch's shoulders sagged with relief. "Thank the Maker."

Squeezing his eyes shut, Duncan hugged Quatina to his chest and buried his face against her neck for a long time, feeling Rannoch put a comforting hand on his back.

"Come on, lad. Let's move her back behind th' tables down the corridor," Rannoch suggested in a quiet voice.

Lifting his head, Duncan wiped the tears from his cheeks, realizing that Rannoch was right. Sitting in the middle of the entryway wasn't the best place to be. He lifted Quatina into his arms and followed Rannoch down the corridor and settled her on the floor behind the tables. Removing his tunic, he bunched it up and put it under her head as pillow and picked up a weapon.

They hunkered down and waited in silence for Terien's return.

⋆

Oblivious to the drama unfolding outside the dome they were in,

Terien, Elek and Makhani had accomplished the descent down the stairs and were now moving single file amongst the trees and potted plants, weapons at the ready as they hunted for the three guards they had spotted from the catwalk.

They were stealthily snaking their way between two rows of bushy flowering shrubs when they caught sight of one guard to their left. His back to them as he squatted behind a low berry bush, he went down without a sound as Elek snuck up from behind and chopped his hand down on the back of the man's neck. Finding some discarded twine, Elek bound him hand and foot and gagged him for good measure, making sure the man could still breathe before rejoining Terien and Makhani.

Continuing on their grim search with Makhani now in the lead, they crossed a narrow a isle between two rows of long seedling tables, crouching low. Making it safely across the open a isle, they were just coming up to a dense stand of dark green trees that were reminiscent of young keyta trees when a guard leapt out at them. Swinging the gardening implement he held like a club, he bashed Makhani straight in the forehead, sending him flying backwards into Terien. The two went down in a tangle, but Elek roared in, swinging the blade of his sword in a ferocious arc that connected with the handle of the implement and splintered it in two. Flinging the broken shaft at Elek, the guard darted away.

Elek was about to give chase when he was stopped by Terien's shout. "Forget him!"

Sheathing his sword, Elek backtracked to where Terien was leaning over Makhani who was lying flat on his back, arms and legs splayed out. A cut in the middle of his forehead was leaking blood at an alarming rate, sending rivulets spilling into his blond hair. More frightening was that his eyes were open and blinking but unfocused.

"Tell me your name," Terien ordered Makhani as he drew a handkerchief from his pocket and pressed it to the cut. "Come on! Answer me, damn it!"

Makhani licked his lips and tried to focus his eyes. "The name's Makhani," he replied weakly. A slow smile blossomed on his lips. "And you're the Royal Boy."

Elek laughed out loud and knelt beside Terien. "He has a hard head," he joked.

"I heard that," Makhani mumbled, lifting one hand in an attempt to touch his forehead.

"Don't touch," Terien admonished, catching his hand and gently pushing it back down. "You're concussed. Just lie there quietly and be a good boy."

Sitting back on his haunches, Terien removed his outer tunic and laid it over Makhani to keep him warm. Elek also removed his and folded it into a wad. He gently lifted Makhani's head and placed the folded tunic underneath.

Terien sighed and looked at Elek. "We can't leave him here alone."

"You go. Find Aurori. I'll stay with him," Elek said.

Terien smiled and slapped Elek's shoulder. "Wishing we'd left you behind on the shore yet?"

Elek grinned. "Wouldn't have missed this for anything," he said with a laugh. His expression became grave. "Go. Just be careful."

"You, too. There're still two guards out here somewhere. Maybe more," Terien cautioned.

They clasped each other's wrists, then Terien leaned over Makhani. "You have to stay awake, Makhani. Keep talking to Elek. Sing for all I care, just don't you dare go to sleep. You hear me?"

Makhani gave him a frail smile. "Oh, goody. I get to sing for Elek. What a nice turn of events."

Giving Makhani's chest a quick pat, Terien rose and nodded once to Elek before he hefted his sword in one hand and an energy weapon in the other and stole away between the trees, intent on finding Aurori and the treacherous Director Maxen.

Chapter Twenty One

Maxen was pacing nervously back and forth behind Aurori who was sitting on an overturned plant pot, a beatific smile on her lips since hearing a man's angry roar echo through the bay several minutes ago. Until then she had been filled with worry and anguish, her stomach in knots as her imagination ran wild with images of Terien and the others staging a breakaway from the guards and ending up wounded or worse. Now, the worry was still there but a shining ray of hope had started to untie the knots in her gut, for she had recognized the angry roar as Elek's booming voice.

Casting a glance back at Maxen who had given up trying to contact his men outside and was now on the verge of a panic attack, Aurori eyed the long wooden handle of the gardening implement propped against the table just a few steps to the right and back, mentally choreographing a way to get at it. Unfortunately, Maxen was in her way at the moment. Cursing as he coughed and sputtered, he desperately needed another dose of his medication but hadn't had the foresight to bring it with him.

Aurori was about to chance making a grab for the gardening tool when the trees to the right of the path shook a bit.

Maxen immediately grabbed Aurori from behind and she gasped when his arm tightened around her upper chest as he forced her to her feet. He pressed the muzzle of his weapon to her side.

"Who's there?" he demanded loudly.

Aurori didn't know whether to laugh or cry when Terien stepped out from the trees, his own weapon leveled at them. His face was flushed and his dark bangs hung limply, making it clear that it had been a struggle to reach her. His tunic was missing, too, leaving him in only his black undershirt. Wondering if he was alone or whether the others were lying in wait behind the bushes, Aurori stubbornly refused to consider any other scenario.

"You!" Maxen hissed.

"Let her go." Terien's eyes were steel as he glared at Maxen across the distance between them. "It's over," he said, knowing full well that wasn't true. There were at least two guards somewhere out there and he had no doubt they would eventually show themselves, but he hoped to bluff Maxen into releasing Aurori before they did.

Only the sound of Maxen's labored breathing underscored the tense silence. Terien couldn't fire on Maxen without hitting Aurori, and Maxen couldn't fire on either one without leaving himself open to attack from the other.

His eyes darting from tree to tree in search of one of his guards, Maxen was just beginning to loosen his hold on Aurori when he caught a hint of movement off to Terien's left. His eyes didn't linger on the spot, but Terien's concentrated study of Maxen's face was such that the Director of Merani Base might as well have shouted and pointed at his guard.

Terien dived for the safety of the trees just as a beam of energy lanced out, searing through the space he had just occupied. Rolling into a crouch, he returned fire in the direction the shot had originated and missed hearing the approach of the second guard because of the whine from the weapon. The same man who had attacked Makhani, the one whose weapon Maxen had appropriated, lunged at him from the side.

Terien went down hard and the energy weapon flew from his hand, ending up in a nearby stand of bushes. He still had hold of his sword, but it was useless in close quarters. Letting it go, he brought his hand up and planted it on his attacker's face, forcing him back far enough so he could wriggle free his other arm which had been pinned between them when they landed. Shifting to grab either side of the man's head, Terien gave his attacker a head butt that sent him rolling away, but both quickly kicked to their feet and charged each other. Coming together with bone-jarring force, they began to wrestle back and forth while the other guard now rose from his crouch, smiling as he watched the show.

Meanwhile, with his arm firmly in place around Aurori's chest, Maxen was backing them away from the fight when Aurori noticed that his weapon had wavered away from her side and was now loosely aimed in the direction of the fight. Sinking her teeth into his forearm with as much force as she could muster, she was rewarded by Maxen's howl of pain. He flung her away with more force that she had anticipated and she stumbled over a potted plant. Cartwheeling over it, she tumbled to a stop right where she had hoped to. Snatching up the gardening tool, she sprung to her feet and whirled it in an arc as she would a quarterstaff, snapping Maxen's wrist like a dry twig. He toppled to the ground, hitting with enough force to jar the weapon from his numb fingers and send it bouncing out of reach.

His body racked by another coughing fit and holding his broken wrist to his chest, Maxen still had the determination to reach his weapon and was scrabbling towards it on elbows and knees. Stepping lightly past him, Aurori scooped the weapon from the floor and held it on Maxen, a triumphant smile lighting her face until Terien's primal howl split the air. Mistaking his cry for one of pain, she whirled around in time to see Terien deliver a flying kick to his opponent's head, sending him falling one way and his attacker the other, but she failed to notice the other guard now emerging from his hiding spot, weapon already drawn and aimed at her. Intent on ending the fight, Aurori turned her weapon on Terien's attacker and fired on him, hitting him with her first volley by pure chance.

"Aurori, get down!" Terien yelled.

Time slowed to a crawl as Aurori automatically hurled herself to the ground. Even as she fell, she could feel the crackle of hot energy shoot past her and was dimly aware of Maxen's agonized cry. The beam intended for Aurori struck him mid-chest as he was rising to make a grab for her during her distraction. His already weakened body seized and convulsed horribly under the onslaught of the energy discharge.

Managing to maintain her grip on the weapon in her hand when she fell, Aurori now fired round after round on the remaining guard, her hands shaking. One shot finally found its mark as the guard was desperately ducking and weaving in his attempt to get away, sending him plowing head first into a wooden table filled with dirt. He shuddered once and lay still.

Out of breath and trembling after his fight, Terien got to his feet and pressed an arm against his aching ribs as he turned worried eyes to Aurori who was leaning over Director Maxen and feeling for a pulse at the base of his throat.

"Are you okay?" Terien asked, already moving towards her.

Her expression shifting with her conflicting emotions, Aurori pushed to her feet and half ran, half stumbled into Terien's arms. Catching her up into a fierce embrace, they silently stood in each other's arms, tired and breathless.

"Oh, Terien! I was so afraid," Aurori whispered, tears brimming in her eyes as she leaned away from him without taking her arms from around his waist. Her expression suddenly crumbled and the tears spilled over as she buried her face against his shoulder once more. "He's dead," she said, her voice hollow.

Terien looked to where Maxen lay and sighed. He ran his hand down the back of Aurori's head, catching up her braid. "I hate to sound cold-hearted, but he got what he deserved, Aurori. He's been holding the whole population of Merani Base hostage for almost thirty years. And he wasn't planning on sending me and the others back to the surface. He was planning on killing us."

Aurori lifted her head, a chill running down her spine.

"I'll tell you about it later," he promised, bringing her braid forward and letting it fall. As he did, he caught sight of something unexpected hanging around her neck. His expression flickered between confusion and disbelief as he reached out and delicately lifted the cylinder between thumb and forefinger.

Aurori followed Terien's gaze downward and the blood seemed to drain from her head and into her feet when she found her key in his fingers. "I... I wanted to tell you," she stammered. "I was planning on... I was going to tell you. I just couldn't... find the right moment," she finished, her voice fading to a whisper as he let the key fall from his fingers and released her from his embrace. The look of astonishment and betrayal on his face was heartbreaking. "I'm so sorry," she murmured, bowing her head.

Terien turned away and looked up at the ceiling, rubbing a hand across his face. "I thought for a moment it might be Quatina's key," he said hoarsely. "How blind I've been. How...

unobservant." He sighed and shook his head. "There were times I suspected you might be the other Chosen, but I kept telling myself that if you were, you would have told me." He looked sideways at her and gave a short, self-deprecating laugh. "I must have looked pretty stupid to you in Glaybor, inviting you along as the representative for Eristea. Bet that was worth a laugh."

"It wasn't like that at all," Aurori protested. She took a hesitant step towards him and put a hand on his back. "I was… afraid."

"Afraid? Of what?" he asked incredulously, spreading his hands in a helpless gesture as he turned to face her.

Aurori self-consciously lifted her cylinder and nervously fiddled it between her fingers. All the things she had planned to say, all the reasons she had held for not telling him – they sounded so lame to her now. If only he hadn't found out by accident like this.

"All the reasons don't make sense anymore. Not even to me. I just didn't want… anyone to know. In case I decided to leave the group. Then I decided to stay, but was afraid that if you knew, you might insist on sending an escort with me."

"I would never have done that to you, Aurori. You should have known that," he said, bitter disappointment in his tone.

"I know, I know!" she said miserably. "And the longer I kept the secret, the harder it was to find a way to tell you." She couldn't even meet his eyes now. "I'm so sorry," she whispered again.

Terien closed his eyes and stood hands on hips for a second, but then his eyes flew open. "Damn it!" Terien exclaimed, angry at himself for letting himself lose focus on where they were and what was going on. He grabbed Aurori's hand, ignoring her gasp of surprise as he pulled her along behind him and broke into a run. "We'll talk about this later," he said over his shoulder. "Right now Makhani needs you."

"What… what happened to Makhani?" Aurori asked, struggling to keep up with him.

"Head wound. I think he has a concussion. When I left him with Elek he seemed in pretty good shape, but you'll have to be the judge of that." He glanced back at her. "You might want to hide that key again," he said flatly.

As Aurori jogged behind him, she caught the bouncing key in her hand and considered his words. The Observer was supposed to keep her identity a secret to allow her to move freely through the populations of the cities she encountered, but she had taken the decree too seriously and had included her friends in it. Her heart sank at the thought. Friends. Could she still call them that once they knew, or would they feel as betrayed as Terien? No matter. She was through hiding from them.

She let the key fall free to bounce against her chest once more.

When they finally came across Makhani and Elek, Makhani was still awake and singing softly to himself while Elek sat at his side, his face awash with a look of long suffering. Elek jumped to his feet and grabbed Aurori up in a bear hug the moment she and Terien appeared, but he quickly let her go so she could examine Makhani.

Clasping Terien's hand and shaking it vigorously, Elek gave him a wicked grin. "Glad to see you're both okay, but I gotta tell you – I'm gonna kill you for suggesting that Makhani sing for me!"

Terien laughed. "What's wrong? He has a better voice than you?"

"Yeah, he does!" Elek grumbled.

Aurori leaned over Makhani and slowly lifted a corner of the blood soaked handkerchief that was still plastered to his head wound. She smiled down at him. "Well, you must be okay if you're driving Elek crazy," she teased him.

Makhani returned a feeble smile. "Tell that to my headache," he said, then raised a hand to catch Aurori's cylinder as it swung past his face. He studied it for a second, then looked up and saw Aurori's apprehensive expression. "Chosen?"

"Your hand-to-eye coordination seems fine, anyway," she said without humor, gently removing her key from his hand. She sighed. "Yes. I'm the other Chosen."

Elek's head turned so fast that Terien was sure it would twist right off.

"Chosen? You're the other Chosen?" he asked, his voice rising in pitch. When Aurori nodded her confirmation, he laughed and folded his arms across his chest. "I just knew it! Man! Wait until everyone hears about *this*!"

Terien blew out an exasperated breath. "Can we discuss this later? There's a revolution going on just outside, in case you've forgotten," he said, stooping to remove his tunic from Makhani and slipping it on.

"It's been pretty quiet out there for a while now," Elek informed Terien. He helped Aurori get Makhani to his feet, then picked up his tunic and shook it out, frowning. "Hey, you wrinkled it!" he complained to Makhani as he put it on.

"Don't fuss. At least I kept it warm for you," Makhani smirked. His knees suddenly buckled and Elek lunged forward, catching him up into his arms.

"He's not going to be able to walk out of here, Elek," Aurori said. "You'll have to carry him."

"This is embarrassing," Makhani protested. "I feel like a child!"

"Shut up and enjoy the ride," Elek growled.

Terien was beginning to lose patience. "Argue later! Come on. Let's find Duncan and the others."

There was a tense moment when they arrived at the main doors to find that several people were spilling out onto the catwalk above, and Terien thought for a moment that they would have to fight their way free until Rannoch and Jos appeared at the rail.

"Well, if ye four aren't a sight fer sore eyes!" Rannoch called down, waving. "Hey, what's Makhani doin' gettin' a free ride?" he yelled, his teasing words warring with the concern in his voice.

"He's fine," Terien called back before Makhani could make a barbed retort. "What's happening out there?"

"I'll tell ye what's happenin', lad! The rebellion is over! We were coming to see if ye needed a hand, but it looks like ye've got things under control."

"Where's Director Maxen?" Jos wanted to know.

"At the back of the dome. He's dead, Jos. Accidentally shot by one of his own guards," Terien reported. "There're three guards in here, too. Unconscious but alive."

At Terien's grim announcement, several of Jos's compatriots cheered and took off down the stairs at a jog, but Jos just leaned

heavily against the catwalk's rail and closed his eyes for a moment. It was finally over.

Inhaling deeply to clear his thoughts, Jos opened his eyes and pointed down towards the main doors. "There's a red button on the panel in the wall over there. Press it and the doors will unlock and open for you," he instructed.

"See ye downstairs!" Rannoch told them, waving as he disappeared after Jos through the doorway at the top of the catwalk.

Terien went to the lock panel by the door and pressed the red button as instructed. With a sigh, the doors opened to reveal several people clustered around just outside, including one very welcome and familiar face.

"You're alive!" Duncan cried out happily, throwing his arms wide.

Unabashed, the two men hugged and slapped each other on the back. When they stepped apart, they held each other at arm's length.

"I have a lot to tell you," Duncan said.

"Me, too," Terien replied tiredly, casting a look back at Aurori.

Aurori looked away, and as her eyes fell on a familiar dark-skinned form lying unmoving behind a couple of overturned tables, her mortification evaporated. "Quatina!" she cried, running to her friend's side and falling to her knees.

"It's okay, Aurori," Duncan assured her quickly. He knelt beside her and reached out to touch Quatina's cheek. "She was hit by one of those energy blasts, but Naneve says she'll be fine in a few hours."

"Who's Naneve?" Terien asked from behind them.

Duncan gave him a broad smile and stood up. He caught hold of Terien's elbow and turned him to face a petite older woman who was just now approaching them.

The top of her head only came to the middle of Terien's chest and she was pleasantly plump. Wide-set brown eyes burned with intelligence from beneath wispy strands of gray hair that she was even now trying to tuck back into her bun. Her warm smile instantly told Terien that he would like her.

"This is Naneve," Duncan introduced. "Jos's mother and the

mastermind behind the rebellion."

Stunned to find that such a dainty little woman was responsible for a successful overthrow of such an entrenched government, Terien nonetheless gave her a small bow. "A pleasure, madam. Though I am puzzled by the brevity of it, my congratulations on the success of your rebellion."

The corners of Naneve's eyes crinkled with delight. "The fight went out of the guards once they realized that they were facing more than only a few armed citizens. My people have reported that many of the guards simply gave themselves up, saying they weren't being paid enough to risk their lives."

Duncan chuckled. "That and they didn't appreciate having to fight while their fearless leader hid himself away."

Naneve turned back to Terien. "It's a relief to find you alive and well. And an honor to meet you, Chosen."

"Just call me Terien," he told her with a smile. "I would say that you and I have a great deal to talk about."

Naneve nodded, giving him an impish smile that took years off her. "That we do, but I think it can wait. I don't know about you, but it's far past my bedtime and I'm exhausted." Her smile faded and she sighed heavily, suddenly looking much older once more. "We still have many wounded to tend to before we can even think about rest, though. We were fortunate that Maxen did order his men to use setting one on their weapons. If not for that, we'd be facing a good deal more than a few broken bones and lacerations."

The men of Jos's group who had gone into the dome were just now emerging from the trees, carrying Director Maxen's body between them. A hush fell over those gathered as they stopped by Naneve who placed her hand on the Director's chest and bowed her head. She closed her eyes for a moment, silently offering a prayer to the Maker for Maxen's soul, then withdrew her hand and nodded for the men to carry Maxen away before turning back to Terien.

"My only regret is that you were forced to become a part of this," Naneve told Terien.

"That was Maxen's doing, not yours. You have nothing to regret on that account."

Naneve gave him an apologetic smile and bowed her head. "I know you must be tired, but I could really use your help."

He'd been running on adrenaline for so long that he hadn't given it a thought, but it had to be the middle of night by now. He had to stifle a yawn at the thought. "Just tell me what I can do to help."

"Young man, you're going to regret having said that," Naneve said with a quiet laugh.

Chapter Twenty Two

It had taken hours to get things settled down. The medical bay in particular had been a scene of controlled chaos as the less injured were shuffled into the nearby labs where extra beds were assembled to make room for the more seriously wounded. Aurori had been pressed into service early on, handling the lacerations and more serious injuries while the fleet of medics Brennai had trained tended the broken bones and minor wounds.

Without credible medical skills, Elek and Duncan had been put to work setting up a secure detention area in one part of the laboratory dome for Maxen's former security guards, while Terien and Rannoch helped maintain order as the non-combatants and uninjured were ushered back to their homes in an attempt to get everyone accounted for and off the streets.

The main dome's lights had just come on for the day as called for by their automatic cycle when Elek and Duncan had finished securing the last of the prisoners, including Garel who sported a black eye after Jos's punch. Upon learning of his father's death, Garel had clammed up and refused to talk to anyone or answer any questions. He sat on the floor in the corner of the cell he had been placed in, hugging his knees to his chest and rocking back and forth, a vacant look in his eyes. Without his father to give him direction, he was quickly sinking into a deep depression as the magnitude of facing a life of imprisonment played on his mind.

With nothing to be done about Garel for the moment, Duncan and Elek left him and the other prisoners under the watchful eyes of the Merani citizens who had helped create the jail, and made their way to the medical bay where Duncan had a happy reunion with Quatina who had awoken from her artificial sleep.

Smiling so hard that his face felt as though it would split, Duncan caught Quatina up and hugged her to him. "Lady, you sure scared the hell out of me!"

Laughing, Quatina threw her arms around Duncan's neck and pulled his head down, kissing him full on the mouth. Surprised, he nonetheless returned her kiss, feeling for a moment as though they were the only two people in the world until Elek cleared his throat loudly.

Stepping apart, Duncan blushed crimson while Quatina shyly held a hand to her mouth to cover her embarrassment. Everyone in the room was smiling at them.

"It's about time you two got together," Elek said, slapping Duncan's back. "But enough of the mushy stuff, Duncan. Tell her about Aurori!"

Duncan's eyes flicked to where Aurori sat on the edge of Makhani's bed at the other end of the room, just now finding the time to seal the wound on his forehead. He looked much better now that the blood had been washed from his hair, but he was obviously still feeling groggy and his eyes were narrowing into sleepy slits despite Aurori's ministrations.

"I don't know. Maybe she'd rather tell Quatina herself," Duncan said, his eyebrows rising in question.

Quatina looked back and forth between Elek, Duncan and Aurori for a moment, then understanding lit her face. "Aurori has finally revealed herself as the Observer?" she asked excitedly.

Duncan and Elek exchanged a glance, looking crestfallen.

"You mean, you knew?" asked Duncan.

Quatina's chin came up and she grinned at them. "I am her best friend," she stated proudly.

Duncan yawned. "Figures."

Naneve suddenly bustled into the room, took one look at Duncan and Elek and planted her hands on her hips, glaring at them. "I've been looking for you two," she said. "You've done a fine job converting the labs into temporary holding cells and I'm very grateful, but it's high time you got some rest." She stalked forward and caught each of them by the elbow, the unexpected strength bundled into her compact frame catching them by surprise as she pulled them along towards the door.

Casting helpless looks at Quatina who giggled and shook her head in amazement, they mutely followed Naneve from the medical bay and soon found themselves outside the door to the room they had been given by Director Maxen.

"Naneve, we can sleep later," Duncan protested when she opened the door and tapped her foot impatiently, waiting for them to enter. "There's still a lot to do!"

"None of which needs doing by the Chosen or his companions. Except the Healer, of course, and I fully intend to make sure she gets some rest as soon as she's finished tending the serious cases. Your help has been invaluable, but the people of Merani need to learn to rely on themselves if we're going to survive," Naneve replied. "Now, I've already sent Terien and Rannoch off to get some sleep. Are you going to argue with me or do I have to ask Aurori for a sleeping potion for you two?"

Elek grinned at Naneve and sketched a bow. "Madam, I can see now how you successfully led a rebellion. You mothered them through it!"

Naneve returned his grin. "Never underestimate the power of a mother figure," she laughed, then turned on her heel and strode off.

Laughing, Duncan and Elek entered their room and shut the door.

Hours later, feeling much better after a good sleep and a shower, Terien left his room and walked over to the open area in the middle of the main dome. Intending to kill some time by taking a stroll through the park before his meeting with Naneve, Terien caught sight of a familiar figure sitting on one of the benches. Knees drawn up to her chest, Aurori was sitting with her back to him, head resting on the back of the bench as she watched the overhead view of the ocean and its ever-moving display of life. She was still wearing the silk outfit from dinner the night before and both the skirt and blouse were rumpled and dirt stained. He stopped and just watched her for a minute, hands stuffed deep in his pockets.

All through the night, even while directing people to their homes and assisting with the wounded, his mind had kept coming back to that one moment in time when he had discovered who Aurori was. He had been angry and hurt to think that most of what she had told him about herself and her life in Eristea was an elaborate lie designed to conceal her identity, and it left him feeling like he didn't know her at all now. It had felt like the person he had grown so fond of and cared so deeply for had ceased to exist at that moment.

It wasn't until Naneve had ushered him to his room and he had lain on his bed, staring at the ceiling for what seemed like hours, that it had occurred to him that Aurori hadn't changed at all; only his perception of her had. Peasant Healer or Chosen, she was still the same person. Only the details of how she had lived were different. Her personality, her intelligence, and the charm of her presence hadn't changed, and he had seen the proof of it himself when he caught a glimpse of her tending the injured in the medical bay. Her warmth and caring had not been diminished, nor had her gentle wit or natural grace, and he had found his feelings of betrayal melt away. All he was left with was a vague uneasiness about her reasons for not telling him. He needed to know if they were the truth or whether there was more to it than what she had told him in the garden dome.

Removing his hands from his pockets, Terien steeled himself by taking a steadying breath and strolled in her direction. At his approach, Aurori's head lifted from the back of the bench and she turned to look at him. There were dark circles under her eyes and she looked totally worn out. Unsmiling, she averted her eyes and seemed to shrink even further into the wooden bench.

"Are you okay?" Terien asked.

"Terrible. Thanks for asking," Aurori muttered tiredly.

Terien chuckled in spite of himself. "Seriously, you look... terrible. Didn't Naneve hustle you off to bed, too?"

"She did, but I couldn't sleep," Aurori admitted. Her posture reflecting her inner anguish, she hugged her arms around her knees, squeezing into a tight ball. "I couldn't stop thinking about how close Maxen came to ruining the Final Reunification because of me. How close he came to killing you." She let out a shaky breath. "And I couldn't stop thinking about how stupid I had been, not telling you who I am." She hung her head dejectedly. "I don't blame you for being angry."

Terien took a seat on the bench beside her, sitting on the edge with his hands gripping the front of the seat on either side of his knees. "I was so angry with you. And hurt. You said you were afraid that I might have tried to force you to stay or send an escort with you. I can see where you might have worried about that at first." He scuffed the toe of his boot at a piece of grass growing through a crack in the hard surface of the walkway. "What I don't understand is why you didn't say something later, after you got to know me better."

Tears welled in her already red-rimmed eyes and her words spilled out in a rush. "I don't know. Part of me liked having everyone think I was just a peasant Healer. I liked being treated no differently than anyone else and I was afraid that if you knew – if the others knew – they might stop treating me like a friend and act differently towards me. Like they do with Sahala."

Terien relaxed his grip on the bench and let out a breath he hadn't even been aware of holding. The truth wasn't as bad as he had feared it might be. In fact, it was somehow charming to find that Aurori was a little insecure.

"Like Sahala," he echoed. "Not likely unless you start ordering everyone around and demanding that someone sleep at your feet," he said with a lopsided grin.

Aurori gave a little laugh, but the sound was almost mirthless.

Sobering, Terien cocked his head to the side. "Would it be safe to assume that you're not just a peasant Healer, then?" He paused for the span of a heartbeat. "Princess?"

Aurori nodded miserably. "First daughter of King Olen of Eristea," she confirmed.

"Now *I* feel foolish," Terien said. "My father visited Eristea eight years ago, as I'm sure you know. He talked for days about King Olen and his three daughters, but I wasn't interested at the time. I was seventeen and couldn't see any point in paying attention to a kingdom we had no plans of opening trade with. I even refused to accompany him." He made a vaguely apologetic gesture. "I think he mentioned your name, but I didn't put two and two together when we met."

"At least you didn't lie like I did," she said in a small, breaking voice. "What you must think of me! I can't believe you're even talking to me after what I've done!"

"Look, Aurori," he said, placing a hand on her knee, "I can't say that I'm happy you didn't tell me sooner, but – I know now. And I want you to know that I'm not angry anymore. Or hurt. Just a little confused." He shrugged one shoulder. "I feel like I know you, yet I feel that I don't know you. Does that make any sense?"

Aurori nodded and squeezed her eyes shut against the tears building up in her eyes, unable to speak past the constriction in her chest. If anything, Terien's easy acceptance and forgiveness made her feel that much worse, and she covered her face with one hand, a sorrowful sob escaping despite her best effort to hold it back.

Confused and dismayed by Aurori's seemingly excessively emotional reaction, Terien found himself wrapping his arms around her. He pulled her to him, resting her head against his chest as he leaned back against the bench. She sagged against him, her body shaking with silent sobs. As he thought about it, though, Terien realized that Aurori was still running on adrenaline, hadn't slept, probably hadn't eaten, and had spent hours tending the injured of Merani Base, all after having faced permanent imprisonment and the potential death of her friends at the hands of a madman. He hadn't thought much of it when she said it a minute ago, but she also seemed to feel she was responsible for Maxen's treachery.

"You can't blame yourself for what Maxen tried to do, Aurori," he whispered. "No more than I blame you for being afraid of revealing your identity."

Her hand clutched the material of his tunic. "If I hadn't been with you, none of this would have happened," she whimpered. "Maybe I shouldn't have come with you at all."

Terien sighed and caressed her back. "After I said I wouldn't have tried to force you to stay…" he muttered to himself. "Aurori, I really do think we're stronger together than we are apart. As for Maxen and his twisted plans – well, you were planning on coming to Merani even if you'd been alone, right?'

Aurori nodded mutely.

"If you had, you would have ended up down here as a permanent guest. The revolution would still have gone ahead, either before, after or during my visit, and who knows what would have happened." He took her by the shoulders and held her away. "Who's to say it wasn't better this way? We're all alive, you're free and so are the citizens of Merani. If you keep thinking about the what-ifs and might-have-beens, you'll drive yourself crazy." Placing a finger under her chin, Terien tilted her head up until she met his eyes. "You're exhausted and not thinking clearly. I know. Before Naneve herded me off to get some sleep, everything looked so bad I wasn't sure how I was going to face you or the rest of the journey, but once I had some sleep everything looked a lot brighter. It will for you, too. I promise."

Aurori wiped at her eyes with the back of her hand and took a shuddering breath. "Maybe you're right."

Smiling, Terien pulled her to her feet and tucked her hand in the crook of his elbow. "When the guards came for us at dinner, I promised you that everything would be fine," he reminded her as he escorted her to her room. "And I always keep my promises."

Leaving Aurori at the door of her room, Terien hurried off in search of the office once occupied by Director Maxen, stopping only long enough to ask directions from a passer-by.

Finding the door open, he strode in and took note that Duncan and Jos were already seated in front of the desk, as were two other men that had been introduced during the course of the night as being two of the rebellion's spies within Maxen's police force – Farnash, whose large, callused hands looked better suited to the back-breaking work of the gardens than the spy business, and Dern, a mousy man whose talents as an engineer had been employed in rigging the minisub for the planned "accident". Naneve herself was seated behind the large desk, now cleared of all Maxen's things, looking like she belonged there.

"Sorry I'm late," Terien apologized as he took the empty seat between Duncan and Jos. "Healer trouble," he said in a low voice and got a knowing look from Duncan.

Naneve smiled and dipped her head in acknowledgment as she leaned her forearms on the desk. "I would like to start by saying how much we appreciate your assistance in overthrowing Maxen and paving the way for freedom and hope to thrive once again in Merani Base," she said, her eyes taking in both Terien and Duncan. "I also want you to know that I have already met with the leaders of the resistance cells and that we have decided on a representative to accompany you to Quayvern." Her chubby face lit with a proud smile and she looked to Jos. "My son was unanimously voted as that representative."

Terien offered a pleased smile of his own and extended his hand to the dark haired young man. "Congratulations, Jos. Welcome to the party."

Beaming, Jos bowed his head in humble acceptance and shook Terien's hand. "It's an honor."

Naneve cleared her throat. "I understand that Jos has already given you a brief history of Merani Base and Director Maxen's rule. Now, let me fill you in on the details about the rebellion and our plans for the future."

Gathering her thoughts, Naneve clasped her hands before her and took a deep breath. "The failed coup attempt three years ago was spearheaded by my husband, Arthinian. He and his fellow workers in garden bay one, thought it would be possible to overthrow Maxen's guards by using the simple gardening tools they were allowed and staged an attack, hoping to take the guard's weapons and continue on to the Director's office to confront Maxen. But the guards panicked and before Maxen could order them to make sure their weapons were set to the lowest setting, my husband and several others were killed." She shook her head sadly and wiped away the single tear that was coursing down her cheek. "My husband was an idealistic man," she said with a fond smile. "The idea of overthrowing Maxen was on everyone's mind, but without proper weapons and the support of the whole population, his coup was doomed to fail. I tried to talk him out of it, but he wouldn't listen," she said softly, her voice breaking with emotion.

"Mom and I didn't want his death to have been in vain and decided to take up his cause," Jos put in, taking over for Naneve. "This time, we planned a rebellion that would include every able person and every dome of Merani. We knew that our only chance of success would be to arm ourselves, so we started by convincing several of our most trusted compatriots to present themselves to Maxen as traitors who wanted to join his hired police force," he said, indicating Farnash and Dern with a nod.

Dern smiled and crossed one leg over the other. "It took two years of waiting, but the time finally came when Maxen trusted us turncoats enough to let us in on some of the secrets of his operation and gave us increasing responsibilities, including access to the energy weapons."

"When the Sky Lord came to Merani Base to announce the impending arrival of the Chosen, we knew it was time to act," Naneve continued, pushing away from the desk and coming to stand at the side of Jos's chair. "The spies on the police force started tampering with the energy weapons, forcing Maxen to discard them as being inoperative. Once out of circulation, instead of destroying the weapons, they would be retrieved, repaired and hidden away for the day they would be needed. It was a slow and dangerous process and took longer than we anticipated, resulting in the delay in staging the rebellion." She put a hand on her son's shoulder. "Jos can tell you – I felt we weren't ready even when word came two weeks ago that you would be arriving shortly," Naneve told Terien. "When we heard about Maxen's plan to engineer a minisub accident and kill you, however, we knew we had no choice but to proceed with the rebellion, ready or not. The rest, as it's said, is history."

Terien leaned forward. "That you staged the rebellion for our benefit even when you felt you weren't fully prepared is humbling. We're eternally in your debt for what you've done for us."

Farnash rose from his seat and went to stand behind Naneve, putting a hand on her shoulder. His fondness of her was transparent. "I think I speak for everyone when I say that we're actually in your debt, Chosen. It was because of the threat to your life and the lives of your companions that the people rallied so strongly. I know you didn't plan on this happening, but we really believe that it was your presence that inspired the people. Not only was their own freedom at stake now, but the future of Primus."

Embarrassed by Farnash's kind words, Terien smiled and immediately changed the subject. "Speaking of the future, what do you have planned?"

"For one thing, we're already making plans to build a town out on the shore," Naneve said. "Aurori has confirmed that the stiffness, bone pains and high susceptibility to fractures that is so prevalent among our population is due to a lack of a certain vitamin in our bodies, caused in great part by having been shielded from the suns for so long. Fresh air and sunshine are what the people need most, and the fleet of minisubs Maxen had kept in storage are about to get a good workout, shuttling people back and forth to the surface." With obvious delight, Naneve warmed to the topic. "The citizens of Merani will be free to travel between the new town and Merani, while the people who had been abducted to work in the gardens will be given the choice between returning to their former homes or staying on if they wish."

"Only Maxen's former guards present a bit of a problem," Farnash said. "We agree that they should pay for their part in holding an entire city captive for so long, but we don't have proper facilities for keeping them incarcerated. Besides, after being held captive under the ocean for so long ourselves, we're not happy with the notion of denying even our former captors the opportunity to go outside."

After giving it a bit of thought, a slow smile spread across Terien's face. "The town of Mayquire is just a little up the coast to the north and is allied with Kaethos. The former guards could be shuttled there and then transferred to one of the logging camps in the area. One of my men could accompany you and explain the situation to the authorities."

Naneve exchanged looks with Farnash and Dern. "I would hate to pawn our problems off on someone else," she said, shaking her head.

Terien laughed. "Hardly. Finding workers has always been difficult for the camps. They'd be more than happy to have an infusion of fresh workers. I know. They were more than happy to accept the four men who had captured Aurori and planned to sell her off as a slave."

Dern sat forward abruptly. "What's this about the Healer?" he asked with interest.

It was here that Terien told them about how he had met

Aurori and what had happened to her abductors. In turn, Farnash offered a startling revelation.

"When Brennai died and Maxen realized that he couldn't survive without a Healer to keep his lung disease under control, he instructed his surface operatives to put out a handsome reward for anyone capturing a Healer," Farnash told them. "Maxen knew from Brennai that the Healers frequently went on journeys to other lands and hoped someone would come across such a Healer and be willing to cash in on the reward."

"He couldn't just go to Eristea to ask for a Healer's help because he didn't want anyone to find out about what he was doing down here," Dern remarked with a shrug that said he didn't quite follow Maxen's reasoning.

"Twisted thinking," Duncan commented, then turned to Terien. "It looks like Aurori was about to end up a permanent resident of Merani at the time we first met her."

Terien nodded thoughtfully. "If Maxen had a network of operatives on the surface, I imagine you'll be hearing from some of them. What do you plan to do when that happens?"

Naneve heaved a sigh and shrugged. "We haven't thought that far ahead yet, to be honest. We'll just have to play things very carefully and see what we can learn from them as they contact us."

"There's a lot to do, that's for certain," Jos said. He stood and looked to his mother. "Are you sure you don't need me to stay here?"

Naneve stood on her toes to give her son a hug, tears suddenly brimming in her eyes. "You know I'd like nothing better than to have you stay with me, but you and I both know that you can best serve our people by representing us at the Final Reunification."

Terien and Duncan also stood now.

Pulling away from the embrace with her son, Naneve wiped away her tears with the back of one hand and faced Terien. "You must be anxious to move out and continue on to Quayvern. As soon as you're ready, I'll have two minisubs ready to take you back to the surface."

"Thank you, Naneve. For everything," Terien said, holding his hand out to her.

Naneve ignored his outstretched hand and gave him a motherly hug instead. "You just take care of yourselves. And I'm not only talking about Jos." She stepped away from him and gave him a stern look. "Just promise that you'll call me from Quayvern."

"I promise," Terien told her, thinking that he would rather do anything but disappoint this powerhouse of a woman.

Chapter Twenty Three

Terien had planned to leave Merani Base shortly after his meeting with Naneve, but changed his mind and ended up staying another night when he and Quatina checked in on Aurori late in the afternoon. Utterly exhausted after her ordeal, they could barely rouse her and decided it might be best to leave her to her much needed rest. The men on the shore weren't expecting them back for another day, anyway, and there were still many interesting places to explore in Merani.

Accompanied by everyone except Aurori and Makhani (who was still zonked out in the medical bay), Terien was given a leisurely tour of the rest of Merani Base by Jos, who was all too happy to spend some time getting acquainted with some of his new traveling companions before heading to the surface. With distinct pride in the accomplishments of his people, Jos showed them how they had managed to keep their under-water home functional after so many long years, and took special care in explaining how the base's power plant was operated and maintained, explaining as well that smaller versions of the fusion generator were used in vehicles such as the minisubs and hovercraft.

The concept of fusion was clearly baffling to Terien and his group, but they caught on enough to become excited when Jos told them that a fusion generator produced energy in much the same way that the suns did, and that all the Hidden Cities had such generators.

"So that's what they meant," Duncan said, his tone charged with excitement. "The Cohalili must have had to leave Alatesh because their power generator failed. Their 'small sun died'."

"That's one mystery solved," Terien remarked with a smile aimed at Quatina.

"Yes! I can hardly wait to tell my people of this," Quatina said, breathless with wonder as she stared down into the huge sunken room, unable to take her eyes off the pulsating colors swirling across the banks of machines far below the walkway they stood on. "At last we know the true reason our ancestors left the Hidden Home – Alatesh."

Jos suddenly looked a little nervous. "You mean to tell me that the fusion generator at Alatesh failed?"

"Apparently so," Terien said. "Why?"

Jos chewed at his lower lip. "How long ago?"

Shrugging, Terien looked to Quatina for an answer.

"We are not certain anymore, but it was many generations ago," she said.

"Is something wrong?" Elek asked, concerned by the look of worry on Jos's face.

Hesitating over an answer, Jos looked down at the banks of machinery far below. "Not really, but I should tell Mom about this." He glanced at Terien. "There are records in our archives showing that Merani Base and Alatesh kept in communications contact with each other long after the comets fell, but that they suddenly lost contact. It was assumed that their communications gear malfunctioned. Now you're telling me that their generator failed." He shrugged one shoulder, trying to appear casual and not quite succeeding. "These generators were designed to last for a couple of thousand years, but if the one at Alatesh failed..." Jos said, his voice heavy with implied meaning.

A chilling thought that brought with it visions of being plunged into inky blackness at the bottom of the ocean.

Terien stubbornly shook the vision away. "We still don't know why the generator at Alatesh failed," he reminded everyone. "Maybe there was an accident or something."

Jos nodded absently. "You're right. And we monitor ours very closely." He laughed nervously and rubbed a hand through his hair. "I guess I'm just being paranoid after Maxen had Dern rig the generator on the minisub to fail."

"More than likely," Duncan agreed.

"Let's go. Mom should already be waiting with dinner ready," Jos said as he turned and led the way out of the generator room. Still, he cast a wary glance back at the banks of machines, making a mental note to have his mom ask that Dern examine the fusion generator very carefully.

Seated once more in the banquet room, this time in the company of Naneve and the other leaders of the rebellion and without a weapon anywhere in sight, Terien found that he still couldn't quite force himself to relax completely. Images of their last sojourn in the room were too fresh in his memory, and he could still see Aurori standing opposite from him, fear and uncertainty filling her green eyes with tears. He blinked and glanced around, noting that the other members of his group were apparently also having a similarly difficult time with being back in the banquet room. Duncan was holding Quatina's hand so tightly his knuckles were turning white, and Rannoch looked green around the gills. Only Elek seemed unaffected, but Terien knew better. The big man was good at hiding his discomfort, but his smile looked forced.

Exhaling slowly, Terien turned to Naneve and found her watching him with a look of apologetic concern. She gave him a smile and patted his hand, then stood.

"It seems to me that this room is far too formal for friends to share dinner and conversation," she said. "Might I suggest we move to the cafeteria in the main dome?"

Without fuss or commotion, everyone hastily agreed and exited the room, heading out into the main dome. As they walked, Terien slipped an arm around Naneve's shoulder and leaned close.

"How did you know?" he asked quietly.

"That you were feeling uncomfortable in the room you had been forcefully taken from?" Naneve huffed out a breath. "Motherly intuition."

Terien chuckled. "You're good."

Naneve glanced sideways at him and shook her head. "Silly boy. I have eyes, don't I? It was obvious how you and your people felt about being in the banquet room. I apologize for not considering it beforehand."

"Not your fault," Terien assured her. "Actually, I'm a little surprised by our reaction. You'd think that a hardened bunch like us wouldn't have given it a second thought."

Naneve put her arm around Terien's waist and chortled softy, scoffing at his statement. "Hardened my eye. You may be skilled warriors, but you're anything but hardened. No wonder you were selected as the Chosen. You have a keen mind and a soft heart. A good combination."

Blushing, Terien wisely declined to challenge her assessment of his character and simply followed her into the cafeteria.

Comfortable now that they were seated in simple surroundings, conversation flowed freely and stories were happily exchanged. Dinner was not quite the sumptuous feast it had been the night before, but no one seemed to notice, caught up as they were by the cathartic release of tension allowed by sharing their experiences with people who had intimate knowledge of their troubles.

The garble of voices fell silent in unison, however, when a man came running into the room, wild-eyed and breathless.

"Naneve! The communications panel in your office just came on! Someone's calling!"

Chairs clattered as Naneve and Farnash bolted to their feet, followed by Jos, Terien and Duncan. Dashing out of the room, they sprinted between the buildings and surged into Naneve's office, all crowding around the crackling communications panel.

"*Come in Merani Base. Do you read me*?" The voice was male and slightly distorted by static, but its clipped, precise enunciation made it clear enough to be understood.

For the first time since Terien had met her, Naneve was at a loss for what to do. She wrung her hands and stared at the panel as though it was about to jump up and bite her.

"He won't be expecting a woman's voice. I might scare him off," Naneve declared. Her hand lashed out and caught Farnash's arm, dragging him closer to the panel. "You answer. Be vague. Tell him Maxen is ill and that you took over for him."

"*Come in, Merani Base*," the voice said again, impatience now creeping into the man's tone.

Farnash swallowed hard and nodded, then pressed down on the transmit button. "Merani Base here."

There was a pause and one could almost imagine the person on the other end reacting in surprise to an unfamiliar voice.

"*Merani Base, I would like to speak to Director Maxen.*"

Farnash locked eyes with Naneve and activated the transceiver again. "This is security chief Farnash. Maxen has taken ill and I've taken over for him at the moment."

Another pause.

"*I see. Then let me speak to Garel.*"

"Garel's tied up at the moment," Farnash said, suppressing a smile at the wide-eyed looks he got for his ironic statement. "We had a bit of trouble last night and he's out making sure everything's settled. Nothing serious. Is there anything I can help you with, or shall I have him call you back?" he asked, hoping that such an invitation might allay any suspicions.

It seemed to work.

"*Trouble, you say? With… guests?*"

Eyebrows rose throughout the room.

"Yeah. Unwanted guests, at that," Farnash replied, warming to his part. "Look, let's quit dancing, shall we? I know all about Maxen's surface dealings. What do you want?"

The aristocratic voice took so long to respond that Farnash feared he might have gone too far and scared the guy off, but the panel still crackled with the sound of the open line.

"*I seriously doubt that you are privy to all of the Director's 'surface dealings' as you so quaintly refer to them,*" the man replied. "*However, I suspect that you know enough about Maxen's plans to tell me how his guests fared.*"

You could have heard a pin drop in the office.

"Who is this guy?" Jos whispered even though the man couldn't hear him unless Farnash held down the activation button.

"Why would Maxen tell someone on the surface about his plans?" Duncan wanted to know.

"We knew about Terien's arrival in advance," Naneve reminded them, then settled her gaze on Terien. "Maxen had to have had someone on the surface watching for you."

Farnash shushed them harshly and pressed the button down. "Oh yeah, I know all about them. My partner and I were responsible for making the arrangements," he said, putting some swaggering pride in his voice as he stalled for time. He released the button and raised his eyebrows at Terien. "Are you alive or dead?"

Terien's mind worked furiously. If he was declared dead they may never find out what this was about. Declared alive, the rest of the journey potentially became that much more dangerous. What if Maxen had a contingency plan in place? Still, he had to know who wanted him dead and why.

"Alive," Terien said quickly. "We escaped. Don't give him more than that, though."

"They escaped. Tricky devils, I can tell you…" Farnash was saying when the transmission was suddenly cut from the other end, plunging the office into cold silence.

Terien shivered. "So much for that. I was hoping he'd have more to say."

"Whoever he was, he was only interested in hearing whether or not Maxen's plan was a success or not," Farnash observed.

Naneve stepped in front of Terien and laid her palm on his chest. "Your mission is in danger."

"Not necessarily, Naneve. This guy might just have been curious to know how things turned out," he told her.

"No!" she said urgently. "It's more than that! Maxen would have just ordered him to call when he spotted you, not let him in on his plans for you. There's more to this, Terien. Someone on the surface wants you dead, which can only mean that they also want your mission to fail."

Naneve's hand slipped from his chest as Terien turned away and went to the communications panel, leaning one arm against the wall above it as he stared at the device and considered what he just heard.

"The questions just keep piling up, don't they?" he said softly to no one in particular. "Who would want to stop the Final Reunification and why? Not one of the kingdoms or lands we've been to so far. Someone from a place we have yet to go?"

"We have to find a way to tell the Sky Lords about this," Jos said suddenly. "Maybe they could help."

Terien pushed away from the wall, coming alive with hope. "You can do that?" he asked.

"Theoretically, yes. I would assume that Lady Idona would

have given Maxen the frequency needed to contact her," Naneve replied, frowning.

"But?" Duncan prompted.

"We don't know it," Naneve confessed, her whole body going slack with disappointment. "I've been all through this office and haven't seen any numbers written anywhere. Garel might know the frequency, but short of torturing him, I doubt we'll get anything out of him. He refuses to talk to anyone."

Terien recoiled at the mention of torture. "And I would never condone such a measure."

"Nor would I," Naneve said firmly. "I merely meant to emphasize how impossible it would be to solicit help from Garel."

Anger flashed in Terien's eyes as he paced in front of the communications panel. "I won't discontinue my mission because of this and I won't be bullied." His expression softened and he glanced between Naneve and Jos. "But I will understand if you or any of the other representatives decide not to accompany me."

"I will not be scared off by anyone," Jos said angrily. "Not even you. Your journey may or may not have become more dangerous, but we didn't abandon you when Maxen tried to kill you and I won't abandon you now."

Terien smiled at the young man and was about to comment when a familiar voice boomed from the doorway.

"And we'll nae be abandonin' ye, either, lad!" Rannoch said, adjusting his glasses on his nose as he strode through the doorway.

"Nor will I," Quatina said defiantly, coming in behind Rannoch.

Makhani came into view as well and leaned against the door jamb, arms folded. He still looked a little groggy, but his eyes glittered with determination as he glared at Terien. "I'm not that easy to get rid of, either, Royal Boy. Looks like you're stuck with us for the duration of the journey."

Terien looked to each of those assembled and felt his heart swell with pride. Someone out there might have designs on putting an end to his mission and the Final Reunification, but they had already failed. Even with the group incomplete, there

was enough trust and determination between those he had already gathered to ensure success no matter what happened.

"Thank you, my friends. I know that together, there's nothing that we can't face," he said, a slow grin spreading across his face. "We leave in the morning. And woe to whoever is out there."

★

In a fit of pique, Leander swept an arm across his desk, sending almost everything on it crashing to the floor or flying into a wall. Coming to his feet with enough force to send his heavy chair toppling over, he stalked to the front of his desk and glaring angrily at the communications panel set on it, hammered a fist down on it as he let out an inarticulate bellow of pure rage.

Idona took a couple of steps further back until she bumped into the wall, her face an unreadable mask as she watched Leander destroy his office.

"The idiot failed! He actually failed!" Leander shouted, whirling on Idona. "He had the manpower, the weapons, everything! And he failed to contain six lousy, insignificant men!" His breathing ragged and fast, sweat beading on his forehead, Leander scooped up the one remaining item on his desk – a small statuette made of plaster – and hurled it at the wall opposite Idona, making her jump slightly as it shattered loudly. "I planned it all. I set it up perfectly. He should have caught them totally unawares. And they escaped. They escaped!" he hissed angrily.

"There must be another way," Idona said quietly, hugging her arms around herself. She had never seen Leander so angry and it frightened her. "There has to be."

Straightening his rumpled jacket, Leander took a deep breath and let his arms fall to his sides, hands still clenched into tight fists. "There are always other ways and other plans, but none as easy and perfect as I thought this one to be." His lip curled into a sneer. "This Chosen is more clever than I gave him credit for. A truly worthy opponent, it seems. But I will not allow him or this Final Reunification stand in the way of my plans. The key to Soloth's undoing is the failure of the Final Reunification, and it *shall* fail."

"What will you do now?" Idona asked, finding the courage to take a step or two closer to him.

Leander's self-control was tenuous at best and he snapped at Idona with enough anger to send her scuttling back once more. "Whatever it takes, you little twit!" Stooping to snatch up a shard from the shattered statuette, he held it up in one hand, its sharp edges cutting into his palm as he crushed it to powder. Drops of blood leaking between his knuckles, Leander fixed Idona with a cold stare, his expression now as bland as though he were considering a stroll in the park. "I am through dealing with outsiders. It's time to solicit aid from Albeon and Edegan," he announced, eyes narrowing to slits. "What we do next must be done carefully and quickly. A decisive strike that will leave the populace of Quayvern reeling and Soloth politically bankrupt."

Leander opened his hand to let the bloody powder rain to the floor.

"That is when they will turn to me for guidance and Quayvern will be mine."

Chapter Twenty Four

Having been split into two groups for the return trip to the surface in order to make room for Naneve, Farnash and Dern who had come to see Jos off, Terien, Aurori, Makhani and Rannoch stepped off the minisub and into the warm light of the morning suns breaking over the horizon, stretching and inhaling deeply of the salt air as the second sub surfaced nearby and crawled ashore. By the time everyone had exited the subs, the men who had been left on the shore had already come running, overwhelming them with both their exuberant welcome and questions about their experiences in the under-water city. The story of their ordeal was quickly shared in broad strokes with all members of the group breathlessly adding their piece to the puzzle of events they had weathered.

Alarmed and angered by what they were hearing, the men who had remained ashore were upset to find that they had been sitting safe and bored during the one time on the journey that they had been sorely needed, but their bitter complaints fell silent when, woven into the tale, was the startling disclosure of Aurori's true identity.

Shyly fidgeting with her cylinder, Aurori murmured apologies for not having told them sooner, wondering all the while how they would react to her now that they knew. Whatever reaction she had been expecting, their joyful acceptance wasn't it. Inundated by a throng of beefy warriors all intent on hugging her, Aurori laughed and cried at the same time as they practically smothered her, while Terien, laughing all the while, gave her a wink when her eyes sought his.

Promising a full account at a later date, Terien cut short the telling of the tale and introduced his men to Jos, Naneve, Farnash and Dern. Awed, the men listened in silence as Terien recounted the most important aspects of the visit to Merani, including the appalling revelation that someone had designs on ruining the

Final Reunification. Unsurprisingly, the men loudly declared their willingness to continue the journey, to which Terien responded by giving the order to strike camp and prepare for departure.

With the men dispersed to their tasks, Terien stood with Aurori and Duncan before the minisubs, discussing a few final details with the three leaders from Merani.

"Duncan will see to asking one of the men to accompany you to Mayquire with your prisoners as soon as we've got everything loaded on the hovercraft," Terien told them.

"I hate leaving you a man short. Are you sure you can spare someone?" Naneve asked, hanging onto her son's arm.

"We can. Don't worry, Naneve," Terien replied with a broad smile. "We're hardened warriors, remember? We'll be fine."

Naneve gave Dern a signal and he disappeared into one of the minisubs, returning with a sack slung over his shoulder.

"These are for you, Terien. Our need for them has just decreased, but I fear that you may have need of them," Dern said, holding the sack out for Terien's inspection.

Terien swallowed when he looked inside to find the sack filled with energy weapons. "You're most generous. Now it's my turn to ask – are you sure you can do without these?"

"Absolutely," Farnash assured him. "We still have more than enough to keep our prisoners in line. Even after we start building our town out here, I can't imagine that we'll be needing that many weapons. From what you've told us, the folks in the area are pretty nice. Wouldn't mind meeting this Empress Sahala, though. Just to say hello to a new neighbor. Think that can be arranged?"

Terien laughed. "In all the commotion I forgot about her," he said, eyeing the camp behind him. "I wonder where she is?"

"Probably holed up in her tent, refusing to come out until someone removes the sand from the beach," Duncan snorted.

"Come on, we'll go find her," Terien said.

Naneve took Terien's arm as they walked. "I thought you might like to know that I've already asked a couple of my people to open the archives and see if they can find record of the frequency Quayvern uses," she said. "Barring that, I intend to try every frequency the communications panel can generate. It might take some time, but we'll let the Sky Lords know what has happened."

"Maybe you should call Petrava. They might have the frequency we need," Terien said.

Naneve gave Terien a bewildered look. "Petrava?"

Blinking in surprise, Terien drew to a halt. "The other Hidden City – the one in the Kescate Mountains," he said.

"I've never heard of such a place," Naneve told him.

"Neither have I," Farnash added.

Giving them a brief account of what Lord Soloth had told him about Petrava, Terien could see that his description of the city built into the Kescate Mountains to the north wasn't bringing so much as a glimmer of recognition to his friends from Merani.

Shrugging, Terien resumed walking towards the camp. "No matter. We'll be arriving in Petrava soon enough. If you haven't gotten through to Lord Soloth by then it really won't matter. Once we leave Petrava we'll be heading directly to Quayvern, anyway."

Naneve's furtive glance at Farnash spoke volumes about her renewed fears. "Perhaps so, but now I worry about what you'll find in this other Hidden City, especially considering we've never heard of it. You just be very careful when you approach it!"

Assuring Naneve that they would be, Terien was about to call out to ask where Sahala was when she came running from behind one of the supply carts. Ignoring the fact that Terien was hardly alone, she threw herself at him, pinning his arms at his sides with her fierce embrace.

"I just heard the men talking about what happened down there! How terrible," she breathed. "I'm so happy you made it back safely!"

Before Terien could extricate himself from her stranglehold, Sahala stood on her toes and covered his mouth with hers, kissing him passionately. Abashed, stunned and caught totally off guard, Terien didn't quite return the kiss, but stood frozen in place, eyes bugging out for the few heartbeats it took for him to mobilize his frozen brain and pull his head away.

"Sahala... please... don't..." he stammered haltingly as he now squirmed and wriggled to get free.

Releasing him and turning with quintessential nonchalance to Terien's companions, Sahala offered her hand to Naneve. "You must be the leader of Merani Base the men have been talking about. It is a pleasure to meet the woman who saved Terien's life."

During the display, Aurori had stood agape, practically apoplectic. Now, at Sahala's smug smirk aimed in her direction, she blinked back the tears she felt coming on and turned her afflicted eyes on Terien, only to find he was studiously avoiding her gaze. Jealousy and anger flamed to life within her and she knew she had to get away before she said something she would later regret.

Aurori spun to face Naneve. "If you'll excuse me, I have to go and pack," she said tightly. "I'll talk to you again before we leave."

Striding away without a backward glance, her hurried steps kicked the sand up in her wake as she left them to their introductions and conversation. Going straight to the supply cart where her belongings had been stored before her trip to Merani Base, she swept up her pack in one hand and grabbed up her other parcels with the other, then stomped over to where Quatina was sitting in the sand, neatly folding her own possessions before placing them in her travel bag. Plopping herself down beside Quatina, she wordlessly started stuffing items from one bag into another.

"You are overreacting," Quatina said without preamble.

"Oh yeah? And what, precisely, am I overreacting to?" Aurori growled.

With an impatient sigh, Quatina sat back on her haunches and regarded her friend with beetled brows. "Sahala kissed Terien, not the other way around. Do not hold it against him."

Aurori's frantic packing efforts slowed but she didn't stop and wouldn't meet Quatina's eyes. "I don't. It's just... not fair," she said plaintively. "She can just waltz right up to him and... and... kiss him like... *that*," she spat, sweeping a hand in Sahala's direction, "while I don't even know how to approach him now!"

Tucking the last of her things into her bag, Quatina stood and patted the top of Aurori's head, giving her a devilish smile. "You'll figure it out," she said, then slung her pack over her shoulder and walked off towards her equine, leaving Aurori to stare after her, frowning in bewilderment.

Unseen by either woman, Makhani came around the side of the supply cart and folded his arms. He cast a sympathetic glance in Aurori's direction, then narrowed his eyes as his gaze shifted to where Terien stood, still talking with Sahala and the group from Merani Base. His hands curling into fists, he pushed away from the cart, fuming as he headed for the hovercraft.

"We'll just have to wait and see, Royal Boy, but I think your day is coming."

Chapter Twenty Five

The image of Naneve standing there clutching Farnash's arm, tears streaming down her cheeks as she waved and watched her beloved son leave her behind, was still fresh in Terien's mind as the hovercraft skimmed across the open terrain hours later, bringing to mind his own emotional departure from Kaethos and his parents. The only bright point had been seeing the look of contained delight on the face of Dellin, the man who had agreed to remain behind and present Merani Base's prisoners to the logging camp at Mayquire. As much as he had insisted that he would rather continue on to Quayvern, there was no mistaking his happiness. He was going home!

With Naneve's promise to search the archives of Merani Base to see if the frequency for contacting Quayvern could be found, Terien held on to the hope that the remainder of their journey would be a success despite the likelihood of encountering resistance along the way. Now that everyone was armed with both their traditional weapons and the energy weapons from Merani Base, he kept telling himself that they would be able to face whatever came their way. He couldn't quite convince himself enough to keep his eyes from constantly scanning for danger, however, even as day after day passed and the routine of travel once more assumed a familiar rhythm – which included Haren's nightly grousing about camping outside Sahala's tent. Morale was generally high and conversation remained fixated on the events of Merani as new details were brought to light and certain events embellished, particularly by Rannoch who took special delight in telling and retelling the tale of his heroic assault on six (then eight, then ten) guards.

Conversation also strayed towards the topic of what Aurori had observed in the cities of each representative, causing her some discomfiture as she found herself pressed for her opinion. While it was easy to tell Makhani and Rannoch what she thought of

Glaybor and Brinbourne, it wasn't quite as easy to explain how she felt about Pergase and its second-class citizens living in poverty, especially since Sahala seemed to be going out of her way to snub Aurori after finding out she was both Princess and Chosen, adding to the existing tension between the two Chosen.

After Sahala's enthusiastic kiss, the wall of uncertainty had once more arisen between Terien and Aurori. While they had managed to regain a semblance of the camaraderie they had previously known and did have occasion to discuss Aurori's life as a Princess in Eristea, it was painfully clear that they were terribly uncomfortable in each other's presence, principally because Terien had Sahala adhering to him much of the time. Despite his polite attempts at making her aware of his annoyance with her uninvited advances, the Empress of Pergase stubbornly remained glued to him. No one made mention of this, even in private, but Makhani's disgust was all too evident in the way he had reverted to treating Terien with barely contained contempt as the pair maneuvered the hovercraft across the increasingly verdant terrain.

Joining up with the road that ran between Pergase and Chihook, they were able to travel for another few days by hovercraft before they were forced to abandon the machine when they came to the lower slopes of the Kescate Mountains and were faced by thick stands of lush trees and a narrowing of the road.

"I hate having to leave the hovercraft behind," Duncan complained as they unloaded. "Maybe the road widens again up ahead," he speculated, turning to Sahala.

She shook her head. "I was in Chihook a few years ago. The road actually becomes more narrow further on and winds between the Kescate Mountains. It will be difficult enough for the carts to make it through in some places, let alone this monstrosity," she said, thumping a fist against the hovercraft.

Rannoch sighed theatrically and pressed his cheek to the side of the machine, fondly caressing the deck. "Well, ol' girl. It's been nice knowin' ye," he said, eliciting laughs all around.

Although the speed of the hovercraft was sorely missed, the more leisurely pace of the felinae and equines did allow additional time to spend enjoying the view. The semi-desert around the coast had been beautiful in its own way, but the lush greenery of the Kescate Mountain Range was positively breathtaking.

Virtually untouched by the comets' destructive rain, the northern reaches of Primus had also been all but uninhabited and remained so even now, for the region was best described – and perhaps too mildly at that – as rugged. Towering mountains with jagged, windswept peaks and arboreal slopes dominated over deep valleys filled with streams and rivers that coursed through the old growth forest. With a canopy so dense that it virtually blotted out the light of the suns, the forest closed in on the road and made it seem that they traveled down a long tunnel. The air was oppressive at times, hot and humid with not a breath of wind, forcing them to strip down to only the most basic of clothes as they continued on.

Evening was approaching when they finally came within sight of the city of Chihook after cresting the plateau they had ascended during the day, and Aurori felt a pang of homesickness the moment she saw it, for it bore a passing resemblance to Eristea. Cradled in a lush valley and backed by a deep gorge over which spanned a mammoth iron bridge with graceful support towers and sweeping arches, Chihook was a breathtaking city aglow with inner light. Squat buildings and homes, all fashioned from native wood, were interspersed throughout the ageless trees on both sides of the gorge. Leaving a great deal of the vegetation intact, the Chihookians had built their city *into* the forest and not simply cleared space for it, making it appear as though each home, each building was a part of the natural surroundings and belonged to the forest itself.

Unwilling to make the descent into Chihook when night was fast approaching, Terien's group made camp that night amidst the greenery, not too far from a cheery brook that meandered downhill from the mountain slope abutting the plateau they were on.

Assigning himself the task of fetching water before dinner, Terien left the bustle of the camp, bucket in hand, and pushed his way through the foliage until he came to the brook. With the dying light from the setting suns suffusing the trees with an other-worldly glow, he set the bucket on the ground and stood hands on hips, head tilted back as he drew in a deep breath of loamy air.

Hearing someone coming through the trees behind him, Terien was just turning to see who was coming when a fist lashed out and caught him on the jaw with just enough force to knock him flat onto his back. He landed in a daze, furious as he pushed up on one elbow and massaged at his offended jaw. "What the hell did you sucker punch me for?" he growled.

Glowering back, Makhani sucked on his bruised knuckles and flipped his long blond hair over his shoulders with his other hand. "When you had just won your fight in the Penaro village, you apologized to me for having been a smug little twerp in the past and told me I should deck you if I ever caught you acting that way again," he said evenly.

Terien made an impatient gesture. "I remember! But I don't recall being a smug twerp recently, so you'd better start explaining, Blondy. Real fast!" he said dangerously.

Folding his arms, Makhani adopted an air of indignation. "A blind man could see how much Aurori cares about you, yet you keep avoiding her while you let Sahala hang all over you – even though it's plain that you can't stand it. The whole camp has been hoping you'd come to your senses, but you're too thickheaded. Can't you see that Sahala's playing with you and enjoys taunting Aurori with her control over you? She has been since the first night we had dinner in Pergase."

"She does *not* control me!" Terien spat, kicking to his feet and advancing on Makhani until they were almost nose-to-nose. "You don't get it, Blondy! She's an Empress and a representative for the Final Reunification. How the hell am I supposed to brush her off – and Maker knows I've been trying – without risking her backing out in a royal fit? You know what she's like."

Makhani would not back down, but the haughtiness left his stance and he put a hand on Terien's shoulder. "You're making excuses, Royal Boy. Forget your fears and listen to your heart for a change, not your head," he said peaceably.

The anger seemed to evaporate from Terien and he took a startled step back as Makhani's words hit home. He had been afraid – terribly so – ever since Lord Soloth had come to announce him as the Chosen – afraid of the responsibility placed on him, afraid of failing, and certainly afraid of how he could possibly open himself to caring about Aurori when so many others demanded his care and attention. It had been easier to keep her at arms length, put her in the same category as all his other friends and not admit that it was her safety, her well-being that mattered most to him, like it or not.

"Duncan has been trying to tell me the same thing, but I wouldn't listen," Terien said, looking down at his boots. "I didn't want… was afraid… my feelings for Aurori might cloud my judgment. I didn't want anyone thinking I was… more interested in her safety than theirs."

Makhani chuffed out a low laugh. "If you thought about it this much, I doubt you're in any danger of doing it," he said. "Give us some credit for brains, would you? I don't think there's even one member of this group who doesn't know you'd do everything in your power to protect all of us." His eyebrows went up. "Remember the incident with the wild felinae? I didn't see you running off to see how Aurori was. Or how about all the times you warned us to be careful when we reached Alatesh? Or in Merani Base? You left Elek behind to stand watch over me when you knew damn well that the guards were more than likely protecting Maxen and you might need his help to rescue Aurori."

Terien couldn't help but grin. "All right, all right! So I'm a total idiot who over-thinks everything!" His face suddenly fell into a deep frown. "Still doesn't mean you had to sucker punch me!"

Makhani shrugged. "You're hard-headed. I thought it might take some doing to knock some sense into you." He offered Terien an unrepentant smile. "As long as I got through to you and you plan on telling Aurori how you feel about her – well, if it'll make you feel better, punch me back."

Considering it, Terien had just thrust a finger at Makhani's chest, mouth opening in prelude to a reply, when the trees behind Makhani rustled loudly.

⋆

Having just tied Mystafire to a nearby tree, Aurori gave her Appaloosa mare a rub on the nose and pulled a sweet fruit from her pocket, letting the equine nuzzle it from her outstretched hand. With a tired sigh, she slapped at her bare arm as an insect buzzed in, hoping for a meal. Reflecting that the sleeveless silk shirt she had bought in Pergase was cooler but gave the bugs a better chance at her, Aurori ambled over to where Benem was removing the bridle from Snowdrift's ginger muzzle and stopped to scratch Shangra under the chin. In response, Shangra dipped his head and began licking her arm, sending shivers through her at the roughness of his tongue.

"Nice night," Benem commented as he picked at a bramble in Snowdrift's coat.

Aurori pulled her arm out of Shangra's reach and rubbed at her abraded skin. "Certainly is," she said, then swatted at another bug, annoyed. "Except for these blasted insects."

Benem gave her a rueful smile. "Wait until we get the fires going. The bugs won't be as bad," he said.

Smiling her agreement, Aurori caught sight of Terien moving off into the forest, bucket in hand. Heaving a sigh, she turned and made her way into the camp, only to be confronted by Quatina who thrust a bucket at her, forcing a huff out of her when it hit her stomach.

"What?" Aurori said, bewildered as she glanced between Quatina and the empty bucket now in her hands.

"We need water," Quatina replied.

Aurori glanced over her shoulder to where Terien had disappeared. "No, I saw Terien going for water," she replied.

Posting her hands on her hips, Quatina gave Aurori a flat stare. "So you did. And he went alone, I might add."

Aurori frowned, shaking her head as she thrust the bucket out to Quatina. "Oh, no. No. If you think I'm going to go after him on the lame excuse of getting more water, you're crazy, girlfriend."

Quatina pushed the bucket back. "I am giving you an opportunity to talk to him," she growled. "This nonsense has gone on long enough. So, talk to him!"

Stubborn, Aurori held out the bucket. "Come on, Quatina! How am I supposed to strike up a conversation?" Aurori snorted. "It's… too embarrassing."

Shoving the bucket back, Quatina gave her a pointed stare and said nothing. She spun on her heel and strode away, leaving Aurori clutching an empty bucket, her thoughts racing.

Heart pounding, Aurori turned and took one step towards the bushes, looked back over both shoulders to make sure no one was watching and took another step. Her feet seemed to have a mind of their own and she was already entering the thick brush before she realized it. Steeling herself, Aurori fought to quiet her thundering heart by taking a breath and telling herself that she would just be casual. Be cool. No one said she had to make any grand statements of undying love, after all. Just have a casual conversation.

As she followed the sound of the brook, Aurori became aware of a voice speaking just ahead and stopped, breaking out in a cold sweat. She recognized the voice as Terien's, but who was he talking to? Creeping forward as quietly as possible, she was sure he would hear her heart beating as it now threatened to leap right out of her chest. Then she heard Makhani's voice and let out a shaky breath of relief. Stealing closer, she crouched behind a thick bush and strained to hear what they were saying as she gingerly parted the bush's leaves to peek out at them.

"Duncan has been trying to tell me the same thing, but I wouldn't listen," Terien was saying. He looked down at his boots as though reticent about sharing his thoughts with Makhani. "I didn't want... was afraid... my feelings for Aurori might cloud my judgment. I didn't want anyone thinking I was... more interested in her safety than theirs."

Aurori's breath caught and she had to plant a hand on the ground to keep from pitching forward. To hear that he had deep feelings for her shouldn't have been a surprise, but somehow managed to stagger her anyway. Should she keep listening or leave or what? Lower lip trembling with suppressed emotion, she repositioned herself into a more stable stance and leaned into the bush once more, angry at herself both for being curious enough to eavesdrop on a private conversation and for having just missed a piece of it in the time it took to settle herself.

"All right, all right! So I'm a total idiot who over-thinks everything!" Terien was saying, that infuriatingly charming smile of his suddenly giving way to a brow-furrowing frown. "Still doesn't mean you had to sucker punch me!"

Confusion, then understanding flickered through Aurori's mind and she had to suppress the urge to giggle. Considering the topic they had been discussing, it sounded like Makhani had decked Terien. But why?

Makhani shrugged. "You're hard-headed. I thought it might take some doing to knock some sense into you," he told Terien. "As long as I got through to you and you plan on telling Aurori how you feel about her – well, if it'll make you feel better, punch me back."

So, Makhani had played gallant knight on her behalf. The notion was rather charming until Aurori realized that her feelings had been so transparent that Makhani felt he had to intervene. A rush of blood hit her cheeks at the thought, followed by a warm, dizzying sensation that came from knowing Terien cared for her. She didn't have time to appreciate the feeling, though. She could see that Terien was actually giving consideration to Makhani's offer, and she couldn't let him do something he would regret later.

The bushes rustling loudly, Aurori surged to her feet and stepped out, making both Terien and Makhani jump slightly at her unexpected entrance.

"Don't you dare even think about it!" she cautioned Terien, shooting him a fiery look as she marched up to them, bucket swinging from one hand.

His mouth gaping open in a wide "O" of surprise, Terien retreated from Makhani as though he'd been pushed. "Aurori! You… how long were you… you didn't…"

Aurori stopped in front of Makhani, lifted his bruised hand and ran her fingers over his swollen knuckles. She released him and wordlessly caressed the side of his face, giving him a warm smile of thanks before thrusting the bucket into his hands and turning on Terien.

Uncertain what to say, Terien made a helpless palms-up gesture, his shoulders bunching into a shrug of misery. "Aurori… I don't know what to say. I'm sorry… I…"

Aurori didn't let him finish. Emboldened by what she had just overheard, she stepped into his open arms and took hold of his face, pulling his head down until her lips met his in a kiss that was gentle yet deep enough to convey without words every thought and hope in her heart. Stunned but elated, Terien enfolded her in his arms and returned the kiss with his whole heart, wordlessly conveying his own joyous reply.

Smiling smugly, Makhani averted his gaze and cleared his throat loudly. "Ah… I'll just be over there – getting some water…" he said sheepishly, giving the pair a wide berth on his way to the brook.

Parting now, Terien sighed and nuzzled Aurori's forehead. "There's so much I want to say. So much I need to tell you," he said softly.

Aurori leaned back and put her fingertips to his lips. "I know. Me too," she whispered back, looking into his eyes with a tenderness that made him tremble.

His head tilted in the direction Makhani was. "Later, though. Sometime when we can be alone?"

She gave him a playful smile. "Just don't forget where we left off," she said quietly.

"I'll remind him if he does," Makhani whispered loudly as he leaned in on them, full buckets swinging from his hands.

Terien groaned with chagrin. "Now can I deck him?"

"No!" Aurori laughed.

A renewed rustling in the bushes put a damper on their light-hearted exchange as Duncan breathlessly rushed onto the scene. His face flickering with surprise and confusion upon finding Terien and Aurori in an embrace with Makhani standing next to them, he skidded to a stop and stared wide-eyed for a second before waving a hand in front of his face as he shook his head in utter disbelief.

"Never mind. I won't even ask," Duncan said, more to himself than anyone. "You have to come and see this, Terien. It looks like there's a war going on in Chihook!"

"What!" they shouted in unison, astonished.

Stepping away from Aurori, Terien grabbed one of the buckets from Makhani and followed after Duncan who was already disappearing into the brush. He held a hand out to Aurori and gave her a quick smile. "Come on, Chosen. Sounds like there's some observing to do."

Emerging into the camp, they found everyone lined up at the edge of the plateau, looking down at the city of Chihook. Joining them, Terien, Aurori and Makhani stared down at the spectacle. It was unclear from this distance exactly what was going on, but the streets seemed to be alive with people running around carrying torches and their angry shouts could be heard echoing all the way up to the plateau.

When Aurori stepped around Terien for a better view, he placed his hands on her shoulders and drew her against him, resting his chin on the top of her head. "Lord Soloth said there was some unrest in this area," he said.

Aurori craned her neck to look back at him. "Yes, but he also said that he didn't think it would interfere with our missions."

"This is nothing new. The authorities will have this settled down by morning," Sahala said, pushing to Terien's side. She took notice of the way he was holding Aurori and a look of jealous anger crossed her face, but she wisely refrained from commenting. "There are two separate factions in Chihook. The Chihookians, who live on this side of the bridge, claim they have lived here since before the Great Division and therefore have the right to live and work on either side of the gorge. The faction on the other side, the Goloto'o, settled there after the Great Division, having been displaced from their native land by the comets. They deny that their neighbors have any right to govern them or their lands and have been trying to declare themselves sovereign." She shrugged indifferently. "It's a petty dispute, but it has endured for hundreds of years."

"Sounds a little like the Cohalili and the Penaro," Elek commented.

Terien's eyes narrowed. "Yeah. Too much so."

"So why don't they just split the city and let each side govern itself? Or better yet – work together?" Benem asked.

Sahala gave him an condescending look. "They have tried both in the past, I am told, but only in recent years have they managed to form a coalition government. There are many on both sides who are unhappy with the arrangement, however, and tempers flare from time to time when one side or the other feels the voice of their people is being ignored." She nodded at the valley below. "The skirmish below is likely to have started between neighbors who have differing opinions and old hatreds. You'll see. By morning everything will be peaceful once more. Until the next time, of course."

"Well, there's nothing we can do until morning," Aurori said, sighing as she envisioned Terien becoming embroiled in another lengthy round of peace negotiations.

"No. No, there isn't," Terien agreed, his chin lifting from Aurori's head. He sighed and took her hand, leading her back to the camp with the rest following in twos and threes. "We'll just post more guards tonight and hope they don't have blow sticks," he jested without mirth in his tone.

Aurori gave his hand a squeeze and caught his eyes. "Don't worry. Everything will be fine."

Smiling, Terien interlaced his fingers with hers. "I hope so," he said, casting a glance back at Chihook as he wondered what kind of reception they would get. "I hope so."

Chapter Twenty Six

Finding that Sahala had been right and the disturbance in Chihook had been quelled by morning, Terien's group descended the plateau and arrived in Chihook just as the skies started to cloud and a light drizzle began to fall. Finding themselves welcomed at the outskirts of Chihook by two officials from the coalition government who had been alerted to their presence by the city's sentries, they were escorted through the city and passed cadres of guards who now stalked the streets in their drab beige uniforms, long, curved swords at their sides. The presence of the guards, a grim reminder of what had transpired the night before, didn't seem to disturb the citizens who simply ignored them and carried on with their lives. Nor did the presence of the Chosen and his entourage deter them. Reserved in their reaction, the citizens of Chihook would eye the entourage with bland disinterest, giving Terien the impression that they were more concerned about what was happening within their city than with the Final Reunification.

Upon arriving at the government building, a massive wooden structure that had been built around the bases of several gargantuan trees and whose roof was a patchwork of angles and curves to accommodate the growth of the trees, Terien dismounted from Shangra and went into a huddle with his men, a ritual that hadn't been performed since Pergase. Assigning the usual complement of half the men to remain outside, he followed the two officials into the structure with his now expanded collection of representatives.

The inner council chambers of the government building were arranged on much the same design as in Brinbourne, in a horseshoe shape with space in the center for people to gather, but with one significant variation. The massive base of one of the trees occupied the very center of the room, its irregular, curving shape rising through the apex of the vaulted ceiling. Hundreds of candles adorned the trunk, set on an iron rail whose helical shape wound around the tree from floor to ceiling, bathing the chamber in a flickering glow that created an aura of antiquity and made the place feel like a shrine.

Seated at their desks along the far wall of the chamber were the ten members of the coalition government. Five sat to the left of the center and five to the right, leaving a space between them that was occupied by a large iron statue of a large predatory animal of a type Terien didn't recognize. Large as a felinae, the animal represented was a quadruped with a heavy body, short, shaggy fur, a short tail and rounded ears. It was depicted rearing on its hind legs, massive paws clawing the air and jaws open in a fearsome snarl.

Eyeing the statue and wondering about its significance, Terien approached the councilors as an eleventh man stepped forward and gave him a deep bow, positioning himself directly in front of the statue.

"It is an honor to have the Chosen visit the city of Chihook," the man said, bowing so deep that his long gray beard reached past his knees for a moment. He was dressed in a brown robe that was ornately decorated with mysterious hand-sewn symbols. He straightened and gave Terien a sad smile. "I am Gregoro, Presider of this Council. It is my duty to speak the mind of the council once a decision has been reached."

Wondering what that meant in this circumstance, Terien returned Gregoro's bow. "I am Terien, Prince of Kaethos and the Chosen Gatherer for the Final Reunification," he said, repeating the well-used formula once more. A sweep of his hand encompassing everyone gathered behind him, he said, "These are the representatives who have journeyed with me from their native lands," and proceeded to introduce each one. With only one formality remaining, he showed Gregoro and the council his cube with its holographic message, secretly pleased with the looks of mixed awe and sober contemplation it evoked in them.

"It is with sadness that we greet you, Chosen. The Sky Lord who visited us those many months ago said we should prepare ourselves and select a representative to accompany you," Gregoro said, "but after many months of discussion, an appropriate representative could not be agreed upon." He bowed his head. "I must inform you that there will be no representative from Chihook to accompany you to the Final Reunification."

Taken aback, Terien looked from one side of the council to the other, realizing that the seating arrangement reflected the division in Chihook. One side must have been comprised of Chihookians, while the other members were Goloto'o.

"The Empress Sahala has made mention to me of the... difficulties you have been experiencing," Terien said diplomatically. "If the council is so disposed, I would appreciate learning more. I am reticent about simply leaving without being apprised of the reasons you have been unable to choose a representative. Perhaps I may be of assistance in this matter."

Gregoro turned to the council. "I propose that this formal session of the council be dissolved and that an informal gathering in my chamber be entertained so that we may speak with the Chosen off the record. How vote you?"

Their eagerness betrayed in their quick replies in the affirmative, the council members now stood and filed towards a door hidden behind the iron statue.

Gregoro smiled warmly now and took Terien's elbow. "Come, then. All of you," he said, motioning with a bony hand for everyone to follow. "We have much to talk about."

Terien was about to proceed into the chamber when Aurori caught his arm, bringing him and Gregoro to a halt.

"Excuse me, Presider Gregoro, but my friend and I were wondering if it would be permissible for us to explore Chihook and do a little shopping," Aurori said, standing shoulder to shoulder with Quatina. Both were smiling sweetly.

Gregoro chuckled. "Of course, my dears. Just be sure to stay on the main streets." His expression clouded. "You are aware of what took place last night, yes?"

Aurori caught Terien's apprehensive glance and felt a pang of guilt. Of course, he wouldn't like her going out into a city that had seen unrest so recently, but it was her mandate to do so, especially in such a circumstance. She had to know what the people were thinking. "Not the details, no. But I would assume we should be safe enough with the extra guards we saw posted on the streets," she said in reply to Gregoro.

"A sad state of affairs, that." Gregoro said. He had also noticed Terien's apprehension and looked up at him. "She and her friend will be safe enough if they confine themselves to the main streets," he repeated, then tapped his chin thoughtfully. "I suspect that you will not be staying the night in Chihook. A curfew has been imposed because of the fighting last night and the council will perhaps ask that you leave before sundown for your own safety, regardless of the outcome of this informal meeting." He turned to Aurori and Quatina. "Go, children. But step gently and be sure to return well before evening."

Terien's uneasiness was plain to see. Aurori could tell that he desperately wanted to say something to stop her from going and that it was taking every ounce of his will to keep from breaking his promise of not interfering with her mission.

"Have fun," Terien said, forcing a smile. "Just... be careful."

Standing on her toes, Aurori kissed his cheek. "Thank you," she said softly, her words layered with meaning.

Watching Aurori and Quatina go, Terien let out a breath and pressed his fingertips to the spot Aurori had kissed, feeling his stomach knot up with worry.

"Ah. She is your lady," Gregoro said with an understanding nod. His bushy brows arched in question. "I could arrange for a guard to accompany them," he offered.

"No!" Terien said quickly. Aurori would kill him! Resolutely pushing his anxiety aside he gave Gregoro a confident smile. "They'll be fine," he said, unsure of whether he was saying it for Gregoro's benefit or his own.

Following the smaller man into the room behind the statue, Terien was introduced to the ten members of the coalition government, shaking hands with each in turn and trying hard to remember their names. Extra chairs had been brought in for the occasion and everyone took a seat as finger foods and drink were brought in by servants and placed on low tables.

Listening as the councilors took turns explaining the situation in Chihook, Terien's heart went out to these men and women who were trying so hard to negotiate a peace between their peoples. They were constantly finding themselves at an impasse when the people themselves would ignore every new attempt and rise up on their own. The street fight the night before was an all too common occurrence and the joint police force was constantly stepping in, bearing the brunt of the people's ire.

With little hope of being able to intervene in the situation, Terien steered the conversation back to the council's inability to agree on a representative for the Final Reunification. Thankfully, this was one problem that Terien had a ready solution for.

"If the other representatives are in agreement, I would propose allowing Chihook to send two representatives. A Chihookian and a Goloto'o," he said, his glance taking in everyone in the room.

The reaction was interesting. Makhani looked at Rannoch, who looked to Sahala, who looked at Jos. They shrugged in unison, having reached a unanimous decision in a heartbeat.

"We see no problem with that," Makhani said. "Of course, we haven't heard from Quatina. Or Aurori, of course," he said hastily.

"Quatina would definitely agree," Duncan put in.

"As would Aurori," Terien said. He turned his gaze to Gregoro. "Then it's settled. If you can select appropriate representatives from both the Chihookians and the Goloto'o, then both will accompany me." He leaned forward in his chair. "I would like to impose one restriction, however. The two people you select must not be openly hostile towards each other and must at least agree on what Chihook has to offer at the negotiation table."

One of the Chihookian Councilors, Jeson, if Terien remembered correctly, laughed. "You ask much of us, Chosen, but that may be arranged," he said, extending a hand to a comely lady councilor whose strawberry blond hair was swept up in a simple ponytail. "What say you, Corliss? Will you accompany me if the council agrees?"

Corliss stared at his hand as if it might be contaminated by something, one delicate eyebrow arching in disdain. "I would accept for the good of the Goloto'o," she said imperiously.

Gregoro leaned in on Terien, smirking. "Don't let the coolness of her attitude fool you. Jeson and Corliss are husband and wife."

Terien's eyebrows shot up in surprise. "You're married and are both councilors, but represent opposite sides?"

"Must make fer interestin' conversation 'round th' dinner table," Rannoch observed.

Jeson smiled. "I like to think that we are proof that there is hope for Chihook," he said, but when he put his hand on her knee, Corliss gave his fingers a light swat and fired him a disapproving frown.

Terien bit his lip to keep from laughing out loud at the schism between Jeson's words and Corliss's actions. Still, he had to worry a bit – married or not, would these two be a problem?

Before Terien could find a polite way of broaching the delicate subject, Gregoro stood and restated the proposal, then called for a vote from the members. With Jeson and Corliss abstaining, the vote was unanimously in favor of the pair representing Chihook.

Deciding to accept in good faith that the councilors would not have allowed the pair to accompany him if they could not be counted on to represent Chihook to the best of their abilities, Terien stood and addressed everyone.

"Actually, this may be premature. There is something you should know," he said. Collecting his thoughts, Terien began to pace as he recounted what had happened at Merani Base, calling on Jos to verify certain aspects of the rebellion and the subsequent mysterious call and what it portended for his mission. The councilors sat spellbound by it all, wide eyes betraying their shock.

"Have there been any strangers through Chihook in recent months? Anyone who looked suspicious?" Terien asked in the end.

Jeson shook his head. "Few journey to Chihook. Since the Sky Lords were here, only a handful of people have come our way. Traders, mostly, bringing goods from Pergase. A few continued on to the two towns beyond Chihook and have not yet returned, but they hardly looked suspicious."

Duncan caught Terien's eye. "You're wondering if Petrava is where the call originated from, aren't you?"

"I am. If there's only been a few traders through here in the last few months, I can't imagine where else trouble might come from," Terien said. "Of course, it might just be that the call was from one of Maxen's operatives, curious to know what had happened."

Corliss rose from her chair and faced Terien. "Regardless of whether there is danger or not, I will not back out from accompanying you, Chosen. Nor will Jeson," she said, casting a glance over her shoulder and giving her husband a look that told him he'd better not contradict her. "Chihook has much to offer for the Final Reunification. Our craftsmen and engineers are skilled in working with both wood and iron, and while we had resigned ourselves to not sending a representative, your generosity in allowing the addition of an extra representative from Chihook means we will not have to disappoint those who have looked forward to sharing their ideas and work with other lands." Corliss rested a hand on Terien's shoulder and gave him a warm smile, the first he had seen on her lips. "That alone is worth the risk."

★

Taking a casual stroll through the hangar deck on Quayvern, Leander smiled and waved to the technicians as he passed. He stopped twice to chat with a couple of families who had received permission to take out flyers for themselves so they could have a picnic on the surface, wishing them a pleasant day and reminding them to stay well within the boundaries to the north that were uninhabited. Assuring him they would, they waved happily after him, pleased to have had a chance to speak with the Sub-Primary of their city.

Leander watched them leave and then continued through the cavernous bay. There were at least a score of flyers parked on the deck, most belonging to the city itself and maintained for use by qualified citizens who could take them out for personal trips, but there were also a few private vehicles belonging to various councilors or private citizens who maintained them for their own excursions from Quayvern. It was one such flyer that Leander now ambled towards; a silver ovoid without markings of any sort, it was currently being serviced by a technician he recognized as being employed by Councilor Albeon.

"Good day, Krisk. I trust you've been well," Leander said, squatting beside the pale man who had his arms inserted in an open panel on the flyer's side.

"Well enough, Sub-Primary. Thanks for asking," Krisk replied.

Leander stretched to run an appreciative hand on the flyer's silver hull. "Fine machine, this one. Having problems with it?"

Krisk might have shrugged, but his arms were so deep inside the panel that it was hard to tell. "Not really. Just some routine maintenance," he said. "It was time to replace some of the circuit boards."

Leander nodded knowingly. "Of course. We wouldn't want something burning out when the time comes for Primary Soloth to collect the Chosen and their representatives."

"No, sir," Krisk agreed. "You realize, of course, that I'll need to take the flyer out for a bit of spin once I'm done, though. Maybe tomorrow sometime. Shouldn't take long. A few hours at best."

Leander rested his wrists on his knees. "Primary Soloth has a busy schedule tomorrow. I'm sure he won't be needing it."

"I already asked. He said that as long as I had it back before the Chosen reached Petrava he'd be a happy man," Krisk laughed.

Rising and dusting his hands off, Leander smiled. "Well, I'll leave you to your work, then." He turned to go but hesitated and glanced back at the technician. "I must say, Krisk, that it's good to find a man so dedicated to his work as you seem to be."

Krisk extricated his hands from the flyer's innards and picked up a greasy rag from the floor, wiping his hands as he smiled up at Leander. "You must have me confused with someone else, Sub-Primary. I'm doing this for the reward Councilor Albeon promised me. Extra pay for extra work. Know what I mean?"

Eyes narrowing, Leander nodded slightly. "We all do what we must to reach our goals," he said, then spun around and strode away, a cold smile spreading across his face.

Chapter Twenty Seven

Having once again shouldered her pack of potions, hidden her cylinder and assumed the guise of a simple peasant Healer, Aurori, in the company of Quatina, moved out into the city of Chihook. Wandering the streets of a city under martial law proved to be both interesting and disconcerting for the pair, but it seemed to be business as usual for most of the citizens and the market was still crowded with shoppers bartering for the goods on sale in the small stores that lined the main boulevard.

The stores themselves were fascinating, having been built on much the same principle as the government building, which meant they made use of individual trees for the basis of their construction. Some were even carved directly into the huge boles of the largest trees.

Stopping for tea in one such establishment whose cramped interior featured tables tall enough to stand at but no chairs, Aurori and Quatina listened to the conversation between the teahouse proprietress, a wispy little old woman with dusky skin and long gray hair that hung in wiry twin braids that lay across her narrow chest, and a large man whose callused hands engulfed a steaming cup of potent-smelling brew.

"I don't know, Marel. I've about had enough of all this fuss," the man was saying, shaking his head slowly from side to side as he stared into the depths of his mug. "Sometimes I wish the Sky Lords had never brought the Goloto'o to Chihook."

That statement made Aurori's eyebrows rise and she looked over the table at Quatina.

"I know what you mean. You'd think that after all these generations they'd have settled in, but they're such a stubborn people," the woman called Marel said with a sad sigh. She ran a damp rag over the counter behind which she stood. "I heard that two people were killed in last night's riot and that a dozen more were injured. Any truth to that?"

"Don't know for sure. The council hasn't yet released an official statement and there's no point in asking the sentries, they'd just tell us to go about our business. And you know how the rumors can be," the man said with a sour smile.

Shifting her feet, Aurori casually leaned forward against the table, elbows resting on the hard wooden surface while she held her cup of tea in both hands. "Excuse me, but my friend and I couldn't help but hear what you've been saying," she said, glancing apologetically between the man and the old woman. "We've never been to Chihook before, and I was wondering if you could tell us a little about what's going on."

The man looked Aurori up and down, then glanced at Quatina. "Except for your clothes, you look Chihookian. Thought you were, actually," he told her, then shrugged and looked back at Aurori, eyes narrowing. "Are you one of the representatives that came in with the Chosen?" he asked.

"Both of us are," Aurori replied.

"Then you are certainly welcome in my humble establishment," the old woman said with a smile before the man, whose face betrayed open surprise, could comment. She gave the man a pointed look. "Tell them. Maybe they will share what they hear with the Chosen."

"You can count on it," Quatina said, containing a small smile by delicately sipping at the hot contents of her own mug as she eyed Aurori.

The man's mouth turned down into a grimace, but he shifted position to face the two women. "No doubt the Chosen will hear much of this from the councilors, but there are a few details they will most certainly omit," he said, then launched into an account of Chihook's history.

Chihook had once been called the Gateway to the North in the days before the Great Division because its massive iron bridge provided access to the great cities of northern Primus. Then the destructive rain of the comets had changed all that. The far north was hardest hit, destroying the major cities there and displacing thousands from their homes. To this day the far north was an uninhabitable devastation zone, leaving Chihook and the two small settlements further up the road as the only populated areas in the Kescates.

In the days after the Great Division, the Sky Lords had criss-crossed the north in their flyers, relocating refugees to any city or town which was willing to offer them safe harbor. Chihook had welcomed one such group from the city of Goloto'o, generously allowing them to occupy the land to the north of the bridge and even helping them build homes for themselves, showing them how to use the existing trees in their construction.

At first the people of Goloto'o were so thankful just to have survived the Great Division that they lived in peace for many generations, but as time passed and the two peoples began to intermix more and more, tensions arose. Stemming from disputes over land ownership as the Goloto'o population started to expand onto lands previously claimed by the Chihookians for future clearing and use as gardens, and fueled by disparate philosophies and religious beliefs, the two peoples began to fight.

The government of Chihook, who administered the lands on both sides of the bridge, tried first to settle land claims, but ran into resistance when neither side could be appeased and refused to compromise. Riots and skirmishes continued off and on for generations before it was decided to allow the Goloto'o autonomous rule over their side of the bridge. This, too, failed. There were many Chihookians and Goloto'o living on either side of the bridge and they demanded their voices be heard and their needs and rights be addressed. More riots, more unrest, until in recent times the two councils came together and formed the current coalition government. The people were generally happy with the arrangement, but there was a splinter group of Chihookians who refused to give up their claim on the lands to the north, and a faction of Goloto'o who advocated a return to autonomy.

The man broke off his narration as four sentries entered the teahouse and took a look around. They circled through the room, weapons prominently displayed as they eyed the other customers standing at tables and made their way to the counter.

"What's the brew of the day, old one," one of the sentries asked Marel, leaning an elbow on the counter.

Smiling politely, Marel tapped a finger against a fluted

decanter standing on the hot surface of the iron stove behind her. "Nagini root tea. Good for calming the nerves," she said.

The sentries shared a laugh.

"Smart choice, old one. See if you can have some delivered across the bridge!" one of them joked as he tossed four gold chips on the counter and accepted four mugs from Marel. "We'll return the mugs later," he called over his shoulder as he and his companions left the small room.

"Are the sentries all Chihookian or are some of them Goloto'o?" Quatina asked.

"Both, but the Chihookian sentries patrol this side of the bridge and the ones who are Goloto'o patrol their own side," Marel explained. Her expression clouded then with displeasure. "Only when there's a problem will both forces come together, and that is where the problem lies. The council denies it and covers it up, but the sentries often beat innocent people during such occasions, taking advantage of the skirmish to exact a little vengeance of their own."

"Vengeance? For what purpose?" Aurori inquired, looking confused.

The man with the callused hands barked out a laugh. "The sentries are well paid for what they do, but many have given their lives in the conflicts over the years. It's well known that many sentries seek to avenge the deaths of their comrades at the next riot suppression, and that must be brought to an end. The council turns a blind eye to it, though, despite the protest of citizens on both sides of the bridge."

"Everyone had hoped that when the Chosen arrived, we would be able to bring this to his attention and that he and the representatives of the other lands might be able to put pressure on them during the negotiations for the Final Reunification so that they would at least promise a review of the sentry forces," Marel said, hope filling her eyes at she looked to Aurori, then Quatina. "Many are saying that the council has been unwilling to address the issue because they fear the very military forces charged with policing the city may rebel and attempt a coup."

"More coups," Aurori sighed tiredly, swirling the last dregs of her tea around her mug before draining them in a single

swallow.

"Will you at least mention this to the Chosen?" the big man asked as he passed his empty cup to Marel.

Quatina nodded. "We shall, but we cannot offer you assurances that the matter will be discussed at the Final Reunification," she cautioned. "It may be that the issue will have to wait, for the other representatives may not wish to attempt placing sanctions on Chihook when the negotiations are still in their infancy."

Marel and the man exchanged glances and shrugged.

"No matter. If the Chosen will at least be made aware of the problem, then there is hope for the future," Marel decreed, smiling.

Bidding Marel a good day and thanking the man for his informative talk, Aurori and Quatina decided to take a stroll to the other side of the bridge and into Goloto'o territory. Stopping along the way to purchase a pair of colorful scarves that the women of Chihook apparently wore over their heads to repel the rain, they continued on until they reached the bridge.

Crossing the iron behemoth was an experience both exciting and frightening. The wild river that had formed the gorge coursed far below, thundering over a steep wall of rock just to the side of the bridge. The noise from the waterfall drowned out all other sounds as the pair reached the center of the structure and looked down over the rail, carefully keeping themselves at arms length from the edge. Mist billowed through the air, adding to the humidity of the warm, rainy day.

Laughing at their timidity, Aurori and Quatina traversed the rest of the bridge's span and followed the wide road into the heart of the Goloto'o settlement, finding more shops and homes built along the same pattern as those on the other side, as expected. The one striking difference was the way the Goloto'o had decorated the exteriors of their homes. Instead of leaving the wood in its natural state, they had painted it with various geometrical shapes in bright primary colors, making their homes look very cheery, if a little gaudy.

The pair was just approaching a row of shops beneath a thick natural canopy of tree boughs when several people ran past, almost bumping them in their hurry to get somewhere. Curious, Aurori and Quatina cautiously followed them down an alley until the sounds of angry shouts became clear.

Emerging into an open square, Aurori and Quatina stood gaping at the sight before them. Several sentries were lined up in the middle of the square, forming a protective barrier for some of their comrades who were helping three injured men to their feet. The men were bloodied and bruised; giving evidence to the beating they must have received at the hands of the rowdy group who was facing off against the sentries. Unarmed except for rocks and home-made clubs, the group of eight masked hooligans had no hope of standing against the sentries and their curved swords, but made up in rabidity what they lacked in weapons. Shouting and heaving stones at the line of sentries who were holding wooden shields, they were slowly being driven back.

Aurori grabbed Quatina's arm and was pulling her back into the safety of the alley when a stray rock shot her way, clipping her forehead and opening a small cut despite her effort to duck away.

"You're bleeding!" Quatina gasped.

"It's not bad," Aurori assured, dabbing at her forehead with a corner of her scarf. "I want to see what happens," she said, leaning carefully around the corner, alert for any more rocks zinging her way.

The line of sentries, perhaps sixteen in all, were breaking ranks now that the wounded men had been hustled away. Chasing down the masked men, they managed to apprehend four of them that Aurori could see, but the other four and their pursuers had disappeared into the city. Shocked, Aurori watched as the sentries roughly slammed to the ground the four men they had captured, taking a turn each to kick or hit the men before they were hauled to their feet and tied up. Bruised and bleeding themselves now, the captured rioters were crudely led from the square, the sentries laughing and prodding them with their wooden shields.

Sliding out of sight into the alley until the sentries passed, Quatina and Aurori exchanged an uneasy look before stepping out into the square. Already the people were starting to emerge from the shadows and doorways, cautiously glancing around before once more setting about their business.

Bravely walking up to the cadre of sentries who had remained behind in the square, Aurori gave them a shy smile and was relieved when one of them gave her a brief nod and stepped away from his compatriots.

"What can I do for you, miss?"

Deciding that honesty might get her further than deception, she cleared her throat and drew herself up. "I noticed that those three men you were helping were terribly beat up. I am a Healer and would like to offer my services if they are required."

The sentry pursed his lips, considering. After a moment he wordlessly motioned his head for her and Quatina to follow him. Leading them down a series of alleys, he stopped in front of a building that was backed on to the gorge and within sight of the iron bridge. Escorting them past a group of weeping women (no doubt relatives of the wounded men from the square) and into the whitewashed interior of the building, it became obvious that this was a hospital of sorts. There were beds lined against the walls, most filled with people swathed in bandages and moaning softly. Asking them to stay at the door, the sentry moved into the room and went over to speak with a pair of men wearing long beige coats. They glanced in Aurori's direction as the sentry spoke, then broke into wide smiles and motioned for her and Quatina to come to them.

"Welcome, Healer," the taller man with the tousled blond hair and easy smile said. "Your timing couldn't be better!"

The second, shorter man also smiled and shyly extended his hand. "We were just discussing a case that you might have some insight on," he said.

Satisfied that the two women were accepted, the sentry left while the two physicians guided Aurori and Quatina into a separate room. The three men from the square were lying on beds, stoically eyeing them as they approached.

"You were there when these three were attacked?" the tall physician asked.

"No, we came after," Aurori said. "Just in time for the mop

up."

Both physicians nodded knowingly before the short one moved to the bed of one of the men and bent over him, pulling back the bloody bandage to reveal a vicious stab wound in the man's abdomen from which protruded a piece of shiny metal.

"The dagger was obviously forged from inferior metal. It snapped in two, leaving part inside the wound," the physician said. "My colleague and I were discussing the best way of removing it without having him bleed to death. Perhaps you could be of assistance?"

Aurori handed her pack to Quatina and went to examine the man. The wound was deep and only the pressure of the blade was keeping an artery from discharging its precious contents. It would take time and effort, but the man could be saved and she told him so, reassuring him in soft, confident tones as she explained what she had to do. Nodding his assent, the wounded man closed his eyes and seemed to relax.

After anesthetizing the man with a shot from one of her largest darts, Aurori set about performing the delicate procedure necessary to save the man's life, assisted by the short physician while his tall counterpart tended to the other two injured men.

With Quatina looking on and passing a few potions and instruments as asked, time ticked by for what seemed like hours. In reality, only two had passed. Finishing up by neatly sealing the entry wound, Aurori then applied a thick layer of the green salve and wrapped a clean bandage over the man's abdomen. She then pulled up a chair and sat heavily, gratefully accepting a cup of water from her short colleague.

"He's fortunate you were here," the physician said, smiling. "I don't know that we could have saved him."

Aurori gave him a demure smile. "I'm sure you would have." She looked at the wounded man. "Do you know why they were attacked?"

Tall, who stood framed in the doorway, was the one to answer when Shorty only shrugged and chewed the inside of his lip.

"They are Chihookians," Tall said. "Their attackers were from the Goloto'o faction which supports a return to autonomy, and these men were openly declaring their opposition to that notion and denouncing last night's violence when more Goloto'o showed up and decided to... persuade... them to see things their way."

Aurori shook her head sadly. "This is such a beautiful land. It's sad that the people have to endure such... hardships."

"Self-inflicted hardships," Shorty snorted, obviously disgusted. "It is no different than thrusting a dagger into your own belly. Chihookians and Goloto'o alike are stronger if they work together, but the hard-headed minority on both sides insists on trying to disrupt the peace we have finally been able to forge." He folded his arms as though to keep from lashing out in anger. "I only hope the council has the wisdom to ask the Chosen for assistance."

Quatina asked the obvious question about what the Chosen was expected to do and received the same story about police brutality that the man in the teahouse had related. Interestingly enough, the two physicians who had just exhibited such care and expended a great deal of time and energy on the three wounded Chihookians, were both Goloto'o themselves, proving how much a minority the splinter groups truly were.

Swiftly making their way back across the iron bridge after having said their farewells to the two physicians, Aurori and Quatina angled their way towards the government building, only to find Terien and Duncan both furiously pacing outside, flanked by the men who looked equally agitated. Surprisingly, they were all now wearing white shirts with high collars and long, billowy sleeves. A gift from the Chihookians?

"There you are! Where were you two so long? We were beginning to worry," Duncan said irritably, gesturing widely as Quatina ran the last few steps and threw herself into his arms, smiling happily.

"It's a long, long story," Aurori confessed, tiredly shaking her head as she strode up to Terien.

Terien's face screwed up with concern when he spotted the small cut near Aurori's hairline. "What happened?" he cried anxiously, stretching a hand out to touch her forehead.

Ducking his hand, she dropped her pack to the ground in

favor of putting her arms around his waist and resting her head against his chest. "It's nothing," she stated firmly.

Despite his best effort to feel miffed about her unwillingness to discuss what had happened, Terien returned her hug and let the relief of finding her safe (if somewhat damaged) wash over him. Sitting most of the day and listening to the council talk about the history of Chihook would have been spellbinding stuff if he hadn't been fretting about Aurori and Quatina wandering the streets of a city with such a tendency towards outbreaks of violence. His fears hadn't been totally unfounded, he noted without satisfaction, if the cut on Aurori's forehead was any indication. From what he'd been told, tensions were high and more rioting was expected. It would be good to leave before nightfall.

Aware of his men standing patiently behind him, Terien gently took hold of Aurori's shoulders and held her away. "I hope you two are ready to go. We're leaving Chihook."

Aurori looked confused. "But, we just got here. And what about the representative of Chihook? Are they sending one?"

"Yes. Two of them," he said, forestalling the question forming on her lips by holding up a finger. "I'll tell you everything later. Right now we're leaving. The council has asked that we not spend the night. They're expecting more trouble."

"I'd say it's already beginning," Aurori said unhappily.

She recounted for them what she and Quatina had witnessed on the Goloto'o side of the bridge, omitting for now the part about the brutality of the sentries. That and what she had learned in the teahouse and hospital were something she would discuss with Terien in private first.

Duncan looked to Terien for confirmation and then turned. "Okay people, let's move out!" Duncan called out, giving Quatina's hand a squeeze before heading towards Tiagra.

Taking Aurori's hand and giving it a kiss as they walked towards where Mystafire and Shangra stood waiting, Terien smiled and said, "I'm just glad you're safe. I hope you know how hard it was to keep my mouth shut when you asked Gregoro if you could go shopping."

"I know," Aurori told him softly and ran her hand down his

arm, enjoying the feel of the soft material of his new shirt. "Nice shirts. A gift?"

Terien smoothed his hands down the front of his shirt and then gave Aurori a leg-up onto Mystafire's back. "Yeah. Gregoro said the material would keep us cool and that the long sleeves would keep the bugs away." He smiled conspiratorially. "Personally, I think the gift was their way of apologizing for kicking us out of their city," he whispered.

Climbing onto Shangra's back, Terien trotted over to where Gregoro was saying goodbye to Corliss and Jeson.

"We shall look forward to your safe return," Gregoro said to the feuding couple who were just getting on the shaggy furred creatures the Chihookians called llayamas that they used for riding. "Beware of the ursuni. They will be plentiful in the mountains this time of the year."

"What are ursuni?" Terien asked, giving Gregoro a quizzical look as Makhani rode up.

"Did you notice the iron statue in the council chamber? That is an ursuni," Gregoro informed him with a small smile. "It is an animal native to this region and the symbol of our city."

Makhani's jaw dropped open. "Please tell me that statue was an oversize representation."

"Life size," Gregoro replied, his smile growing wider when Makhani groaned mournfully. "The ursuni are generally quite shy and will only attack if they are startled."

Makhani considered that for a moment and then nodded to himself. "So, if we make noise they won't be startled and won't attack. Right?"

Gregoro's lower lip protruded as he nodded thoughtfully. "That would certainly work."

Grinning, Makhani tossed off a salute to Gregoro and reined his equine over in the direction of Elek. "Hey! Elek! Someone has to sing to keep the ursuni away and I've just been elected!" he called out.

Elek's moan was loud enough to be heard by everyone. "Anyone got a gag? Or better yet – anyone got a noose?"

Shaking his head, Terien offered his hand to Gregoro and gave the old man a warm smile just as a booming thunderclap echoed overhead, reverberating across the valley.

"Looks like we're going to have a wet night," Terien commented as the rain started to fall in huge drops. "Gregoro, I want to thank you for everything. The fresh supplies you've given us are certainly appreciated. As are these shirts," he said, plucking at the soft material.

"You are most welcome. May the Maker go with you, Chosen," Gregoro said solemnly, bowing low. "And may your path rise to meet your feet."

Bowing his head slightly, Terien reined Shangra towards the head of the procession and led the way towards the iron bridge and the path that would take them away from Chihook.

Chapter Twenty Eight

Soloth, Primary of Quayvern, sat slumped slightly to the left with his elbow propped on the arm of his chair and his chin resting on his fist, listening as Walem, one of the other councilors, droned on about how one of the spires in his district needed immediate maintenance to its exterior, claiming that it was a disgrace for the people living in that tower to have to put up with such conditions.

Unintentionally tuning the man out, Soloth's eyes wandered over the interior of the circular council chamber. Built like an amphitheater with a forward-sloping floor and a semicircular raised stage on which the fifteen councilors sat behind an ornately carved bench, the chamber had seats for 1,000 spectators, but there were only a handful of citizens attending this session. Who could blame them? The agenda for the day was flat out boring.

Glancing to his left, Soloth met the eyes of his long-time friend, councilor Kell, and they shared a secret smile that said they were both tired of this assembly.

Shifting in his seat and stretching his cramping legs, Soloth cast his eyes back towards the podium where Walem was now engrossed in stating his proposed upgrades for the spire and caught Leander stifling a yawn next to him.

"I quite agree," Soloth whispered as he leaned in on the younger man who had served as Sub-Primary to the council for nearly ten years, fondly patting Leander's arm.

"Not exactly riveting stuff," Leander said with a reserved smile.

Soloth suppressed a chuckle and leaned back into his chair, steepling his fingers as he considered the future. As soon as the Chosen contacted him from Petrava, he would go out and bring them to Quayvern. With the negotiations under way between the representatives of Primus, he would announce his retirement and finish off the rest of his term in office in peace. Soloth knew that he was still the popular choice for Primary and that if he chose to run for the next election he would no doubt win by a wide margin, even over Leander who had also grown in popularity in recent years, but it was time to step aside and let a younger man like Leander have a go at leading the Council.

Twenty-five years was a long time to hold the seat of Primary of Quayvern, and he was finding the meetings increasingly tiring and that the demands on his time were becoming an annoyance. His wife had been after him to retire for two years and he had finally seen the wisdom of her words when he realized that his grandchildren were growing up fast and he hadn't even been able to find the time to take them down to the surface in the last few months.

Twenty-five years, he thought again, suddenly startled at how quickly the years had passed. He smiled inwardly as he considered all he had accomplished in that time. Bringing Quayvern back to Primus. Overseeing the excursions into the lands. Finding out about the legend and helping bring it to fruition. Now, there was an accomplishment he was truly proud of. It would be the crowning achievement of his service as Primary. A good note to retire on, he reflected.

Jolted out of his reverie by the sound of the grand clock chiming the end of the morning session, Soloth rose and thanked councilor Walem, then rang the ceremonial gong. The councilors filed from the room, leaving in small groups through the four doors set in the chamber's curving walls. Sliding out from behind the long bench, he exited through the nearest door, chatting with a few councilors on his way to his private office down the hall.

Closing the door once inside, he went to his desk and sat heavily in the leather chair and was rubbing at his tired eyes when a knock sounded at the door.

"Come in," he called out automatically, straightening.

Idona poked her head through the door, her long red hair swaying. "Care to join me for lunch?" she asked with a smile.

Soloth returned her smile but shook his head. "No, thank you, Idona. I'm just going to have lunch in my office today. Paperwork to review," he said, shrugging apologetically.

"No problem. See you later, sir," Idona said and was gone,

closing the door once more.

Sighing, Soloth opened a drawer in his desk and pulled out the boxed lunch his wife, Kereta, had prepared for him. Opening the box, he pulled out a sandwich and took a big bite, chewing thoughtfully as he pulled a sheaf of papers towards him.

Mouth full and attention on the papers, Soloth almost choked when the communications panel on his desk crackled to life, emitting a shriek of static that sent him shooting to his feet and set his heart pounding. Glaring down at the panel, he set his sandwich aside and fiddled with the adjustment knob for a moment, thinking there was a malfunction, but his hands flew away from the panel when a female voice emanated from it.

"*Merani Base to Quayvern. Please answer. I repeat, Merani Base to Quayvern. Can you hear me?*"

Hands shaking with excitement, Soloth stabbed down on the transmission button. "This... this is... Sky Lord Soloth," he managed to say, remembering at the last minute not to call himself by his title of Primary.

"*Thank the Maker! We finally got through!*" the female voice breathed, sounding relieved. "*My name is Naneve. I'm calling from Merani Base and I have news for you about the Chosen.*"

His blood froze in his veins at her mention of the Chosen and he had to sit down before his jellied knees decided to buckle. "I'm listening," he told her, and was glad he was sitting when she started explaining what had happened.

A short time later, his sandwich forgotten on his desk, Soloth was striding across the deck of the hangar bay, his jaw set with determination as he headed for the stall his private flyer occupied. He was halfway there when he remembered that his flyer had been under maintenance and that the technician had mentioned that he needed to take it out for a test flight this afternoon.

Cursing under his breath, Soloth went directly to the communications panel on the wall and punched in a frequency he often used and was relieved when Kell's lilting baritone responded almost immediately.

"Councilor Kell."

"Kell, my friend," Soloth said urgently, glancing over his

shoulder at a nearby group of technicians taking their lunch. He lowered his voice. "I need to borrow your flyer. No, wait. I need you to come with me, too."

Kell's voice was full of surprise and bewilderment. "Certainly – but, where are we going?"

"To find the Chosen," Soloth whispered. "I'll give you the details once we're airborne, but suffice it to say that there's been some trouble and I want to fly out to talk to him."

"That's... I mean, shouldn't you ask the Council for permission first?" Kell asked.

"No. That will take forever and I won't risk a negative decision," Soloth told his friend. He hesitated, then said, "You'll understand when I tell you what happened. I have to talk to them," he insisted, his voice rising with urgency. "Now, are you with me or must I steal your flyer and go alone?"

Soloth could hear Kell blow out a breath and could imagine his long-time friend considering the ramifications once their little trip came to the Council's attention.

"Oh, hell. I was planning on retiring pretty soon, anyway," Kell said with resignation. "The worst that could happen is that they force me into early retirement, right? I'll be down shortly. Kell out."

Soloth deactivated the communications panel and walked towards Kell's silver and red flyer, trying hard not to think about the uproar his spur of the moment trip would cause within the Council. His had been the strongest voice in favor of allowing the Chosen to make their journey without support or monitoring from Quayvern, and here he was breaking his own rules. Not exactly the proper thing to do, but certainly necessary for his peace of mind.

The Council be damned. There were times when the rules needed breaking. This was one of them.

★

Having made camp for the night just a few miles from Chihook, Terien and his group had spent a wet night huddled in their tents from an early hour as a thunderstorm had rolled in, cutting short their usual after-dinner conversation when the sky began to flash with an impressive display of lightning. Heavy rains and winds buffeted the mountain slope throughout the night, keeping everyone half awake.

By morning the brunt of the storm seemed to have passed, but a steady rain was still falling, leaving the road waterlogged and the trees dripping. They traveled with their cloaks draped over their heads to ward off the wetness, but the air temperature had climbed high enough by afternoon to be annoyingly warm.

"Well, this is perfectly miserable," Benem complained, struggling to keep his cloak raised over his head without actually putting it on.

"Quit bellyaching," Haren growled from where he sat beside Sahala on the cart they were riding, holding her cloak out over her head while trying to both keep himself covered and hold the reins with his other hand. Sighing, he gave up the struggle and sat fuming, getting soaked and looking completely put upon.

"Is it always this wet up here?" Jos asked, riding beside Jeson and Corliss at the back of the entourage.

"At this time of the year, yes. This is the rainy season," Jeson replied, looking completely at ease with the inclement weather. "Sometimes Chihook will get socked in by clouds and it will rain for a month straight. You should see the river rise in the gorge."

"We should watch for mud slides, too," Corliss put in. "The area between Chihook and the two settlements further up the road is fairly rough and is known for flash floods and mud slides."

Corliss's warning about mudslides and flash floods made Duncan break out in a cold sweat as he remembered his own past experience with them, but he forced the horrific memory aside and asked instead about the two settlements she mentioned. "Are these two settlements not allied at all with Chihook?" Duncan asked over his shoulder.

"They were at one time, but not for many generations now," Jeson answered. "Naru and Kral are pretty small and are quite close to Chihook, but they have their own Council of Elders. They do quite a bit of trade with us, however."

Nodding, Duncan turned back around and was about to kick

Tiagra into a trot so he could catch up to Terien who was up ahead and warn him about mud slides and flash floods, but he held back as a familiar whining sound could be heard in the distance.

"You hear that?" Duncan said to Aurori who was right in front of him, riding beside Quatina.

Aurori cocked her head to the side and listened, a slow smile spreading across her face. "It sounds like a Sky Lord's flyer. Naneve must have gotten through to Lord Soloth!" she said excitedly.

Near the middle of the procession, Terien had also heard the sound and was trying to scan the skies to see if he could spot the flyer, but without much luck. The thick canopy formed by the trees made it difficult to see more than a few patches of sky, but the whine from the flyer's propulsion system was loud enough to make it clear that it was getting close. Lord Soloth wasn't likely to see them down here, but up ahead, the road went uphill and broke through into an area where the trees weren't as dense, flanked by a steep hillside to the left and a span of sparse trees edged onto the deep ravine it followed.

Terien pointed up the road. "We have to get out in the open where he can see us!" he yelled above the growing noise from the flyer.

Excited, Rioto and Benem who were at the front of the procession spurred their felinae into a run, followed by Shaygan and Makhani on their equines and Terien trailing behind on Shangra.

Reaching the crest of the hill, Rioto and Benem skidded to a stop and waved wildly, buffeted by a down draft of hot air as the silver flyer swooped by and then banked a short distance away, turning back in their direction just as Shaygan and Makhani were charging up the hill.

Inside the flyer, Krisk grinned and flipped a set of switches on the panel, activating the weapons. "They're making this too easy," he said out loud to himself. "Take 'em out, dispose of the evidence and go home to collect a big, fat reward. Maybe I'll buy myself a nice penthouse suite," he laughed, his finger tightening on the trigger set on the flyer's control yoke.

Rain sleeting down his face, Rioto was centered on the road, still smiling and waving as the flyer finished its turn and lined up on him. Twin beams of energy lanced from the nose of the flyer, one striking him and his felinae, literally incinerating them, while the other tore into the rocky hillside, triggering a small landslide that flushed Benem's felinae off its feet and sent him rolling towards the ravine. Shaygan, who was just cresting the hill at the time, pulled back on his equine's reins, but the startled animal lost its footing in the roiling mud and they both plunged down the ravine after Benem, a large boulder pinning him.

"No!" Terien screamed, as the flyer continued past, then slowed to a hover and began to rotate back around.

Soloth and Kell were following the road below as they searched for the Chosen in Kell's silver and red flyer. After having heard what had happened to the Chosen at Merani Base and the subsequent mystery caller, Kell had agreed that Soloth was within his rights to want to go out and have a talk with Terien. They had been speculating about why someone would want the Chosen dead and had come up blank on that point, but had agreed that there was a high probability that someone on Quayvern itself was involved. The question was – who? There were few people who had opposed the plan to take the Prophecy and use it to help the people of Primus reunite themselves, and no one they could think of who could possibly benefit from its failure.

Still debating the issue as they rounded a mountain, Kell noticed another flyer in the far distance, hovering low over the trees.

"Isn't that your flyer down there?" he asked Soloth, pointing.

Soloth looked, eyes widening in surprise. "Yes, but what's he doing this far out? He should know better than to..."

Both men gasped in shock as the flyer started firing into the forest.

"What's he doing?" Kell cried in alarm.

"Picking up where Director Maxen left off!" Soloth shouted angrily.

They had to act, and quickly.

His eyes narrowing with determination, Soloth's lips curled

back into a predatory scowl as he slammed the throttle to maximum and the flyer shot forward, vibrating with the strain. "Arm weapons and prepare to fire!" he yelled at Kell, then dropped his voice to a menacing growl, his eyes fixed on the distant flyer. "You've picked the wrong man to cross, my friend. The wrong man indeed."

Fury and unspeakable anguish twisting like a knife in his belly, Terien squeezed his heels into Shangra's sides and charged up the hill towards Makhani who had turned his equine around and was skidding towards him, desperately trying to get out of harm's way without realizing that the flyer could still see him and was bearing down on him.

Launching himself from Shangra's back, Terien tackled Makhani off his equine's back just as the flyer passed slowly overhead, strafing the road. Both men narrowly missed being caught by the twin beams and it was only Shangra's incredibly powerful leap into the ravine that saved the big cat from suffering the same fate as the now smoldering corpse of Makhani's unfortunate equine.

Scrambling to their feet, Terien and Makhani watched in horror as the flyer's strafing run continued up the road, the light from the energy beams flashing down again and again, tearing into the road, churning up rock and mud.

"What the hell is going on?" Makhani roared, grabbing Terien's arm and spinning him around. "Why the hell are the Sky Lords trying to kill us?"

Chest heaving, Terien shook his head violently, trying to think straight past the fear thundering through his veins. He had seen Duncan hauling Aurori and Quatina onto Tiagra's back while he dismounted and sent the big cat off into the forest, but even that gave him no relief. The flyer was relentless and his people helpless. How long could they evade those beams?

"How the hell should I know?" Terien yelled back, reaching for the energy weapon strapped to his leg and adjusting the setting to maximum. "But there's no way I'm going to let this happen," he said dangerously. He whistled for Shangra. "I don't care what it takes," he spat, "that flyer is coming down!" He leapt onto

Shangra's back and offered Makhani his hand.

Without hesitation, Makhani grabbed his hand and swung up behind him, drawing his own energy weapon. Bellowing a challenge, Terien kicked Shangra's ribs. The big cat reared back, screaming his own challenge to the sky as his massive hind claws dug deep into the muddy ground and he tore up the hill at his master's command.

Overwhelmed and horrified after witnessing Rioto and Miasma's fiery end and the heart-stopping events that followed, it took Duncan's frantic shouts to mobilize the rest of the group into running for cover. Yanking Aurori and Quatina from their slower-moving equine and onto Tiagra's back as the first paired energy beams struck the road up ahead, Duncan jumped down and gave the cat's rump a hard slap, sending the two women off into the forest while he and Elek stayed near the road, shouting orders for everyone to run for cover into the forest.

"Move! Move! Move!" Elek roared, waving wildly as the beams stabbed closer.

The scene was absolute chaos. Unwilling to abandon the carts, the drivers steered them into the forest, careening between trees as the equines strained to pull their loads over the quagmire of the wet ground. Galloping after them, the riders dashed for cover, some abandoning their mounts who were bucking and whinnying in terror as their feet sank and slipped in the soft earth.

Teeth bared in a grimace, Haren, who had handed over his felinae to Pret and taken his place as a cart driver so he could ride with Sahala, snapped the reins and sent his team of equines bolting for the forest. The wheels of the cart caught on a ridge at the road's edge and the whole cart began to tip over. Realizing that he and Sahala would be crushed, Haren engulfed the Empress in his massive arms and jumped away from the cart, twisting in mid-air so that his own body would bear the brunt of the impact with the ground. Regardless, they rolled in a tangle before Haren's back smacked into a tree, bringing them to a jarring halt. Ignoring Sahala's sputtering protests, Haren bolted to his feet, swept her up and threw her over his shoulder before dashing further into the forest.

Managing to bring Tiagra to a stop, Aurori and Quatina slid

off his back and dove behind the huge rotting carcass of a fallen tree, huddling together.

"This can't be happening!" Aurori shouted, heartsick and trembling as she raised her head above the tree and searched for Terien in the direction of the hill, the image of him tackling Makhani and disappearing into the thick undergrowth burning in her mind.

"Why are they doing this!" Quatina exclaimed, angrily swiping at her stinging eyes as she watched Tiagra bound back towards Duncan who leaped onto the cat's back and rode off with Elek, heading in the direction they had all seen Benem and Shaygan go down.

"Get down!" Haren yelled as he plunged in beside them, yanking Sahala with him. Shielding all three women as best as he could with his own large frame, they hunkered down and waited for the flyer to pass, trying not to listen to the cries of pain and fear that now echoed through the forest.

Strafing the forest itself in random shots that splintered trees and sent clouts of loamy earth flying, the flyer maneuvered overhead, its pilot firing blindly. One stray shot caught one man in the leg as he ran and he went down screaming. Another unlucky fellow and his equine were making a mad dash for the ravine when a beam flamed down, smashing through the spindly trunk of a nearby young tree and sending it crashing down on top of them.

Leaving their llayamas to fend for themselves, Jeson and Corliss joined Jos in sliding down into the ravine. Muck-covered and shivering with fear and cold, they crouched low and hugged the steep bank, crowded together in a tight knot.

Rannoch had just survived having his equine slip on the wet grass and fall out from under him when a beam struck nearby, panicking him into a wild run that ended when he lost his footing and tumbled head over heels down the steep slope of the ravine. Knocking his head on the way down, Rannoch's unconscious, bulky form came to a rest face down in the murky stream at the bottom and he lay unmoving, arms floating out to the sides.

As the sound of the flyer receded, Aurori and Haren poked their heads up to survey the scene, Aurori's eyes once more searching for Terien. Her heart constricted painfully when she spotted him. He and Makhani were at the top of the hill, standing shoulder to shoulder as they fired round after round at the passing flyer.

Terror choking the breath from her lungs, Aurori's worst fear came true as the flyer's energy blast lashed out, surrounding Terien and Makhani in a nimbus of malignant light. Both men flew backwards, sliding on their backs down the rocky incline. When they came to a stop, neither one moved, lying as still as death.

"Terien!" Aurori screamed, her face contorted with agony as she shot to her feet, only to have strong hands grab her waist.

"No! You can't!" Haren shouted at her. He had witnessed what had happened to Terien and Makhani and knew she would run out there mindless of the danger. He hauled her down behind the log and wouldn't let go no matter how hard she struggled. "You're the Chosen! You have to survive!"

"Let me go, Haren!" Aurori raged. "Terien and Makhani need me!"

"He's gone, Aurori," Quatina said gently, pushing Haren aside and taking Aurori's hands in hers. "We all saw what happened to Rioto and Miasma. Do not let your grief overwhelm you. Terien and Makhani would want you to live. You are the Chosen."

"No! There are no Chosen!" Aurori cried, hot tears coursing down her cheeks. "The Sky Lords have betrayed us! Without Terien there's nothing left! Let me at least…"

Her tirade ended abruptly as a second flyer screamed in overhead, the force of its sudden deceleration shaking the trees and sending a shudder through the ground as it opened fire on the first flyer. Propulsion systems whining, both flyers took off, trading shots as they receded into the distance.

A ragged cheer went up just as Jos's pitiful call for help rang out from the ravine.

"Help! Aurori! Help!"

"You are needed, Healer," Quatina said firmly, standing and hauling Aurori to her feet. "There will be time for grieving later. Right now you must help the living go on living."

Disoriented, devastated and wishing she could curl up in a ball and cry, Aurori choked back the bitter sob building in her chest and leaned on Haren's arm for support as he led her to the edge of the ravine.

Becoming aware that rain was pelting his face, Terien opened his eyes and groaned. Every nerve in his body felt as if it were on fire and he was almost sure someone was pounding on the top of his head with a club. Lying on his back (which felt as if Shangra had used it for a scratching post) with his head facing downhill, he had a spectacular view of an impressive silver and red flyer swooping in at high speed, decelerating so fast that the air shrieked in protest and the ground trembled. Like an avenging angel, the new arrival turned on the silver flyer that had been strafing the forest and his friends, firing crimson beams of energy at it and pursuing it away.

His foggy brain finally got the concept and Terien drew a shaky breath. So. The mysterious call they had received in Merani Base had something to do with the Sky Lords. But what?

Realizing that Makhani was beside him and still wasn't moving, Terien was just struggling to sit up and reorient his legs to face downhill so he could check on the blond man when Duncan and Elek clawed their way up the hillside to their position.

"You're alive!" Duncan cried, grabbing Terien by the shoulders. "By the Maker, man! We thought you were finished for sure when we saw that energy beam strike you two! What the hell were you thinking, standing out in the open like that?"

"Heat of the moment," Terien said with a contrite grin. "We didn't actually get hit by the beam. The details are a little foggy, but I seem to remember it hitting the hillside just beside us, then – wham! – it was like jumping into frozen water – every nerve in my body went haywire. I don't know what happened after that," he admitted, wincing as his back twinged. Tucking an arm up behind his back, his hand encountered shredded material and came away sticky with blood. "Actually, I think I'm glad I don't remember the rest," he said ruefully, turning his attention to Elek who was now shouting in an attempt to rouse Makhani.

"Come on, Blondy! Wake up!" Elek said loudly, slapping

Makhani's face gently. Getting no response, he slapped him harder.

Moaning, Makhani tossed his head from side to side, then opened his eyes. "Quit hittin' me."

Elek blew out a breath. "Quit scarin' me and we'll talk," he joked, now helping Makhani sit up.

Relieved that Makhani was okay, Terien turned back to Duncan as a renewed wave of concern surged through him. "Is everyone okay? I mean – aside from Rioto. Quatina? The representatives? ...Aurori?" he asked, afraid of the answer.

Duncan nodded. "I think so. We've got some badly wounded, though. Elek and I had to get some of the guys to help us move a boulder off Shaygan. Don't know if he'll make it," he reported with a sad shake of his head. "And Benem has a broken leg. Looks bad."

Terien didn't feel all that well himself at the moment, but he staggered to his feet with Duncan's help and cast a glance up at the sky. The two flyers were quite a distance away now, still bobbing and weaving as they traded shots. As concerned as he was with the outcome of their fight, he had more pressing matters to attend to.

"Come on. I need to know how everyone else is," Terien said grimly.

When Aurori and Haren reached the edge of the ravine and looked down, there below was Jos, holding Rannoch's limp body, flanked by Corliss and Jeson who were clinging to each other so tightly that it made Aurori's heart ache just to look at them.

"He's not breathing!" Jos wailed.

Galvanized by the helplessness of Jos's tone, Aurori half ran, half slid down the slippery incline and fell to her knees beside Rannoch. Pulling him from Jos's lap so he was now flat on the ground, she felt for a pulse, and finding none, placed her hands over his chest and began compressing it. Alternating that with blowing breaths in through his mouth, she fought to save his life.

Trailed by Duncan, Elek and Makhani, Terien wove his way

through the forest, stopping first where Shaygan and Benem lay being tended. Benem was in fairly good spirits, especially upon finding out Terien was alive, but his left leg was bent at an odd angle and he was in obvious pain. Shaygan, on the other hand, had a massive bruise forming across his chest and abdomen and was having difficulty breathing. Not a good sign. Offering what words of encouragement he could, Terien went on to check on the rest of his men and was dismayed to learn that Cornel had been crushed beneath a falling tree, suffering possibly a broken back, and that Stev had a badly burned leg after a glancing blow from the energy beam.

They had come away from the ordeal better than Terien had hoped and worse than he cared for. One man was dead, as were several equine and one felinae, and there were four men seriously wounded. Even learning that Aurori was alive and well, tending Rannoch who had undetermined injuries, was cold comfort at the moment.

Despite the dizziness and fatigue gnawing at him, Terien forced himself to head in the direction of the ravine, Duncan and Makhani in tow. They were nearly there when Makhani suddenly collapsed on his knees.

"You okay?" Duncan asked, squatting next to Makhani as Terien sunk to his knees beside both of them and braced a hand against a tree. He didn't look much better.

"Sorry. Just... feeling a little... dizzy and... out of breath," Makhani panted, hunched over with his arm across his stomach.

"Must be the after-effects from the beam," Duncan decided.

Terien patted Makhani's shoulder. "It's okay. I don't feel so great either." He cast a glance in the direction of the ravine, then looked at Duncan. "Go see what's happening, will you? We'll be along in a minute."

Duncan nodded and strode off.

Everyone cheered when Rannoch finally drew a breath and began to cough. Aurori hugged him despite his efforts to wave her away, then sat back on her haunches, smiling and crying at the same time. A wave of grief washed over her and she sobbed once, biting into her lip to drive back the urge to cry. She had work to do.

While she had worked to save Rannoch she had still been aware of the cries of pain coming from the forest, and she now struggled to her feet, intent only on getting up there and doing her duty as a Healer.

Turning towards the ravine's slope, Aurori began to claw her way up, gratefully accepting Quatina's hand as she neared the top. Clearing the lip of the ravine, her breath caught and her heart skipped a beat. Duncan was striding towards her and behind him, helping each other to their feet, were Terien and Makhani!

"You... you're alive!" Aurori cried out, and it was only Quatina's firm hold on her hand that kept her from almost pitching backwards into the ravine in her surprise.

"That's debatable at the moment," Makhani called back, giving Terien a gentle shove in Aurori's direction.

Coming together in a rush, Terien swept Aurori into his arms and hugged her tight, burying his face against her neck as she cried into his shoulder. Both exhausted and trembling, they sank to their knees on the soft ground, clinging to each other fiercely as tears streamed down both their faces. They stayed that way for a few moments before Aurori gently pulled back and took Terien's face in her hands.

"I love you, Terien," Aurori murmured quietly, her eyes searching his as she gently stroked his face.

"And I you," he replied tenderly, giving her a gentle smile as he caressed the tears from her cheeks then embraced her once more.

Sharing a warm embrace of their own, Duncan and Quatina shuffled aside as Haren and Jos helped Corliss and Jeson heave Rannoch up from the ravine.

A murmur of disquiet swept through the crowd as the sound of a flyer approaching filled the air and brought everyone to a standstill. The tension in the air was almost palpable. Craning their heads back to catch a glimpse of which one it was, a collective sigh of relief went up when they sighted a flash of silver and red moving overhead.

"I better go see what I can do for some of the injured," Aurori said, giving Terien's back a quick look. Satisfied that he could wait, she gave Makhani a hug and a peck on the cheek, checked his back and checked him out as well, then hurried off to the side of the nearest injured man.

Terien watched her go, then looked over to where the flyer was now landing at the top of the hill. He turned to find Duncan already walking his way.

"Let's go and see if we can wring a few answers out of the Sky Lords," Terien said with hostility.

Striding out to greet the flyer, Terien's face was a study in cold determination as he readied himself to fire off a few pointed questions and not back down until he had some answers. When the door irised open and Lord Soloth stepped out, however, one look at the grief and anguish on the old man's face melted the ice from his heart.

"Terien! Oh, Ancestors! Thank the Maker you're alive!" Soloth cried, enfolding Terien in a fatherly hug. "I thought the worst when we saw that flyer shooting down into the forest!" Taking hold of Terien's shoulders, he held him at arm's length, his expression souring into outrage. "And my own flyer at that, damn it!"

"Lord Soloth, please – tell me what's going on," Terien pleaded, hands spread apart. "Why were the Sky Lords trying to kill us? What's going on?"

"I don't know who's behind this, but I intend to find out!" Soloth growled. "If it weren't for the call I received from your friends in Merani Base, I would never have known anything was wrong until you didn't show up at Quayvern. As it is, Kell and I were only flying out to talk to you about what happened at Merani. We had no idea that another flyer was out here trying to kill you," he said, suddenly feeling weak in the knees as a thought occurred to him and he had to place a hand on Kell's shoulder for support. "By the Maker! What if I hadn't decided to come? Or if we'd been an hour too late!"

"Don't think about it," Terien said grimly, then changed the subject. "You said you spoke to Merani Base. Did Naneve tell you about the mystery call we received?"

"Yes. She told me everything," Soloth said. He shook his head. "The call had to have come from Quayvern, my boy. Or the caller had connections to Quayvern, at the very least."

"That just became painfully obvious," Terien said grimly. "Did Naneve also tell you about how we tricked the caller into revealing what he was calling about?"

"She mentioned it briefly," Soloth said. Puzzled by where Terien was going with this, he was just gearing up to ask when Kell grabbed him and Terien each by the sleeve.

"They are wounded, Soloth," he said, nodding towards the forest. "Shouldn't this discussion wait until later?"

Soloth moved away from Terien and went directly to where Aurori was now examining Shaygan. Despite the panic she felt, a veneer of professionalism had dropped into place and she gave the injured man a comforting smile and a pat on the arm before Soloth drew her aside.

"Tell me, Healer. How bad is it?" Soloth asked in a soft tone.

"Bad enough. There are four men here that I can't do anything for," she whispered hoarsely. "If we were back in Chihook there might be a chance, but not here. I don't have the proper instruments."

Rubbing a hand across his face, Soloth nodded and beckoned Kell forward with a finger. "I want you to take these four men to Quayvern. See to it that their injuries are treated."

"We could call for help. Have more flyers sent and transport everyone to Quayvern," Kell suggested.

Soloth shook his head. "No. We don't know who was behind this. We can't risk alerting the wrong people." He placed a hand on Kell's shoulder. "Fly back with these men and tell Leander what's happened. Have him institute the Emergency Measures Act. Recall all flyers and make sure no one leaves Quayvern. Ask him to also schedule an emergency meeting of the Council for after my return tomorrow. I'll explain everything to them in more detail then."

"You... you're not coming back with me?"

"No. I'll stay here the night. Come back for me tomorrow morning," Soloth told him.

"What are you going to do, Soloth?" Kell asked worriedly.

"Tell them everything. They deserve that much after what's happened," Soloth said angrily. "We would have told them once they reached Quayvern, anyway. I'm just advancing the timing."

His expression softened. "And tell Kereta I won't be coming home tonight, would you? Poor woman will have a fit, but she'll understand when you tell her about all this."

Kell sighed and his shoulders slumped. "I hope you know what you're doing."

"So do I, Kell," Soloth said with a small sigh. "Now go. These men desperately need medical attention."

Terien had listened in on every word and now stepped forward. "Just don't tell anybody the details about the mystery call we received in Merani Base."

Kell looked perplexed. "But… but…"

"Do as he says," Soloth told Kell, but his eyes were on Terien. "What are you thinking, my boy?"

"The caller was told a pack of lies that could be used to trip him up," Terien said. "Farnash made it sound as though Director Maxen was still alive and that Garel was out checking around. He also told the caller that I had already escaped. If only you and Kell know what truly took place, you might be able to use that to trip up any suspects you find."

Understanding dawned on Kell's face. "I'll just say that we received a call from Merani Base to let us know that Director Maxen tried to kill the Chosen. I won't mention more than that."

Satisfied, Terien now instructed his men to move the injured onto the flyer. As soon as they were aboard, Kell had the flyer in the air and angling towards Quayvern.

It was then that Soloth turned to Terien and sighed heavily. "I have much to tell you," he said, but Terien forestalled him with an upraised hand.

"I suggest we tend to the minor injuries we have and get a camp set up first," Terien said. "I have a feeling that everyone is going to want to hear what you have to say."

Chapter Twenty Nine

Except for a few minor abrasions, cuts and bruises, the remainder of the group had escaped the ordeal relatively unscathed and Aurori was able to treat them quite quickly.

After a successful group effort to set right the overturned cart, they divided the work details to round up the scattered equine, set up camp and dig graves for Rioto and the fallen animals. In all, they had lost six animals – Rioto's felinae, Makhani's equine and four more equines that had to be put down after sustaining broken legs in their flight through the woods.

Morale hit an all-time low when they came together to bury Rioto, for that was when the traumatic events of the day finally hit home. Not one person held back his tears as they huddled together to lay their fallen comrade to rest amidst the verdant greenery of the ageless forest, and nature itself seemed to feel the need to ease their suffering by putting an end to the rain.

Finally able to change into dry clothes, they set about preparing dinner after Soloth insisted they eat and refused to even consider giving his talk until they had, and it was during this time that two interesting events took place.

Sahala had been avoiding Haren like the plague ever since the incident with the flyer, going so far as to actually run away from him the one time he tried to approach her to ask if there was anything she needed. She paced around nervously, wringing her hands and looking on the verge of tears, causing everyone to wonder what could possibly have her so worked up until all at once she seemed to come to a decision.

In full Empress mode, Sahala now stalked up to Haren who was quietly minding his own business and giving Elek a hand preparing dinner. Assuming her patented air of regal haughtiness, she slapped him soundly across the face.

"What was that for?" Haren griped, rubbing at his offended cheek.

"For hauling me around like a sack of produce!" Sahala said archly, drawing herself up imperiously.

Just as suddenly, before Haren could make the retort forming on his lips, she rushed in and grabbed his face in her hands, kissing him firmly before throwing her arms around him and pressing her face to his chest.

"What... what was that for?" Haren now asked, his voice high with startled confusion.

"For saving my life," Sahala said in a small, quavering voice.

Looking around helplessly, hoping someone could explain the Empress' outrageous behavior, Haren got a series of raised eyebrows and shrugs in response. Totally confused, he shrugged his own shoulders in resignation and wrapped his arms around her, clumsily patting her back in an attempt to comfort her.

Elek, meanwhile, was so engrossed with the spectacle that he sliced the knife he was using into his thumb instead of the vegetable he was holding, cursing loud enough to draw everyone's attention.

"It's okay! Just cut my thumb," he reported, chagrined.

"Let me have a look," Aurori offered from where she sat by the fire, stirring a pot. Climbing to her feet, she went over to Elek and inspected the profusely bleeding cut. Pressing the tip of her thumb into the first joint of her middle finger, a ritual they had all seen many times by now, she placed her fingertip at the apex of the cut, slowly drawing it over the wound until all that remained was a slightly raised pink line.

"No matter how many times I see you do that, it still amazes me," Elek said, shaking his head and staring at his thumb as he went to wash his hands in a bucket of water nearby before resuming his task of cutting up vegetables.

After also washing her hands, Aurori returned to the fire and now sat beside Terien, letting Quatina take over stirring the pot she had been tending. Taking Aurori's hand in his, Terien ran his thumb gently over the tiny raised scar he found on her finger and silently raised an eyebrow.

Aurori looked at Terien apprehensively, but the question she expected wasn't being asked and she ultimately gave a small sigh.

"Implants," Aurori said, curling her fingers around Terien's hand.

Terien looked at her, perplexed by the suddenness of her statement. "Excuse me?"

"Not all Healers have them, but those who are about to go on long journeys have tiny mechanical devices implanted in their fingers," Aurori explained. "There are two of them; one in the index finger that's used to make incisions, and one in the middle finger used to seal a wound." She looked up as several people drew nearer, amazement on their faces, and gave them a small smile. "We think that Eristea used to manufacture them before the Great Division and we still have stockpiles of them. From what I've seen, they work on the same principle as the energy weapons Naneve gave us, or the energy beams we saw today," she said, her voice trailing off as she shivered at the memory of the flyer firing down on them and she slid her hand out of Terien's to stare at her own fingers, suddenly feeling that she, too, had a part in the suffering of her friends simply by possessing a technology with such deadly potential.

From where he sat across from her, Soloth nodded thoughtfully, recognizing her discomfort. "Precisely so, but you must remember that this technology is neither good nor bad. It is a tool whose use depends on the intention of the user."

Aurori nodded absently. "I know, but – I don't think I'll ever be able to use my implants again without thinking about what happened. Or hating the… pain… when I do."

Taking her hand once more, Terien looked at it questioningly. "It… hurts when you use the implants?"

"When I activate them, they either cut or burn through my fingertips. It doesn't last long and the beams are actually very narrow, but, yes, it does hurt – until I deactivate them and they close the wound as they shut down."

"Lass, that's terrible!" Rannoch blurted out.

"A small price to pay for being able to heal wounds, don't you think?" Aurori asked in reply, embarrassed.

"Perhaps so," Makhani reflected. "I am puzzled, however. Why did you feel you had to tell us this? You know none of us would have asked despite being curious about how you are able to… do what you do," he finished, making a helpless gesture.

"Healers don't usually reveal their secrets, but have been known to let their friends in on it from time to time," Aurori told him, then looked at Terien. "I suppose I just wanted to let go of the last secret I was holding."

Terien gave her hand a squeeze and smiled at her, then accepted the bowl of steaming stew Elek passed to him.

Also accepting a bowl, Soloth leaned his back against the log behind him and looked around. Everyone had settled in for dinner, squeezing together in a two-tiered circle around the single fire. He sighed heavily. "You speak of wishing to let go of secrets," he said, setting his bowl aside. "It's time I let go of mine."

Terien shook his head and swallowed his mouthful quickly. "You said after dinner," he reminded Soloth. "Don't you go breaking your own rule?"

Soloth laughed outright at that. "I've already done so once this day," he replied, but relented and picked up the bowl. He shoveled a spoonful of the stew into his mouth, chewing pensively. "Still, a little dinner conversation couldn't hurt," he said with a sly smile.

"You already know all about the history of our planet. How the world before the Great Division was filled with technology and how that came to an end when the comets fell," Soloth said. "You most certainly have heard the Legend about how the Sky Lords were credited with amazing acts of heroism and piety in the months following the cataclysm, relocating refugees and helping people escape the devastation."

"That is a matter of history, not simply a part of the Legend," Corliss interjected. "The Goloto'o are proof of that."

"Quite true," Soloth agreed, taking the opportunity to have another spoonful of the delicious stew. "There is more to that story, however. You see, Quayvern was originally a multinational research and development platform before the cataclysm, populated by scientists and scholars from all over Primus. It was from Quayvern that the comet had first been sighted by astronomers using a powerful new telescope they had built," he said. "As you can imagine, Quayvern survived the comet shower simply because of its mobility. Afterwards, the scientists did all they could to help the survivors, relocating many to some of the other cities that had also remained intact by virtue of being built underground or underwater.

"Such as Alatesh, Merani Base and Petrava?" Terien asked.

"Exactly! Those cities could only accept so many refugees, however, and many more were transported to places like Chihook," Soloth said with a nod in Corliss and Jeson's direction. "There was one problem, though. Many of the displaced citizens were angry at having been placed in the surface cities where the technology was in ruins when so many others were being allowed to live in places like Quayvern and Merani Base where technology survived intact." Soloth sighed and set his empty bowl aside. "I do not know all the details because my ancestors chose to erase the records pertaining to what truly happened, but about sixty years after the cataclysm it was decided to leave Primus and go out in search of other survivors on other continents."

"Also a matter of legend," Makhani said impatiently. "Or history, as is the case. The Legend tells that the Sky Lords left Primus because the people were angry and jealous of them and that they would not return to fulfill the Prophecy until the people of Primus had mended their ways." Makhani offered an elaborate shrug. "So far you're not saying much that we don't already know."

"What did they find on the other continents?" Elek wanted to know.

"Much of this planet remains a devastation zone," Soloth said quietly, his words creating a buzz of disbelief. "There are whole continents out there that are nothing but vast wastelands, devoid of any kind of life, even after all the hundreds of years that have passed."

"Then, where have the Sky Lords been all this time? Everyone knows Quayvern only reappeared over Primus approximately a year ago," Jos said, shifting to lean forward with his hands resting on his upraised knees.

Looking uncomfortable, Soloth rocked forward and slowly got to his feet. He inserted his hands into the opposing sleeves of his robe, now becoming very formal. "Quayvern has been landed on several continents over the centuries, the most recent being Heretallia, where my people have lived for the last 200 years.

Heretallia, much like Primus, survived the cataclysm relatively intact and my people chose a secluded, uninhabited area to settle," he told them. "I was still a young lad when people began talking about returning to Primus and the idea captivated me. So, when I later ran for election to the Council, I promised that if I were voted in as Primary of Quayvern, I would see to it that Quayvern returned to Primus. That proposal garnered me great support and I won by a wide margin. A year later we left Heretallia and arrived back over Primus." Soloth paused, pursing his lips as he looked around at the intent faces around him. "That was almost twenty-four years ago."

Open astonishment rippled through the camp and Terien finally had to stand up and quiet everyone down, for they were all talking and asking questions at once.

"Calm down, everyone," Terien pleaded, then turned to Soloth. "Okay, so the Sky Lords have been on Primus longer than we thought," he said, gesturing with one hand. "Why didn't you reveal yourselves before now? Was this prescribed in the Prophecy?"

Soloth scratched at the back of his neck, looking decidedly uneasy. "We're... not actually... Sky Lords," he said haltingly, his words creating a buzz of disbelief.

Rannoch pushed to his feet and quickly shushed everyone. "What makes ye say that?" he asked, heavy gray brows knitting in consternation.

Soloth looked like he was in agony now and began to pace back and forth. "When we returned to Primus and liked what we saw, we decided to stay. But we were uncertain about what kind of welcome we would receive after so many hundreds of years and chose not to reveal ourselves. For years we remained hidden in the far northern regions, occasionally making journeys into the cities, disguised as traders. It was during one of these outings that I first heard about the Legend and the Prophecy, and I was stunned to find that not only was the city of Quayvern mentioned, but that our people were being called 'Sky Lords' and were expected to select two Chosen who would help reunite the people of Primus," he told them, looking terribly apologetic.

"Go on," Rannoch said, gesturing.

"I put forth the proposal that we fulfill our prescribed roll in the Prophecy and the people of Quayvern voted in its favor." He began to pace, a few feet this way and a few feet that way. "We only wished to help you bring the leaders of the cities together so that the Final Reunification could be brought to fruition." He hung his head contritely. "We did intend to tell you the truth once you reached Quayvern, despite our fear that you may take a dim view of our participation in the fulfillment of the Prophecy once you learned that we're just ordinary people. We hoped that after being together through the inevitable hardships of the journey, you would want to continue on with the Final Reunification despite our meddling."

"Fer pity's sake, man! Are ye sayin' that ye deny bein' the Sky Lords because ye feel unworthy of th' title?" Rannoch asked incredulously.

"We're just people like you. Nothing more," Soloth said quietly, shaking his head. "We never intended to deceive you. We just... wanted so much to help you reunite yourselves."

"Tell me this – did you make-up the Legend and the Prophecy?" Jos asked.

"Certainly not!" Soloth denied vehemently. "We had no part in creating them and have no idea how they came to be."

Jos laughed. "Then you didn't meddle in the Prophecy. You fulfilled your part in it, just as was foretold. Just as Terien and Aurori are. As we all are," he told Soloth, getting sage nods from everyone gathered. He stood and addressed his fellow representatives. "The people of Merani Base have known about the Legend and the Prophecy for generations, but we, more than anyone else could, also knew that Quayvern was a city not much different from our own," he said, now advancing to Soloth and placing a hand on the older man's shoulder. "No one expected the Sky Lords to be gods. We expected you to be... just as you are. People of high moral standing who would one day return and fulfill the Prophecy."

"But... we're not..." Soloth was starting to protest.

"Yes, you are," Sahala interrupted him, shooting to her feet. "You're missing one important fact. The Prophecy explicitly names Quayvern as the city of the Sky Lords. Whoever the author of the Prophecy was, they gave the people of Quayvern that title for a purpose," she reasoned.

"I was going to say that we're not of such high moral standing," Soloth said. "Look at what happened this afternoon."

"The people of Chihook understand, more than we would like to," Corliss said sadly, placing a hand on her husband's arm and giving him a meaningful look. "The people of Quayvern – the Sky Lords – obviously suffer from the same problem we do. There are always those who will oppose something right and good for the sake of their own agenda."

"What it comes down to, Soloth, is that we believe you are the Sky Lords and that you've fulfilled your part in the Prophecy whether you feel worthy of it or not," Makhani asserted. "Nothing you can say will change that and we fully intend to carry on with this journey and the Final Reunification," he said, looking to his fellow representatives who loudly made known their agreement. "What we do want to know," Makhani continued, "is who tried to kill us and end the Final Reunification, and what they possibly stood to gain by it."

"I don't know," Soloth said dejectedly. "I truly don't. Kell and I were speculating about that and could not come up with an answer. Unfortunately, the flyer's pilot refused to answer our calls and the reason for his attack died with him when we shot him down." Soloth spread his hands in supplication. "All I can tell you is that there were some people who opposed our participation in the Prophecy's enactment, but that the vast majority voted in favor. I can only offer my sincere regrets for what has happened and assure you that we will do all we can to bring the person or persons responsible to justice."

"I can live with that. For now," Sahala said, fixing Soloth with an imperious stare that said he'd better have some answers for them when they reached Quayvern. "What I want to know is how you selected the Chosen. Why did you decide on these two?" Sahala asked, nodding at Terien and Aurori who traded embarrassed glances as every eye in the group turned to them. "The Prophecy was explicit about what kind of people they would be and I can't argue with your choice, but how did you find them when you were supposedly hiding back here in the hills?"

Soloth relaxed a bit. At least this was one question he had no compunction about answering. "Remember that we had been making excursions into the cities for several years, so we had a good idea where to find a pair of young people who would fulfill the requirements," he told them. "We then sent our representatives out to announce the coming of the Chosen, asking that they pay close attention to whom they would choose to fill the roll of the Chosen. When they reported back, six candidates were put forth and the Council then made their selection from that list." Soloth now turned to Terien and Aurori but found them avoiding his eyes. "Aurori was selected as the Observer primarily because she proved to be a very observant individual," he said with a shrug. "She possesses many of the characteristics that were laid out in the Prophecy and her status as Healer ensured that she would be able to journey across Primus without drawing much attention. Terien, on the other hand, was the obvious choice for the Gatherer. Having recently been through negotiations with Glaybor, he would be familiar with the process. In addition, he, too, possessed the lofty qualities demanded by the Prophecy."

"Careful, now," Makhani cautioned, smiling wryly. "All this high praise is likely to give Royal Boy a swelled head."

Everyone laughed at that.

"I just have one question," Quatina said, speaking for the first time since the discussion began. "Do all the Sky Lords – Quayvernians – wear such handsome robes despite the heat, or is it cold on Quayvern?" she asked innocently.

Soloth laughed and looked down at himself. He did look rather ridiculous, clothed in a hot and heavy robe on an evening that was pleasantly warm and humid. "My council robes. We usually wear them only for Council meetings," he said, abashed. "We decided they made us look more distinguished for our portrayal of Sky Lords, but I don't imagine that I need to perpetuate that deception any longer." He now unbuttoned the royal blue robe and removed it to reveal the light gray suit and high-collared white shirt he wore, sighing with relief to be rid of its hot bulkiness.

Sahala suddenly gasped in surprise and pushed past Jos to get to Soloth, her wide eyes fixed on the crest embroidered on the breast pocket of his jacket as she reached out uncertainly to touch it.

"What is it, child?" Soloth asked her.

"This emblem… what does it mean?" Sahala asked in a choked whisper, now looking up at Soloth with afflicted eyes.

Perplexed, Soloth looked down at the crest – a stylized circle featuring a bird in flight with a torch and a sword crossed over its breast. "It's the crest of Quayvern," he replied, then looked at her. "The letter 'Q' with a dove of peace to symbolize our peaceful quest for knowledge and truth, which are in turn symbolized by the torch and sword. You… recognize it?"

Sahala nodded and slowly pulled her hand away. Reaching behind her head, she unfastened her hairpin and held it out to Soloth with trembling hands. "This was my mother's. She told me that my father gave it to her before I was born," she said tearfully, shaking her head. "Everyone believes that I was conceived during one of my mother's tours of the towns allied with Pergase, but the truth is that my father was a stranger traveling through Pergase. He told my mother he was from a great land faraway and he gave her this, promising to return one day, but he never did." Sahala wiped her face with her sleeve. "When I was a little girl I always dreamed of one day traveling all over Primus so I could find him," she said, sounding pitifully like a little girl right at that moment.

Soloth took the pin from her and turned it over in his hands. "I'm sorry, child. This pin is definitely from Quayvern, but it would be difficult to find out who it had belonged to. I can think of several young men who would have passed through Pergase those many years ago that we were exploring Primus," he said, shaking his head. He pressed the pin back into Sahala's hand and folded her fingers over it. "However, I could make a few discreet inquiries, if you like."

"No. It's okay," Sahala said. "I didn't mean to… I was just hoping…" Her voice failed her and she ran off to the edge of the forest where she slowly sank down onto a log and sat hunched over and crying, staring at the hairpin in her hands.

"How terribly sad for her to find out where her father comes from and still not know who he is," Quatina commented quietly, casting a glance at Sahala.

Moved by pity, Haren rose and went to Sahala. He sat beside her on the log and put an arm around her, talking softly to her as she leaned against him and sobbed quietly.

"Let's leave them alone, shall we," Aurori said, drawing everyone's attention away.

"I suggest we bring Soloth up to date on all we've experienced so far," Terien said. "Particularly the part about Merani Base."

"Indeed," Soloth agreed, settling himself by the fire along with everyone else. "Naneve was only able to give me a brief account of what had transpired."

"And then you can tell us what we can expect to find in Petrava," Makhani added, then looked at Soloth with narrowed eyes. "Never mind. Just tell me that the people there aren't led by a madman bent on our destruction."

Everyone laughed nervously at his comment, but they still looked worriedly at Soloth who laughed and clapped his hands.

"You're in luck! I was the one assigned to go to Petrava to make the announcement about the Chosen," he said, still chuckling. "I can assure you that there will be no surprises in store for you there. Their leader, Elos, is a fine young man who was actually one of the six being considered for the roll of the Chosen Gatherer," he told them with a wink, but his expression quickly grew somber once more. "I have no doubt that you will make it safely to Quayvern," he said in a low voice, "but I worry about your arrival. I can't promise that we will have everything resolved by the time you get there."

Terien met eyes with every representative he had gathered and found his own determination mirrored there. Looking last to Aurori, he took her hand. "Then we'll just have to be prepared for anything," he replied resolutely.

Chapter Thirty

Leander left his own office and walked down the corridor with a bounce in his step, his green ceremonial robes swishing around his legs and a placid smile on his lips.

Upon Kell's return to Quayvern and after the four injured men from the Chosen's entourage had been hastily taken to the medical bay, Leander had been outraged to learn that his carefully laid plan had failed. The Chosen were still alive, having been rescued by Soloth himself after Merani Base had apparently called to tell him what had transpired there. Kell had deplored at length what had happened while conveying Soloth's orders and it had been all Leander could do to keep the rage from his face until Kell let slip that Soloth intended to announce his retirement as soon as the Chosen reached Quayvern. His rage had instantly transmuted to an overwhelming feeling of joy and victory. True, a great deal of time and effort had gone into plotting Soloth's downfall and had been all for naught, but the victory was just as sweet. Quayvern was his.

All that remained was to weather the storm of questions and investigations that would follow. Albeon and Edegan, as well as Idona, had been near panic the night before when they had met together and Leander told them what had transpired, but he had calmed them by telling them that since it was he himself who was to lead the investigation, events could easily be dead-ended or colored as necessary. The key was to keep suspicion firmly placed on Krisk, the technician who had repaired Soloth's flyer, and they had chosen to involve Krisk for two very important reasons: his violent past history and his lust for mayhem. It would be all too easy to pin blame on the dead man.

Now, with the return of Soloth and the emergency meeting of the Council less than two hours away, Leander stepped into the ante-room of Soloth's office suites and exchanged a victorious smile with Idona who was at her usual post behind her desk, dressed in the drab pale blue skirt and jacket she often wore for her secretarial position. Giving her a confident wink, he went to the door set in the far wall and, tucking the report he carried under his arm, knocked briskly.

"Enter," came Soloth's voice from within.

Doing as he was bidden, Leander entered the office and closed the door behind him, noting that the dark blue ceremonial robes Soloth was just putting on looked a little rumpled after his night in the woods with the Chosen.

"You look well after having spent a night under the stars," Leander commented cheerily, advancing towards Soloth's desk.

"Thank you, Leander," Soloth returned, forcing a weary smile as he settled himself into his high-backed chair. "You said you wanted to speak to me before the meeting. I assume this has something to do with the fiasco with the Chosen?"

"Indeed it does," Leander said, producing with a flourish the record he had brought. He laid it before Soloth on the tidy surface of the desk. "This," he said, tapping the report's cover, "is my preliminary report on my investigation into the matter. I felt you should be apprised of what I have learned before the meeting."

Soloth's forehead wrinkled in surprise. "You've started an investigation already?"

"I started as soon as Kell told me what had happened. How could I do otherwise under the circumstances?" he said earnestly, putting as much concern on his face as he could manage.

Indicating that Leander should pull up a chair, Soloth leaned forward and planted his elbows on the desk. "What have you found, then?"

Leander settled into the high-backed chair and leaned forward with his elbows resting on his knees. "The body you brought back this morning from the wreckage of the flyer is still being examined by the coroner and she expects to have a positive identification sometime this afternoon, but Krisk was the only person reported missing yesterday and I proceeded on the assumption that it was he who was on board the flyer. It was only logical, considering that he had supposedly taken the flyer out for a test flight," Leander said with a shrug, leaning back into his chair and crossing one leg over the other as Soloth now pulled the report closer and opened it. "My investigation is far from over, of course, but the preliminary evidence suggests that Krisk may have been working alone," Leander said, waving a hand in the direction of the report. "As you can see from Krisk's personal record, he had a long history of being treated for a psychological disorder. He was given to fits of extreme anger and bouts of depression and had been admitted to the medical bay on several occasions after having been arrested for disorderly conduct. Each time, he had been charged with assault and remanded for psychiatric assessment and counseling."

"Interesting, but hardly incriminating," Soloth replied, frowning.

"Ah, but there's more. Krisk was also a vocal detractor of our participation in the Prophecy. He has no family on Quayvern, but I did speak with several of his co-workers. He apparently had told them several times that he hoped the Chosen didn't survive the journey and that someone on the surface, and I quote, 'would take the bastards out'."

Soloth felt a chill go down his spine. He closed the cover of the report and sighed. "There were a handful of people who had opposed our participation in the Prophecy on the basis that we were meddling in the fate of others, but I can't imagine that anyone would feel so strongly as to wish the Chosen or the representatives any harm."

Leander nodded slowly. "One would have thought that anger would have been directed at the Council, not the Chosen," he agreed. "However, it appears that was not the case."

"I can accept that Krisk may have been a... troubled individual who harbored hate for the Chosen for his own reasons and saw an opportunity to strike at them, but there is the matter of what happened in Merani Base."

Leander's head came up at the mention of Merani Base and a momentary torrent of apprehension made his palms sweaty. He had assured his partners that, if necessary, he would be able to incriminate Krisk in those events, as well, but Soloth was hardly a blithering idiot. The old fox was a sly one. He would have to work hard to stay one step ahead.

"Yes. Kell told me that you received a call from them to tell you that the Director of Merani Base had attempted to kill the Chosen and the representatives and was himself overthrown in a rebellion. He also recounted how the Director had been keeping the citizens of his city under house arrest and had used guards culled from the surface cities as his personal army," Leander said tightly. "Nasty business, that; but are you trying to tell me that you suspect the two events may be related?" he said, sounding shocked.

Soloth chewed the inside of his lip for a moment. "Possibly." He felt slightly guilty holding back information from Leander, but in the light of his promise to Terien that he would not reveal the circumstances of Merani Base's mystery caller, he decided he had no choice at the moment. "I was told that after the Chosen had escaped, Merani Base received a call from a man who was very interested in knowing whether or not the Director's plans had succeeded," Soloth said at last. "Apparently Director Maxen had contacts on the surface with whom he dealt, and they surmised that he might simply have been one of those contacts calling in out of curiosity, but the way he suddenly broke contact made them suspicious that he might try to complete Director Maxen's work and go after the Chosen." Soloth shrugged sheepishly and looked away to the window for a moment. "I was concerned that Terien had no idea that there was a possibility that he and the representatives could still be in danger, and I decided to fly out to warn them."

"In the light of what happened with Krisk, your actions were justified," Leander replied firmly.

Soloth turned back to Leander, ignoring the comment. "It may be that the two events *are* unrelated, but I couldn't take the chance that there wasn't a connection. Hence, my order to ground all flyers."

"A prudent move. I can see now why you're wondering if the two events may be connected in some way. Unlikely, but I wonder..." he said, rising from his chair to pace the confines of the room. He held a finger to his lips, gently tapping them as he made a show of giving deep consideration to what he had heard, while Soloth silently watched him wide-eyed.

"Could Krisk have been working with Director Maxen?" Leander mused aloud. "The Director had... contacts... on the surface. It would be reasonable to assume that he had a means of communicating with these operatives," he murmured just loud enough so that Soloth could follow along. "It's a matter of record that Krisk made many trips outside Quayvern, ostensibly to test-fly the flyers after repairing them. Could he have intercepted a communication between Director Maxen and one of his operatives? Perhaps... perhaps..." he muttered, still pacing and thinking.

"What are you thinking, Leander?" Soloth said with barely contained agitation.

Leander stopped pacing and looked up at Soloth as though he had forgotten he was there, his hand falling away from his mouth. "I think you may be on to something. It's possible that Krisk and Director Maxen had somehow... met and collaborated in an effort to kill the Chosen."

"But for what possible purpose?" Soloth asked angrily and pounded his fist on the desk out of frustration. He blew out a breath and scrubbed a hand across his face. "Perhaps you're right. Maybe they *are* unrelated."

Leander had to stifle a laugh. This was going to be easier than he anticipated. All he needed to do now was make sure Soloth believed he was ardently willing to explore every contingency.

"As I see it, there are three possibilities," Leander said, resuming his seat. "One," he said, lifting a single finger, "is that the two events were unrelated. In which case we must entertain the probability that there still exists a threat to the Chosen from an unknown party on the surface and that they won't be safe until they reach Quayvern. Moreover, we must accept that we may never know what motivated Director Maxen in his attempt to kill the Chosen. Second," he said, lifting another finger, "is that Krisk and Director Maxen were working together for some unknown reason. Remember, this Maxen fellow held the citizens of his city captive, proving himself as twisted an individual as Krisk. If, by chance, the two managed to hook up, the purpose of their collaboration to kill the Chosen may have held some unknown reward for the Director, but we can assume that we know Krisk's motivation. Regardless, the threat to the Chosen has been eliminated. And third," he said darkly, holding up a third finger, "is that there was a mastermind behind both attacks – someone on Quayvern with a vested interest in the failure of the Final Reunification."

Soloth was taken aback by the suggestion. "Who on Quayvern could possibly benefit from such a thing?" he cried.

Leander relaxed and let his hands fall into his lap. "No one I can think of, and for no reason I am aware of," he said. "However, I would be remiss in my duties if I failed to give at least passing consideration to the possibility." He cast a glance at the door to Soloth's office and lowered his voice. "Was it not Idona who journeyed to Merani Base to make the announcement about the Chosen's imminent arrival?"

His mouth dropping open in shock, Soloth blinked several times, unable to believe what he was hearing. "Surely, you don't suspect Idona of such... such treachery!" he whispered hoarsely.

Leander laughed softly and held up a placating hand. "Hardly, my friend. However, I feel that the possibility of Krisk and Director Maxen working together deserves closer investigation and I would like to enlist her aid. She might have some insight into it after having been to Merani Base."

Soloth visibly slumped with relief and let out a long sigh. "I can see you've given this a great deal of thought, Leander." He looked down at the report still lying on his desk and stretched out to finger its cover. "Thank you for briefing me on what you've found."

"May I?" Leander said, indicating the report under Soloth's hand. "There's still a bit of time before the meeting and I would like to add the other two theories to my report."

"Of course, of course," Soloth agreed readily.

Standing, Leander straightened his robes and picked up the report, smoothing his hand over it as he hesitated for a moment.

"Was there something else?" Soloth asked.

"Yes, there was," he replied, straightening. "Kell mentioned that you intended to announce your retirement. I wanted to say that you will be sorely missed at the Council meetings."

Soloth gave him a wry smile. "Good old Kell. Just couldn't

keep a secret."

Leander laughed. "Don't be too hard on him. He was overwrought after what had happened. I think it just… slipped out."

Now Soloth laughed and rose from his chair. "At any rate, I thought you would be overjoyed to hear I was retiring," he said, still grinning.

Giving Soloth a bow of his head in acquiescence, Leander gave him a puckish look. "Of course, my friend. You and I have been doing battle during the elections for fifteen years and I have lost soundly each time! I expected a repeat performance in the next election, but now have a real hope of succeeding. Still, I must say that serving with you as Sub-Primary has been no less rewarding."

"Bovine dung!" Soloth laughed. "You've been itching for a chance at the Primary's seat for the last ten years and don't you dare deny it!" He fixed Leander with a mock scowl. "You were probably wondering how long it would take for an old codger like me to finally step aside."

Leander returned a small smile. If only Soloth knew how right he was. "Personally, I've always thought of you as an old fox, sly and wise," he intimated, feeling rather magnanimous now that his victory was at hand. "You've proven that with your management of the Prophecy and the Chosen. I can only hope that my turn at the Primary's seat will be as productive as yours has been."

Soloth accepted the praise with his customary aplomb and extended a hand to Leander. "Of that I have no doubt," he said.

They shook hands and Leander was halfway to the door when Soloth stopped him with a startling remark.

"You'll have a taste of the Primary's seat soon enough, Leander."

Leander turned back, a puzzled look on his face.

"I wasn't going to announce this until the meeting, but it's only fair that I give you warning," Soloth said. "After I have brought the Chosen and the representatives to Quayvern, I will step down as Primary. You will fill in for me until the formal elections and oversee the Final Reunification."

Leander blinked in honest surprise. "What would make you

do such a thing?"

"I went out to speak to Terien without consulting the Council, thereby breaking the rule of non-interference we agreed on."

Leander shook his head. "Under the circumstances..."

"No. The ends cannot justify the means," Soloth insisted.

Leander locked eyes with Soloth. It was obvious that Soloth would not back down on this decision, and in truth Leander had no real desire to talk him out of it. "I see you've already made up your mind," Leander now said. "If the Council sides in favor of such action, then I will be honored to serve," he said, bowing from the waist.

"Thank you, my friend. Now go, finish your report. I'll see you at the meeting."

Leander left Soloth's office and paused by Idona's desk, giving her a conspiratorial smile.

"How was your meeting with Primary Soloth," Idona asked nonchalantly, playing well the part of a courteous secretary.

"It went very well, thank you," Leander replied politely. "I have asked Soloth's permission to enlist your aid in my investigation and he has generously agreed. Would you be so kind as to meet me in my office after the meeting?"

Smiling coquettishly, Idona ran her tongue over her lips. "Will this be an informal session?"

"Certainly. You needn't overdress for the occasion," he replied in a husky voice, then strode from the office of the man he had worked so hard to unseat through deception and murderous plotting, feeling not the least bit of remorse for having needlessly done so.

Watching him go, Idona settled back in her chair and toyed with a strand of her hair as she considered her future. Want for power, wealth, and respect had been the motivating factors throughout her life. Unable to obtain them on her own, she had connived a way to finally realize them through another. Once Leander was elected Primary of Quayvern, she would have everything she had ever wished for. And more.

Smiling to herself, Idona rose from her desk and went to Soloth's office door to ask if there was anything he needed of her before the meeting, pleased with the thought that soon she would be the one whose needs would be attended as she lived in the lap of luxury.

Chapter Thirty One

With Kell's return for Soloth the next morning had come the welcome news that the four men who had been injured would all make a full recovery and would remain on Quayvern until the group's arrival on the floating city. Soloth had expressed again his deepest regrets over what had happened, but Terien and the representatives reassured him that they did not hold him responsible, stating that it would be enough if he would investigate into who had been behind the attack.

Once Soloth and Kell had departed, Terien had given the order to break camp and move out. They resumed their journey, stopping in the two towns of Kral and Naru that lay to the north of the city of Chihook. Finding themselves welcome, they stayed a night in each and met with the Elders of both villages who were thrilled to listen to the stories Terien and his people told. However, when Terien invited them to submit representatives for the Final Reunification, both towns politely refused, saying that they had little to offer and were happy enough with the amount of trade they did with Chihook. Promising to share the goods and services they stood to gain from the Final Reunification, Corliss and Jeson told the Elders of Kral and Naru that they would see to it that the coalition Government of Chihook was made aware of this and that more formal trade agreements be enacted in the future.

Continuing northward, Terien was astounded to find that the road did not simply end in Naru. Though it became increasingly rough and narrow, having been overgrown and unused for countless years, it wound higher and higher into the mountains on a course straight for the Hidden City of Petrava. Navigating the road proved treacherous in some places where heavy rains had caused rockslides to block the road, but they were able to either move some of the smaller obstacles or find a way around the larger ones. Though this added a few days to their journey, no one seemed to mind. A few wary souls in the group kept casting glances at the skies from time to time as though expecting another flyer to attack, while others still kept a watchful eye on the thick woods in case they were being followed over land, but overall, the mood was relaxed and casual despite the recent events and the loss of Rioto.

Only Sahala seemed more subdued than usual. After having found out where her father had come from and being painfully reminded of his abandonment of her mother, it was as though the lonely little girl she once was had now taken control, making everyone speculate that her earlier attitude and actions had been her way of making sure no one could ever get close enough to hurt her as her mother had been hurt. Preferring to keep to herself now, she seemed to have lost a good deal of her imperial bluster, even to the point of telling Haren that he need not sleep at her feet any longer. Despite Sahala's quiet protests, night after night Haren would roll out his sleeping bag at the entrance to her tent, his passive defiance making it clear that he, at least, had no intention of abandoning her.

Pressing on, the air of excitement increased as they started to slowly ascend the mountain marked on Terien's map as being the site of Petrava. The road they followed eventually became little more than a winding dirt path that disappeared altogether one sunny afternoon as they approached a sheer cliff face that lay two-thirds of the way up the mountain. Thousands of feet wide, its base had an accumulation of silt and debris from a recent flood deposit, making them question whether they were at the correct spot.

"If Petrava is supposedly a thriving city – and Soloth said it was – why hasn't its entrance been cleared?" Duncan wondered aloud, shading his eyes with a hand as he looked up at the towering wall of jagged rock.

Rechecking his map, Terien bore a puzzled look. "This is definitely the right place," he confirmed. "Maybe they just don't come out very often," he offered, rolling up the map once more.

"Whatever. Let's just look for the lock mechanism," Makhani growled testily, jumping down from his borrowed equine and stalking off towards the cliff.

"What's with him?" Terien asked, frowning.

Rannoch struggled down from the back of his own equine and stood with his hands braced against the low of his back, grimacing as he stretched the kinks out. "Th' lad's not happy with the equine he's ridin'. Keeps complainin' it leans t' the left."

Laughing, Terien dismounted from Shangra and motioned everyone towards the cliff. "You know what to look for. Call out if you find it."

While everyone else fanned out along the base of the cliff and hunted high and low, Aurori remained near the carts and animals, considering something she had noticed as they had emerged from the tree line. The road may have all but disappeared, but there was still a faint break in the trees leading up to the cliff, wide enough to have allowed the carts through. What if the road had once led directly to the door? Using the break in the trees as guide, she walked over to the cliff face and began searching for the lock on a direct line of sight from where she now suspected the road had once run.

She had paced back and forth several times and was beginning to think her idea had been unfounded when she spotted an odd-shaped stone that lay against the wall at her feet, half hidden in a collection of silt and twigs. She stooped down and ran her fingers over its exposed edges, then picked up a stick and dug around it until she had cleared some of the hardened mud away. Tingling with excitement, she let out a delighted whoop.

"I found it! I found it!"

Aurori was still digging furiously when everyone else came running on to the scene, practically tripping over one another as they gathered around.

"It can't be the lock, can it?" Quatina said, crouching next to Sahala. "It's so low on the wall!"

"It has to be. I think it's just been buried by the mud slide that came through here," Terien remarked, his knit brows expressing puzzlement as he knelt beside the two women. "I wonder why no one from Petrava came out to clear this away?" he muttered under his breath as he examined the lock more closely. "It's plugged up with mud," he reported. Picking up a small twig, he began to ream out the hole.

"I hope it still works after this," Quatina worried.

"Only one way to find out," Terien said when he had cleaned out the receptacle as best he could. He turned to smile at Aurori. "Well, Princess – care to make use of that key of yours?"

Aurori's eyes lit up. "It would be a shame if its only purpose had been as a tattle-tale," she said with a lopsided smile aimed at Terien.

Grinning at her allusion to the way he had discovered who she was, he moved aside to allow her access to the lock. Removing her cylinder from around her neck, Aurori slowly inserted the key into the receptacle. She had to push hard on it to get it seated past the mud's residue, but it still emitted a faint click that told them it had made contact with the mechanism inside the lock.

Expecting the side of the cliff to open as it had at Alatesh, they stepped back a few paces, not thinking that the lock might not have been purposely placed at the base of the cliff. The familiar sound of machinery whining to life from within the mountain evoked a chorus of excited shouts that petered out as the ground beneath their feet started to crack and tremble. A small section of the cliff had indeed begun to open, but it was half buried behind the mudslide!

Now that the door was opening, the unstable mass of dirt and debris was losing its support and was spilling into the cavern beyond as they scrambled to move off the slithering mound they had been standing on. Almost everyone made it safely away. Only Aurori, Quatina and Terien weren't as fortunate. Losing their footing, the three let out startled yelps when they fell and were borne along on a wave of dirt, rolling and sliding into the darkened cavern beyond, while Duncan and the others looked on helplessly, shouts of alarm rippling through their ranks.

Heedless of any potential danger, Duncan, Makhani and Elek started down the unstable slope, their boots skidding in the loose dirt, calling out the names of their three friends in voices high with concern.

"We're fine," Terien reassured as the three men came within view.

Looking shaken but unharmed, all three were covered in dirt and were slowly sitting up, coughing from the dust now floating

through the air.

"Watch your step on the way down," Terien warned as more and more of his men started to come down the slope.

"You scared the hell out of us," Elek grumbled as he and Makhani went to give Terien and Aurori a hand getting to their feet while Duncan, who clearly looked panic-stricken, assisted Quatina.

"Tell me about it," Terien complained. Shrugging Elek away, he turned to Aurori and took her shoulders in his hands. "You okay?" he asked, looking her over.

"I'm fine," she assured him and reached out to wipe a smudge of dirt from his cheek. She looked down at herself and pouted her lips. "You know, I'm really starting to hate white," she commented dryly as she looked from her own visibly dirt-smudged clothes to Terien's cleaner-looking black ones.

"Why do Healers wear white?" Quatina asked from where she stood with Duncan, effortlessly dusting the dirt from her own greenish leather ensemble.

Duncan's eyes were wild and his breathing was ragged as he staggered back a step from Quatina. "This isn't exactly the time or place to discuss fashion!" he exclaimed in exasperation.

"It was *not* a fashion question!" Quatina said hotly, folding her arms. "I am simply curious to know the significance of a Healer's white clothing."

"I'm sure there's a fascinating story to it," Duncan retorted, his voice starting out mild and rising as he spoke, "but in case you hadn't noticed, you three were just caught up in a landslide! You could have been buried or broken something or even been killed!"

Quatina opened her mouth and held up a finger, but Duncan wasn't done ranting.

"Not to mention that this place is as deserted as a schoolhouse at recess! Why is it so dark in here? Where is everybody?" he shouted, throwing his hands in the air.

Aurori and Quatina converged on Duncan, attempting to calm him. Whatever they were whispering to him as they led him aside and settled to the floor with him seemed to be working. He was taking deep breaths, his hands clenching and unclenching in his lap, but he was no longer wild-eyed.

"What's with him?" Makhani whispered to Terien.

"He and his parents were buried in a landslide when he was fourteen. Their whole house slid down the hillside it was built on after Kaethos experienced a bout of torrential rains one summer. Took hours for rescuers to dig them out, and when they did, Duncan was barely alive and his parents were… well, they didn't make it," Terien whispered back. Makhani made a condoling sound in his throat while the rest of the men from Kaethos gathered around, nodding sympathetically. They knew well the story of what had happened to Duncan. "I think he's having an anxiety reaction to our fall," Terien said after a moment, watching, while Duncan now nodded and smiled weakly as Quatina enveloped him in a comforting embrace.

That was the moment the lights in the overhead panels flared to life, startling everyone, and a deep male voice called out to them from down the tunnel they could now see at the far end of the featureless rock cavern they were standing in.

"Greetings, my friends!" called the tall man approaching at the lead of a procession of six people coming down the tunnel. Clothed in red, his pants were wide-legged and his long-sleeved tunic was loose fitting with a simple white cord cinching it around his narrow waist. His skin was smooth and darker even than Quatina's, and he was entirely bald. Eyes as dark as midnight and filled with open concern took in the small landslide that had spilled through the door and then fixed on Terien on whom he advanced. "Were any of you injured?" he asked.

"No, we're all fine," Terien said, then cocked his head to the side. "We are full of questions, though. You must be Elos," he said, extending his hand to the taller man.

"And you are Terien, the Chosen Gatherer," Elos replied with a smile as they shook hands. "This," he said, indicating a smaller man dressed in bright blue clothes, "is my aide, Detata."

Terien in turn introduced the pair to the representatives and his own men, including Duncan who had now fully recovered from his momentary bout of anxiety.

"I apologize for the state in which you found this door," Elos said with a deep bow. "We had not realized it had rained so hard," he said, turning to his aide with a questioning look and getting a shrug in response.

"It doesn't usually rain so hard on this side of the mountain," Detata replied. "I will go and bring more men and some shovels."

"*This* side of the mountain?" Terien echoed as Detata disappeared back down the tunnel. "I'm afraid I don't understand."

Elos laughed; a warm, rich sound that echoed slightly in the confines of the cavern. "You might say that this is the back door to Petrava and is rarely used. Lord Soloth felt that although the road you just took was a little more difficult, the other road between Petrava and Chihook winds along the western coast and is far longer, and he hoped to save you time on your journey."

"The only other road is the one that leads to Eskai," Jeson piped up, looking confused as he turned to Terien who looked equally at a loss. "We do occasional trade with Eskai," he explained. "It's a small town north-west of Chihook that's situated at the foot of the Kescate Mountains where they border on the Merani Ocean."

"You know it as Eskai," Elos said with a broad smile, "but it is actually a suburb of Petrava," he said, his smile fading at Jeson and Corliss's doleful expressions. "I am sorry we have kept this secret from your people all this time. I hope you will understand when I tell you that we were truly not looking to hide anything from you. We only wished to leave as much of our remaining technology behind as we possibly could." Elos glanced over his shoulder as many men with digging tools approached through the tunnel behind him and he spread his hands in an all-encompassing way, his smile returning. "Perhaps once you have seen Petrava you will have a better understanding of my people and their motivations. Come, let's get the doorway cleared of debris so that you may get your animals and carts through."

Chapter Thirty Two

Many hands made short work of clearing the landslide and Terien's group was able to get their animals and carts inside the cavern. The back door and tunnel, Elos told them, had never been intended as anything more than an emergency exit and it was a bit of a tight squeeze for the carts to traverse the tunnel's length. It was worth the effort once they emerged from the passage and stood on a wide landing near the apex of the cathedral ceiling of the main chamber. A murmur of awe swept through the assemblage as they looked out over the city.

Hollowed out in the heart of the mountain, Petrava was a work of art. The main chamber itself was enormous and had eight levels to it, each with its own series of interconnecting landings. On every level there were entrances to other chambers that lay beyond, and the walls themselves bore sculptures and bas-reliefs carved into the luminescent silver-white rock. Intricate crystal chandeliers hung from the ceiling and cast an ethereal pale blue light throughout the gargantuan chamber. Far below lay an open plaza filled with small stone buildings centered around a pristine lake that reflected the deep blue of its crystal bed. A graceful arched bridge made of interlocking stones spanned the lake and a pathway of the same interlocking crystal stones led to the far side of the chamber and disappeared into a passageway. People walked amidst the grandeur of the plaza, all dressed in the same loose-fitting clothes as Elos, but in varying colors and patterns that made it seem as though butterflies flitted across the floor below.

"It's… magnificent," Aurori breathed, coming to the edge of the landing and gripping the rail with one hand and Terien's arm with the other.

"Aye, lassie. I've never seen th' like o' it!" Rannoch whispered as he pushed his glasses higher onto his nose for a better view.

Everyone now pressed forward to the rail to stare out over the main chamber in hushed wonder. The sound of voices far below echoed softly through the chamber, as did the resonation of the crystal chandeliers and the barely perceptible thrum of machinery hidden deep within the viscera of the mountain.

"It was not always so beautiful," Elos confessed in a quiet voice as he gazed out over the city he governed. "Petrava was originally an iron mine more than a thousand years ago. Then, at a time when the world's need for iron and other metals was at a low point, a multinational consortium bought the mine and turned it into a factory where textiles were produced. At the time of the Great Division, Petrava was in decline and being used mostly as a warehouse, but all the chambers that had been converted into living quarters for the factory workers were still in place and it was here that the Sky Lords brought many refugees." A look of unmistakable pride shone in his dark eyes as he turned to Terien. "Our ancestors decided that they would make Petrava their home and resolved to remake the caverns and chambers into a place worthy of the name. They set about sculpting the rock, transforming the featureless passageways and chambers into what you see here. A place to be proud of."

"It's certainly inspiring," Terien enthused, his own voice barely audible as he stood entranced by the beauty of Petrava. "It must have taken them decades to complete."

"Indeed it did," Elos said with a grin. "There is more, however. The textile consortium never resurfaced, of course, leaving Petrava with chamber upon chamber filled with bolts of every kind of fabric, thread and yarn imaginable, along with the machines necessary for their fabrication. We have been slowly trading these with the other lands over the years since the Great Division, but lacked the desire or the wherewithal to do more than trading in small quantities."

"I purchased a white cloak from a seamstress in Donellin that's made of the most exquisite material I've ever seen, and she told me that the material she used came from a faraway land that still held the technology for making such fabrics. This must be the place that fabric came from," Aurori said excitedly.

"Most likely," Elos said, tipping his head to her. "Now that the Final Reunification is at hand, Petrava would offer more trade of the fabrics and materials we have on hand. Later, I will show you the supplies we have on hand. I think you will be amazed by what you see."

"You certainly have a lot to offer for the negotiations," Jos remarked, glancing longingly between his own drab blue suit and Elos' bright red clothes. "I know my people would be all too happy to get rid of these old styles and colors Director Maxen forced us to wear."

"Do you still mine iron?" Jeson asked suddenly.

Elos' eyebrows went up. "Not much, no. We don't have a need for it. However, there are a few chambers that could be returned to active mining."

"You and I will have to discuss the possibilities further," Jeson said, then jumped as Corliss pinched his thigh and shot him a dirty look. "*We* will have to discuss the possibilities," he amended, frowning at his wife's angelic expression as he rubbed at his stinging thigh. "Chihook has several forges and many skilled blacksmiths who would jump at the opportunity to have a ready supply of ore. We currently operate a small surface mine not too far from Kral, but the grade of ore is poor and quantities are limited."

"Some of the old equipment is still functional, as well," Elos told Jeson, then turned back to Terien. "Which reminds me – we have quite a few land cars and cargo hover decks in storage that Soloth thought you might want to have a look at. He mentioned that you had activated an old hover deck at Alatesh and might find use for them."

Makhani exchanged a look with Terien and Duncan. "If you're talking about the hovercraft we used – you bet we're interested!" Makhani replied enthusiastically. "Just think how much easier and faster it would be to transport goods between our lands if we had more hovercraft!"

Rannoch trundled forward and cuffed Makhani's shoulder, leveling a condescending look at the blond man. "Bright as ye are, ye're forgettin' that we had t' abandon the hovercraft 'cause the road was too narrow an' windin'. What do ye propose we do about that?" he asked archly.

Makhani rolled his eyes and blew out an impatient breath. "That's simple, Rannoch. We improve the roads!" he cried, his expression fervent as he threw his arms wide.

"An' which o' us do ye expect to see footin' the bill for all th' manpower that'll take?" Rannoch huffed.

"Ah… guys?" Terien broke in, waving a hand between the two. "Can we maybe table this discussion for a later date? Like once we're on Quayvern?"

Looking chastened, Rannoch and Makhani looked at each other irritably and then both folded their arms and turned away from each other.

Shaking his head at the pair, Terien leaned casually against the rail and regarded Elos thoughtfully. "I'm curious about something. You just said that Soloth mentioned our use of a hovercraft to you. When did you and Soloth get a chance to talk about all this?"

Elos shuffled his feet uneasily. "From the text of the Prophecy, the people of Petrava have always known that we would have the honor of being the Chosen's last stopover before Quayvern, but only upon Soloth's arrival to announce your coming did we find out how great our honor would be," he said humbly. "Soloth gave us portable communications equipment so that we might be able to contact him upon your arrival. In truth, we have had contact with him off and on since the beginning of your journey," Elos admitted with a self-effacing smile. "His most recent call was about a week ago. He told me about what had happened to you at Merani Base and about the flyer in the forest."

Terien pushed away from the rail. "Speaking of Merani Base – it had its own communications equipment built right into its walls," Terien said. "Petrava doesn't?"

"No," Elos said, shaking his head. "Merani Base, Alatesh and Quayvern were all facilities belonging to the old government that existed before the Great Division and had far more in the way of technological devices than we do. Petrava was privately owned. I believe we may have had a communications device at one time, but I have never seen the proof of it."

"That explains why Merani Base has never heard of Petrava," Duncan said with a sideways glance at Terien.

Terien nodded reflectively and looked over the edge of the rail. "Anyway, it doesn't matter anymore. Naneve was able to get through to Soloth and we've made it safely to Petrava. The journey is almost at an end."

Everyone knew that to be true, but somehow it hadn't seemed possible or real until Terien had said it out loud. Now, they stood once more in silence, each lost in his or her own thoughts, this time looking at each other instead of the spectacular view of Petrava's main chamber.

"Well," Rannoch finally spoke up, getting their attention, "I only have one more question, then." They looked at him expectantly as he glanced down at the plaza far below, then turned back to Elos and shot him a pointed look. "How in blazes do we go about gettin' down from here?"

After the laughter had died down, Elos and Detata led them to an oversize cargo elevator that had once been used to move cars of iron, and later, pallets of textiles. Amazed by the new device and elated by the opportunity to experience the workings of a new piece of technology, everyone took turns operating the elevator and asking questions about it. It took several trips to get everyone and everything down, and once they had, Elos led them in procession across the fantastic lake amidst a fanfare of happy shouts and waves from the citizens inside the plaza.

Navigating down a series of wide, downward inclined passageways, they emerged into a cavernous bay with massive doors that opened onto another surprise – the town of Eskai.

Hugging the base of the mountain, the coastal settlement lay scattered through the dense foliage, its small buildings and dirt streets charmingly lackluster compared to the grandeur of the city of Petrava. The homes and businesses were constructed mostly from native wood and looked so new that Terien commented on it.

"Our ancestors long ago decided that they didn't care for living underground," Elos explained as they moved through the streets. "So, once the disastrous weather brought about by the cometary bombardment had settled down, they built Eskai. This close to the coast, however, there are still the inevitable natural disasters. Eskai was rebuilt four years ago after the last hurricane came through."

Stopping in front of one home, Elos told them to wait outside for a moment while he went in. He came out a few minutes later with a strikingly lovely woman and three adorable children in tow.

"My wife, Lakila, and my three boys, Betar, Chel and Zeref," Elos introduced. "Lakila is one of our physicians," he said with a proud smile.

Lakila smiled warmly and offered her hand to Terien. "It is an honor to finally meet you," she said, then moved on to greet all the representatives before coming to Aurori and giving her a spirited handshake. "Though we have never had the honor of a Healer's visit, we have heard many tales from the traders and I know my colleagues would be thrilled to meet you! You simply must come to our medical facility," she told Aurori. "Would you be willing? There are so many things I would like to ask you!"

"It would be my pleasure," Aurori laughed. "Let me just go and get my pack."

"Before you and Lakila bury yourselves in work," Elos interrupted, placing a hand on his wife's shoulder, "I would like to ask you where you would like to spend the night. Which would you prefer – to spend the night in Eskai or inside Petrava?" he asked.

There was no real need to consider the two options; everyone agreed that Petrava was too unique to pass on the opportunity to stay within its sculpted magnificence.

"I guess we stay in Petrava, then," Terien said, laughing at the looks of giddy excitement on the faces around him.

"I thought as much," Elos said, laughing along with him. He motioned for Detata to come forward. "Detata, please see to it that the Chosen's animals and carts are stabled here in Eskai and then escort his men to the chambers reserved for them. When you are done, please join us in the council chamber."

Watching as his men moved off behind Detata while Lakila and Aurori disappeared with Quatina in tow, Terien turned to Elos with a sigh. "You know, I doubt we'll be able to take the animals and carts with us when we go to Quayvern tomorrow. Could you possibly..."

Elos held up a hand. "Of course, my friend. They will be well taken care of until your return," he said, then looked to the remaining representatives before gesturing back towards the open doors of Petrava. "Come. I will show you to your rooms. After you have rested, you must tell me all about the journey you have made!"

"Elos, you have no idea what you're asking. We have enough story to keep you up half the night!" Terien laughed.

"An' then some!" Rannoch boomed, slapping Elos on the back as they moved off.

Elos thought about that for a moment, then a slow smile spread across his face. "Then we will have a celebration tonight. One where your people and mine can eat and drink, share stories and songs!" he said, then gave Rannoch a conspiratorial wink. "My people make a delightful fruit wine that I guarantee will make our celebration a feast to remember!"

Makhani groaned out loud. "I hope they also make it in large quantities," he muttered to Terien and Duncan when Elos and Rannoch had moved out of earshot.

"Makhani! You surprise me!" Terien said with a frown. "You didn't seem all that interested in drinking when we were back in Brinbourne."

Makhani shook his head. "I'm not, but Elos mentioned sharing songs and stories. I was thinking that Elek's singing sounds better when he's had a few!" he said with a wicked grin.

Laughing, Terien, Duncan and Makhani hurried to catch up with the others.

The feast Elos promised wasn't quite as elaborate as the one in Glaybor nor as rowdy as the celebration in Brinbourne, but it was thoroughly enjoyable all the same and attended by hundreds of Elos' people who were all decked out in their finest attire, as were Terien and his entourage. Held in a stunningly massive chamber inside Petrava, they sat for hours, recounting in detail for their hosts all the things they had experienced on their journey, all while sharing an abundance of locally grown food and intoxicatingly delightful drink.

Later, tables and chairs were hastily removed and an orchestra struck up lively tunes that had everyone dancing and singing. Including Makhani, who, despite his loud protests, ended up singing a duet with Elek whose voice was in fine tune after a couple of glasses of the strong wine.

As the night wore on, Terien was chatting with another set of dignitaries when he spotted his men all clustered around Aurori, Rannoch, Makhani and the other representatives he had gathered together, talking animatedly about something. A wave of melancholy washed over him as he realized with a start that the happy group was close to going their separate ways. Once the Final Reunification was completed, each representative would return to their respective lands and the odds were that they wouldn't see each other after that when the duty of actualizing trade between them would fall to others. As arduous as the journey had been, there was no denying that it had bound them together. These weren't just a group of dignitaries he was leading – these were his friends and he would miss them all.

Suddenly needing to be alone, he stole away from the party and headed outside through Petrava's main doors. The night was clear and warm and the scent of the ocean rode the wind as he walked a short distance from the doors. Standing with his hands stuffed in his pockets, he stood gazing up at the stars and let out a slow sigh, his own despondent mood at odds with the thrumming beat of the orchestra that was filtering out from Petrava.

Terien's breath caught and an electric tingle shot through him as Aurori came up behind him and wrapped her arms around him, startling him out of his train of thought.

"What are you thinking?" Aurori asked softly, pressing her face against his back.

Terien closed his eyes and covered her small hands with his, tilting his head back as he relished the feel of her warm embrace. "Just... about the journey."

"Tell me," she said, releasing him and walking around to face him.

His shoulders came up in a slow shrug, then settled back down again. He looked at the ground and scuffed his boot in the dirt, suddenly feeling embarrassed that he was feeling so sentimental when they hadn't yet reached Quayvern or completed the Final Reunification. "Going back to Kaethos is going to seem kind of... dull... after what we've seen and where we've been," he said, looking away. He shrugged again. "I was just thinking that I was going to miss the… journey… once this is all over," he muttered, shifting his eyes to stare down at his feet.

Aurori tilted her head to the side and folded her arms. "Ah. Of course. The excitement. The danger. The thrill of seeing new places," she said somberly, nodding her head.

"Exactly!" he said, lifting his head to meet her eyes.

"The long hours on the back of a sweaty animal. The thrill of sleeping on the ground. The joys of being shot at," she went on straight faced, tongue-in-cheek.

Terien gave her a wall-eyed stare and raised one eyebrow. "Now you're making fun of me."

She placed her palms flat on his chest and gave him a playful shove, but her eyes were serious. "You're so pathetic!"

"Me? Pathetic?" he said, putting a hand to his chest and giving her a wide-eyed innocent look.

"Yes, you!" Aurori laughed, stepping up to him and hugging her arms around him. "You're going to miss the stuffing out of every single representative you've gathered." She sighed heavily. "We both are."

Resting his cheek on the top of her head, Terien stroked her back and stared out over the lights of Eskai. He had never felt this way before. Not ever. In the past, all the people he cared about were always nearby and no one ever left for more than a few weeks at a time. This was different. Never again to listen to Rannoch's endless but cheerful complaints? Or have to intervene between Makhani and Elek's sparring or watch Haren's long-suffering at the hands of Sahala? "Seems kind of silly to be missing people who haven't even left yet, doesn't it?" he whispered.

"Maybe," Aurori agreed, lifting a hand to brush away the single tear that had escaped as she, too, thought about parting ways with all the people she had come to know. "But it's also a good sign. If the others feel this way too – and I know they do – it means the Final Reunification is already a success."

"Oh, really? And how do you know the others feel the same way?" he asked, pulling away to give her a lopsided smile.

"I asked," she replied with a smug smile. "That's what we

were talking about when I saw you leave. You should have heard Makhani. Maybe it was the wine, but he was really getting emotional," she related, now grinning. "He's really going to miss everyone. Especially Rannoch. And you."

"Me? Blondy's going to miss *me*?" Terien blurted, then gave a short laugh. "You're dreaming, Princess!"

"Royal Boy, you really *are* pathetic," Aurori chided him and stepped away. "Both of you are. You two make a big show of barely tolerating one another, but when push comes to shove, there isn't anything you wouldn't do for each other – and don't bother trying to deny it," she said quickly when he started to protest.

Realizing it was pointless to argue with Aurori – especially when they both knew she was right – Terien ran a hand through his hair and swallowed back the blustery denial he had been about to make. He reached out to brush a wisp of hair away from Aurori's face. "I suppose you're right," he said, "but I do know this much – there are other people I'm going to miss a lot more."

Aurori narrowed her eyes at him. "You'd better be about to say I'm at the top of that list, mister," she teased, poking him in the chest with one finger.

Terien blinked uncertainly. "You most of all," Terien told her softly and drew her into his arms once more. He hadn't thought of it before now, but Aurori must be as anxious as he was to be going home. Eristea and Kaethos weren't all that far apart – a matter of a few days – but the thought of being separated from her for any length of time was almost unbearable.

He pressed his face into her hair and closed his eyes in a feeble attempt to blot out the thought of their being parted just when he'd finally been able to admit how much he cared for her. Better to think about Quayvern and the Final Reunification for now. The future would have to wait.

Chapter Thirty Three

It was early morning, the suns were shining and excitement was the order of the day as the first of the five flyers that came to carry the Chosen and the representatives to Quayvern landed on the beach on the outskirts of Eskai.

Dressed for the grand occasion in his silver-accented black uniform and flowing cape, Terien smiled and extended his hand to Aurori as she hurried towards him down the beach. Adorned in a shimmering white cloak with green trim that the people of Petrava had presented her that morning, she looked every inch the Princess she was. Her hair, freed from the braid she had favored throughout the journey, was swept away from her face and fell free around her shoulders in loose curls that were being tossed about by the wind from the flyers. Together they approached the landed flyer from which Soloth was emerging. Squinting against the swirling sand the other four flyers were kicking up as they settled on the beach not too faraway, they were accompanied by scores of children whose delighted squeals competed with the whine from the engines.

"Terien! Aurori! You look splendid!" Soloth shouted above the noise from the flyers, beaming as he embraced them each in turn.

"I see you're all dressed for the occasion, too" Aurori said loudly, referring to the flowing council robes Soloth wore once more.

"Yes, well, I'm afraid pomp and ceremony are to be expected this day," Soloth shouted ruefully as he made a vain attempt to keep his blue robe from billowing up around him.

As soon as the flyer pilots shut down their engines, the children descended on the flying machines, running their hands over the sleek metallic hulls and chattering ecstatically. "The flyers are as big a hit with the kids as our felinae were," Terien laughed, combing his fingers through his disheveled hair.

Soloth smiled as a group of gangly youths rushed up to him, practically hopping from foot to foot with excitement.

"Can we look inside?" one fair-haired youngster with freckles asked eagerly.

Soloth looked over his shoulder and smiled at Kell who stood at the top of the flyer's extended ramp. "You may. Just be sure not to touch anything," Soloth warned, ruffling the lad's hair before he and his companions charged up the ramp, giggling as they disappeared into the flyer.

"It's good to see you again, Lord Soloth," Duncan said as he, Quatina and Elek came up the beach, carrying their small travel packs over their shoulders.

Duncan and Elek looked dapper in the Kaethosians uniforms they hadn't worn since entering the Teseni Desert, while Quatina was radiant in the long, blue silk dress she had purchased in Pergase. She had even grudgingly traded her sentati-skin boots for a pair of soft silk slippers and allowed Aurori to style her hair into an elegant chignon.

"Much better than last time," Elek said with a hearty laugh.

"How true," Soloth chortled as he shook hands with them briefly before turning back to Terien. "I wanted to ask a favor of you, if I could. The children of Quayvern have heard about your felinae and have been asking if you would be bringing them with you. Would it be possible to transport a couple of them?"

"I don't see why not," Terien smiled. "They seemed to enjoy riding on the hovercraft, so I'm sure they wouldn't mind a flyer ride." He turned to Duncan. "What do you think? Shangra and Tiagra?"

"Sure. Those two love kids," Duncan said with a shrug.

"I'll get them" Elek said and, dropping his pack to the ground, hurried back down the beach.

Soloth clapped a hand on Terien's shoulder. "Wonderful! I was hoping you would agree. Which is why I took the liberty of having the seats removed from the extra flyer I brought for them," he said with an embarrassed little smile, indicating the last flyer in line. The pilot gave them a small wave, looking nervous at the prospect of transporting the two cats. Turning back, Soloth shook his head. "It took a great deal of convincing to get

Councilor Walem to consent to lending us his flyer. He wasn't thrilled with the thought of having his pride and joy partially dismantled to accommodate your two cats, but his granddaughter convinced him otherwise." He said with a wry smile, then sighed heavily. "This would have been much easier if I still had my own flyer."

"Speaking of that," Terien said in a low voice, "do you have any news about who it was that attacked us?"

"We believe that the flyer attack was carried out by a troubled young man with a past history of violence," Soloth said, frowning. "We are still investigating, of course, but it seems that he opposed Quayvern's participation in the Final Reunification and in the twisted depths of his mind, decided the best way to end that participation was to kill you." Soloth shook his head sadly. "As for the events in Merani base, we theorize that Director Maxen wanted to keep Aurori captive to make use of her healing talents and decided it would be best to eliminate the rest of you. We cannot explain the mysterious call, but believe it may simply have been one of Maxen's surface operatives checking in. Tell me, did you encounter anything suspicious on your way to Petrava?" he asked.

"No," Terien said with a negative shake of his head. "The rest of the journey has been uneventful, thank the Maker."

Soloth stroked his goatee pensively. "Then perhaps acting Primary Leander is correct and the two attacks were unrelated," he said. He took a deep breath as though to dispel some lingering doubt. "If that's the case, then the danger has passed and the rest of the Final Reunification should proceed smoothly. Still, guards have been ordered to stand watch at your arrival and at your presentation to the Council of Quayvern," Soloth told them. "Just in case."

Duncan's eyebrows shot up. "Guards? Seems unnecessary considering we're all warriors," he said, then noticed Elos walking towards them, dressed in his now familiar baggy red outfit, carrying a travel pack. Behind him was Rannoch who was also decked out in a new pair of brown slacks, clean white shirt and a short tan jacket. "Well, almost all of us," he amended.

"Wait a minute," Aurori interrupted, her forehead creased in puzzlement. "Did I just hear you say 'acting Primary Leander'? I thought *you* were Primary of Quayvern."

"Sub-Primary Leander has assumed the title of Primary on an interim basis until the next election as I have resigned my seat as Primary of Quayvern," Soloth said with a sad smile. He clasped his hands together in a penitent gesture. "I felt it was necessary in the light of my unauthorized flight the day you were attacked."

"That's ridiculous!" declared Terien, frowning deep and slashing a hand through the air. "If not for your intervention, we would have all been a pile of cinders and there wouldn't be a Final Reunification!"

Soloth placed a calming hand on Terien's shoulder. "I thank you for your support, but it was my decision and one I am compelled to stand by. The Council felt as you do, my boy, but a leader can hardly expect to ignore the very rules he himself fought to legislate," he said with a shake of his head, "and I fought long and hard to leave you to your journey without monitoring or interference from us 'Sky Lords'. Besides, I was planning on announcing my retirement from office as soon as the negotiations were over." A quirk of a smile turned the corners of his mouth upwards. "The fact of the matter is that as Primary I would have formally welcomed you to the Quayvern while another would have been directly involved in the Final Reunification. Now, with the permission of Leander, I am free to act as your liaison to Council," he said, then raised his eyebrows in a hopeful expression. "If you'll have me as such."

A slow smile blossomed on Terien's face and he nodded, considering Soloth's motivations in stepping down as Primary. He offered the older man his hand. "We'd be honored to have you as our liaison," he said, then broke into a wide grin. "I promise we'll try to go easy on you."

"Not too easy, I hope," Soloth said, laughing. "I wouldn't want the Council to think I'm not earning my pay!"

"Knowing this bunch, they'll have you running so much that you'll wish you were still Primary," Aurori teased.

"Speaking of whom, here they come now," Terien said with a nod towards Eskai. He had to smile as they approached. Everyone was once more dressed in their finest, including his men who were all decked out in their black dress uniforms. Sahala, who walked with one arm hooked through Haren's, looked spectacularly regal in a pale lavender silk dress, while Corliss and Jeson were once more wearing their colorful council robes, flanked by Jos in his blue suit. As for Makhani, he looked dashingly handsome in black pants and a starched white shirt over which he now wore a knee-length vest embroidered with an intricate geometrical design. Even Shangra and Tiagra, being led by Elek, looked regal in their own cat-like way, having been brushed until their fur shone.

"Everything's all set," Elek proclaimed with a huge grin as they assembled around Terien and Aurori.

Looking over his shoulder at Kell, Soloth gave his friend a curt nod. Kell inclined his head and disappeared inside his flyer as Soloth now took a couple of steps towards the assembled representatives. He tucked his hands into the sleeves of his robe and assumed a formal demeanor. "Before we depart for Quayvern, I would like to give you a brief overview of what you can expect," he said, smiling. "Upon your arrival in Quayvern, there will be a parade wherein you will be led through the main concourse of the lower level. Then, you will be escorted up to the Council Chambers where Leander will formally welcome you to Quayvern." Soloth's thick eyebrows rose and he turned to face Terien and Duncan. "I should warn you, however, that Council members and guests are forbidden to bring weapons into the Council Chamber. Only the guards are allowed to bear arms, and that is the reason extra men are being ordered into attendance."

"Wonderful," Duncan moaned.

"No need for alarm," Soloth assured him. "My final act as Primary was to hand-pick the guards and I have made certain that these men are ardent supporters of the Final Reunification. As I said, we are not expecting any problems but have increased security regardless."

"I'm sure we'll be fine, then," Aurori whispered to Duncan who returned a nod but still looked unhappy with the arrangement.

"After the formal greeting," Soloth went on, "you'll have lunch with the Council members. From there, I have arranged for you to meet in our arboretum with several classes of children who are quite looking forward to seeing your felinae," he said with a smile. "After that, you will be brought to the private set of suites I have arranged for your stay. I do have a few more social functions planned for the course of your stay, but starting tomorrow morning you will be free to conduct the negotiations during the day." As a distant thrumming now filled the air, Soloth glanced at the triple mountain peaks that bordered Eskai to the north and offered the assemblage a deep bow. "My friends, it is my honor and privilege to extend to you our humble invitation to join us among the clouds for the conclusion of the Final Reunification." He now turned to face north and extended a hand to the sky. "May I present to you Quayvern, the floating city of technology prophesied as the site of that Final Reunification."

On cue, the city of Quayvern rose from behind the triple peaks in all her majesty. The light from the twin morning suns scintillated across the multicolored mirrored panels of her graceful spires as the whole city revolved slowly around her vertical axis, looking for all the world like a precious gem suspended against the backdrop of the deep blue sky. From this distance there was no backwash from her fusion-driven repulser engines, but the sound of their powerful thrust reverberated throughout the Kescate range, drowning out the awe-filled gasps of those assembled. After a couple of minutes, the city moved off into the distance, leaving everyone agape.

"Nice touch," Terien commented to Soloth in a hushed tone.

"I thought so," Soloth said with a smile. "Which is why I suggested the maneuver."

After a few more seconds of staring at the mammoth-floating city, Terien shook his head in wonder and turned to face the gathering. He cleared his throat loudly to get their attention. "I suggest we be on our way, then."

While everyone was directed onto the four waiting flyers which held six passengers apiece, Elek and Duncan moved towards the last flyer in line with the two felinae and led them up the ramp. The pilot, who backed himself up against the control panel, stumbled a bit as he nervously eyed the two huge cats.

"They don't... bite, do they?" the pilot asked in a strained voice.

Elek grinned at him as he secured Shangra's bridle to a cargo hook on the deck. "Naw. They never bite," he said confidently, then rubbed at his jaw as though considering the question further. "Claw a bit, sure, but never bite."

Duncan shot Elek a disapproving look as the pilot swallowed hard and broke out in a sweat. "Don't listen to him. He's just being a pain in the ass," Duncan told the pilot. "They don't bite, claw or otherwise mangle people. If they did, we wouldn't be bringing them to show the kids."

"You… you're sure about that?" the pilot asked in a whiny voice as Tiagra's mouth opened in a gaping yawn. The poor man looked like he was practically frozen in place and his knuckles were white as he gripped the back of his chair.

Duncan sighed, exasperated. "Smooth going, wise guy," he growled as he cuffed Elek's shoulder. "You just earned yourself a ride on this flyer."

Elek made a face. "Me and my big mouth," he muttered to himself as Duncan strode away down the ramp, then he extended his hand to the pilot and gave him a huge grin. "Name's Elek. You are?"

"Barlok," the pilot managed to squeak out in reply, his eyes going wide when Shangra let out a startled roar as he tried to stick his head out of the window and his nose encountered the solidity of glass.

"Problems?" Terien asked as he poked his head into the flyer.

"None at all," Elek said quickly, draping an arm over Barlok's shoulder. "Right?" he asked of Barlok, thumping a hand on the man's chest.

"No problems. None. I'm fine. Just fine," he said weakly as he slipped out from under Elek's heavy arm and melted into his operator's chair.

"Great. See you on Quayvern," Terien said, then eyed Elek. "Just make sure Shangra and Tiagra don't chew or scratch anything," he warned before heading back down the ramp.

Barlok whimpered miserably while Elek covered his mouth to hide his amused smile and dropped into the co-pilot's chair.

Amidst a hail of cheers and shouts from the Petravans gathered on the beach, the five flyers lifted off, spraying sand in their wake as they angled towards Quayvern. Inside the flyers, everyone was pressed up against the windows and talking animatedly. Even those who had gone down to Merani Base in the minisub found the new experience of air travel exhilarating and were comparing the merits of the two.

"This doesn't feel as confining as the minisub ride," Duncan observed.

"Nor is it as dark," Aurori agreed, then shivered slightly as she looked down at the ocean far below. "Mind you, there's something to be said for not being able to see much," she murmured, leaning back away from the window.

"Don't tell me you're afraid of heights," Terien said from the seat behind her, reaching around the back of her seat to place a hand on her shoulder.

"Not especially," Aurori replied uncertainly as the flyer was jostled by a turbulence. "It's just that… there's so much space between us and the ground! It's… a strange sensation."

Sahala, who sat across from Aurori, slumped in her seat and squeezed her eyes shut. "I've always hated enclosed spaces. Now I think I have a new phobia," she murmured miserably, putting a hand to her mouth as the flyer shimmied again.

"Uh oh," Haren intoned, casting a worried glance at Terien.

Soloth swiveled his seat around and quickly strode to the back. He opened a small compartment, withdrew a small pail and a foil package, then rushed to Sahala's side. "Fortunately, we're prepared for such things," he said with a wry smile as Sahala unceremoniously grabbed the bucket from him and thrust her head into it. Tearing open the foil package, he handed its contents – a damp cloth – to Haren who slid out of his seat and knelt beside Sahala. "Also fortunate is that it's a short flight. See? We're almost there," Soloth said, indicating the forward viewport.

Sure enough, the lower levels of Quayvern loomed large before them and Kell activated the communications panel to have the bay doors opened.

"Flyer zero one to control. Please activate main landing bay doors," Kell said.

"*Control to flyer zero one. Opening main doors now.*"

Terien looked over at Duncan. "Just like this morning when Elos called to have the flyers sent. The transmission is perfectly clear."

"Why shouldn't it be?" Soloth asked over his shoulder.

"The call to Merani Base wasn't very clear," Terien explained. "We thought that was normal."

"Ah, yes," Soloth chuckled. "Naneve's transmission was full of static as well. That only happens when a low frequency is used. The communications on Quayvern use high frequency and are always perfectly clear," he explained. "I've taken the liberty of passing this information on to Naneve. Perhaps we can give her a call later and see how she's doing."

Exchanging a raised-eyebrow look with Duncan, Terien settled back in his seat as the massive bay door was opened to admit the flyers. Within the span of a few seconds the flyer decelerated and passed through the aperture, skimming forward above the metal deck for a short time before it slowed to a hover, rotated 180 degrees to face the open doors, then settled gently. When the whine of the engines died off, Soloth climbed out of his seat and went to open the flyer's hatch.

"There now. That wasn't so bad, was it?" he asked with a smile.

"Oh sure. Not bad at all," Sahala muttered, looking decidedly green as she staggered to her feet with Haren's help.

Sharing an amused look at Sahala's expense, Terien and Aurori disembarked from the flyer and gazed around in wonder at the cavernous landing bay. Pipes, tubing and catwalks ran overhead and the entire place was a maze filled with drums, flyers, tools and machine parts. The bay was deserted except for a group of six fresh-faced young guards standing to one side, along with two white-clad nurses standing behind a pair of very familiar people in wheelchairs.

"Benem! Stev!" Terien cried, rushing down the flyer's ramp to clasp hands with both men.

Becoming the center of the attention in short order, Benem and Stev laughed as they were overwhelmed by happy shouts, backslaps and handshakes while enduring Aurori's probing of

Benem's casted left leg and the bandage-swathed burns of Stev's right leg. Everyone was practically tripping over each other in their effort to recount recent events for the pair, including a description of Petrava and the exhilarating flyer flight they had all just experienced. However, the joyous reunion was brought to a screeching halt when Terien asked about the other two injured men who had been transported to Quayvern.

"How are Shaygan and Cornel?" Terien wanted to know.

"Itching to get out of the medical bay," Benem reported. "The physicians wouldn't let them come down to meet you, though," he said, glancing behind him at the pretty blond nurse who had brought him to the landing bay.

"Shaygan had extensive internal injuries and is still recovering from surgery," the nurse told them, "and your other friend, Cornel, had two crushed vertebrae in his back. They're both doing well, but the physicians didn't think it would be wise for either one of them to leave their beds just yet. You can visit them later, if you like," she said, smiling.

Benem suddenly caught sight of Elek shooing the two felinae down the ramp of the flyer. "Hey! Where's Snowdrift?" Benem asked worriedly.

"Safe and sound back in Eskai," Terien assured him quickly. "Being pampered and getting fat, just like you," he joked, poking a finger into Benem's stomach.

Looking on from the sidelines, Soloth folded his arms and smiled. "I truly do hate to break up this reunion, but we have business to attend to. You may leave your belongings on the flyers. I will have them brought to your rooms," he said, looking to Terien. "If you don't mind, I'd like you to be riding your felinae as we move on to the concourse."

"Pomp and ceremony?" Terien laughed as he walked over to climb onto Shangra's back.

"Something like that," Soloth agreed.

Duncan signaled for Tiagra to crouch down, then turned to Aurori. "Might as well have both the Chosen ride in, don't you think?" he suggested.

Aurori patted Benem's shoulder and strode over to Tiagra. Accepting Duncan's assistance in mounting the cinnamon and cream colored cat, she gave the reins a light snap, giving the cat his cue to rise. She then directed him over to Terien's side. "Well, Chosen Gatherer! Are you ready to complete the Final Reunification?" she asked with a smile.

Terien extended his hand to her, returning her smile. "I am," he said softly, then raised her hand to his lips and kissed her knuckles. He turned to look back at the jubilant faces of the representatives they had gathered and felt a warm glow of satisfaction settle over him. Lined up in pairs, they were smiling back at him with pride and confidence. "We all are," he murmured, then gave Aurori's hand a squeeze before letting it go.

Soloth now took position in front of them, accompanied by two guards. "The procession will be quite long, I'm afraid, but it is important for the people of Quayvern to see you. Remember, they've been looking forward to this moment for a long time. Don't be surprised if they're… enthusiastic," Soloth said and moved off towards the doors.

With Soloth and two of the guards leading the way, they wound their way through the landing bay until they reached a set of double doors. At their approach, the doors hissed open and the entourage emerged onto an open-air concourse that curved away in both directions. Lined by glittering low-rise buildings of varying heights whose fronts were decorated with colorful signs and sported goods for sale, the wide walkway was filled with people of all size, age and color who were cheering and waving wildly. Confetti filled the air, raining down from where people were leaning out of windows and hanging over balconies to get a look at the Chosen and the representatives as they slowly moved out, following the concourse around to the left. From the backs of their two majestic felinae, Terien and Aurori waved and smiled, as did the representatives and Terien's Honor Guards who strutted proudly while craning their heads to get a better look of the city.

It was impossible to tell for certain from their low vantage point, but it seemed that Quayvern may well have been built in concentric circles. The buildings at the outer edges were no more than two or three storey, while the ones behind them were three or four storey higher and so on, with the tallest sky-reaching spires being at the center of the circle and approaching heights of about 200 feet. Each building was slightly different from its neighbor in both color and design, but each shared one common element – they were all constructed of the same reflective glass.

Coming to the end of the concourse where it butted into a building, the procession continued around to the right and it quickly became apparent that the concentric circle theory was correct with the addition of one detail. The streets between the buildings were a series of interlocking mazes and the next access point to the third row of buildings lay in the middle of the block, cutting between the buildings themselves.

Following the twisting path, they noticed that the crowds were beginning to thin out. Still, it was some time before they entered the heart of Quayvern where a cluster of seven spires stood, their bases surrounded by a broad expanse of green parkland featuring a shallow simulated stream, statuary, park benches and tables. As they proceeded through the park, Soloth halted the procession and called their attention to the tallest and most central spire.

"If you look at the central tower, you will see a bulge near its top. That is where the Council Chamber is housed. It is a circular amphitheater surrounded by an open-air observation platform," Soloth explained, pointing. "Directly above the Council Chamber is the main control center for all of Quayvern. From there, operators can direct Quayvern's journeys and have a 360-degree view of both the city and all that lies beyond. Even when Quayvern is stationary, as it is at present, one technician is on duty at all times, monitoring thrust and making minor adjustments for atmospheric conditions."

"In other words, someone has to make sure the city doesn't get blown into a mountain by a strong gust of wind," Jos said, chuckling. "So, where are all the machines that power Quayvern?"

"The power plant and all other systems are housed one level down from the landing bay you arrived in. I'd be happy to give you a full tour another day," he said, smiling. "Right now, however, the Council is waiting."

Making use of all six of the elevators in the tower, two of which had to be employed for the massive felinae, they arrived simultaneously on the top floor of the shining blue-tinted tower.

A light breeze was blowing as they spread out across the observation deck, peering down from the dizzying height to gaze upon the magnificent city while Terien and Duncan settled the two felinae against the curving wall of the Council Chamber where they contentedly lay down to bask in the warmth from the suns.

Soloth looked slightly embarrassed as he came up to Terien. "Don't forget, your weapons must remain outside the Council Chamber," he reminded them.

Nodding, Terien signaled for his men to disarm. "Leave your weapons here beside the felinae," Terien ordered as he unbelted his sword scabbard and gun holsters.

"Now I feel practically naked," Elek complained as he laid his sword and energy weapon down.

"Thank you for ruining my day with that interesting mental picture," Makhani commented dryly as he too laid his weapons on the floor.

"I just feel totally defenseless," Duncan muttered, then shot an apologetic look at one of the guards. "No offense."

The guard smiled and patted the energy weapon holstered at his side. "Don't worry, sir, we've got you covered," he assured them smugly. "If anyone wants to get in the chamber, they'll have to go through us first."

Haren, who towered head and shoulders over all six of the young guards, made an acerbic face and leaned over to Elek. "Oh sure. As if these six scrawny youngsters have ever seen battle," he growled quietly.

"Don't be paranoid," Terien hissed at them, casting a glance at the guards. "They may look young and inexperienced – but they might be able to toss you on your ass for all we know," he said, smirking.

"Besides, Soloth doesn't seem to think we're in any danger," Duncan added before Haren could rebut Terien's statement. "These guards are just a formality."

Terien pursed his lips and sighed. "Sure. But keep your eyes open. Just in case."

"Now who's being paranoid?" Makhani laughed softly.

Terien shrugged and looked away to where Soloth was getting

everyone lined up in front of the chamber's main doors. "I'm not totally convinced that there isn't more to the attacks."

"Forget about it," Duncan said, squeezing Terien's shoulder. "Come on, Chosen. Time to get on with the program."

With a nod, Terien straightened his tunic and walked over to where Aurori stood in front of the doors. Her hand found his and she interlaced her fingers with his as the doors parted.

Led by two of the guards, they entered the Council Chamber and walked in procession down the center aisle. The remaining four guards took up position outside the chamber's four doors which now slowly began to close, sliding down from top to bottom. The chamber was empty except for the thirteen councilors seated at the bench on the semicircular raised platform at the head of the room, all dressed in their colored robes and smiling broadly as Terien, Aurori and the representatives approached. Off to one side of the platform, a tall, thin man in green robes stood at a speaker's podium. Beside him, sitting at a large semicircular desk, an attractive redhead regarded them solemnly.

"That's Leander, Acting Primary of Quayvern," Soloth whispered to Terien, indicating the man with a curt nod as they walked down the sloping floor of the chamber's center aisle. "The woman at the control desk is – was – my aide, Idona. She is responsible for recording these proceedings."

Soloth brought the procession to a stop a few feet from the platform with Aurori and Terien standing slightly forward of everyone while the representatives took up position one step behind in a semicircle. The two guards who had led them into the chamber now moved off, climbing short flights of stairs on either end of the horseshoe-shaped platform. One took up position at the far end of the raised platform, facing outward, while the other gave the redhead a brief smile before planting himself between her desk and the speaker's podium.

Soloth stepped in front of Aurori and Terien, clasped his hands before him and bowed low to the Council, then turned to look up at Leander.

"Primary Leander, distinguished members of the Council, it is my honor to present to you the Chosen Gatherer and the Chosen

Observer for the Final Reunification," Soloth intoned loudly, his rich baritone carrying throughout the amphitheater. "Terien, Prince and heir to the throne of Kaethos," he introduced, "and Aurori, Princess of the Healers' Kingdom of Eristea."

Amidst a hail of applause and a standing ovation, Terien took two steps forward. "Primary Leander, allow me to introduce to you and this venerable Council the representatives for the Final Reunification," Terien said with a formal bow. Starting with the first person standing to his right, he indicated each. "Sahala, Empress of Pergase, Quatina, First Speaker of the Cohalili and the Penaro, Elos, Prime Legislator of Petrava, Rannoch, First Councilor of Brinbourne, Makhani, Vizier of Glaybor, Jos, Leader of Merani Base, Corliss, Speaker of the Goloto'o, and Jeson, Speaker for the Council of Chihook." He turned back to face Leander, inclining his head. "And, of course, my Honor Guards, warriors of Kaethos."

After another round of applause had died down, Leander spread his arms wide in an all-encompassing gesture. "On behalf of this august assembly," Leander proclaimed loudly with a glance at his fellow councilors, "I am delighted to welcome each and every one of you to Quayvern." He clasped his hands in front of him and bowed his head. "It is with our most sincere hopes for the success of your efforts at the Final Reunification that we humbly offer you the services of ourselves and our city."

At Leander's very first words, Terien's blood ran cold. The room seemed to spin and the whole scene suddenly took on a surreal mien as his mind flashed back to that evening in Merani Base when, standing in Naneve's office, he had first heard that aristocratic voice with its precise, clipped tones. Even with the distorting static of the transmission, Terien had known he would never forget the pitch or quality of the caller's voice, and there was no doubt in his mind that he was hearing that same voice right here, right now, in the Council Chamber of Quayvern.

"It was you," Terien said in a voice barely more than a whisper, his eyes locking on Leander and narrowing to accusing slits. "You were the one. Yours is the voice of the mystery caller of Merani Base."

Chapter Thirty Four

"I… beg your pardon," Leander stammered, taking an involuntary step back as the shock of Terien's quiet accusation thundered through him.

The room went deathly quiet and an eternity passed before Terien dropped his head a fraction to pin Leander with a venomous stare, his hand instinctively going for the weapon usually holstered at his side. Belatedly remembering that his weapon wasn't there, his finger curled into a tight fist.

"You heard me. You were the one who called Merani Base. Yours was the voice we heard," Terien stated flatly. "And if that is true, then it's also possible that you were behind both the attack in Merani Base and the flyer attack in the forest."

A low murmur of incredulity swept through the chamber. Near the far end of the platform, Albeon and Edegan exchanged anxious looks and mutely turned to stare at Leander whose face had become a pale, unreadable mask as he desperately struggled to think his way out of the predicament he was in. He had been duped. The Chosen hadn't escaped. He had to have been in the room at the time of his call to Merani Base if he recognized his voice. Still, the transmission had been low power and filled with static. Perhaps he could use that to his advantage.

Steeling himself, Leander returned Terien's steady gaze. "You're mistaken, my friend," he said in a reasonable tone. "I assure you, I have never been in contact with Merani Base."

The lie was so smooth and sincere, so devoid of apprehension, that Terien's expression was starting to soften until Duncan angrily pushed in-between him and Aurori. "You're right, Terien," Duncan growled. "It *is* the same voice."

Up to now Soloth had been standing frozen in place, rooted to the floor by disbelief and shock. With Duncan's corroborative statement, he took a hesitant step forward, his angular features drawn into a pained look of confusion and betrayal as he regarded the Acting Primary of Quayvern. "Leander? Is this true?" he whispered hoarsely, his hands making a gesture of helpless supplication.

Leander's jaw muscles worked as he bit back the urge to blurt out the truth to the old fool. Instead, he spun to face the other councilors who were glancing between him, Soloth and Terien, trying to make sense of what was happening. "This is absurd! Am I to understand that you actually believe this accusation?" Leander snarled, turning back to Soloth. His expression abruptly shifted to one of bitter affliction and he lifted his hands in entreaty. "You know me," he said to Soloth, then turned around to face the councilors once more. "You all do. How can you possibly give credence to this allegation? It is hardly more than conjecture." Seeing the looks of skepticism pass between the members of the council as they murmured amongst themselves, he turned back to Terien and Duncan, confident that he could cast doubt on the veracity of their testimony by calling its source into question. "How dare you! What proof have you that it was I who called Merani Base?" he asked loudly. "The proof of your ears alone?"

"I know what I heard," Terien said evenly. "I know *whom* I heard. What proof have you that I am wrong?"

Leander placed his hand over his heart. "I beg you to rescind your accusation," he pleaded. "Do you really wish to accuse me of such treachery based on a single static-filled communication?"

Duncan looked away, ashamed, but Terien's lips slowly curled back into a predatory grin. "Why, Primary Leander? In my recent experience with communication systems, transmissions are generally quite clear. How did you know that the communication with Merani Base was plagued by static?"

A shocked hush fell over the room and all eyes turned to Leander as the significance of Terien's simple question was driven home.

"Why, Leander?" Soloth whispered, shaking his head at Leander who had been rendered speechless as he realized the terrible mistake he had just made. "How could you do this?"

Realizing that Soloth was moments away from ordering Leander's arrest, Idona came to her feet behind her desk. There was no way her involvement in her lover's plans would go unnoticed, and while Quayvern had no death penalty, she, Leander and their two co-conspirators could expect to be imprisoned for the rest of their lives. If she didn't act now and act quickly, they would be finished.

Before anyone could move or say another word, Idona's hand snatched the weapon holstered on the left hip of the guard beside her desk. Caught totally by surprise, the hapless fellow barely had time to register what was happening before Idona fired into his back. While he slid silently to the floor, stunned by the weapon's incapacitating beam, Idona raised the muzzle and fired three shots in rapid succession, striking the guard at the other end of the horseshoe platform in the chest just as he was taking aim at her.

Cold fury settled like a stone in Terien's stomach and he took a step towards the platform, only to be held back by Duncan and Aurori.

"Everybody get down!" Idona shouted. With a flick of her thumb, she advanced the weapon's setting to maximum and started firing into the floor below the platform.

Pandemonium reigned. Terien shoved Aurori down, shielding her with his own body as everyone dived for cover, shouting warnings or crying out in shock. Shrieking, the terrified councilors sought refuge by ducking under their raised bench as Idona now turned and strafed the wall behind them.

"That's enough!" Leander yelled. He stepped to Idona's side, smiling as he grabbed her trembling hand and removed the weapon from it. "Well done, my dear. Well done, indeed," he said to her, then flicked his eyes towards the fallen guard at the other end of the platform. "Retrieve the other blaster," he ordered her.

As Idona went to do as she was bidden, Soloth raised his head and followed her with his eyes, stricken with disbelief and grief. He had known Idona and Leander were secretly seeing each other. He had seen their covert glances. Had taken note of their frequent meetings. Why had he not foreseen her involvement the moment Leander's guilt became apparent. "Why, Leander? Why have you done this?" Soloth asked, his voice full of bitter betrayal.

A furious pounding sounded on the doors to the chamber and

the communications panel flared to life.

"*Constable Folker to the Council! Can you hear me? What's happening in there?*" one of the guards outside the locked doors shouted.

Ignoring Soloth's question, Leander went to the control desk Idona had been sitting at and punched in a few commands that cut Constable Folker off. Leander pulled a flat card from his pocket and inserted it into the computer interface. While casting wary glances down at where everyone lay motionless on the floor below him, silently glaring up at him with impotent fury, he continued to type on the computer. He spared a glance in Idona's direction and caught sight of Edegan poking his head out from under the bench. Leander shook his head and clucked his tongue. "Albeon! Edegan! Did you really think I had forgotten about you?" he called out to them as he finished typing in the command path he had been working on, hitting the last keystroke with a flourish before removing the card and pocketing it.

"This is madness, Leander!" Edegan called back, shaking his head vigorously from side to side. In truth, he *had* held some dim hope that he and Albeon would be forgotten in the chaos, but such was not to be. "You'll never make it out of here alive! And if you do, where will you go? There's nowhere to hide on Quayvern!"

"Listen to him," Albeon urged from where he crouched beneath the bench. "End this, I beg you. Our plans have failed. It's better to accept defeat and live than to carry this further and risk death! We won't be a part of this any longer!"

"Coward!" Leander cried, firing a shot into the desk just beside Edegan's head. He managed to duck for cover just in time, but a jolt of alarm rippled through the room as it became clear that Leander was fully willing and capable of using the weapon he held. "I will *not* be caged like some animal!" Leander screamed, his face contorting with horrible rage. Chest heaving, he angrily motioned Idona to his side. He grabbed her by the shoulder, roughly turning her to face out into the room. "Watch them!" he commanded, then angrily stripped off his council robe and threw it aside. He boiled down the steps to the audience level and came to stand over Soloth, his lips curling back into a sneer as he

pointed the weapon at Soloth's head. "This is *your* fault, old man. All of it. If you had confided in me, if you had simply told me you planned to retire, then none of this would have happened," he said, his voice deadly calm.

Soloth blinked up at him, gray brows knit together. "Is that what this was all about?" he asked incredulously. "You were seeking the seat of Primary?"

"I have been seeking the seat of Primary for fifteen years, Soloth. *Fifteen years*!" Leander shouted, his finger tightening on the trigger. With a visible effort he managed to get himself back under control. "And I have been defeated every time. By you. By your cleverness. By your accursed ability to come up with a platform that the people find appealing," he said, galled by that fact. "I knew I had no choice but to tarnish your image, topple your popularity. What better way than to plot the failure of the Final Reunification that you had worked so hard for? I would have succeeded if not for that idiot, Maxen. And you," Leander growled menacingly, turning a scorching stare on Terien who returned a defiant glare. "I should kill you, Chosen. End your miserable life here and now," he said under his breath. "But I won't. I'd rather you lived, knowing how, in the end, I defeated you and your mighty warriors with no more than a single ally and a quick mind."

"Leander! We have to go. They must have called for reinforcements by now." Idona whined with urgency, glancing at the doors. The guards had long since given up pounding on the doors and were most likely working on a way to get them open.

"Not to worry, my dear. I've shut down all communications in the tower," Leander said, his tone now cheery. He raised his weapon away from Soloth. "I also locked out all the elevators and stairwell doors. No one goes anywhere without my permission." He spun on his heel and strode over to where Rannoch lay. "You. Get up," he ordered, waving him to his feet with the barrel of the gun. And you," he ordered Sahala, reaching down to grab her by the scruff of the neck and forcing her to her feet.

"Let her go!" Haren shouted angrily, surging to his feet and lunging at Leander.

A beam of energy flared out from Idona's weapon and Haren

flew backwards, landing in a heap, his chest smoking. Ignoring the danger, Duncan, who was closest to where Haren had fallen, belly crawled over to him.

"Haren!" Sahala screamed, struggling for a moment until Leander pressed the muzzle of his weapon to her throat.

"You bastard!" Terien hissed, struggling against Aurori and Makhani's restraining grasp on him. "You'll pay for this. I swear it!"

"Perhaps, but not today," Leander laughed as he backed away towards the side door. "Idona," he called out, "it's time to set off my little surprise."

Idona stabbed a finger down on the keypad of the control panel and immediately the sound of sirens wailing could be heard from beyond the Council Chamber walls. She then stepped down from the platform and grabbed Rannoch around his ample waist, holding him in front of her as she, too, made her way over to the side door.

Taking up position on either side of the door, Leander nodded to Idona and inserted the card he had programmed into the control panel set in the wall, unlocking and activating the doors to the chamber. Two of the four guards immediately rushed in, only to find they faced a hostage situation.

"Drop your weapons!" Leander shouted to them. "Now! Or she dies."

"You can't!" Aurori cried out, raising herself onto her hands and knees. "She… she's your daughter."

Leander's expression didn't even flicker. "A good attempt at distracting me, Chosen Observer. Very well played. But ineffective. I wondered at the possibility myself when I first saw her, but it hardly matters. She means no more to me than her mother did."

Sahala's choking sobs were all but drowned out by the blare of the sirens outside as Aurori miserably settled back to the floor, tears of remorse streaming down her cheeks. Her desperate ploy had not only backfired, but had ended up hurting Sahala deeply.

Leander narrowed his eyes at the two guards. "Your weapons. On the floor. Now." The two guards slowly bent to deposit their energy weapons on the floor, keeping their eyes on him the whole time. "Very good, gentlemen. Now, kick them towards me." As they complied with his order, Leander raised his voice and called out to the other two guards outside. "There's no point in playing hero, gentlemen! Come in where I can see you. Slowly, with your hands and weapons raised!"

The last two guards eased into the room, their sour expressions making it clear what they thought of the whole situation as they lay their weapons on the floor and kicked them in Leander's direction.

"Over there," Leander said, motioning towards the middle of the room with his head. "Lay down with the rest of the sheep." Once the four guards were face down on the floor with everyone else, Leander smiled at Idona. "Let's go. And don't forget the doors."

As the pair slipped out of the door with their hostages, Idona yanked the keycard out of the control panel on her way out, setting the doors to closing once more.

Springing to his feet the instant Idona and Leander were out of sight, Terien sprinted for the main doors, ignoring Aurori's startled shout of his name. He launched himself into a flying leap the last few steps and sailed beneath the closing door, skidding on his side until his upper body impacted with the retaining wall of the observation platform. He scrambled to his feet and threw himself back towards the shelter of the convex curving wall of the Council Chamber, narrowly missing being drilled by a blast from Idona. As he stood there panting, in the periphery of his vision he saw another figure edging around the wall to his right. He was preparing to tackle the figure when he caught sight of long blond hair blowing in the breeze.

"Spit! What the hell are you doing here, Blondy?" Terien bit out angrily.

"What do you think, Royal Boy? I came to help!" Makhani fired back. "In case you hadn't noticed, we're the only two who made it out before the doors closed!"

Blowing out an annoyed breath, Terien slowly advanced towards where the elevators and stairwell were, eyes peeled for another blast that never came. The observation deck was empty. Idona and Leander had managed to escape with their two hostages.

Jogging past the two cats who had been roused from their slumber by the wail of the sirens, Terien went to the elevators and tried the call button. Finding it unresponsive, he then went to the stairwell door. Its lock was glowing red hot from being fused by an energy blast and would not open. Venting his anger on the metal door, Terien smacked his palms against it. "Damn it!"

"*Terien? Makhani? Can you hear me?*" Duncan's voice came through from a communications panel set in the wall by the main doors.

Makhani, who was closest to the door, stabbed a finger down on the intercom button. "*Yes! We hear you. You've got communications restored?*" He had to raise his voice to be heard above the alarms blaring across the city.

"*No. Soloth says this panel is just a two-way speaker between the inside chamber and the observation deck. He's working on getting everything restored even as we speak,*" Duncan said, glancing over his shoulder to where Soloth was working furiously over the control desk's computer interface. "*Are you guys okay?*"

"*We're fine, but Leander and Idona got away. They melted the lock on the stairwell door. We're stuck out here,*" Makhani reported.

"*Never mind us,*" Terien said. "*How's Haren doing?*"

"*He's alive. In poor shape, but alive. Aurori is with him right now. She figures he must have the constitution of a bovine. He should be dead, but he's not,*" Duncan said, shaking his head even though they couldn't see him. "*You two sure surprised the hell out of us by running for the doors. Elek and Jos tried to follow, but they didn't make it. Elek's nursing a bruised forehead and Jos broke his wrist when the doors closed in their faces.*"

Soloth slammed a fist down on the control panel. "Damn it! When Leander shut down the communications and the elevators in this building, he password protected his sabotage." He blew out a frustrated breath and scrubbed his hands across his face. Then, giving his knuckles a good cracking, he let out a slow, deliberate sigh and started pecking at the computer console once more.

Outside, Terien paced back and forth until a thought struck him. "*Soloth, why would Leander have initiated the alert?*"

"*Running around with two hostages would not go unnoticed. I suppose he hoped to cover his escape without arousing suspicion,*" Soloth's voice said from the intercom. He sounded weary. "*Though, where he expects to escape to is beyond me.*"

"*He's heading for the landing bay,*" Terien said. "*There's nowhere else for him to go. He has to leave Quayvern.*"

There was a pause on the other end, then Soloth's voice called out again, this time sounding elated. "*Excellent! Leander may have locked me out from accessing command functions, but he didn't block out sub-system commands. By rerouting through the waste disposal subroutines, I should be able to override his programming. It will take some time, though.*"

Terien went to the rail and leaned his elbows on it, looking defeated as he stared down at the city below. There was confusion below, that much was obvious. People were running through the streets, probably trying to figure out what the sirens meant and what they should do.

Makhani came to stand at Terien's side and joined him in looking out over the city. "Don't worry. It's a long way down the stairwell to the bottom of the building. It'll take quite awhile for Leander and Idona to get down there, especially dragging Rannoch and Sahala with them. I'm sure Soloth will be able to sort things out before they reach the landing bay." He sighed heavily. "Too bad we don't have a flyer. We could get down there and stop Leander ourselves."

Terien spared a sour glance at Makhani, then turned his eyes back over the city. He looked down at the rooftop of the nearest building, twenty feet below. Then looked further on to the next building whose roof was about twenty feet below that and felt a tingle run through him. "We don't need to fly," he said, gripping the rail with both hands as he straightened. "We can jump."

"Whoa, Royal Boy!" Makhani blurted, holding his hands up in a cautioning gesture. "Let's not get suicidal!"

"Not suicidal. Just using my head," Terien told him. "Being around all this technology has made me forget about the natural resources we already have."

"*What* resources?" Makhani demanded to know.

In answer, Terien pushed away from the rail and strode towards the two felinae.

Makhani's face screwed up with puzzlement. He glanced from the felinae to the rooftops Terien had been studying, then it dawned on him and his face went slack. "Tell me you're joking."

Bending to heft his sword scabbard, Terien proceeded to belt it around his waist, his expression grim. "No joke, my friend. The felinae can jump in excess of fifty feet. We used to do this all the time in the mountains around Kaethos."

Makhani's expression was pained as he watched Terien pick up an energy weapon and holster, then vault effortlessly onto Shangra's back. He looked over the edge of observation deck and swallowed hard. Then, squaring his jaw, he tugged down on his long vest and strode over to snatch up his sword and an energy weapon. He then went to Tiagra and was about to mount the great cat when Terien stopped him short.

"Don't even think about it, Blondy," Terien growled menacingly. "You've never done this before."

"I won't let you go alone," Makhani shot back, glaring up at Terien defiantly. "You're not familiar with the layout of the landing bay and there're two of them and you are alone. The chances of both of us stopping them are slim enough. By yourself, you're just asking for trouble."

A dark cloud passed over Terien's face as he considered the validity of what Makhani was saying. He hated to admit it, but Makhani was right. "Fine. You come," Terien stated flatly. Makhani's hands went to Tiagra's back and he was about to haul himself up. "But you ride with me."

Makhani's jaw dropped. "You *are* crazy, Royal Boy. Two of us on one felinae?"

"Done it before, Blondy," Terien said with a shrug, then flashed Makhani a wicked grin. "Trust me," he said, holding his hand out.

"I'm going to regret this, aren't I?" Makhani mumbled as he clasped the proffered hand and let himself be hauled up into position behind Terien.

"I guarantee it," Terien laughed. "Just hold on tight to me and squeeze your legs around Shangra's belly. And remember to lean back a bit so we don't both pitch forward over his head."

Makhani licked his lips nervously. "Uh, shouldn't we tell

them what we're doing?" he asked, motioning towards the Council Chamber. "In case… in case…"

Terien shook his head. "They'd just try and talk us out of it," he said as he directed Shangra over the edge of the observation deck. Makhani's arms tightened around his waist and he could hear him breathe fast and hard. "Don't worry. We'll be fine," he assured him.

"Who's worried? I'm not worried. Do I look worried?" Makhani babbled.

"Just hold on," Terien growled.

For a long moment they stood there with the wind whipping through their hair. Far below, the sound of sirens wailing and the faint shouts of confusion drifted up to them. Terien's eyes narrowed with determination as he focused his every thought, his every ounce of concentration on the first rooftop far below.

Entwining one hand into Shangra's thick neck fur, Terien tugged lightly on the reins and backed the big cat away from the rail. Then, with a gentle kick of his heels that inspired the big cat to let out a deafening roar, they bounded over the rail and were airborne, wind whistling past them in free fall.

Chapter Thirty Five

Inside the Council Chamber, blissfully unaware of Terien and Makhani's dramatic departure, Soloth worked feverishly over the computer console while the councilors milled about, discussing the day's events in muted, weighty tones. Every now and then they would cast a glance towards where three of the guards stood watch over Albeon and Edegan, then shake their heads and continue their conversation. Soloth, too, would look up from time to time and have a quick look at where one of the guards was half immersed into the access panel they had opened, desperately trying to get the door open by hot-wiring it.

Aurori took note of all this without comment. She sat on the floor next to Haren and the two unconscious guards, feeling totally useless and helpless. While the two guards were only suffering the "stun effect" of the lowest setting of Idona's weapon and would be fine in a few hours, Haren was not so fortunate. The more powerful energy blast he had received had left a ragged, gaping hole in the heavy material of his uniform tunic and penetrated to the flesh underneath, leaving a blistered, charred third-degree burn in its wake. According to the guards, the beam should have burned through his chest and out his back. By rights, he should be dead. But it hadn't and he wasn't. Luck? A glancing blow? Miraculous intervention? Whatever the reason, it hardly mattered. Without her pack of potions, there was nothing she could do for his injuries, and to make matters worse, his eyes were fluttering open. Once he awoke to the full sensation of pain, what was she to do?

Haren moaned softly and weakly lifted one hand towards his chest. Aurori caught his hand and held it, exchanging a worried look with Quatina and Elek.

"Sahala?" Haren whispered, his voice a pale ghost of its normal robust bass.

"She's going to be fine, Haren," Aurori told him in as

confident a tone as she could manage. It could have been a bald-faced lie for all she knew, but she simply couldn't let him consider any other outcome when she needed him to focus on staying alive. "I'm sorry, Haren. I know you're in a lot of pain, but there's nothing I can do to help you right now. I promise – we'll get you to the medical bay as soon as we can." She smoothed a hand over his forehead as he nodded and closed his eyes, then she looked over to where Duncan stood beside the intercom. "Any luck?" she asked.

Duncan shook his head. "None. They're still not answering," he reported. "I know Terien would have told us if he got the stairwell door open, so I have to assume that Constable Folker's fiddling with the door controls somehow cut off the intercom," he said with an annoyed glance downward at the man.

"You want the door open or not?" Folker growled back irritably, grimacing as he struggled to inch his arm into the panel a bit further. "Here it is – wait a second – got it!"

The doors to the chamber started to rise and a cheer went up. Rushing out onto the observation deck, Duncan looked around in confusion when he found it empty except for Tiagra who stood in the corner by the elevators.

"Where the hell…?" Duncan spat. He jogged around the curve of the chamber to the far side then back again. He marched past Aurori and Quatina who were emerging from the room and tried the door to the stairwell. It was still fused shut.

"Where could they have gone?" Elek wondered aloud as he pushed past Aurori and Quatina.

Duncan went to the rail and looked down. Off in the distance he could see a white shape bounding across a rooftop. It made a spectacular leap across empty air, landing nimbly on the roof of the next building. "Well, all right!" Duncan crowed, punching a fist in the air. "Way to go!"

Aurori rushed to the rail and looked down. Her heart skipped a beat as Shangra bolted across the roof of another building and sailed across the gap between it and the next building in line. "Oh, Maker. They're crazy," she breathed.

Duncan slapped his hand on the rail and went to the open door of the Council Chamber. "Soloth, how soon do you think you'll have this thing beat?"

"Not too long. Ten, fifteen minutes at best before I can get the elevators operational," Soloth replied without looking up. "Longer until I can get communications online. If Terien's right and Leander plans on leaving Quayvern, I want to stall him by denying him access to the landing bay. I'll worry about getting communications back online after that."

"Too long," Duncan muttered. He turned on his heel and strode over to where they had deposited their weapons. He picked out two energy weapons and started strapping them on.

"What do you think you're doing?" Quatina asked, frowning.

"Going after Terien and Makhani. They might need me."

Aurori and Quatina looked at each other, then at Duncan as he swung up onto Tiagra's back. Quatina's lips compressed to a thin line. She knew that trying to talk him out of following Terien and Makhani was pointless. "Please be careful," she said, laying her hand against his leg. He nodded silently and cupped her chin in his hand for a moment, then maneuvered Tiagra over to the rail.

As Duncan repeated Terien's careful survey of the rooftops, Aurori wrung her hands and glanced back into the Council Chamber where Haren lay surrounded by his fellow warriors. Staying here with nothing to do was starting to drive her crazy, and worrying about Terien and Makhani – and now Duncan – was sure to put her right over the edge.

"Take me with you," Aurori said, turning pleading eyes to Duncan.

He was about to refuse. He had thought about asking one of the other warriors to accompany him, but one look at the determination etched on her lovely features changed his mind. She might not be the best fighter, but what she lacked in skill she more than made up for with sheer spunk. He held out his hand to her. "Welcome aboard, Princess. Just remember," he cautioned as she settled in behind him, "It'll be a wild ride."

"As if I care," Aurori told him as she wrapped her arms around his waist. She then looked over at Quatina and Elek. "Promise me that the minute those elevators are working, you'll get Haren to the medical bay."

"You have our word," Quatina replied.

Without further comment, Duncan backed Tiagra up a bit, then kicked his heels into the cat's sides. Hind claws raking the deck, Tiagra ran at the railing and launched himself over. For a moment they seemed to be suspended in mid-air, then gravity took over and they fell towards the rooftop below. Aurori's scream of abject terror battled for supremacy with the sirens of the citywide alert, then ended abruptly as Tiagra's massive paws made contact with the rooftop, sending a jolt through her whole body. Before she could take another breath, they were tearing across the roof, heading for the next wild leap.

Terien and Makhani had made it down to the roof of one of the buildings lining the concourse that ran on the outside of the landing bay and were getting set to make the last leap down when they caught sight of Leander and Idona. The pair were moving through the throngs of people, heading for the landing bay's main doors. They were alone.

"Oh, Maker! I hope Rannoch and Sahala are okay," Terien whispered.

"Don't think about it. Just get us down there before they get away!" Makhani yelled in his ear.

With a final shaky leap that told Terien the big cat was near the end of his endurance, they landed on the concourse, startling the passers-by. Apologizing as they went, they bulldozed their way through the crowd as fast as they could and arrived at the bay doors mere minutes after Leander and Idona had passed through.

Jumping down from Shangra and leaving the weary animal to its much deserved rest, they ran to the doors where Terien frantically slammed the heel of his hand down on the activation panel. Much to his surprise and disappointment, the doors failed to open.

"What the hell? It won't open!" Terien shouted.

"They must have locked it from the inside," Makhani snapped, thumping his fist against the door.

"Fine. Then we do this the hard way," Terien said, pulling his energy weapon from its holster.

Watching Duncan and Aurori's progress from the rail, Elek and Quatina exchanged a wry look as, behind them in the chamber, Soloth let out a triumphant hoot.

"I've done it!" Soloth shouted. He shot to his feet. "The elevators are operational and the landing bay has been locked down! Let that snake try and escape from Quayvern now!"

"Figures," Elek said with a shrug as he strode to the chamber doors. "Okay, let's move Haren out to the medical bay. Gently, now, boys. Gently," he cautioned as four of Haren's burly compatriots lifted him.

"I'll remain here and work on restoring communications," Soloth said, settling himself in front of the computer again.

"You do that," Elek said. He and the others stooped to pick up their weapons, then proceeded on to the elevators.

"I'll show your men to the medical bay," Constable Folker said as the elevator doors closed.

"Fine. The rest of us will head over to the landing bay in case we're needed," Elek said.

Leander and Idona ducked inside the landing bay, but not before sighting Terien and Makhani leaping down from the rooftop not too faraway. While Leander locked the door from the inside, Idona clutched at his arm.

"Did you see that? The Chosen is right behind us! What are we going to do?" Idona whined.

Leander grabbed her shoulder and steered her away from the door. "By the time they find a way in, we'll be long gone," he said with a smug smile.

Taking Idona's hand, Leander led her towards the far end of the bay where his private flyer was docked. They had made it two-thirds of the way there when the sound of footsteps approaching sent them scurrying into the shadows. A squad of six guards was coming around the curve of the bay. Idona raised her weapon, but Leander pushed it back down. "Leave them to me," he said, tucking the energy weapon into the waistband of his pants and pinning his jacket to conceal it. He stepped from the shadows. "Constable! Thank the Maker we've run into you and your men!" Leander called to them.

"Primary Leander, what's going on?" the lead guard asked as they approached.

"It's the Chosen and their representatives! They tried to hold the Council hostage and take over Quayvern," Leander told them smoothly. "They forced Lord Soloth to activate the alert and cut off all communications from the Council Chamber. Administrator Idona and I were the only two who managed to escape."

"The... the Chosen did that?" the guard asked incredulously, exchanging glances with his teammates. The news was hard to believe, but considering that it was Primary Leander himself who was doing the telling, the six guards had no reason to doubt his word.

Leander shook his head somberly, looking wholly perplexed and aggrieved. "It was terrible. Simply unbelievable! A couple of them chased us down here. We've locked the bay doors, but they may find a way in," Leander said with a worried glance over his shoulder.

"Not past us, they won't," the guard assured them grimly as he and his companions pulled their weapons. "Get yourselves to safety. We'll take care of things." The guard turned to his men. "You three guard the main doors," he said, pointing to three of them. "The rest of us will take up position near the middle of the bay in case they come in one of the secondary doors."

While the guards trotted off, Leander chortled softly and shook his head once they were out of earshot. "Quayvern's finest in action," he said sarcastically, then turned and headed for his flyer.

Terien aimed at the landing bay's panel and fired three shots at it in rapid succession. The door didn't open, but the panel's cover did fly off. It clattered to the deck, twisted and scorched.

"Damn, damn, damn!" Terien cursed. "Just like in Merani Base! These stupid weapons just won't do the job!" Angered, he fired one more shot into the exposed circuitry of the door panel and actually jumped back in surprise as the panel sparked and snapped, then burst into flames. This time the doors began to open. "Heh. Learn something new every day," Terien muttered.

A shadow crossed his handsome face as he traded the weapon to his left hand and drew his sword. "Come on, Blondy. We've got work to do."

Pressing close to the wall, both men moved into the dimly lit cavern of the landing bay. Leander and Idona were nowhere in sight, but they could hear muffled voices in the distance. Unaware that the sirens had stopped and the landing bay doors had closed behind them once more, they kept to the shadows as they silently crept forward. Becoming aware of footsteps coming their way, they concealed themselves behind the wide body of a flyer while a trio of armed guards came into view.

"How do you want to play this?" Makhani whispered to Terien.

"I'm not sure. Leander and Idona probably just waltzed right past them. Remember, these guys have no idea what's going on," Terien whispered back. The three guards came to a stop and fanned out, taking up defensive positions facing the bay doors. "Uh oh! Looks like they're expecting company."

"Yeah. Us." Makhani shook his head. "Leander's a crafty bastard. Who knows what he told these guys."

"Probably twisted the whole story about what happened," Terien whispered back angrily.

He and Makhani poked their heads out and scanned the area. The flyer they were hiding behind was inside a three-sided alcove. Once they reached the wall at the far end, they would have to veer back out onto the main aisle and run a good thirty feet before they could reach another safe haven. There was no way the guards would fail to notice them once they were exposed.

Makhani leaned his back against the flyer and sighed. "Next time I insist on going anywhere with you – just shoot me."

"Better yet – I'll return that punch I owe you," Terien said, grinning. He smacked a hand down on Makhani's shoulder. "Ready?"

Makhani took a deep breath and nodded. They slunk forward, following the gentle curve of the flyer's hull.

Aurori had long since stopped screaming and found that she was actually enjoying the wild ride in a kind of terrified, heart-stopping way. Clinging to Duncan, she spared a glance sideways as they bounded down to the rooftop of one the buildings on the concourse and caught sight of Shangra curled up outside the landing bay's main doors.

"They must have made it inside," Aurori said loudly just as the sirens finally fell silent.

"Hah! Soloth did it!" Duncan shouted. "If he's ended the alert, I'll bet anything he was able to seal the landing bay, too."

"Let's hope so," Aurori said.

"Come on, Tiagra. One last jump," Duncan said to the panting, trembling cat.

Sidling up to the edge of the roof, Tiagra crouched down and leaned forward, gingerly putting one front paw then the other on the vertical surface of the building while holding himself back with his powerful hind legs. Easing into a stretch that shortened the distance to the ground, he jumped. Landing hard in the street below, he let out a low "mew" of discomfort.

"That's it. Enough riding," Duncan announced when Tiagra favored his left front paw after a few steps. Dismounting, he helped Aurori down then circled in front of Tiagra and inspected the cat's paw. "Just a sprain," he proclaimed after a moment.

"Can he make it over to the doors?" Aurori asked.

"Sure. Come on, boy. Just a little bit further," Duncan said as he took up the reins and led the cat down the concourse.

Passing bewildered citizens who wandered the concourse as they slowly returned to their homes and businesses, Duncan and Aurori quickly arrived at the bay doors where they settled Tiagra in beside Shangra before turning their attention to the closed doors.

"Panel's shot to hell," Duncan stated flatly. "Terien's handiwork, I'd bet. So, how do we get in?"

Aurori looked up and down the concourse. "There must be another entry somewhere. Come on," she said, heading off along the curving wall.

They didn't have far to go before they found another door, but it was locked. Pulling out one of the weapons he had brought, Duncan started firing at the panel before Aurori could stop him. After several shots, the metal cover of the panel was scorched and warped, hanging on by just a couple of melted bolts. One final shot sent it zinging away.

"There was an easier way, you know," Aurori said as Duncan strode up to the panel and inspected its innards. "Didn't you pay attention to how Constable Folker opened the panel in the Council Chamber? He removed the bolts holding the cover in place," Aurori said with a bemused look.

"Same effect," Duncan said absently. He fingered a few circuits and wires, then shrugged, took a step back, and fired a bolt of energy into the works. As the door slowly began to grind open, they could now hear the sound of weapons discharging. "Oh, hell!" Duncan breathed as he held his weapon at the ready and dashed inside.

The area of the bay the side door opened on to was filled with stacks of crates, pipes and machine parts. Crouching low, they moved forward until they could get a better view. What they saw made Aurori's blood run cold. Terien and Makhani were running across an open expanse of aisle, dodging and weaving as three guards fired at them every step of the way.

Duncan checked his weapon, made sure it was on the lowest setting, then raised it and started firing in the direction of the guards. From his angle of attack, he was able to hit one guard, taking him out of commission. It was enough of a distraction to allow Terien and Makhani to reach their objective which lay across the aisle from his position. Somersaulting behind a row of some sort of equipment, they sprawled on the floor, safe.

"Duncan! Keep them busy!" Terien shouted above the whine from the guards' weapons. Without waiting for a reply, he and Makhani got up and started threading their way through the clutter, heading for the far end of the bay.

Keeping the two remaining guards pinned down wasn't an arduous task. They'd fire at him, he'd fire at them. If anything, Duncan was getting bored with it. He turned to offer Aurori his spare weapon and found she wasn't there. Uncertain of when she'd left or where she'd gone, he fired another blast in the direction of the two guards and scanned the immediate vicinity. She was nowhere in sight.

"Oh, hell."

In a fit of rage, Leander hammered his fist repeatedly against the unresponsive control panel, his lips peeled back in a vicious snarl. "He locked me out! That bastard Soloth locked me out!" he screamed.

He gave the panel a final thump and stood away, chest heaving with fury and frustration. He and Idona had made it to his flyer easily enough, but when he went to one of the auxiliary control panels and tried to open the outer doors, he found that the whole system was off-line, password protected and refusing to allow him access.

"Leander, stop! Please!" Idona pleaded as his face screwed up once more and he raised his fist to hit the panel one last time. She caught his hand and held it. "Let me go to the main panel. I can easily override Soloth's work from there," she said soothingly.

"Sorry. I'm sorry," Leander murmured. He let out a slow breath and his face slackened into a neutral expression as he reached out and stroked the side of Idona's face. He caught her up with one hand and held her close to him. "Go. I'll wait for you here," he told her, then kissed her hard. When he released her, he gave her a shove in the direction of the control room which lay towards the middle of the landing bay. "Hurry!" he called after her, then turned and headed for his flyer.

While Terien and Makhani skirted along on one side of the bay, they were being shadowed by a figure moving along on the other side. Aurori was having trouble negotiating her way around a mechanic's cluttered work area and decided the best way was to climb over the top. As soon as she started to clamor over a piece of equipment, her elevated vantage point gave her a better view of the area ahead and her heart skipped a beat. Three guards were concealed up ahead and Idona was heading towards a computer console standing against the wall on Aurori's side of the bay. Knowing Terien and Makhani wouldn't see the guards from where they were until it was too late, Aurori did the only thing she could.

"Terien! There're three guards up ahead!" she yelled. Immediately, the three guards swung their weapons in her direction and started firing. Plunging headlong off the equipment,

Aurori gritted her teeth as she tumbled and bounced to the floor. Bruised and hurting, she lay for a few moments, catching her breath while energy splashed off the machinery she lay behind.

Crouching behind a stack of crates, Terien looked in the direction Aurori's warning had come from but couldn't see her. Worry clawed at him as he wondered whether she was okay, but he resolutely swallowed down his fear for her and forced himself to assess the situation. There was no way past the guards up ahead. To move forward meant exposing themselves, and going back was out of the question. Scanning the area of the bay they were in, Terien noticed a metal ladder set in a towering piece of equipment standing against the wall and followed it up with his eyes. The crane's gantry arm was diagonally extended out high above the guards' heads and stretched to the far side of the bay.

"Wait until I'm up on top of that machine," Terien told Makhani, pointing, "then create a diversion so they won't hear me when I pass over their heads."

Makhani glanced up at the crane, then at Terien. "Good luck, Royal Boy," he said solemnly.

As soon as Terien had scaled the ladder and moved out onto the gantry arm, Makhani leaned out from behind the crates and started firing his energy weapon, pumping the trigger as fast as his finger could go. The response was immediate. The three guards broke off their sporadic fire on Aurori's position and peppered Makhani's hiding place. Small fires erupted here and there throughout the pile of crates and splinters of wood sprayed in all directions. Outgunned, Makhani huddled behind the crates and snapped off intermittent rounds as he could. He didn't dare peek out to see how Terien was faring, but mentally crossed his fingers and willed his friend to make it safely across.

Free to move again, Aurori eased up onto her knees and took a quick look around. She could see a snippet of Makhani's long vest sticking out from behind the smoldering crates and assumed Terien was somewhere back there as well. With both men pinned down, it fell to her to try and stop Leander's escape, and she knew exactly where to start. She had seen Idona heading for a computer control panel not too faraway, which meant that Soloth had succeeded in locking down the landing bay. Idona was obviously going to try and override that lockout, and Aurori was going to do everything in her power to make sure the woman didn't succeed.

Keeping low, Aurori scooted from one hiding place to the next until she was moving along the concave curve of the wall. Dodging under hanging pipes and around obstacles, she snuck up to where Idona stood anxiously pecking at the computer console. Scanning around for some sort of weapon, Aurori silently cursed when she couldn't find anything readily available until she spied a low conduit pipe running horizontally just a few feet away from Idona. At head height, it offered Aurori a perfect opportunity. All she had to do was distract Idona's attention.

Hefting a discarded tool, Aurori lobbed it high over Idona's head. When it clattered to the floor, Idona snatched up the weapon she had laid on the computer panel and spun in that direction. Aurori made her move. Charging forward, she hooked both hands on the conduit and swung her feet up, her heels connecting with the back of Idona's head. Idona lurched forward, smacked face first into a support strut, then fell backwards, unconscious. On impact with the floor, Idona's gun hand bounced once and a shot issued from the weapon. It narrowly missed Aurori's left hand and cut right through the conduit. With a screech of shock, Aurori felt the conduit give way and she fell, landing flat on her back. Her head struck the floor and the last thing she thought before the bay went dark was that at least she had foiled Idona's attempt to get the landing-bay doors open.

Having successfully traversed the length of the gantry, Terien looked down from the end of the crane's arm and spotted Leander not too faraway, pacing back and forth on the far side of his flyer. Unable to get a clear shot, Terien muttered a curse and stowed his weapon into its holster. Lowering himself through the framework of the crane, he grasped the thick cable hanging from the end and began to climb down. He wasn't even halfway to the floor when what sounded like a stampede erupted at the other end of the bay.

Curious about what was going on and impatient for Idona's return, Leander stepped around his flyer. His jaw dropped open as he spied Terien shinnying down the cable. For an eternity the two men glared at each other across the distance separating them. Terien was caught. He was too high off the floor to risk dropping the rest of the way and Leander was only a few feet from the ramp of his flyer. He would never make it to the floor before the treacherous Acting Primary of Quayvern made good his escape.

Both men went for their weapons at the same time. Terien, clinging to the cable one-handed, drew awkwardly from the holster strapped to his left side while Leander drew his in a graceful single pull from his waistband. It was no contest. Terien barely had his weapon out before Leander fired with pinpoint accuracy and shot it from his hand.

Cackling with glee, Leander took a step in Terien's direction. "Surprised, are you?" he taunted.

Terien winced in pain and hazarded a look at his hand. The shot had been a glancing blow, but it still had been enough to char and blister the skin on the back of his hand. "Nothing about you surprises me, Leander," Terien ground out past the throbbing in his hand. His grip on the cable faltered and he slipped down a short way, the rough cable abrading the palm of his hand. "A man who would be willing to commit murder just to gain authority over a city is capable of anything." Sweat beaded on Terien's forehead and trickled down into his eyes with the effort of holding on to the cable. He slipped down another few feet. "Only a maniac would be so blinded by the desire to control people's lives that he wouldn't understand that true power can only be bestowed, not taken by force."

"Ah! Of course. Spoken like a true Royal," Leander sneered, edging closer. "You say I am blind? I would counter that it is *you* who are blind, O Prince and heir to the throne of Kaethos!" His tone became mocking. "You were born into a royal family. Born into power and privilege. You think yourself high-minded? Power means nothing to you? Then give up your kingdom!"

"My family *governs* over the lands and peoples belonging to Kaethos in fairness and justice," Terien spat, "we do *not* rule for the pleasure of it. And we have always – *always* – included representatives from the people in all major decisions affecting them or their lands!"

Leander barked a laugh. "You *are* blind, aren't you? We have more in common than you realize. Certainly more than you'll admit to. You and I are both deep thinkers. Keen strategists. Your escape from Merani base, your entrapment of me and your success in getting this far prove your cunning. We are always one step ahead of the others, plotting, deliberating, and planning. We think alike in that respect."

"We are nothing alike!" Terien shouted angrily. "I would never kill to obtain or remain in power." His eyes narrowed and locked with Leander's. "I would rather die than become a power-hungry bastard like you," he said in a quiet voice filled with adamantine conviction.

The sound of running footsteps could now be heard coming their way. Leander's nostrils flared and his jaw muscles tightened. "It's a pity to be forced to destroy a keen mind like yours," he said with a sad shake of his head, "but, I do intend to leave here alive."

At the same time Leander raised and fired his weapon, Terien drew his sword in one fluid motion. Terien had spent long hours practicing with many kinds of weapons, but the sword had always been his weapon of choice, the one whose use he was most proficient in. Without conscious thought he held the sword up and tilted its shining blade. The energy beam deflected away at the perfect angle. Reversing course, it stabbed into Leander's right thigh. With a scream of fury and pain, Leander fell to the floor while Terien, ignoring the fiery pain that lanced through his hand, slid down the cable until he was close enough to the ground to drop the rest of the way. He tucked and rolled away as Leander fired erratically after him while hobbling up the ramp of the flyer.

Terien's men, accompanied now by Quayvernian guards, swarmed into view just as Leander retracted the ramp and closed the door. They did fire multiple shots, but those only succeeded in scorching the hull of the flyer.

Leander did what no one was ever supposed to do within the confines of the landing bay. He advanced the throttle to maximum, filling the bay with a deafening roar. The backwash from the engines blasted through the confined space, sending objects both large and small whirling into the air and knocking everyone off their feet. The heat from the fusion drive choked the air as Leander now released the braking assembly and tore out of the open bay doors.

Terien sprang to his feet and ran to the door. Framed within the rectangular opening with the golden and red sunset as a backdrop, the wind rippled his hair and clothes as he stood staring after the retreating flyer, his sword hanging loosely in his hand. There was defeat and anguished disappointment etched on his face and in the slump of his shoulders. Behind him, his men silently got to their feet and came to stand behind him. He could feel their own sense of defeat radiating over him.

Terien lifted his shoulders and took a deep breath. It was too easy to dwell on this small defeat and forget the greater triumph – as he and his men were tempted to do. Leander was right about one thing – holding a position of authority did give one great power over people, and that power could be used to hurt or heal. To lead or mislead. It was all a matter of one's intentions and purpose.

Turning to face his men, Terien met each one's eyes. "Any battle lost is a bitter thing," he said softly, "but the war was already won the moment we set foot on Quayvern. Bringing Leander to justice would have been a satisfying ending, but life is rarely so neat and tidy." A smile he truly felt on the inside found its way to his lips and into his eyes. "And if that's true, then we'll just have to settle for a perfect ending instead. The Final Reunification is at hand and nothing now stands in our way."

Amidst a hearty round of applause and enthusiastic cheers, Elek came running out from behind a pile of clutter.

"Terien! Come quickly! Aurori has been injured!"

His heart was beating faster and harder now than at any point during the long battle as Terien dashed after Elek. Skirting around a pile of crates, his heart flip-flopped when he saw Aurori sitting up with Quatina's help. Looking disoriented and glassy-eyed, she had bruises on her arms and face and was holding a hand to the back of her head. Rushing to her side, he dropped to his knees and took her into his arms. Holding her close, he squeezed his eyes shut against the tears welling in them. The warm feel of her breath against his neck made all the cares of moments ago evaporate.

"Hey, Princess. How are you feeling?" Terien asked in a soft whisper as he held her away and stroked her cheek.

She gasped in surprise when she suddenly noticed the state of his hands. "What happened?" she asked, gently taking his hands in hers and inspecting their burns and abrasions.

"It's nothing," he said softly. "I'm more concerned about you."

Aurori gave him a look of exasperation. "My head hurts and my ears are ringing," she said, then smiled over at Elek and Makhani who were looking on with concern. "I've felt worse. Usually when those two get together and sing."

Elek and Makhani exchanged a wounded look. "There's a critic in every crowd," Elek said with mock disdain.

"One would think that a noble-born Princess would have a ear for fine music," Makhani sniffed, assuming a regal air.

Terien shook his head and glanced in Idona's direction. "Looks like you were busy," he said with a small smile. The faithless Primary's Aide was still lying unconscious on the floor, a dark bruise marring the center of her forehead.

"Yeah, but by the sound of things I didn't stop her in time," Aurori said with a sigh. She looked at Terien with eyes full of regret. "Leander got away, didn't he," she said softly. The way she said it made it clear that she knew he had and that she also knew Terien felt keenly disappointed and abashed by his failure to stop it from happening.

"Yes. He did," Terien said, then surprised her by shaking his head and saying, "It doesn't matter. What does matter is that you're okay and that the Final Reunification will still go ahead." His face clouded and he turned to Elek. "Does anybody know what happened to Rannoch and Sahala?"

"They're going to be fine," Elek said, grinning. "We found them at the bottom of the stairwell. Stunned unconscious, but alive and well. I had some of the boys take them up to the medical bay."

"Which is where we should head," Terien said. He moved to take Aurori up into his arms, but she gently pushed him away.

"Not with those injured hands, you don't," Aurori told him,

frowning as she waved him away and got to her feet. "I can walk, you know."

"Who said anything about walking?" Terien asked with a smile, then stood and whistled loudly. From the other end of the landing bay, Shangra came running.

"No! Oh, no," Aurori laughed, holding up a staying hand. "I've had quite enough of felinae rides for a long, long while!"

Terien's brows knit into a deep frown and he narrowed his eyes at her. "You didn't!" he said, then turned a piercing look on Duncan. "Tell me you didn't!"

Duncan grinned wolfishly and shrugged. "Okay, I won't."

"How else were we supposed to get down here when the elevators weren't working?" Aurori asked mildly.

Terien shook his head without comment and laughed, then offered Aurori his arm and led the procession out of the landing bay.

Chapter Thirty Six

Aurori stood at the rail of the terrace outside the banquet chamber on the top floor of the second tallest spire on Quayvern, glass of bubbly fruit wine in hand as she stood looking over at the tower across the way that housed the Council Chamber. The last rays of the setting suns were casting shadows throughout the city and lights were coming on in the buildings as her eyes retraced the path across the rooftops Terien and Makhani – then she and Duncan – had taken more than three weeks ago in their desperate attempt to stop Leander.

Immediately after Leander's escape, Soloth had ordered flyers to go out and hunt for him, but days of searching had turned up nothing. It was as though Leander and his flyer had simply vanished. They had initially harbored some hope that he may try and contact Idona or return for her, but they abandoned that line of thinking once they had a chance to interrogate her and Leander's other two co-conspirators.

Albeon and Edegan had been smooth-talked into believing that their own power bases would expand under Leander's leadership of Quayvern and that they stood to gain great wealth. Greed had been their downfall, whereas Idona had been driven to take part in Leander's schemes by both a misplaced love for him and her own desire to attain a position of power and glory. Every step of the way, Leander had told the three exactly what they wanted to hear, getting them to do his bidding by skillfully making them believe he truly cared about them. However, as the story of his violent swings of mood and rough treatment of them came to light, it became apparent that he had, in the end, simply used their own desires against them.

The final proof of Leander's cold-hearted self-centeredness lay in his callous dismissal of Sahala. By his own admission he had suspected she may be his daughter, yet he had shown no more regard for her than for anyone else. In point of fact, when Sahala had discovered that it was possible to find out for certain through medical testing, she had eagerly submitted herself to the blood test, insisting that she had to know the truth. Upon finding out that Leander was indeed her biological father, her reaction had stunned those who knew her. She had simply let out a slow sigh of relief and remarked that at least one mystery had been solved. As for why Leander had seduced Sahala's mother and what he had gained by it – that remained a mystery that would likely remain unsolved until they found Leander. If they ever did.

Determined not to dwell on sad thoughts, Aurori sighed and turned away from viewing the city to look back into the open doors of the banquet chamber where the celebration marking the fulfillment of the Prophecy by the successful completion of the Final Reunification was taking place. Filled to capacity with revelers, the room was a hubbub of music, dancing and feasting, and as Sahala and Haren glided past on the dance floor, Aurori had to smile as she remembered back.

She and Terien had just arrived in the medical bay after the fight in the landing bay when Sahala had awakened. Uncharacteristically for the Empress, her first concern had not been for herself but for Haren. Driving back the physicians with her usual imperial high-handedness, she had rushed to Haren's bedside and wept genuine tears of grief until he had opened his eyes and smiled up at her. Sahala had surprised everyone in the room by tenderly kissing Haren's forehead and telling him right then and there how much she loved him. The pair had been inseparable ever since.

Aurori sighed contentedly and leaned her back against the rail. The Final Reunification was complete. The trade agreements had been negotiated and signed and the representatives would be taken home soon. Only she and Terien, in their capacity as the Chosen, were still expected to continue their travel from land to land to be present for the implementation of the trade agreements. However, while Terien was being given a flyer for the task and would spend most of the next month learning to pilot it before he would have a chance for a brief visit to his home, she would be free to return to Eristea and spend the time with her family. While she was happy to be going home, she found she was already looking forward to the time she and Terien would spend together and she smiled at the thought.

"Hey Princess!" Terien said as he walked through one of the open doors and came to stand beside Aurori at the rail, leaning both elbows on it as he joined her in looking back into the banquet hall. "You look happy," he commented when he noticed her smiling.

"I was just thinking about the Final Reunification," she told him, idly reaching out to straighten one of the folds of the cape draped over his shoulders. "And the future."

Terien caught her hand in his and looked into her eyes. "You know, I've been thinking..."

"So, this is where you two wandered off to," Sahala proclaimed loudly as she and Haren walked out over the terrace to Terien and Aurori at the rail. Releasing Haren's arm, she smiled up at him and then positioned herself in front of Terien and Aurori. "I wanted to thank you – both of you. For everything," she said softly, bowing to them both. "This journey has forced me to grow up, and I now realize how... foolish I have been. Many of the lessons I learned were hard to bear and I know I have caused both of you great discomfort through my earlier words and actions. I want you to know how sorry I am, and how thankful I am to you both. Most especially for your patience with me," she said, looking pointedly at Terien.

Terien blushed and averted his eyes. "Patience is hardly one of my virtues, Sahala. If anything, I should be thanking you – and everyone else – for teaching me to be more patient."

"An' the Maker knows we tested th' limits o' th' poor man's patience over th' last few weeks," Rannoch laughed as he and Makhani materialized through the doorway with Corliss and Jeson one step behind.

"Yep. There were times I thought Royal Boy was going to blow a blood vessel," Makhani teased, grinning. "Especially once we started in on how much of what kind of goods and services we each had to offer and were willing to trade. Face it, we're ten different lands and eleven representatives. That's a lot to juggle." His grin mellowed into a warm smile as he looked at both Terien and Aurori. "You two did a great job considering you had to mediate and act as representatives of your own lands at the same time. I bet there were times you just wanted to tell us all to shut up when we'd all start talking at once."

"It wasn't that bad," Terien insisted, then cocked his head to the side and gave them a lopsided smile. "Well, almost. Not quite, but almost."

"Hey guys," Jos called out as he and Elos stepped out, drinks in hand. "What's going on?"

"Just talking about the Final Reunification," Makhani told them. "We were saying how hard it must have been for Terien and Aurori to deal with all of us."

"Oh yeah!" Jos chuckled. "You know, the best part was last week when Soloth announced that the citizens of Quayvern had voted to stay permanently on Primus and wanted to join the negotiations for the Final Reunification. The looks on Terien and Aurori's faces when they realized they had to renegotiate Quayvern into the picture were priceless!"

"I am still somewhat ashamed that we even had the wherewithal to make the request so late in your discussions," Soloth said from the doorway of the banquet hall. "Unfortunately, holding a referendum on such short notice was no easy task. But we were able to come to a consensus quickly and with such an overwhelming majority voting in favor of staying on Primus…" Soloth shook his head and smiled. "I must admit to being utterly flabbergasted. I had assumed Quayvern would have to approach you on the matter long after the fact."

"Actually, we're glad it happened now rather than later," Aurori said, laughing. "Look at how much we benefit from having the use of your flyers."

"So, when's the big date for landing Quayvern?" Terien asked Soloth.

"Quayvern is still up in the air over that, I'm afraid," Soloth said, smiling at his own joke in spite of the groans all around him. "Landing the city not only requires a large, relatively open area, but we also have to test potential sites for geological stability among other considerations. I don't think we'll be ready to land for at least a month or more."

"About the same time the trade agreements will be ready for

implementation," Jos mused out loud.

"Yes. I expect Petrava's fleet of hovercraft to be operational and ready for delivery by then," Elos said, but his tone sounded uncertain.

"Uh oh! I don't like the way you're saying that," Terien said.

Elos sighed and shook his head. "I was just thinking that Soloth's proposal to use Quayvern's flyers to airlift the hovercraft to each land could present a problem if we don't get started immediately. We are approaching the rainy season here in the north and that usually means we can expect periods of high winds. Slinging hovercraft would be impossible if weather conditions are unfavorable, and I doubt that we could widen the road between Eskai and Chihook within a month." Elos shrugged apologetically. "I'm sorry, my friends. I had not thought of this before."

"In other words," Corliss said with a sigh, "what happens if there's a delay in getting trade moving?"

"I would say that it does not matter," Quatina spoke up loudly as she and Duncan stepped outside from the banquet room. "Whether we wait a month or two or three is irrelevant. The point is that the trade agreements have been signed and the Final Reunification has been accomplished. There are bound to be minor difficulties. That is to be expected." Quatina's dark eyes sparkled with pride as she came to stand before Terien and Aurori. "What matters is that for the first time since the Great Division, our lands and peoples have come together as one and have taken the first step towards making our continent a better place for all. This is an accomplishment that would never have come to pass without the two Chosen, and I for one think it is time we recognized them for what they both have suffered to bring us together."

As a chorus of agreement rustled through the assembly, Terien's men now showed up. Among them were the four who had been injured, looking hale and hearty once more. The terrace was now filled to bursting as Quatina turned to the representative of Glaybor and gently cuffed his shoulder. "You have been with the Chosen the longest, Makhani. I think it should be your honor to propose a toast."

Makhani's head came up and his eyes went wide. "Me?"

"Oh, aye. There's a fine choice fer ye," Rannoch grumbled sarcastically. "Th' lad's bound to have something witty t' say."

Makhani glowered at Rannoch for half a second, then cleared his throat and stepped to the center of the circle of representatives. "It's no secret that Terien and I have had our differences in the past. But, that was the past," Makhani said with a glance at Rannoch. "It has been an honor to be with the Chosen from the beginning. Even if I didn't know at first that I was traveling with both," he said with a smile in Aurori's direction that made her blush. "We have all seen evidence of their courage and their compassion and know what lengths they have gone through to see the success of the Final Reunification. Leaving family and home, facing both the dangers of the journey and the pitfalls of having to deal with such a diverse bunch of representatives as we turned out to be – they still answered the call of duty as laid out by the Prophecy. For that, we thank you and will be ever in your debt." Makhani raised his glass and bowed from the waist. "May the Maker never forget what you have done for the people of Primus. We never shall."

Everyone raised their glasses to Terien and Aurori and drank in their honor. In the silence that followed, Terien lifted his glass and caught the eye of every one of his men in turn as he spoke. "I would also like to propose a toast to the warriors of Kaethos who accompanied me – for their bravery, loyalty, and companionship. To those present here and those who are no longer with us – Maker bless them all!"

The gentle clink of glasses and quiet acknowledgments followed as everyone drank in silence, remembering that not everyone who had set out on the journey was going to make it home. The moment was a heavy one, especially for Terien. It made him remember his melancholy mood the night they were in Petrava and a thought struck him as he looked out over the people assembled on the terrace.

He had come out on the terrace because he had naturally searched out Aurori. Once they were outside, the others had slowly joined them, gravitating together as though drawn by some invisible force they neither felt nor saw. It had been this way for some time, now. They had become more than a collection of strangers compelled to fulfill the Prophecy out of duty or a sense of commitment to their peoples. They had become friends – no, more like an extended family. They truly cared for one another – and perhaps that was the true heart of the Final Reunification.

"I don't think it's enough that we've agreed to meet annually on the anniversary of the Final Reunification," Terien said, the sound of his voice seemingly startling many out of deep thoughts of their own. "The Final Reunification isn't just about what goods we'll get out of the trade agreements. It's much more than that. It's about people coming together to share their experiences and their lives – to share ideas and beliefs." He shook his head. "Our ancestors must have known this at one time. Look at the wonders they accomplished together. They built Alatesh, Petrava, Merani Base and Quayvern," he said, turning to look over the rail at the city. "The peace and prosperity they shared fell apart when the comets fell, but I say it was because they lost sight of what was important. In the end, I think they took for granted the precious gift they had." Terien turned back to the assembly and sighed. "Just as we might have. It's too easy to become wrapped up in the cares of the world – the need to survive and the materialism that drives our lives. We must not forget the lesson of the journey we just completed. It wasn't the food and drink or clothes and wealth that sustained us. They only kept us alive. What sustained us was our faith in the Prophecy and our faith in each other. We need each other."

"Then, let's not waste the opportunity we have here," Aurori said. "I propose that we meet as often as possible. And not only us. I say that we consider some sort of exchange program whereby others in our lands be granted the opportunity to travel to other lands."

"Quayvern can offer flyers for such a venture," Soloth piped up.

"Aye! 'Tis a grand idea, Lass!" Rannoch enthused. "I can think of several youngsters in Brinbourne who would love th' chance t' travel aroun' an' meet people."

"Never mind youngsters! I can think of a few elders who would be just as eager to share some of their stories and experiences," Elos said, laughing.

"Just think – we could start a whole new craze! People traveling all over just to meet people in other lands and get to know how they live," Jos laughed.

"Oh, how our storyteller would love that," Quatina giggled.

"Great. Then it's settled. We'll have to work out the details, though," Terien said. "So, now we just have to decide when and where our next meeting will be."

"That's easy," Sahala said, smiling up at Haren. "How about in Pergase – after the wedding?" When Haren paled visibly and swallowed hard, Sahala's face fell and she looked on the verge of tears. "I… I'm sorry," she whispered to him. "I… I didn't mean to presume…"

Haren laughed and took her hands in his. "No, no! It's not that. It's just that you didn't give me a chance to ask you yet!" Getting down on one knee before Sahala while everyone looked on, he gazed tenderly up into her eyes. "Sahala, I may not be a Prince or a rich man, but I love you with all my heart. I have since the first time you made me sleep outside your tent," he said with a small smile at the memory. "Will you marry me?"

In reply, Sahala threw herself into his arms and whispered the word "yes" over and over again as tears streamed down her cheeks, while joyous laughter and applause echoed over the terrace.

Terien arched his brows and grinned at Haren. "Hmm. Emperor Haren," he muttered, testing out the title his friend stood to acquire. "Just don't expect to be called 'Your Highness' or something equally embarrassing," he said, extending his hand to the big man.

Haren laughed as he and his bride-to-be rose, surrounded by well-wishers. He engulfed Terien's hand in both of his. "Not likely. I have your example to live up to, after all."

As Terien retreated back against the rail between Aurori and Makhani to get out of the way, the blond man chuckled. "Well. That takes care of that meeting, I guess. And I have a feeling the next one won't be too long after that," he said glancing over at Duncan and Quatina who stood by the rail, holding each other. They both averted their gaze but didn't deny his observation.

"You know, Royal Boy," he said quietly, turning back to Terien, "I never thought I'd hear myself say this, but I'm glad King Denid ordered me to accompany you. You've been a good friend."

"You too, Blondy," Terien said. The two men clasped hands, smiling at each other awkwardly.

"You know, I envy you learning to pilot a flyer," Makhani admitted. "Sounds like a lot of fun." He shook his head and laughed. "I guess that's one of the benefits of being the Chosen."

Before Terien could comment, Soloth approached them. "Actually, Makhani, I'd like to talk to you about that," he said loud enough to bring the assembly to a standstill. "Terien will be given one of two spare flyers we have on Quayvern. I can foresee a time when all the lands will have them, but until then it would be a shame to let the other sit idle. If there is no protest from the other representatives," Soloth said, looking around, "I see no reason why Makhani should not learn to pilot a flyer now."

"I'd love to," Makhani whispered, his eyes widening at the prospect as he stood there looking like he would burst at the seams from excitement. He looked hopefully at the faces around him and raised his eyebrows expectantly.

"I certainly have no quarrel with such a proposal," Quatina said with a shrug. "Someone has to be among the first to learn."

"Aye, an' it won't be me, I can assure ye of that!" Rannoch laughed as he turned to face Jos. "What say ye, Merani Base? As long as the lad promises to give us a lift to all th' meetings, I see no reason to put a pin in his bubble."

"Sounds reasonable to me," Jos said, smiling.

"Actually, this might be a time saver," Elos piped up. "If Soloth can gather us northern folk and Terien the southern representatives, Makhani can see to the ones in the central regions."

"Splendid," Soloth chuckled as Makhani broke into a boyish grin. "Now, then. If you'll all direct your attention to the skies, I have a small surprise for everyone." Soloth signaled to someone inside the banquet hall and the lights went out, plunging the terrace into near darkness. Only the pale light from the surrounding buildings cast enough of a glow for them to still make one another out.

“This should be good,” Jeson commented loudly. “Soloth’s last surprise was to have Quayvern rise from behind the Kescate Mountains.”

“You have to admit, the man has a knack for dramatic moments,” Aurori laughed as she and Terien turned to face outward from the rail.

“From the time of the Great Division, the people of Primus have waited in patience and faith for this day,” Soloth intoned solemnly, his rich baritone filling the quiet of the night. “The Final Reunification is complete. May we never forget this night when we came together in peace and friendship to celebrate this great accomplishment and rejoice in the hope of a bright future!”

Muted thumping sounds from far below were followed by keening whistles that cut the silence of the night. Uncertain of what to expect, those gathered on the terrace let out gasps of awe when colorful bursts of light erupted against the dark sky. Sparking and scintillating, the bursts swelled outward and seemed to fall in slow motion before flickering out, only to be replaced by a renewed chorus of thumps and whistles as the spectacular light show was repeated again and again in ever-changing colors and patterns.

“How fitting. The light dispels the darkness of the night,” Aurori murmured as Terien wrapped his arms around her and drew her close. “It’s beautiful.”

“Just as our friendship and love dispels the darkness in our lives,” Terien whispered softly. He caressed Aurori’s cheek, drawing her gaze away from the light display and up into his own eyes. “Remember how I said I would miss you most of all once the Final Reunification was complete and everyone went their separate ways?”

“Mmm hmm. I remember.”

“I don’t want to miss you, Aurori. Ever. I love you too much to let that happen.”

Aurori blinked back the tears brimming in her eyes. “I love you too, Terien,” she whispered, taking his face in her hands.

He tenderly kissed her, then rested his forehead against hers. “Marry me?”

Smiling, Aurori slid her hand to the back of his neck and drew his head down until her lips brushed his ear. "Oh, yes!" she whispered. "With all my heart, yes. But not yet."

Terien pulled back, startled. "Meaning?"

"Meaning – let's keep this a secret until after Sahala and Haren's wedding," Aurori said with a soft laugh. "Imagine the attention our announcement would draw," she said, looking over to where Sahala and Haren stood dividing their attention between each other and the light show. "I would hate to overshadow Sahala's big day. She's been through so much... she deserves every bit of attention she and Haren will get."

"I can live with that," Terien said, then smiled. "As long as the answer is still 'yes'."

"Always, my love. Always," she said, then kissed him and snuggled into his arms.

"I wonder if we'll ever find Leander," Terien said suddenly as a particularly bright starburst of light and sound exploded in the sky.

"Forget Leander. At least for now," Aurori said, laying her head on his chest and returning her gaze to the skies as the sound of another round of whistling creased the air. "The Final Reunification is complete, and the future holds great promise for us all. We have our friends and each other. Nothing else matters at the moment."

Terien rested his cheek against Aurori's head and sighed slowly, letting his eyes drift across the assembly. His friends, both old and new, stood in rapt attention as the bright bursts of colored light sparkled through the skies, their faces reflecting their inner joy and contentment. With so many people willing to pull together, the future looked bright indeed and he was honored to have a part in that.

A final glorious burst of multicolored pyrotechnics radiated light across the entire city of Quayvern. It reflected off every mirrored panel, setting the night sky ablaze.

"Of course. Hope, faith, and love," Terien whispered more to himself than anyone else. "Nothing else matters."